CANDLELIGHT
Ecstasy Supreme™

"DON'T BACK OUT ON ME, HONEY. THIS IS IMPORTANT TO BOTH OF US."

Sarah's contemptuous look said more plainly than words that nothing could be so important that Charles had to wait five years to see her, but she said nothing.

"I haven't kissed you yet . . . and I need something to last me until five thirty."

She opened her mouth to protest, but his lips seized hers in a hungry invasion that made her ferociously greedy for more.

He'd changed. Into a harder, more determined, more ruthless man. It was in his voice, in his touch, and in the rough hunger of his mouth. It would take every ounce of willpower she had to keep her distance from Charles. His appeal was now almost irresistible. It was that simple . . . and dangerous!

CANDLELIGHT ECSTASY SUPREMES

1 TEMPESTUOUS EDEN, *Heather Graham*
2 EMERALD FIRE, *Barbara Andrews*
3 WARMED BY THE FIRE, *Donna Kimel Vitek*
4 LOVERS AND PRETENDERS, *Prudence Martin*
5 TENDERNESS AT TWILIGHT, *Megan Lane*
6 TIME OF A WINTER LOVE, *Jo Calloway*
7 WHISPER ON THE WIND, *Nell Kincaid*
8 HANDLE WITH CARE, *Betty Jackson*
9 NEVER LOOK BACK, *Donna Kimel Vitek*
10 NIGHT, SEA, AND STARS, *Heather Graham*
11 POLITICS OF PASSION, *Samantha Hughes*
12 NO STRINGS ATTACHED, *Prudence Martin*

PAYMENT IN FULL

Jackie Black

A CANDLELIGHT ECSTASY SUPREME

Published by
Dell Publishing Co., Inc.
1 Dag Hammarskjold Plaza
New York, New York 10017

Dell ® TM 681510, Dell Publishing Co., Inc.
Candlelight Ecstasy Supreme is a trademark of Dell
Publishing Co., Inc.
Candlelight Ecstasy Romance®, 1,203,540, is a registered
trademark of Dell Publishing Co., Inc.

ISBN: 0-440-16828-7

Printed in the United States of America
First printing—February 1984

To Charles . . . all three of them—

Most of all to the one who has shared almost all of the years of my life. Secondly, to the one who inhabits these pages and represents many of the qualities I find admirable in a man. And last, to the one who was instrumental in adding touches of authenticity to this fictitious work by sharing with me reference material from his own days in Africa as the son of missionary parents.

I also want to express my appreciation to *The Wall Street Journal* for their series of informative articles on the problems, both political and economic, facing the emerging nations of Africa today.

To Our Readers:

Candlelight Ecstasy is delighted to announce the start of a brand-new series—Ecstasy Supremes! Now you can enjoy a romance series unlike all the others—longer and more exciting, filled with more passion, adventure, and intrigue—the stories you've been waiting for.

In months to come we look forward to presenting books by many of your favorite authors and the very finest work from new authors of romantic fiction as well. As always, we are striving to present the unique, absorbing love stories that you enjoy most—the very best love has to offer.

Breathtaking and unforgettable, Ecstasy Supremes will follow in the great romantic tradition you've come to expect *only* from Candlelight Ecstasy.

Your suggestions and comments are always welcome. Please let us hear from you.

Sincerely,

The Editors
Candlelight Romances
1 Dag Hammarskjold Plaza
New York, New York 10017

CHAPTER ONE

Charles Trainer, his tall, athletic, impeccably clad body moving with an indolent grace that denied the weight of the heavy bag he carried and the hours of airline travel from the African continent he'd just endured, stepped past the row of waiting taxis outside John F. Kennedy Airport, scanning the occupants of the stream of cars flowing past with his startlingly clear blue eyes. Just as he got to the end of the row of taxis, the expression in those eyes sharpened, displaying for an instant a formidable intelligence that was normally cloaked somewhat by a translucent candor, usually the first thing people noted and responded to about him.

A nondescript sedan glided to the curb. Charles opened the back door and tossed in his bag, then got in the front seat in one smooth motion. Before the car door closed behind him, the car was already gathering speed and departing the area with circumspect haste, while Charles slanted a brief smile at the hard-eyed driver whose cynical gaze was turned briefly in his direction.

"Perfect timing as usual, Foster," Charles approved. "How's it going?"

Foster shrugged, looking as though he dwelled in a perpetual state of boredom until one noticed that his deep-set dark eyes were never still, never less than completely alert, and they displayed an intelligence that matched Charles's, though the cold expression in them was considerably less charming than his passenger's.

"Same as usual," Foster replied in a gravelly voice that matched his rough face. "Hurry up and wait."

It was Charles's turn to shrug then, though as he did so a look of weary impatience clouded his expression momentarily. "Hazards of the trade," he commented dryly, his tone edgy.

"Yeah," Foster said absently as he turned the wheel of the car to take a curve. When he was once again heading down a straight street, he flicked Charles a cool glance. "But that's something you won't have to worry about too much longer, right?" Then, without waiting for a response to his remark, he asked, "How'd you manage to get out of traveling on the royal jet?" The cynicism in his tone was apparent, but the faint hardness in his eyes said that he wasn't making idle conversation.

"Don't worry," Charles said wryly. "I made it look good."

Foster flicked up one shaggy eyebrow. Trust was not one of the commodities he dealt in normally, but over the past five years, he had learned that if Charles Trainer said something, it could be counted on to be accurate.

Charles shifted in his seat impatiently, his restless eyes scanning the area around them without interest. "We are going straight there, aren't we?" he asked Foster pointedly, the edginess in his voice more pronounced.

The tensing of Foster's jaw was the only sign he gave that he disapproved of the reason behind the question. When he spoke, his tone was casual, however. "Sure. I got your message." All inflection left his voice as he added, "But I wonder if you've thought long and hard enough about what you're doing. It isn't that easy to get out of this business when you've been in it as long as you have."

A faint, harsh smile tugged at Charles's firmly chiseled lips. "Oh, I expect my years in 'this business,'" he said mockingly, "will affect me for the rest of my life. But I only made a commitment for five years, and they're up—almost," he added with impatience in his tone, an impatience that spelled out his need to have this part of his life over and done with. "I've paid my dues," he finished inflexibly. "I want to get on with the rest of my life."

If Foster had been a man given to sighing, now would have been a good time to give a big one, but he was not, and he did not. Instead, he gave Charles a resigned look tinged with regretful respect. "For someone who doesn't like the work, you're

12

damned good at it," he said grudgingly. "We're going to have a hell of a time replacing you."

Charles shrugged, his movement clearly expressing the attitude that that was not his problem. Foster, a professional to his toes, firmed his jaw grimly but refrained from direct comment. He dealt in reality, and Charles Trainer was not the sort of man one could browbeat into an unwanted course of action. Foster did not, however, refrain from commenting indirectly.

"I hope she's worth it," he said in a tone that clearly spelled out his disbelief that such could be the case. "I admit she's got the look of a woman who could keep a man wanting her for five years, but in this business you're a fool if you let anyone get to you enough to interfere with—"

"I knew her before I got into this business." Charles cut him off in a clipped tone, his look coldly implacable. "I gave her up for this business," he added harshly, the sound of his voice making even the redoubtable Foster shoot him an uneasy glance. "I've paid my dues," Charles repeated, more quietly, but no less firmly. "I want out!"

There was a brief silence between the two men as Charles stared stonily out the window and Foster contemplated how to approach him again. Finally Foster said with calm reasonableness, "But you don't even know if she'll have you back. What if she won't?"

Since Charles's head was turned away, Foster didn't see the brief spasm of pain that clouded Charles's blue eyes momentarily, and Foster was not sensitive enough to hear it in Charles's level voice when he replied. "I'll face that when I come to it," he said quietly, before facing Foster again, suddenly all business. "Now, do you want a report or do you want to keep hashing over my love life . . . or lack of one," he added curtly, the barest hint of bleakness in his tone.

Perhaps surprising even himself, Foster did sigh then before letting his face close up in its habitual expression of blank impassivity. "We're almost there, and your lady won't be arriving for work for a while yet. Let me get parked, and then we'll have at it."

Charles nodded, only the unusual tenseness of his large, superbly modeled frame testifying that he was under a great deal of strain. He made a conscious effort to relax, stretching his long legs out in front of him and leaning his shoulders against the seat. He closed his eyes against outside distractions and composed his thoughts so that he could give Foster a clear, concise report about the latest developments in the government of the African country where he worked, ostensibly, for an American oil firm.

The oil job was a cover, of course, though he was more than good enough at it to justify holding the position of chief financial officer for that particular branch of the multinational firm. Ordinarily his comparative youth—he was only thirty-two years old—would have prevented his obtaining the job, but the oil firm had been willing to cooperate with the United States government in providing it and had never been disappointed with the results. Charles's reputation was by now such that, regardless of whether he continued to work for the government, he was assured of a position somewhere with the firm, though they would prefer him to stay where he was, since, having grown up in the country, the son of missionary parents, he was uniquely equipped to serve there.

Charles's long, gold-tipped lashes flickered as he felt Foster pull the car to a stop. Opening his eyes fully, he saw that they were in an alley that afforded them a view of an office building across the street while keeping their own position relatively unnoticeable. He sat up, his gaze sharpening as he studied the pedestrians hurrying along the sidewalks at this early hour.

"Relax," Foster advised him dryly. "She won't be along for a while. I've been watching her long enough to know her habits, and since this is Monday, she's likely to be a little late."

Foster seemed unprepared for the steel in Charles's tone as Charles switched his gaze to him. "Why?" he asked in a deceptively quiet voice that made a slight chill run along even the seasoned Foster's back. At Foster's inquiring look, Charles clarified his question. "Why is she likely to be late because it's Monday?" he asked in a low, dangerous tone.

Foster relaxed then, looking wryly amused, a look that died when Charles's returning gaze remained stony. "Don't get your hackles up," Foster said with a grunt of disgust. "I've told you there's no man in her life now. There hasn't been in a couple of

14

years, and even then, the guy didn't last long. She's as crazy as you are!"

His tone made it evident he couldn't fathom why two people as attractive as Charles and the woman they awaited didn't take their pleasures where they found them. He knew it wasn't from lack of opportunity. He himself would secretly have given his eyeteeth for a night with the woman Charles Trainer had had him keeping an occasional eye on for the past five years. And he had inside knowledge enough about what went on back at Charles's assignment to realize that what few suitable women crossed Charles's path would be equally eager to claim his exclusive attention for however long he was willing to grant it.

"Then why is she late?" Charles persisted, ignoring Foster's comment while he relaxed somewhat at being reassured that what he had been told before about Sarah Bailey still held true.

Foster answered with lugubrious patience. "Remember I told you about that acting class for underprivileged children she sponsors?" At Charles's nod Foster went on. "Well, on Sunday nights they have long, drawn-out rehearsals. It's the only time she can spare them without interruptions. She gets home late, so I presume she sleeps late on Monday mornings." He shrugged. "Satisfied?"

Charles nodded curtly and turned his head away to stare across the street once again, his expression unrevealing, though had Foster looked closely enough into the blue eyes, he would have seen a thawing warmth there that transformed the younger man from being merely good looking to having such charm, he would stand out in any crowd.

"Okay, then, let's get down to business," Foster grunted. "What's new with Lugubu? Is he still up to no good?"

Charles stirred, shifting his body into a more comfortable position, taking a moment to get his thoughts back in order before he began to speak with crisp clarity, though his eyes never left the building across the street.

"Yes, and more so than usual. He's had some pretty suspect visitors lately, and unless I miss my guess, the meetings are connected with the fact that World Oil's agreement with the government comes up for renegotiation soon. Nothing would please him more than to kick us out and give the rights to his Slavic friends. You know that."

"Sure." Foster shrugged, one eyebrow lifting laconically. "Everybody knows that. What we need to know are the kind of tactics he'll be using this time. What do you think he has on his mind?"

"I'm not sure yet," Charles said thoughtfully. "I was hoping to get a report from one of the people I planted in his office, but it didn't come through before I had to leave. But all the signs are pointing to the fact that he's going to go to work on Njomo in earnest."

Foster frowned, pursing his lips into a thoughtful expression. "I thought Njomo didn't trust him?" he ventured.

Charles shrugged. "He doesn't. But Lugubu is as sly as a snake, and it's beginning to look like he's trying to engineer a marriage between his son and Njomo's granddaughter. If he succeeds, we may be in trouble."

Foster's shaggy eyebrows twitched in an expression of skepticism. "Why would that make such a difference with Njomo? I thought he had his head screwed on pretty good."

Charles looked impatient with Foster's lack of understanding for an instant. "He's a decent, intelligent man," he answered, his respect and affection for Njomo apparent in his tone. "But though he's worked for his country for a good many years, he's old and he's getting tired, not to mention the fact that he loves his family as much as he does his country. If Lugubu should become part of that family . . ." Charles shrugged one shoulder expressively. "Who knows what might happen? Even I can't predict which way Njomo will jump if Lugubu has the chance to work on him consistently and with the advantage of being an inside member of the tribe. And just being part of Njomo's family will increase Lugubu's stature."

For the next few moments Charles and Foster discussed the matter in more detail, but Foster, upon becoming aware that as the minutes ticked by, Charles's attention was beginning to wander more and more, finally closed the small notebook he had been using to take notes.

"Hell," he said with resigned disgust when Charles had neglected to answer a question Foster had asked twice. "It's a good

16

thing you're not Superman or you would have irradiated that building with your X-ray vision by now," he said dolefully. Giving an amused shake of his head, he suggested, "Why don't I go get us a cup of coffee while you keep watch?"

Charles's lips curved into a slight smile, but his attention never wavered from the view in front of him. "Yeah, you do that, Foster," he agreed absently, raising a strong, tanned hand to rake long fingers through his mane of thick, blond-streaked hair. "I'll give you a more thorough briefing this afternoon after I've seen Sophie."

Foster, who was halfway out of the car, turned back in puzzlement. "Sophie?" he questioned quizzically. "Her name is Sarah, isn't it?"

Charles, his mouth curving in a reminiscent smile, flicked his companion an enigmatic glance. "To the world she's Sarah," he said quietly. "To me, she's Sophie." He shrugged his magnificent shoulders, which were clad in a light blue summer suit that matched his eyes. "It's a private joke, Foster," he said negligently, but in a tone that invited no further questioning.

Foster stared at Charles for a moment longer, then, shaking his head, he climbed out of the car and shut the door. Leaning his head back in the window, he inquired, "Black or white? Sugar?"

"Whatever," Charles answered absently, his attention plainly not on how he drank his coffee.

Foster raised his eyes to heaven, then strode off in a deceptively ungainly gait to a corner grocery where he disappeared inside to purchase the coffee. Charles, meanwhile, kept his gaze roving the street in front of him. Abruptly he froze as he caught sight of a tall, slender woman racing toward the building he had been watching. She was clutching her full, gaily patterned skirt in one hand against the gusting breeze while she carried a briefcase in the other.

Charles swallowed, the tanned, smooth skin of his throat rippling with the effect as the wind suddenly ripped the skirt from the woman's hand, exposing one long, beautifully curvaceous leg for an instant before the skirt was impatiently pulled down again. His eyes traveled the length of that leg, up to the flat stomach and slender waist, the ample, warmly enticing bosom, the slender

17

neck, the firm, rounded chin, the full, generous mouth, the straight nose, the huge, gold-flecked brown eyes and the mass of windswept, vibrantly glowing sable hair.

"Sophie . . ." Charles breathed the one word, his eyes opaquely hungry as he sat remembering the silken skin, the enticing planes and angles and hollows and smoothly rounded femininity of that body. It was a body he had explored from the tip of the shining head to the soles of the slender, arched feet, even to the one slightly crooked little toe she had inherited from her mother's family. He had buried himself in that body, exulting in it, worshiping it, conquering it again and again with Sarah's hot-blooded, warmly encouraging cooperation. It had belonged to him totally at one time, as had the loving heart beating within it, the unique, highly individualistic intelligence that directed it, and the soul that gave it life.

"Sophie . . ." He said her name again in a whisper, the sound intoned with bleak yearning, the ache in his heart and in his groin threatening to force him out of the car and propel him across the street to make all of that his again then and there.

His fists, which he had been clenching unconsciously against the desire to do just that, slowly relaxed as Sarah, after giving the lopsided grin he remembered so well and a greeting to a younger woman approaching from the opposite direction, disappeared inside the doors and out of his view, if not out of his mind and heart.

"God, Sophie!" Charles muttered under his breath, after taking in a deep breath of air to fill lungs that had been deprived of it since the instant he had spotted the woman he had come to see. "You're more beautiful than ever! How is it some other man hasn't taken you away from me before now?"

The thought made him run a restless hand over the back of his tanned neck. "Have you been waiting for me, my darling Sophie?" he murmured, realizing even then that such a possibility was so remote as to be impossible. He had made a strong effort to burn his bridges behind him when he had left her five years before for the job his conscience demanded he take. For the first time in their relationship, he had hurt her, hating every moment of it and making a thoroughly bad job of it, because at the time he hadn't had much experience with the art of deception. He was

18

much better at it now, but he had never developed a taste for the practice, and he knew that as far as Sarah was concerned, he would never do it again, not even to save her from the pain of knowing he was putting himself in danger.

But five years ago he had been determined not to ask her to wait, knowing she would have if he asked, but also knowing the wait would be a very long one, or even a fruitless one. The Agency had been very careful to spell out the dangers of his assignment, and he knew enough about the death of his parents to believe their warnings.

So he had been cruel, and he would never forget the look in Sophie's eyes. It haunted his dreams to this day, accusing him, loving him, not understanding why he was hurting her so when she had given him everything she was and had to give. But even that look, though it had branded him like a flame, had failed to deter him from his duty.

Now, however, he considered he had given more than enough of himself to still the pangs of his conscience, and as his eyes bored into the building Sarah had entered, they glittered with a combination of anticipation and fierce determination.

"I'll make it up to you, Sophie," he promised beneath his breath, his mouth hardening with purpose. "I can't give either of us back the years we've lost, but I'll make the ones to come so good, we'll forget about the empty ones."

Foster's voice intruded into his thoughts as the older man thrust a cup of coffee into the open window.

"Here's your coffee," Foster grunted.

He took the coffee, feeling the tension within building once more, and as Foster trod around the car to enter the other side, Charles thought wryly that food or drink was the last thing on his mind at the moment. He wanted sustenance of a different kind—the sort only Sarah Bailey could provide.

As Foster clambered into the car, Charles straightened his shoulders, making an effort to appear relaxed and normal. He was well aware of Foster's opinion concerning Sarah, as well as how Foster viewed what he considered Charles's defection from their mutual employer. And though he didn't give a damn about Foster's opinions, he did need to get himself under control for the forthcoming meeting with Sarah, and now was as good a time to start as any.

After taking a gulp of his coffee, Foster peered through the windshield. "Any sign of her yet?" he inquired.

"She's in the building," Charles answered with a brevity that was just short of being curt.

Foster shot him a surprised glance, then grinned without mirth. "What'd you think of her?" he asked curiously, sounding callous. "Does she still get to you?"

Charles turned his head and stared at Foster through eyes that were suddenly so glacial that Foster automatically tensed into a defensive position as though he were waiting for a physical attack. Charles let his expression thaw slightly, though his voice was cold when he answered.

"She'll always 'get to me,' as you put it, Foster. Keep your questions to yourself from here on out, will you?"

The request was perfunctory, the tone of it spelling out that Foster could disregard it at his own peril. Foster eyed the still dangerous light in the icy eyes of the man beside him, pursed his lips thoughtfully, and let himself relax, thinking Charles Trainer was one man he wouldn't care to cross unless there was a damned good reason for doing so.

"Relax, Trainer," he said in a level tone. "I didn't mean anything you have to take offense to." After a moment's silence he asked with a careful lack of inflection, "How are you going to handle it? Remember, you can't tell her anything yet. In fact, it would be a hell of a lot better if you waited until you're out of the business entirely before you approach her at all."

Charles's expression hardened. "I'm not waiting," he said tersely. "I'll handle it, Foster, don't worry." He knew Foster was right—it would be better to wait until he was entirely free before seeing Sarah. But Foster wasn't the one who was being prodded by the need to see and touch and talk to Sarah, a need which had been growing with increasing ferocity since a month before, when he had learned he would be coming to New York for the final two months of his tour of duty. And no matter how unwise it might be, Charles knew he was incapable of waiting ten minutes more, much less two months, before he reestablished contact with Sarah. He had kept his own personal desires under tight

20

control for five long years. He wasn't prepared to do so any longer.

Foster shook his head fatalistically. "All right, Trainer," he said in weary tones. "Then I guess you'd better get to it. She's a busy woman. If you don't get in there soon, that little bit of a secretary of hers will manage to keep you from seeing her at all."

Charles's mouth pulled up at the corners in a hard smile and his eyes, when he turned them on Foster, were implacably determined. "Want to bet?" he asked softly, his tone harsh for all its quietness.

Foster, remembering in a brief flash how Charles had been five years ago—a charming, idealistic, almost innocent but formidably intelligent young man whom Foster privately had viewed with the skepticism of a seasoned veteran—grinned ruefully. "No, I won't bet with you, Trainer," he said wryly. "I would have when you started with us, but you're not the same man now. I wouldn't take you on in much of anything anymore."

For an instant the hard planes of Charles's face tightened, while his eyes went bleak. He knew Foster considered what he had said a compliment, but Charles couldn't help wondering if Sarah would view it as such. But there was no going back to the man he had been. He would just have to concentrate on making her love the man he now was.

"I'll pick you up in an hour," Foster said as he bent to turn on the ignition. "We have a lot to go over, and the chief wants to talk to you too. Can you get it done by then?"

"Part of it," Charles answered as he straightened his tie and pulled down his shirt-sleeves. "The rest of it will have to wait until tonight. Don't make any plans for me after five o'clock, all right?"

Foster started to say something in protest, but Charles was already getting out of the car, and in the end Foster said nothing, though his dark eyes reflected the fact that he resented being the one who would bear the brunt of the chief's displeasure at learning Charles Trainer would not be attending the intimate dinner the chief had planned for the express purpose of trying to talk Charles out of ending his involvement with the agency.

"Suit yourself," Foster muttered, thinking Charles wouldn't

hear him. He was surprised when Charles bent to peer in the window at him, a boyish light in his remarkable blue eyes.

"From now on, I intend to," Charles answered with a devilish grin Foster envied, knowing its effect on women must be earth-shaking. "See you later, Foster." Charles started to take his leave, but then he paused, his expression completely different from the chilling one Foster had seen several times since picking Charles Trainer up at the airport. Now it was calm, purposeful, and determined, containing a hint of the boyish charm Foster remembered from years ago.

"Thanks for the lift, Foster," he said, his light tone tinged with gratitude. "And thanks for keeping tabs on Sarah for me all these years. I appreciate it." The words were quietly sincere.

Despite Foster's hard veneer of cynicism and determined lack of emotionalism, he found himself grinning back at Charles. "Oh, believe me, Trainer, that was no hardship. I'm a sucker for a pair of beautiful legs, and that woman of yours has a pair of the best I've seen in years. It beat tracking the scum I usually get stuck with all to hell."

Charles smiled a slow, effortless smile, but his eyes went slight-ly cool at the remark. "Looking doesn't hurt, I guess," he said levelly, but with an inflection that made Foster feel sorry for any man who did more than look at the woman Charles Trainer considered his own.

"See you later," Charles drawled as he pivoted to stride across the street.

He might have grinned had he seen Foster pause to watch him start on his way to recapture something he'd lost a long time ago. And he would have laughed if he'd heard Foster's thoughts as the man took in the purposeful set to Charles's broad shoulders. "Funny," Foster muttered quietly to himself. "I would have said he didn't have a chance of getting that woman back after all this time. But I wouldn't bet against him now. That is one hell of a determined man!" And shaking his head philosophically, Foster put the car in motion, surprised to find himself wishing he could be there to see the coming meeting between Charles Trainer and the woman he had come halfway across the world to claim.

CHAPTER TWO

"Thaaat's right . . . drink it all up," Sarah Bailey crooned to the thirsty rubber tree she was endeavoring to coax into turning from a midget into the splendid tropical magnificence she had envisioned when she had bought it. "Mama's sorry she forgot to water you Friday, but she was in a hurry. No need to droop like that. She won't forsake you again."

Sarah's secretary, Chelley, paused in the doorway on her way into the office with the appointment book and lifted an eyebrow at Sarah's monologue.

"You're wasting your time with that ungrateful weed," Chelley remarked with a disapproving sniff. "You can water it and fertilize it and croon to it until doomsday, and it'll still just squat there soaking up all your tender loving care and refusing to put out so much as a sprout just out of sheer nastiness. Why don't you toss it out the window and be done with it?"

Sarah flicked Chelley a stern frown over her shoulder. "Shhh . . ." she hissed. "Enrico will hear you. You know how sensitive he is."

"Huh!" Chelley snorted disdainfully, crossing to the desk and slapping the appointment book down on it. "You ought to hear how I talk to him when you're not here. He thrives on it! It suits his nasty personality."

"Murderer!" Sarah said absently, straightening up and placing a hand on her back to rub a spot that had begun to ache as she'd bent over to water Enrico. "You've probably destroyed every bit of his incentive to grow with your hostility."

"No such luck," Chelley drawled, leaning against the desk and crossing her arms over her chest. "Enrico's about as sensitive as Lila Benton, who, incidentally, is going to be walking through

23

that door in about five minutes demanding you cast her in that part in Bal Henderson's new play, for which, in my opinion, she is totally unsuitable."

Sarah cast Chelley an absent look before turning back to finger a place on one of Enrico's stunted leaves that looked suspiciously yellow. "You're wrong, Chelley," she said musingly as she looked dreamily into space. "Lila's exactly right for that part— once I talk Bal into changing the character a bit," she added thoughtfully. "In fact, I wouldn't be surprised if she wasn't the hit of the season in it."

Chelley raised her eyes to the ceiling in a fit of exasperation. "And just how do you think you're going to get Bal Henderson to change the character, might I ask? He's got an ego the size of the Rock of Gibraltar, and he doesn't take kindly to suggestions from anybody." Sarah turned around and started to open her mouth, but Chelley talked over her. "And besides, why would you want to go to the trouble for Lila Benton anyway? She's never been anything but a pain in the . . ."

Sarah raised a finger and placed it over her mouth, her beautiful eyes sparkling wickedly. Chelley broke off what she'd been about to say with a disgusted shrug. "You're too softhearted, Sarah," she complained irritably. "I've told you that a thousand times!"

"Yes," Sarah said with innocent gravity. "I thought I'd heard it somewhere before." Chelley looked unrepentant, and Sarah moved her long, graceful legs in the direction of the desk and sat down to slouch low on her back with her legs straight out before her, crossed at the ankles, and her head supported on the back of the chair.

"One," she held up a graceful, pink-tipped finger, "Bal is a pushover when you know how to approach him, and two"—she held up another finger—"I don't cast parts on the basis of whether I like someone personally or not. I cast them on my judgment of whether they're right for the part. Lila will be stunning as Marilyn Mason whether you or I or anyone else likes her real personality or not. Take my word for it."

Chelley sighed, looking resignedly woeful. "I guess I'll have to," she said grudgingly. "You're the boss. Besides, you never

24

seem to be wrong." She flashed her employer a scowling look and complained, "That gets irritating in case you didn't know it."

Sarah met the look with a grin. "Come on, Chell," she coaxed her secretary playfully. "It keeps a roof over our heads, doesn't it?"

"Barely," Chelley replied with the pessimism of one who never seemed able to figure out her own balance sheet. "Which reminds me," she added, brightening somewhat. "Can I have another advance on my salary? Saks had this darling dress in the window last night, and I just couldn't re—"

"Where is everybody?" A low, sultry voice sounded from the outer room, interrupting Chelley's request. The voice sounded petulant, and Chelley gave a barely audible groan as she gave Sarah a long-suffering look over her shoulder.

"In here, Lila," Sarah called out, cautioning Chelley with a wicked grin to behave herself.

Chelley shrugged, pasted a bland look on her pixieish face, and pushed herself away from the desk. "Be firm!" she hissed over her shoulder at Sarah in a whisper before she crossed the room, arriving at the door at the exact moment it was filled by the voluptuous, sensationally dressed form of a dramatic-looking blonde.

"Oh, hello, Chelley," Lila Benton said with gracious condescension as she struck a pose for Sarah's benefit that exactly parodied one made famous by a now deceased actress whose life was the subject of Bal Henderson's new play.

"Hello, Sarah," Lila then drawled in a voice that was uncannily like that of the same actress.

"Hi, Lila," Sarah answered, barely containing her laughter at the trouble Lila was taking to impress her with her capabilities for playing the part in question. Still, those capabilities were impressive, and if Sarah hadn't already made up her mind to try to get Lila the part, she would certainly have begun considering it strongly after this display.

Lila sidled into the room, her tight, white silk dress molding her ample curves so closely, there wasn't a crease or a crevice of her body left to the imagination. Sarah quirked an eyebrow, though her eyes turned serious as she studied how closely Lila was imitating the other actress's walk.

25

"You've almost got it, Lila," she said thoughtfully, getting straight to the point as was her habit. "But Marilyn put a little jounce in her step you haven't quite got right yet. Fala Dalton's got the edge on you there, I'm afraid."

Her deliberately inflammatory statement was greeted with all the outrage she had known it would inspire.

"What do you mean Fala's got the edge?" Lila shrilled in a voice that was as far from the sultry low one she had used earlier as it could possibly get and still come from the same human being. "Are you giving her the part, Sarah?" she demanded as she abandoned the sidle and stomped toward the desk, her unsupported breasts joggling with every step. "You can't be serious!" she stormed as she leaned across the desk threateningly. "She can't hold a candle to me on stage!"

"Now, now, Lila," Sarah soothed, lifting a hand to stem the invective still sputtering on Lila's crimson lips. "I haven't given the part to anybody yet. I'm just telling you what you need to work on if you want to be seriously considered for it."

Inwardly Sarah was giving a weary sigh, wishing there were some other way to get her points across to Lila. But the woman had a head as hard as a block of granite, and Sarah knew from long experience that the only way to get through to her was to bludgeon her with her own insecurities and jealousies. Otherwise, Lila would never listen to the direction that was responsible for lifting her talent from the merely ordinary to the occasionally brilliant.

Lila fumed for a moment, her pouting lower lip stuck out like a delectable piece of fruit just waiting to be devoured by any starving male within a twenty-mile radius. Farther, actually, as it was that mouth that was responsible for Lila's burgeoning fame as the latest sex symbol—that mouth and a few other, more generous attributes she flaunted as easily as she breathed.

Switching tactics, Lila began to whine. "Sarah, honey, you know I need this part," she coaxed in her best little girl voice. "That last picture of mine was a real dud, and I want to show those Hollywood characters I really can act when I've got a decent script to work with."

Her impossibly long black lashes beat a tattoo over her languid blue eyes, and Sarah felt like telling her she was wasting her time using that tactic on another female. It should be saved for the other, more gullible sex. Instead, she gestured toward the chair on the other side of her desk.

"Sit down, Lila," she invited casually. "Have you got the script with you?" At Lila's eager nod, given as she arranged herself to the best advantage in the chair, Sarah drawled, "Have you had a chance to read all of it?"

"Oh, yes," Lila breathed with gusty eagerness, "and there's one scene that's made for me, Sarah. Let me read it to you," she said, her voice growing abstracted as she flipped the pages of the script.

Sarah said nothing, though she knew exactly which scene Lila would read because the actress was right—it was written as though the author had Lila in mind. Unfortunately, it was the only scene in the whole script that had been so written, however, and Sarah knew that unless she could talk Bal Henderson into changing the focus of the character slightly, Lila had no business in the play at all, a fact that was discouraging since Sarah didn't know of one single other actress in the whole profession who could play the part as it was now written.

Sarah leaned back in her chair, watching Lila through half-closed lids and listening with total concentration as the woman read the scene. Midway through the reading, Lila got so caught up in the role, she was up out of her chair and striding liquidly across the room, her beautiful face completely transformed into an almost unnerving resemblance to that of the actress she was portraying. Sarah sat, nodding unconsciously. When Lila got things so right, it was sheer pleasure to watch and listen to her. When at last Lila sank down to the carpeted floor, tears streaming from her vivid blue eyes as she ended the scene, Sarah gave an emphatic nod and clapped her hands enthusiastically, giving Lila her due.

"Excellent, Lila!" Sarah praised her, getting up to come around the desk and lean on the edge of it. "You've done your homework, haven't you?"

Lila tossed her head up, a complacent smile curving her voluptuous lips as she raised a languid hand to pat her rioting blond curls. She wiped the tears away from her cheeks with a prosaic gesture as she got to her feet and straightened her tight skirt around her hips. "Don't I always?" she asked smugly.

Cocking an amused eyebrow, Sarah nodded, her warm brown eyes smiling at Lila as the other woman came back to the chair to gather up her things.

"So have I got the part?" Lila asked confidently. Her frown was thunderous when Sarah quietly said she did not have it . . . yet.

"Lila," Sarah said gently, "it's a little more complicated than being able to play one scene to perfection."

"What!" Lila squawked indignantly. "What do you mean, Sarah Bailey?" Lila placed her fists on her curvaceous hips and glared at Sarah, transforming herself into a fishwife preparing to indulge in a brawl on a wharf.

"Calm down, Lila," Sarah said with no answering hostility in her patient tone. She was impervious to Lila's histrionics, having been subjected to them too many times in the past. "I have to have some discussions with Bal Henderson before I cast that part. Give me a couple of weeks and I should be able to tell you definitely one way or the other."

"A couple of weeks!" Lila flared, bright spots of red beginning to color her smooth cheeks. "I need to know now!"

"Why?" Sarah asked with a shrug, her brown, winglike eyebrows lifting inquiringly.

"Because . . ." Lila paused, pouting again as she eyed Sarah petulantly before she squared her shoulders and lifted her chin in a defensive movement. "Because Jocko Norwood has asked me to go on a cruise on his yacht, that's why!"

Sarah just looked at her steadily, trying to keep the disappointment she was feeling out of her expression. It was not her place to pass judgment on her clients.

"You needn't look at me like that!" Lila flared up. "Just because you're the frigid witch of the East doesn't mean everybody else has to be!"

Raising both eyebrows in amusement now, Sarah's lips twitched with the urge to tell Lila that frigid was definitely not an adjective Sarah would have applied to herself. But then Lila couldn't be expected to know about the dreams that still occasionally plagued Sarah's sleep even after five years. Lila could only know that Sarah's lack of a love life was common knowledge in the trade.

"I'm not judging you, Lila," Sarah said gently to the other woman. "You're old enough to know the chances you're taking by getting mixed up with someone like Jocko Norwood. It's your life."

Lila's pale cheeks flushed slightly at that, but her defensiveness remained unabated. "You're darned right it's my life, Sarah," she sulked as she grabbed up her things and headed for the door. She flung it open with one red-fingertipped hand, then turned back in a dramatic movement to fling her last shrill comment back into the room.

"You get me that part, Sarah!" she demanded in harsh tones, unaware that behind her Chelley was getting to her feet with a belligerent, protective look on her face, while the outer door to the offices was just closing behind a tall, blond, extraordinarily attractive man who paused where he was, his cool blue eyes assessing the situation.

"You know I'm right for it, and I want it!" Lila continued in a threatening tone. "What's more, I expect to hear from you in one week, not two!"

With that, Lila swung around, teetering dangerously on her ridiculously high heels, a stormy look of hostility distorting her beautiful features into an unattractive grimace. She started across the room, only to stop dead upon catching sight of Charles where he stood, his expression sardonically amused, preparing to open the outer door for her.

Lila gaped up at Charles's heavy-lidded eyes for an instant before she recovered herself, her expression changing from astonished surprise to pleased female speculation with startling rapidity.

"Well, hello," she cooed in dulcit tones that were so different from the shrill ones she had been using that Charles's pupils opened a little wider in surprise.

"Hello." He returned her greeting with calm self-possession, while Chelley, having just become aware of his presence, reacted with a startled jerk of pleasure at hearing such deep, sexy tones issuing from a man whose appearance alone was enough to seduce a woman on sight.

29

"Where did you come from?" Lila purred, blinking her false eyelashes at Charles and letting her famous lower lip pout provocatively. "I haven't seen you before, have I?"

"I'm sure you haven't," Charles replied with grave politeness, though his blue eyes moved restlessly to the door behind Lila. "I've been out of the country for quite some time."

"Well, welcome back," Lila teased flirtatiously, moving her body slightly to regain Charles's attention and distract him from his perusal of the door leading into Sarah's office. "Are you an actor?" she persisted when her ploy didn't accomplish the desired effect.

Charles switched his gaze back to her briefly, one eyebrow rising as he took in the look he was getting that, had he been less self-confident, would have made him feel like a piece of meat hanging in a butcher's window for inspection.

"No," he replied, his clipped tone denoting his growing impatience with the conversation. "Excuse me," he said with bare politeness as he moved to step around Lila, his eyes once again turning to the open door behind her.

Lila frowned while Chelley hastily moved to intercept Charles. "You can't go in there without an appointment, sir," she started to say, and then her voice died as Sarah herself appeared in the doorway, her face white, her unusually large, soft brown eyes widening even farther as she saw Charles pause on his way to her, his clear blue gaze burning with an intensity that seared her from several feet away.

"Charles . . . ?" Sarah's voice, sounding as if it came from deep within her, cracked somewhere in the middle of saying his name. With a wide, staring look, she took in his appearance from the top of his thick, gently waving, blond-streaked hair all the way to his expensively leather-clad feet. Then her gaze returned to the bronze perfection of his face, moved over the impressive width of his shoulders in the pale blue suit down to his trim waist and flat stomach, and finished at the muscular tension of his well-shaped thighs.

"It is you," she breathed in a choked voice. "I thought I heard your voice, but I couldn't believe . . ."

She stopped, helplessly dazed by the sight of the only man she had ever loved standing unexpectedly in the middle of her offices,

30

looking as tightly coiled as a spring about to unwind—in her direction.

"Hello, Sophie." Charles's tone, though very quiet, was rough with some emotion that feathered the spine of every woman in the room, including Sarah. His crystal-clear blue eyes held Sarah's warm brown ones locked in a gaze of such intense unspoken communication that Sarah went weak at the knees. They stared at each other for a long, long moment, oblivious of the interested stares they were getting from Lila and Chelley, until Charles looked toward her office and spoke again.

"I need to talk to you, Sophie. Can we go into your office?"

Temporarily released from the spell he had cast, Sarah came to herself with a start. Her eyes darted to where Lila and Chelley were watching her reactions with avid curiosity, and she cleared her throat.

"Of-of course, Charles," she responded shakily. "Chelley?" She turned to her secretary, her eyes blindly unaware that Chelley's eyes were dancing with mischievous glee. "Will you hold my calls for a while?" She neglected to wait for Chelley's response before she added vaguely, "Oh, and what time is my next appointment?"

"Not for another hour, Sarah," Chelley answered with suspicious deference. As Sarah started to turn away, however, Chelley ventured to ask, "But what if Mr. Henderson calls? You know he doesn't like to be kept waiting." Though her tone was innocently inquiring, her hazel eyes reflected deep satisfaction when Sarah's reply came, still in that abstracted tone.

"He'll have to wait this time, Chelley. Tell him I'll get back to him when I can." Sarah's attention reverted to Charles as he started toward her, his body expressing inexorable purpose with every step he took, and she began to back into her office under the force of his almost tangible aura of determination.

Sarah was surprised to find she hadn't tripped over her own feet when she at last came to a stop in the middle of her office as Charles shut the door behind him with a decided click.

Sarah's huge eyes, nakedly revealing without the smoky glasses she had left on her desk, raked his form with something like despair in their golden-flaked depths. She had always known Charles was the kind of man who could grow only more striking as he got older, but she hadn't realized he would turn out to be quite this striking. In fact, she hadn't counted on ever seeing him again at all, and his abrupt appearance here had her whole body quaking inwardly.

As Charles turned to face her, she noted half hysterically that his movements were as gracefully sensual as they were purposeful, more so than they had ever been. His thick hair, which she had always loved to thread through her fingers, was more streaked now, as though he spent a good deal of his time outdoors. And his deep tan, which set off his beautiful blue eyes with startling effect, confirmed her deduction.

"Sit down, Charles," she croaked, privately cursing her acting skills for deserting her temporarily in her time of need. She felt as if her insides had begun to melt into an indistinguishable mass and that at any moment they would start to flow out through her feet, leaving her even more empty and vulnerable than she felt already.

Charles swept his gaze over her from head to foot, cutting into her and over her like a laser beam. "I'd rather stand, Sophie," he answered with quiet firmness, the tension she had sensed in him earlier becoming even more pronounced as he stood stock-still, his whole attention focused on her until she found it increasingly hard to breathe. "I want to look at you," he added softly.

Sarah stood frozen to the spot while he did just that, her breath coming faster and faster as his gaze roamed every inch of her. There could be no mistaking his feelings at that moment. He wanted her, all of her, just as much as he ever had when they'd lived together. Perhaps more so, Sarah thought helplessly as she felt all the old responses to him coming alive inside her against her will. She couldn't recall ever seeing him look at her this hungrily. He seemed as though he had to hold himself back with all his considerable willpower to keep from devouring her whole.

When she could stand his inspection no longer, and feared she would give in to the heat he was generating just with his eyes, she stammered, "Don't, Charles!" She swallowed as he lifted his gaze to hers. "Don't look at me like that," she whispered achingly.

"Why not?" he asked, his voice husky. "What you're seeing is exactly what I feel."

32

Sarah stiffened then, all her old resentment and anger and anguish surfacing just in time to save her from making a fool of herself by running into his arms.

"And what you're seeing is exactly what you could have had five years ago," she clipped out raggedly. "You didn't want it then. Why should you want it now?"

Through a hazy cloud of remembered pain, she saw Charles's beautifully formed mouth tighten, while his expression turned to one of haggard regret. Fighting hard against the weakness that look instilled in her beleaguered heart, Sarah turned away, pivoting to move behind her desk and put its protective bulk between herself and the man who had once taken her to heaven and then cast her down into hell within the space of a few hours.

"You're wrong, Sophie," Charles answered low-voiced, moving to close the gap between them and making Sarah very glad she had put the desk in his path. "I did want you five years ago. I want you even more now. That's why I'm here."

Sarah stared at him, noting with half her attention how sensuously appealing he looked standing there, his body seemingly relaxed until one noted that his hands were clenched into fists and his shoulders were tensed like a tightly drawn bow ready to snap him in her direction.

She forced herself to smile wryly, blessing her years of theatrical training. She was not a working actress now, but all the moves were still there, and right now she needed them badly.

"I find that hard to believe," she said in dry tones. And then in self-defense she made herself try to hurt him the way he had hurt her in the past. "But then, you do seem to have trouble being consistent. Five years ago, if I recall correctly, it took you less than a day to go from being a devoted lover to a nonexistent one. Forgive me if I find it difficult to take you seriously now."

She hoped she had sounded lightly casual. She hoped her face was under control and not displaying the agony she felt at the memory of how Charles had shattered her hopes and her love with no warning. Indeed, he had made passionate love to her throughout the night before he had faced her the next morning with the news that he was leaving her for good.

So why was he here now? she wondered, her anger growing. Now that the shock of seeing Charles again was dissipating,

33

there was room for other emotions, and they were swamping her like a floodtide.

The strength of her responses to Charles—both positive and negative—literally staggered Sarah. She had thought she was well and truly over him at last and had been for some time, despite the recurring dreams that took her unawares occasionally. And she was furious to discover that it was taking only a few moments in his presence to bring him thudding back into her emotions with a force that was agonizingly unfair!

"Sophie, you have a right to feel as you do," Charles said, his voice deeply timbered with regret. "I hurt you badly. I hurt myself as much. Will you give me a chance to show you that I never stopped loving you?"

Stunned by his declaration, Sarah stiffened, drawing in upon herself to block out the appeal in his voice and in his words. Out of a deep need for self-protection, she ignored his question and flared, "Don't call me that! My name is Sarah!"

Charles held her eyes with his own as he murmured, "Not to me. Never to me, Sophie."

His words slashed at her heart, and Sarah had to struggle desperately to keep herself under control. "Stop it, Charles!" she demanded, her voice ragged with her conflicting emotions. "Please, just stop it!"

Her tone was barely civil, but there was an unconscious plea underlying it as well, and at hearing it, Charles came around the desk, moving quickly and purposefully. He stopped Sarah's instinctive movement away from him before it was half started, pulling her into his arms with a force that stunned her.

"Sophie . . . Sophie . . ." Charles breathed her name against her hair while his hands traveled over her, remembering, cherishing, wanting. "God, I've missed you so much!" he ground out raggedly as he tipped her head back to stare with blazing intensity into her tortured eyes. "You can't imagine how much I've needed you!"

In the space of an instant Charles's words transformed Sarah from a molten mass of sensitized nerve endings to a coldly angry woman with bitterness blazing from the depths of her brown eyes.

"Can't I?" she asked with unnatural harshness as she wedged

her hands in between them. "Do you really think I handled your desertion without a moment's pain? Do you think I didn't miss and need you too?" she asked witheringly.

To her angry surprise, her denunciation didn't have the desired effect. True, there was pained regret in the clear luminosity of Charles's eyes. But she wanted far more from him than regret. She wanted explanations, and perhaps revenge as well. She opened her mouth to flay him with words, but he put a finger over her lips.

"Shhh . . ." Charles whispered huskily as she tried to sputter against his restricting finger. "I know I handled things badly when I left you, Sophie. Preachers' boys don't get much practice at deception." His eyes teased as he shared an old, unspoken, private joke between them, one that caused a dart of combined pain and pleasure in Sarah's breast.

"I'm a lot better at concealing the truth now than I was then, Sophie," he continued, sad bleakness in his tone. "But I don't intend to lie to you ever again. If I can't answer you truthfully from here on out, I won't answer you at all." And as he noted the puzzled, resentful expression in Sarah's eyes, he shook his head in frustration. "I have to talk to you privately, Sarah, without interruptions." His look indicated the office didn't fulfill those requirements. "And soon," he added, returning his gaze to her. "Tonight in fact. Are you willing to listen?"

Sarah regarded his strongly planed face warily, noting that where once Charles would have teased and cajoled her with delightful beseeching humor, now he simply waited for her answer with a tense calmness. Her protective instincts told her she would be a fool to make herself vulnerable to him again by spending any more time with him. Already, after only a few minutes in his company, vulnerable was too weak a word to describe the effect he was having on her. But if she didn't see him again, how would she ever understand why he left her and what he was doing here now?

"Come on, Sophie," he murmured in a low, husky, sexy voice. "I'm not going to hurt you again. I never want to hurt you again."

The sincerity in his voice had Sarah momentarily wanting to believe him before she repressed the reaction, cursing her susceptibility to his brand of deception. Still, she had her own reasons for wanting to see him again, chief among them the chance to vent her long bottled up feelings of outrage at his betrayal all those years ago.

"I . . . all right, Charles," Sarah gave in, telling herself she was compelled by her own reasons, not by Charles's persuasion. "We can have dinner tonight," she added coolly. "You can pick me up at five thirty."

The last statement was meant to sound coldly businesslike, but Charles destroyed the effect by choosing that precise moment to pull Sarah's lower body closer to his in an instinctive movement of relief and joy.

Charles's gaze warmed at seeing the involuntary closing of her eyes. "I'll be here," he promised in a very soft, very deep voice. "Don't back out on me, honey," he prodded, giving her a searching look that told her that even if she tried to back out, he would find some way to see her. "This is important, Sophie," he added huskily. "To both of us."

Sarah widened her eyes and flashed him a contemptuous look that said more plainly than words that if he had waited five years to see her, nothing could be that important, but she said nothing. Instead, she gasped when he then said, with a smile that twisted her emotions yet more, "I haven't kissed you yet, Sophie, and I need something to last me until five thirty."

She opened her mouth to protest, but she didn't have time to say anything before Charles's lips seized hers in a hungry invasion that for Sarah shattered the present into a thousand pieces and thrust her back five years. Suddenly a hunger of her own enveloped her with an intensity she hadn't experienced in so long, she had actually forgotten, consciously at any rate, what it felt like to have every cell of her body awake and alive and ferociously greedy for all the sensations Charles had honed to perfection when she had belonged to him.

He withdrew from her slightly to stare into her eyes, his own fiercely blue with passion. "God, Sophie!" he choked out in a strangled tone. "It's all still there! Nothing's changed! It's only gotten stronger!"

He had been a man five years ago, but now Sarah became aware he'd changed to a harder, more determined, more ruthless man. It was in his voice, in his touch, and in the rough hunger of his mouth as it closed over hers again, forcing her lips apart so that his tongue would have access to the sustenance she provided. In the past he had been so very gentle, so sweetly loving, and yet so completely masculine. Now he was so dominantly forceful, she had little choice but to submit to his kiss, and as she did so, and as she became increasingly alarmed by the way the heat she felt in him was igniting her own fires, she realized with a sinking, helpless feeling that it was going to take every ounce of willpower she had to keep her emotional and physical distance from Charles. His appeal was now almost irresistible. It was that simple . . . and that dangerous!

He was straining her to him so intensely as he forced her curves into the hard planes of his body with kneading, wanting hands, that it came as a shock to Sarah when he finally thrust her back from him and held her inches away in a hurting grip that told her how hard it was for him to break contact with her. His eyes were glinting sleepily with passion, his jaw was set in a harsh mold, and his mouth was forming into a harsh line where seconds ago it had been warmly full as a result of their kiss.

"If I don't get out of here now, I'll take you on the floor!" he ground out in a rasping husk.

Sarah stared at him mutely as he started toward the door. "We'll talk tonight, Sophie," he said with an abrupt raggedness that told her he was still fighting for control over his arousal. "I can't be with you anymore right now. Not like this."

He paused at the door with his hand on the knob and turned his body toward her, a look in his eyes that was like an exquisite touch of fire. And then he said it. He said the words she had dreamed about, tried to make herself forget she'd ever heard, and never expected to hear again.

"I love you, Sophie," he said with quiet ferocity. "I loved you when I left you, and I love you now." He paused, but at seeing that Sarah was too shocked to respond, he smiled at her, a crooked, purposeful smile that echoed the intent in his eyes. "And I intend to hear you say the same to me again, Sophie," he added very softly. "I'll make you feel it again, and then I'll hear you say it again, or . . ."

But he didn't spell out what the consequences might be. In-

37

stead, he jerked the door open and let himself out while Sarah stood frozen where she was, shaken to the core by his words and by the sheer dominance of the man he now was. As she stood there, she wondered what in God's name had happened to him to turn him into such a man. The question echoed over and over again in her mind, making her oblivious to the fact that Chelley had come into the room and was inspecting her with a wicked, knowing smile and a great deal of sparkling curiosity.

"*Who* was that?" Chelley finally broke the silence, making Sarah drag her attention back to the present. "I'd cast him as my leading man any day of the week," Chelley added archly.

Sarah gathered her shattered composure together, managing a faint smile. "A man from my past," she answered calmly enough, though it took a great deal of effort. In order to forestall the questions she saw hovering in Chelley's sparkling hazel eyes, she gave her secretary an order, speaking with unusual curtness.

"Get me Bal Henderson on the phone, Chelley. Lila's right for that part, and I need to start working on Bal to land it for her before she gets herself into trouble."

Momentarily diverted, Chelley replied in an exasperated tone. "I heard what she said to you, Sarah, and it made me good and mad! Don't you think she needs to learn that instant gratification isn't always possible in this business?"

Irritated unreasonably by Chelley's tendency to argue every instruction, Sarah practically snapped at her secretary for the first time since Chelley had come to work for her.

"Just get him on the phone, Chelley!" she said with gritting patience. "I'm not in the mood to discuss my methods of handling clients right now!"

Chelley blinked in surprise before her gaze grew speculative as she contemplated the reasons for her employer's uncustomary bad humor. Then, with a shrug, she turned away to go to the telephone, but when she came back with the news that Bal Henderson wasn't in his office just then, her hazel eyes glinted with her determination to have her say.

"I don't know what's going on between you and that blond Viking who was just in here, Sarah," she began, "but if you want my opinion, you'll get him out of your past and into your future fast!" And with a gleeful chortle, she scuttled out the door to escape Sarah's withering glare.

When Chelley was gone, Sarah sank down into her chair, feeling as though all of her bones had suddenly decided to play hooky from the job of supporting the rest of her. She felt as though she'd just finished running a marathon, but as tired and disoriented as she felt, she still had the strength to maintain the remnants of her anger. How dare Charles reappear out of the blue to turn her well-ordered life upside down, to stir up emotions—good and bad—she would have preferred to let sleep? And damn him for still possessing the power to stir her as no other man ever had.

She clutched her head in her hands, besieged by conflicting thoughts. Was it really possible that Charles still loved her?

Puzzled, outraged, and frightened by the impact Charles had had on her, Sarah groaned and leaned back in her chair to stare grimly at the wall across from her. "I won't go tonight!" she gritted softly to herself, gathering her self-defensive anger about her like a shield. "I won't be here when he comes to pick me up. Let him wonder where I am and whom I'm with . . . let it tear him apart the way he tore me apart, damn him!"

But remembering the way Charles had kissed her, and the sound of his voice when he had told her he loved her, she knew she wouldn't back out of their meeting that night. For even though she was almost terrified at the thought of becoming vulnerable to him again, she felt an inner excitement building she hadn't felt since the year they'd lived together. She told herself she was just eager to at last obtain the answers to questions that had plagued her for years, and to take this opportunity to express the anger and heartache that still burned inside her even after all this time.

But as she gathered her composure together to get through the rest of the day, a still, small voice inside her was mockingly calling her a fool, while Charles's image—the sound and touch and smell and impact of him—stayed with her throughout the hours with a vividness there was nothing she could do to dispel.

CHAPTER THREE

A few minutes past five, Sarah waved Chelley out of the office, having gotten her to leave on time by giving her a requested salary advance, and encouraging her to use her time spending money rather than earning it.

As she returned to her own office to get her makeup kit from her purse, Sarah felt no pangs of conscience at employing such a subterfuge. Chelley was entirely too curious and outspoken to refrain from badgering Sarah to the point of insanity if Chelley had known the "Viking" would be returning to the office in a few moments.

As Sarah touched up her makeup, applying shaded browns to her lids, a smooth blush to her high cheekbones, and a tawny peach lip gloss to her mouth, she studied her face absently, wondering what there was about it to attract Charles enough to bring him back to her again after all this time. But as she pulled a brush through the lushness of her long sable hair, she reflected that he had been attracted to her from the first moment they literally ran into each other as each had rounded a corner in the Administration Building at the university all those years ago.

Of course, it might just have been the fact that they were both older than most of the students crowding around them, since both of them were working on their master's at the time. But that didn't wholly explain the immediate spark that had ignited as blue eyes met brown in surprise and consternation after their collision. And hard on the heels of Sarah's rather stunned "Sorry," Charles had taken all of her in in a measured look, smiling a smile that had dazzled her with its sweet charm, before replying, "My fault, can I buy you a cup of coffee to make it up to you?"

That had been the start of a relationship that had gone from immediate attraction to a mutual blazing desire within the space of a few hours, a desire that soon had Sarah so frustrated, she almost seduced him.

They had been sitting in her cramped Volkswagen in a parking area fronting a moonlit lake exactly one week after they'd met. Each was breathing hard after a short, explosive bout of petting that had done little but make the two of them writhe with ragged frustration, when Sarah, after taking all her courage in her hands, said, "Charles, do you want to make love to me?"

He had given her a look that reeked of male incredulity that she had had to ask such a question, but Sarah, despite the evident physical signs that Charles wanted her, had been fearful that his early upbringing as the son of missionary parents might make him hesitate or, worse, reject her. And she had had to quell her nervous tremors as she persisted, "Then why don't you?"

"God, Sarah!" he had answered, his voice taut with frustration. "Do you think I wouldn't have already if you hadn't told me you're a virgin? We haven't known each other long enough to think about marriage, and even if we had, I'm in no position to ask you. I'd lose my scholarship, and though that wouldn't matter so much if I wasn't already three years behind where I should be because of—" But he had broken off there, and after an almost infinitesimal pause, he'd continued. "It just doesn't make sense to add another year's delay because I can't keep my hands off you."

This last had been accompanied by a rueful, burning gaze that had made Sarah want him to take her in his arms again. Instead, she had taken a deep breath and plunged over the deep edge.

"My virginity is mine to give, Charles," she had said, softly sincere. "Something's always stopped me before, but not with you. You're the one I've been waiting for." And at Charles's startled, intensely wondering gaze, she had plunged onward. "I know it's too soon to think about marriage," she said with shaky quietness. "But that doesn't mean we can't have what's possible, and I want it! I want you! Please, don't let me sit here feeling like a fool much longer. Tell me you want me."

The silence that had greeted her suggestion had stretched her nerves to the breaking point before Charles had answered, his

41

voice lightly teasing, though there had been a serious, tender undercurrent as well.

"My parents warned me about falling into the clutches of scheming temptresses who might try to seduce me and lead me into a life of sin and degradation, and here I am, just as they feared, being propositioned by an actress, no less." The mockery in his tone had been loving, however, and as Sarah turned to look into his face, not knowing whether to feel offended or amused by his words, he had bathed her with an expression of such sensuous tenderness, she had had to catch her breath against the love she felt for him.

She had managed to respond with shaky pertness. "And my Aunt Sarah, God rest her soul, who raised me after my parents were killed, warned me about tall, blond, preacher's boys who smile like angels and kiss like devils." And then she had let her smile die and faced Charles with her soul in her eyes. "Are we going to ignore all those warnings, Charles? Are you going to make love to me?"

"The sooner the better," he had responded with a grin and a lusty growl in his voice that had made her thrust herself into his arms with relief and happiness and a growing sense of anticipation that made her tremble.

They had both been so innocent, Sarah remembered now, reminiscent sadness in her eyes as she stared at herself in the mirror. Their first time together, after they had finally found a tiny motel that fit their combined budgets, had been beautifully eager and tender, if a trifle inept. Somehow, in a world of sexual liberation, they had remained innocent, Charles perhaps because of his upbringing in another world under the tutelage of loving, but morally strict, parents, and Sarah because some deep inner instinct had warned her time and again to wait, until Charles had appeared in her life, and her instincts had dissolved into a glorious recognition that the waiting time was over.

Charles had delighted in teasing her about what knowledge she did have, gained from gossip and her omnivorous reading habits, and as their hunger for each other had grown, he had laughingly encouraged her to obtain ever more detailed "dirty" books, as he termed them, since he was the ultimate recipient and more than willing coexperimenter in what she learned from them.

Their decision to live together had been inevitable, Sarah reflected as she stood blindly staring at her own image in the mirror while she relived her memories. And again, she had been the one to suggest it. Neither of their living arrangements allowed them to be together in the way both wanted. But when she had brought up the matter, Charles had hesitated, distressing her with his reluctance. When he realized he'd hurt her, he started to make an explanation, but then broke it off, and when he took her into his arms to tell her he agreed, he had the look of a man who knew he would pay later for taking what he wanted in the present.

But Sarah had been so happy, she'd soon forgotten that look, and as their relationship deepened day-by-day, as the joy they found in each other increased until Sarah actually forgot most of the time that they weren't married, she gave herself totally to the man who could make her laugh, and cry with tenderness, and brighten her days in a way she'd never known was possible.

Sarah shifted where she stood as she approached the point in her memories where everything had changed, and her complexion paled as she forced herself to live that last night, and that last, devastating morning, she and Charles had spent together. The remembered pain might help her be strong tonight.

Their last night together had been one long explosion of loving eroticism. It had started in a celebration. The term was over and each had obtained the degrees they sought, a master's in drama for Sarah, a master's in finance for Charles. And it had ended in bed, with Charles's loving becoming almost desperately demanding and intense throughout the night. Sarah had attributed the unusual intensity of his lovemaking to his relief that the grueling year was over now, and the two of them could make their life together permanent.

In the mirror Sarah saw her eyes grow bleak as she remembered the morning after the loving. She had woken late to find Charles sitting beside the bed, fully dressed, watching her with a tight, bleakly forbidding expression that had startled and worried her. That expression hadn't changed when, in an attempt to make it go away, Sarah had stretched luxuriously, then held out

43

her arms to him, a smile of bemused, sleepy pleasure curving her love-softened lips.

"What are you doing dressed?" she had mumbled teasingly. "It's Saturday. Come back to bed."

"No, Sarah," Charles had answered in a harsh voice, as though he held himself on a tight rein he dared not relinquish. She had been surprised, not only by his use of her given name rather than the special one they used between them, but by the coldness in his eyes. "I have to leave," he had added so abruptly that Sarah had had to blink away her astonishment.

"Leave?" she had asked in a bewildered tone. "For where? I didn't know you had a trip planned."

"It's not a trip, Sarah!" Charles had answered as he thrust himself from his chair and paced toward the window to stand with his back to her. "I'm leaving for good."

Sarah, growing more alarmed by the moment, had stared at his broad back for a long time, so completely caught off-guard, she couldn't believe she had heard him correctly.

"I don't understand," she had managed to say at last, sitting up to reach for her robe. "What's wrong, Charles? I don't know what you're talking about."

He had turned then, the icy gaze in his blue eyes freezing her in the action of climbing from bed. "It's over," he had said with a quiet inflexibility. "After this morning, you won't be seeing me again."

Feeling that suddenly her world had turned upside down, Sarah had clutched her throat, her huge eyes wide and staring, as she mumbled, almost incoherently, "What have I done?" And then in a thick voice filled with panic overlying her pain, she had pleaded with him. "Charles, tell me what I've done! If I know, I can fix it! I love you, Charles . . ." With a gulp to swallow down the sob rising in her throat, she had begged him with her eyes. "Please." She had buried all her pride. "Please, don't leave me, Charles."

With a film of tears obscuring her vision, Sarah had never been sure she had actually seen the flicker of something approaching agony in Charles's blue eyes. But she had certainly heard the note of finality in his voice when he had replied.

"You haven't done anything, Sarah," he had said with ragged

fierceness. "And there's nothing you can do to make me stay. I've had a job offer, and I'm taking it." And then he had fore-stalled her plea to take her with him by adding immediately, "I can't have you with me. You'd just be in the way."

The cruelty in that last statement had devastated her. She had stared at him mutely, feeling more disoriented than she ever had in her life. She would have staked her life on the belief that Charles loved her as much as she loved him, and that he had planned to marry her now that they had their degrees. But the look on his face, the tone in his voice, the cutting cruelty of his words, convinced her in one agonizing, soul-destroying moment that she had been wrong. Charles didn't love her.

When she was finally able to speak, she had mumbled, in a voice as devoid of emotion as she felt, "If you're going, go. There's not much point in staying around now, is there?"

"Sophie." She looked at him. The pain in his voice had been matched in his eyes. "I did this all wrong," he had muttered wearily a muscle in his jaw flexing with some strong emotion. Sarah thought it must be self-disgust. She knew it wasn't love for her. He couldn't possibly love her and still hurt her this way.

"I thought if I was cruel enough, you'd put me behind you sooner," Charles had tried to explain while Sarah had just stared at him, her eyes blank with shock. "I . . . there are things I have to do with my life," he had begun a faltering explanation. "Com-mitments I've made that I have to keep. Sarah, I had no right to love you. No right to make you love me the way you do. But damn it, I'm only human!" he had ground out. "And from the first moment we met, I couldn't help myself. When you asked me to make love to you, I couldn't help myself. And every moment we've had together is a gift—a treasure I can't regret even now!"

He'd stepped back from her then, his expression haggard. "Don't look at me like that, Sophie," he'd whispered raggedly. "I'm sorry. If it weren't for the things I have to do . . ."

But his incomplete explanation had just made things worse as far as Sarah had been concerned, and she had cut him off abrupt-ly.

"Then go do them," she'd said, the unnatural calm in her voice overlaid with bitterness. "You're right. Your cruelty will make me forget you sooner. I'll get over you if it's the last thing I ever do."

She had had the hollow satisfaction of seeing Charles flinch, as though he'd received a physical blow. And she had remained unmoved, considering that the blow she had delivered was mild in comparison to the one she'd received.

Then he had gathered himself together, and she would never forget the way he had seemed to draw on some deep inner well of strength she knew she herself didn't have. He had stepped back from her, and said with quiet ferocity, "I hope you do, Sarah. It's the best way. Forget me. Consider me dead if it helps. Use anything you have to to put your life back together again." And with his face looking as though it had been carved in stone, he had turned away from her, leaving the room and the apartment and Sarah, his back straight, his step firm, his shoulders rigid.

Sarah sighed, grimacing at her image before she put her make-up away and crossed to the window to stare down at the city street below which was now jammed with homegoing traffic. Everything was bathed in a golden, late afternoon light that matched her mood of anticipation. In nature, the waiting was for the cloak of night to fall. In her case, the waiting was undefined, characterized by a restless, anxious sense of anticipation and dread combined.

As she stood there remembering those times with Charles, she could only hope with all her heart, that she was stronger now, strong enough to sit across from him in a restaurant while she listened to what he had to say. Strong enough to say no if he really wanted her back. Strong enough to put him in the past where he belonged once and for all.

Sarah jumped reflexively as she heard the outer office door open and close again, and she swung around just in time to see Charles fill the door to her inner office. For long seconds the two of them simply stared at each other, Sarah unaware that her features were expressing fierce hostility, while Charles's expression became quietly impassive, with only his blue eyes seeming to be alert and alive, and just as fiercely determined as they had been that morning.

"Are you ready, Sarah?" he asked at last in a quiet, almost

formally polite tone, his use of her given name emphasizing that strange formality. Still, there had been a quality to his question that made Sarah uneasily aware that he might be asking something more meaningful than whether she was ready to go out and dine with him.

Straightening her shoulders, she faced him with a steady serenity she was far from feeling. "I'm ready, Charles," she replied levelly, hoping she was replying to any question he might have been asking.

After an infinitesimal pause, Charles slowly lifted his arm and extended his hand to her. "Then let's start," he said simply, though there was an unspoken word at the end of his suggestion that pounded in Sarah's brain as she moved toward him. The word was *over*. Charles had not finished the sentence, but as Sarah placed her slightly shaking fingers in his firm, warm hand, the convulsive pressure of his strong fingers as they closed over hers spelled out what he'd really meant. He had meant Let's start over, and as he drew Sarah close to him and tucked her hand over his arm so that she could feel the warmth of his body through his suit, she could only pray that the conflict over what he'd meant, and what she intended, would be resolved in her favor.

CHAPTER FOUR

At this early hour, the small, secluded restaurant Charles picked was almost deserted, and the isolated booth with high, red leather sides, enhanced Sarah's nervous sensation of being completely alone with him. There was room in the booth for her to put a reasonable distance between them, but after Charles had seated her on one of the outer curves, he disconcerted her by sliding in the other side and shifting to within a foot of her, far too close for Sarah's peace of mind. She could feel his knee almost touching hers beneath the table, and indeed, occasionally she felt the actual brush of it against her own, a sensation that, every time it happened, succeeded in distracting her from her desperate determination to hang on to her anger and her common sense.

A black-suited waiter approached them with alacrity, and without asking her preference, Charles ordered for both of them, choosing a white wine Sarah had always favored when he had known her before. She felt a waspish desire to ask him if he didn't think her tastes might have changed over the years, but she decided to save such barbs for when she might need them more desperately.

Charles merely watched her while they waited for the waiter to return with their drinks, his eyes roaming her stoically composed face as though he wanted to commit every pore of her skin to memory. In reaction to Charles's concentrated inspection, Sarah at first determinedly let her eyes travel the room around them. But at last, in an outward fit of exasperation, she gave in to her own strong desire to examine him as closely as he was watching her, and turned to boldly let her eyes travel his face. Immediately her gaze was caught and held in a vise of shimmering blue intensity which, contrary to what might be expected of

48

such a cool color, warmed her from head to foot with an exclusive intimacy she remembered so heartbreakingly well.

The returning waiter broke up their mutual absorption as he set glasses on the table and chattered cheerfully about the weather.

"Leave the bottle," Charles instructed him quietly, his suave, authoritative calmness making the waiter bow respectfully. "In an hour," Charles continued, "we'll have the beef Stroganoff with a green salad and the house dressing. Until then, we don't want to be disturbed."

The waiter murmured his acquiescence and walked away, and when Charles turned back to Sarah, it was to see her brown eyes snapping angrily at him. "That was rather a cheap shot, Charles," she managed to speak with reasonable composure, though her hand shook as she reached for her glass of wine. "Are you going to do that all night?" she queried, hating the quiver in her voice.

Charles clasped one strong, warm hand over her wrist as she toyed with the stem of her glass. "It wasn't meant to be a ploy to make you remember our past together, Sophie," he said with deep-toned sincerity. "I simply didn't want to waste time looking at a menu, so I ordered what I knew you used to like so much." He pressed his fingers into her wrist lightly. "Relax, honey," he said softly. "Let go of your mistrust for a little while. Try to listen with an open mind."

Sarah cast him a wary, hostile look, hoping against hope that he wasn't aware of the reason for the fluttering of her pulse beneath his fingers. But of course he was, she thought despairingly when Charles's eyes swept over her with the same sleepy passion he had displayed in the office earlier that day. But after giving her wrist one last squeeze, he removed his hand to lift his own glass of wine to his lips and drank deeply.

Sarah did the same before she eyed him curiously, noting that he was refilling his glass after having drained it in one swallow. "Have you taken up drinking, Charles?" she asked soberly, so unnerved by the indications she was picking up that underneath his familiar exterior, Charles was a different, harder man now, that she forgot to curb her tongue.

Charles flicked her a look that was so self-assured, she had

49

trouble believing his answer. "I drink more than I used to, Sophie," he drawled. "But tonight I'm drinking for courage." He shrugged, making her aware of the breadth of his shoulders. "I could get drunk just on the sight of you, but you aren't ready yet for the consequences of that, are you?"

"Hardly," Sarah said stiffly, though she was dismayed at feeling a surge of heat as she thought of the implications of his question.

"I meant it when I said I love you, Sophie," he said in a low tone of rough sincerity. "And you've got to believe that I loved you when I left you. In fact, it was because I loved you so much that I had to leave you in the way that I did."

The slight hesitation before the last few words, and the tone of self-disgust Charles imparted to them made Sarah weaken, and she had involuntarily lifted a hand toward him before she realized what she was doing, and jerked it back.

Charles reached across and seized it in his own, his grip almost as painfully intense as was his steady gaze, which held her own, forcing her to look into his eyes. "Do you believe me, Sophie?" he asked in a voice roughened by emotion.

"I . . ." Sarah had to stop and swallow, besieged as she was by the power of Charles's personality, the seductiveness of his hand on hers, and the faint scent of his aftershave that enveloped her in memories. His body, though he held it still, was so threateningly sensual, she could feel an answering stir of arousal deep within her.

"No, I don't, Charles," she managed to answer, a lie prompted more by her need to protect herself than from an overt desire to deny the truth. For she did believe him, she realized with an inner wail of incredulity at her own foolishness. But how could she trust herself? She had believed him once before, and she had been so disastrously wrong.

She felt a zing of empathy when she saw the pained disappointment in Charles's eyes, and she hastily took him up on the rest of his statement. "It makes no sense to me that after what we'd had together—" She stopped, deeming it foolish to make the assumption that Charles had viewed what they'd had together in the same way she had. "I just can't imagine any possible reason why you should have had to be so cruel about the way you left me because you *loved* me," she finished in a tone of cold disbelief as she regathered the folds of her protective anger about her again.

Charles sighed, giving her hand a squeeze before he leaned back against the cushions of the booth, seeming to prepare for a long discussion. "I had a job to do, Sophie," he said in his smooth, deep voice. "A job I couldn't turn my back on. I owed dues. My education was paid for with the expectation that I would devote at least five years to . . . well, to a job I was uniquely qualified to handle, and which for personal reasons, I wanted to take on. It was a nasty job in some ways," he continued in rather a sad, musing tone, Sarah thought. "But a necessary one."

He held her gaze intently as he went on, and Sarah, unable to look away, tense with the knowledge that she was finally going to get some answers to questions that had plagued her for years, stared back at him with total concentration.

"To this day I can't tell you what the job is all about," Charles said, making Sarah's full mouth twist into a spasm of disappointment. "I would if I could, darling," he assured her firmly. "But I haven't the right. All I can tell you is that if I had married you, as I wanted to do, I still couldn't have taken you with me. It wouldn't have been permitted, and the restriction was a wise one. I couldn't have functioned for worrying about you."

He hesitated before continuing. "And I couldn't ask you to wait. I knew I would be gone at least five years, which I have been," he added with harsh longing for those lost years coloring his tone. And then he startled her into frozen attention by adding so softly she wasn't sure she had heard him correctly, "That is, if I was able to come back at all."

She was certain she hadn't mistaken his meaning. He wasn't talking about not being able to come back for any mundane reason. He was talking about not coming back to her because he might be dead.

Sarah felt faint for a moment, and her white face must have shown her disturbance because Charles frowned, then let go of her hand so that he could place his own on the back of her neck. He rubbed her nape with disturbingly tender roughness. "Are you all right, Sophie?" he asked in a voice made harsh by concern.

51

Sarah shuddered, then took a deep breath to restore her equilibrium. "Yes," she said faintly. "But I need a drink."

Charles thrust her glass of wine into her hand and watched as she raised it shakily to her mouth and drank deeply of the contents. When she set the glass back down, it was empty, and she flicked a glance at the bottle. "More, please," she said on a breathless gasp.

Charles frowned again, hesitated, then reached for the bottle to refill her glass. When he had done so, Sarah carefully lifted it to her mouth, sipping this time rather than gulping, while Charles stayed silent, his gaze almost as grim as his voice when he finally spoke. "Your reaction just now convinces me I was right not to tell you anything before. Do you see why I made such a mess of saying good-bye?"

Sarah gazed at him, her heart in her eyes, her generous mouth starting to tremble with the emotions that gripped her. "If you knew all that time that you were going to have to say good-bye someday . . ." She faltered, but her look was accusing.

"Why did I get involved with you in the first place?" Charles finished for her, his face full of resigned self-condemnation. And at Sarah's mute nod, he sighed. "I knew it was wrong, Sophie," he said softly. "But it was more than I could do to walk away from you then. When we first met, I didn't know I was going to fall head over heels in love with you. I was lonely, and I'd been through—" He stopped, shaking his head angrily. "Never mind," he clipped out. And then he was back to a tone of gentle remembrance.

"When we ran into each other, I didn't intend to get as involved with you as I did. I simply wanted to spend some time with a beautiful young woman, have some laughs, lead a semblance of a normal life for a change. But before I knew what was happening, you were part of me."

With a deep sigh Charles locked his gaze into Sarah's and went on. "I knew that living with you was only going to make it harder to say good-bye someday. But I wanted you with me for as long as possible, in every possible way. So instead of being strong and brave, I was human and weak. I'm sorry I hurt you, Sophie," he finished softly, roughly sincere. "But I'm not sorry we had that time together. The memories have sustained me for five long years—the memories and the hope that someday we'd get it all back."

As he lapsed into silence, Sarah's continued confusion was clearly evident in her anguished expression. And then she brought an answering look to his face by whispering, "It hurt so much, Charles. I thought I'd die of it."

Charles moved closer, put his hand on the back of her neck, and tipped her chin up with his thumb.

"I know, baby," he rumbled from deep in his chest. "I'd have given anything not to have it so."

Slowly his mouth came closer until Sarah's eyes fluttered closed and her breath sighed in her throat as his lips gently closed over her own. It was not a sensuous kiss, unless one counted a sincere desire to offer comfort and an exquisite capacity for gentle tenderness as seduction of a special kind. Sarah obviously did, because by the time Charles raised his head again, her eyes had grown sleepily luminous, and her mouth stayed parted as though waiting for more of Charles's brand of sweet seduction.

He smiled at seeing that look, but he didn't renew the kiss, though it obviously cost him a lot to deny her. "We're in a public place," he murmured with loving teasing in his voice. "Otherwise, I'd accept what you're offering. I do intend to, though, once we're out of here."

Sarah blinked at him, slowly coming out from under his spell. Finally she sat straighter, her cheeks blooming with a lovely color as Charles continued to watch her with his special look of sensuality she remembered had always preceded his lovemaking in the past.

"It isn't that easy for me, Charles," she breathed in a quavering voice. "I never thought . . . I never suspected . . ." Suddenly she raised stricken eyes to his, their soft brown depths swimming with unshed tears. "I thought you'd used me, Charles," she accused him. "And it shook my faith in everything and everyone for so long." She gave a short, harsh laugh, ignoring the concern for her Charles was showing. "After all, if I could misjudge you after having lived with you for a whole year, during which I was certain you loved me, only to have you walk out without a

53

second thought . . ." Sarah took a deep, steadying breath. "Well, I was obviously no judge of human character, was I?"

She flinched at the sudden savage anger in Charles's blue eyes, which quickly turned to regretful frustration, though his expression was still hard.

"God damn it, Sophie, don't ever say that to me again," he rasped in a tone that wrapped Sarah in a chill. "I never used you! And as for walking out without a second thought . . ." Charles shook his head in an expression of disbelief, and his hand trembled slightly as he raked it around the back of his tanned neck. "Hell, I've never been so torn up about anything in my life except—" But again he bit off what he'd been about to say, and Sarah, growing used to his mysterious silences now, was seized by a sudden, half-hysterical desire to laugh at the sense of unreality his reticence imparted to their conversation.

Then Charles took her hand in both of his, and Sarah was utterly conquered for the moment by the absolute sincerity in his voice and eyes as he spoke. "Sarah, that year with you was the best of my life, before or since. I wanted it to go on forever. And if I'd had any choice in the matter, it would have. Can't we make that happen now? Can you forgive me, put aside the past, accept that I love you and try to love me again?"

Charles's gaze warmed as he saw Sarah weakening, then grew bleak at her answer.

"I'm . . . not ready for that yet, Charles," she said, darting a look at him that half begged for his understanding, yet was still defiantly wary. "You really haven't told me very much about this . . . this job that split us apart, and until I know more about it, how can I judge the strength of the love you say you feel for me?" She shrugged, a shivering movement that spelled out the inner turmoil she was feeling. "How can I know that you won't let another job come first—before me?"

The strong planes of Charles's face tautened. His look was level, and his voice firm when he answered. "Sarah, I've told you all I can tell you about the job." And at her look of withdrawal, he grimaced with frustration. "Honey, a man is not much of a man if he walks away from commitments that involve his honor." He sighed, again frustrated, when Sarah's look told him he had had a commitment to her that, in her opinion at least, he had dishonored.

"I know, baby," he said levelly. "But from the beginning of time a man has been expected to put aside his own desires, and those of his family, when he has a duty to perform. That was the choice. Either I took what I selfishly wanted for myself and for you, or I did what my conscience told me was right. I can't say that won't ever happen again, but as of right now I feel that I've done my share. I want a normal life for a change. I want to share it with the woman I've loved all these years. I want to own you again, Sophie," he said with quiet intensity. "And right now I want to know if I have a chance of getting all that. I love you. Are you willing to take a chance on loving me?"

Unable to make the commitment he was asking for, Sarah seized upon only part of his statement. "I suppose I should resent the way you put that," she dissembled, trying for lightness and failing. And at Charles's slightly disconcerted, inquiring look, she clarified what she'd meant. "Your saying that you want to *own* me again. Is that how you thought of it?"

Charles's sensuous mouth curved as he held her gaze with his own. Electricity seemed to vibrate in the air between them. "Isn't that how it was?" he asked with lazy meaningfulness in his deep voice. "I know you owned me. And I know I'm looking forward to having you hold me in bondage again."

Sarah swallowed, certain now in her own heart that she wasn't going to be able to walk away from this unexpected encounter with Charles without giving him the chance he was asking for but unwilling somehow to capitulate verbally with such pride-shattering rapidity. "I . . . I can't imagine any woman owning you, Charles." She tried a diversionary tactic. "At least not now. You're—different."

There was a pause, during which Sarah broke away from the magnetism of his gaze by dropping her eyes to the tablecloth.

"Yes, I'm different, Sophie," Charles said quietly, making no apologies. "But not where you're concerned. You can always count on my love, Sophie." He paused, and then in a voice that caressed her, he asked, "Can I count on yours?"

Seized by a sudden fear, Sarah didn't want to make this decision at all. Not yet, not until she knew this new Charles better and was certain he wasn't going to betray her again.

She spoke quickly. "Charles, I can only promise that I'll see you again. Not that I'll love you again." She averted her gaze so that she wouldn't have to see the disappointment in his face, but when he remained silent for several moments, she was forced to turn back and see his reaction. To her surprise, his disappointment seemed mixed with patient, understanding acceptance.

"All right, Sophie," he said quietly. "I guess that's all I can expect." And then his stunning smile broke out, and the determined purposefulness she'd seen in him earlier reappeared, somehow more intense than ever. "I guess it's up to me to use the time you've promised to give me to the best effect. Starting now." He picked up his glass of wine and his eyes reflected a devilish charm as he toasted her with it before bringing the glass to his lips. "Get ready, sweetheart," he chuckled softly when he'd set the glass down again. "You're going to be courted like you've never been courted before, by a man who's been hungry for you for a very long time now. And I'm betting I won't have to go hungry for very much longer. In fact, I'm counting on it."

And as Sarah answered his light tone with an unsteady smile and a toast of her own, she found that excitement that had started in her office growing by leaps and bounds, and not even her strongest attempt to hold on to her common sense and her anger was proof against the seductive charm Charles employed for the rest of the evening, a charm that was all his own and as potent as the wine they drank far too much of before Charles escorted Sarah to her door.

When he'd unlocked the door for her and pushed it open, Sarah looked up at Charles with a wary, defensive gaze. She'd only just rediscovered now that they were at the real danger point of the evening.

"Don't worry, sweetheart," Charles said softly as he took her into his arms. "I'm not going to ask to come in, though I won't deny I'd like to." He paused, his gaze focusing on Sarah's trembling mouth, the blue of his eyes deepening with desire. "But I am going to take a good-night kiss," he murmured huskily. "If I'm going to lie awake all night anyway, I should at least have something to daydream about."

Sarah watched as Charles's mouth came closer and closer to her own, and though she would have liked to deny it, she was forced to admit that she wanted his kiss very badly. And when she felt the at first feathery-light sensation of his lips on hers, she shuddered and gave in to the desire to experience again the heady, one-of-a-kind electric sensation only Charles had ever been able to elicit from her.

"Oh, baby," he murmured against her mouth at feeling that shudder. "Oh, God, baby, you really don't know how hungry I am or you wouldn't encourage me like that!"

And then he gathered her up into his arms in a possessive, yet sheltering embrace, that made Sarah feel like she was a precious, hotly desired treasure and Charles couldn't make up his mind whether to crush her or treat her with the delicacy he would show a fragile, easily breakable object of value.

His mouth displayed that same ambivalence as he alternately caressed her lips with teasing lightness and seized them in an invasion so demandingly intense, Sarah thought she might faint under the intensity of the sensations he provoked. And all the time he was kissing her, his hands were taking the same sort of inventory, raking over her with desperate seeking, or barely brushing her body as though she possessed a tangible aura he could feel without pressing too closely.

When he at last drew back, Sarah's huge, drugged eyes inspected the strained lines of his face, and the electric blue of his eyes in a dazed fashion, as though she couldn't believe he could still have that effect on her.

"Why not?" he answered her unspoken thoughts in the way he always had, just as though the years when they'd been apart from each other had never existed. "We were always meant for each other, Sophie," he whispered softly. "It was always like this and it always will be. And the sooner you accept that again, the sooner we can go the rest of the way to paradise together."

He took a shaking breath then and steeled himself to let her go, though it was obvious to Sarah that it took all of his control to make the effort.

"I'll see you tomorrow night, Sophie," he said. "And every night after that until you can't send me away anymore." A flash of humor lightened the taut, strained lines of his face as he added, "And I hope to God you make that decision soon, because I won't be able to survive many nights like this one."

And with that Charles turned away and strode down the hall to the elevator, while Sarah stared after him, wanting desperately to call him back, but too much afraid of the consequences to take the risk.

CHAPTER FIVE

The next day Charles began to make good on his promise to court Sarah as she'd never been courted before. She was awakened after a night of tossing and turning by the ring of the telephone. And when she'd answered with a grumpy "Hello!", the first thing she heard was a soft, affectionate chuckle.

"You didn't use to wake up like that," Charles teased in warm tones tinged with the evidence that he'd spent a sleepless night himself. And then his voice dropped to a lower, huskier register. "When I'd kiss you awake, you used to smile and stretch and kiss me back. You were always as warm and sweet as a kitten until I'd turn you into a demanding tigress. Remember, honey?"

The trouble was, Sarah remembered all too well, and she wasn't proof against the seduction in Charles's tone and in his words, any more than she'd ever been proof against the actions he was recalling to her mind.

"I remember," she found herself responding in a tone that matched Charles's, even as she cursed the liquid warmth that was spreading throughout her body, making her wish Charles would take the decision of whether to accept him again out of her hands by appearing at her door and demanding what he wanted—and what she was beginning to want with increasing fervor.

"Sophie, you could have been awakened like that this morning," Charles murmured over the phone. "You know that, don't you?"

"I know," she whispered back achingly.

"And you're wishing you had been, aren't you, honey?" he said huskily, desire and gentle understanding and love all mixed up in his caressing voice to weave a hypnotic spell around Sarah where she lay weak and vulnerable and aching with desire for him.

"Yes, Charles," she admitted on a sigh. "Oh, yes . . ."

An infinitesimal pause followed her admission, and then Charles spoke more urgently. "Then trust me, darling," he coaxed. "Let me come over now. A lifetime isn't long enough for us to make up the years we've lost. Do you really want to waste another minute of the time we have left?"

Sarah hesitated, torn by the desire to give in to the loving urgency she heard in Charles's tone and her as yet unresolved doubts and fears. A glance at the bedside clock resolved the dilemma for her temporarily, by recalling to mind the fact that she had an appointment that morning she couldn't afford to miss.

"Charles, I can't," she said, unable to keep the regret she felt out of her voice. "I have to be at the office in an hour and a half for an important meeting."

A disappointed silence greeted her denial before Charles spoke again, this time with weary understanding. "All right, sweetheart," he said quietly. "But it's going to be a long day before I get to see you again."

"Yes, I know," Sarah answered, surprising herself with her candor. But her resistance was at its lowest in the morning, as Charles well knew, and yet she had the feeling her answer would have been the same had it been midnight rather than seven A.M.

"Do you, darling?" Charles said, a smile in his voice. "Does that mean I'm getting through to you?"

"You've . . . always been able to get through to me, Charles," Sarah responded fatalistically as she began to accept that he was going to be able to do it again.

"And you to me," Charles said with simple honesty. "That's why we belong together." And then with a sigh of resignation he concluded the conversation. "I'll pick you up at five thirty again, Sophie. Not a moment later. That's as long as I can wait."

"Yes," Sarah answered, unwittingly admitting that she felt the same. And even when she'd realized what she'd done, she couldn't regret having done it. She was simply too tired and too weakened by the indefinable bond that still existed between the two of them to fight him any longer.

"I love you, Sophie," Charles rang off huskily. "Remember that."

"I'll remember," Sarah answered quietly, but it was more than she could do to give him the words he was obviously waiting for with undisguised impatience. But that she would be saying those words to Charles before too long was already clear to her, and Sarah accepted the knowledge with a sense of destiny fulfilled. She could argue against her feelings until hell froze over, but that wouldn't make them any less real, or the inevitable conclusion to Charles's reentrance into her life any less imminent.

All through that day, even as she conducted business as usual, Sarah pondered what Charles had told her the night before and considered her options, and weighed her justifiable anger against what was possible between a man and a woman who responded to each other as though they had been created to belong to each other.

When she thought of him telling her that there had been a possibility he might not have been able to come back to her at all, she discovered the truth only those who have faced their own mortality, or that of someone they love, can appreciate—that all else fades in importance when the specter of death presents itself in all its indisputable finality. And she discovered something else. Anger—no matter how justified—runs a poor second when pitted against love.

By the end of the day, in the few minutes she had alone following Chelley's departure and before Charles's arrival, Sarah sat thinking very hard and very honestly. Suppose she did lose Charles to duty or to death or to any number of other possibilities that faced any human being in the course of a lifetime? Nothing was ever guaranteed—nothing was ever certain from one day to the next. Was it foolish or wise to do as Charles had done and seize the opportunity for happiness when it presented itself, even knowing that someday a terrible price might have to be paid?

Her decision was already half made by the time Charles appeared in her doorway, looking heart-shakingly attractive in a tailored gray summer-weight suit, a white shirt, and a beautifully patterned red and gray tie.

His smile was as warm as sunlight, and it was all for her, and

Sarah's smile echoed that warmth, making Charles catch his breath at the beauty it imparted to her already lovely face.

"God, Sophie, I'd kill to keep that smile on your lips if you mean it the way I hope you do!" he said with low-voiced fervency.

At that, Sarah laughed outright for the first time since Charles had reappeared in her life. "What a frightening thought!" she teased with almost the same lightheartedness she'd displayed in their earlier days. "I'd hate to be the cause of a homicide simply because I felt a bit grumpy."

Charles's grin imparted a boyishness to his handsome face that made it Sarah's turn to catch her breath. "Then I'll have to make sure you never feel grumpy, won't I?" he teased back meaningfully, referring to their conversation of that morning. "I don't want to go to prison when I could be living with you."

Sarah let that go by, merely smiling as she got up from her chair and crossed to meet Charles in the center of the room. "Where are we going tonight?" she asked lightly, and then the lightness disappeared to be replaced by an expectant softness in her large brown eyes as Charles seized her waist in his large hands.

"Nowhere until I've kissed you hello," he responded softly an instant before dipping his head to take her mouth in a warm, enveloping kiss that feathered her senses with all the subtlety of dynamite.

When he raised his head he was breathing unsteadily, and the blue in his eyes had darkened to a midnight shade. "I think we'd better get out of here," he whispered shakily. "For some reason this office affects me in the strangest way . . . or maybe you're the cause?" he asked mockingly, with a sensuous smile. "Maybe we ought to test the question by making love here someday?"

"Maybe," Sarah answered huskily before stepping out of Charles's arms and heading toward the door. "But not tonight. Tonight I'm hungry for food, and I hope you planned to feed me because otherwise I *will* get grumpy, and we've already decided that the consequences of that are too severe."

Charles chuckled as he accompanied her out the door. But when they reached the outer one, he stopped her briefly, and his eyes were gleaming with a combination of mischief and tender humor as he said, "Why don't we really start over, Sarah? Let's go to the same restaurant we went to last night, and I'll ask the same questions, and this time, you'll answer them differently. Do you agree?"

Sarah eyed him with bland calmness, though her heart was thudding at a rate that pushed the blood through her veins with alarming speed. "I agree to go to the same restaurant," she rejoined smoothly. "As for the rest of the evening . . ." She shrugged, feeling a little ashamed of her desire to make Charles pay, in however small a way, for the pain he'd inflicted in the past. And when his eyes clouded momentarily with disappointment, her shame increased, but still she maintained a stubborn sense of justice about her refusal to give him what he wanted.

But it seemed Charles was determined not to let his momentary disappointment spoil the evening for either of them, and his mood was determinedly light, and thrillingly tender as he escorted Sarah to the same restaurant, and even the same booth they'd shared the night before.

After they'd ordered—and this time Charles was careful to ask Sarah's preference—Sarah took a deep breath, and determinedly asked the question that had preyed on her mind all the preceding night and day.

"Charles, please tell me more about why you had to take that job. I still don't understand. I *need* to understand," she added quietly but firmly, her brown eyes unflinchingly on his, willing him to tell her the truth.

A shutter seemed to veil Charles's normally clear blue eyes for an instant, then he muttered a soft curse and captured her hand in his.

"Sarah, I'm not going to lie to you," he said with quiet ferocity. "But there's very little more I can tell you without compromising myself and others. All I can say is that it was something I had to do, something I was especially equipped to do." He stopped, giving a soft sigh of frustration at the puzzled intentness in Sarah's brown gaze. "But it's almost over anyway, honey," he added, seeming to be pleading for her understanding. "In two months it will all be behind us, and we can concentrate on each other for a while without any distractions."

When Sarah's eyes widened at that information, a slow smile

63

lit Charles's face, lightening his eyes to a translucent blue. "What would you say to a honeymoon in Mexico?" he asked Sarah. "If I recall, you always wanted to go there, and I've heard of a little place that is breathtakingly beautiful, if I decide to give you time to look at it." The low meaningfulness in his tone made Sarah's eyes widen farther, and Charles's smile broadened.

"Come on, honey," he said softly. "You knew that was coming, didn't you? You don't think I would have found you again with anything less in mind, do you?"

Sarah lifted a trembling hand to rub a temple, the look in her eyes slightly glazed and disoriented. "Ch-Charles," she stumbled over his name as she tried to get her chaotic thoughts in order and make sense. "You're going so fast. I mean, you've obviously had time to think about all this, but I . . ."

And then at a sudden thought, her eyes cleared and she looked at him with wondering astonishment. "How did you know I wasn't already married to someone else?" She saw that same shuttered look begin to close him off from her, and she reached over and grasped his forearm, willing him to stop it. "After all, it's been five years, Charles," she uttered forcefully. "What made you think I would be waiting for you?"

The veil dropped then, and Charles looked at her, his expression thoughtfully calm. "I never thought you'd still be waiting for me, Sophie," he said levelly. "I thought some other man would have snapped you up long ago. But I . . . checked . . . from time to time, and now that's it's so close to the time I'll be free, I couldn't wait any longer. I thought you would at least give me a hearing. It means too much to me not to try everything in my power to win you back."

"And what would you have done if I had married someone else?" Sarah asked bleakly. "You knew that could happen when you left me. You obviously meant for me to live my life as though you were never coming back. What would you have done, Charles?" she persisted, not sure herself what answer she wanted from him.

His answer, when it came, was delivered in equally bleak tones, as though he were thinking, as Sarah had been, what a disaster such a thing would have been.

"I honestly don't know, Sarah," he said quietly. "I've never stopped loving you or wanting you. I suppose it would have depended upon how happy you seemed to be with someone else." The sudden harshness in his voice spelled out his jealousy of the nonexistent "someone else." "I do know," he continued, "that it would have taken all my willpower to leave you alone, whether you seemed happily married or not. I seem always to have had the idea that you and I would get back together again one day, and that would have been an awfully hard dream to give up."

A shiver ran down Sarah's back as she contemplated how much, how very much Charles had changed. In the past he would never have considered violating the sanctity of a marriage. But then, Sarah reflected wonderingly, Charles had never acted predictably where she was concerned, not even back then.

The waiter appeared then, surprising Sarah with his intrusion, especially since her hunger had disappeared. When the waiter had finished bustling around them, Sarah contemplated the food in front of her with little appetite, but she dutifully picked up her fork and began to eat, and Charles did the same.

They ate in silence for a few moments, neither of them displaying much of an appetite for food, before Charles abruptly raised his head and fixed Sarah in a glittering blue gaze that stilled her hand as it was lifted halfway to her mouth with a bite of food.

"Did you love the man you—" He stopped abruptly, unable to voice the question in the way he'd envisioned it. And then, much more gently, and to Sarah, much more sadly, he tried again. "Did you love the man who came after me?"

That he knew about Clive caught her by surprise, and she wasn't sure she was capable of answering his question. She reflected bleakly that only yesterday she might have wanted Charles to be hurt by the knowledge that she'd been with someone else, while now that he was displaying his pain openly and honestly, she felt only sadness that she was the cause of it.

Charles never wavered in his steady regard, and as Sarah sought to escape the intentness of his look, he said in a tone of gentle inflexibility, "I want to know, Sarah."

"You have no right to ask me that, Ch—"

He cut her off impatiently. "To hell with rights, Sarah! Answer me! Did you love him?"

Flushing with resentment, Sarah said in a very small voice,

"No." And then with an added flash of rebellion, she added, "But I thought I did before . . ."

But Charles's look told her he didn't believe her, and Sarah had to drop her eyes to keep from revealing that she didn't believe herself either. She had used that excuse for a long time, but the truth was she had entered the relationship with Clive more from a desire to prove that she was free of Charles's memory than because she was truly in love with Clive. And, of course, it hadn't worked, and she had been left with a determination to pour her energies into her career rather than into relationships with men who could never hope to compete with the one man she did love.

"Sophie, I love you," Charles said in a caressing tone.

Slowly Sarah raised her eyes, and what she saw in Charles's melted the last of her resistance. Suddenly it didn't matter that she had reason to resent him and to suspect his sincerity. She had never in her life been capable of holding a grudge, especially against someone she loved, and right at the moment she knew she had never stopped loving Charles. Her lies to herself over the years lost veracity, if they had ever had any, in the face of having him here beside her now, telling her he loved her and always had, showing her with every word and inflection and a wealth of body language that he was hers and always would be.

Her capitulation was delivered with all the soft, direct sincerity that she could give it. "I love you, too, Charles," she said simply, her heart swelling as she saw him suck in a deep breath and close his eyes briefly against the emotions her confession evoked in him. When those blue eyes opened again, his blazing hunger for her scorched its way into her, igniting her own.

"Let's get out of here," Charles suggested in soft, slurred tones.

"Yes," Sarah answered on a deep sigh, telling him everything with that one word.

Charles tore his gaze away from her reluctantly to gesture for the waiter to bring their check. Neither of them responded to the waiter's concerned chatter over the fact that they hadn't finished their dinner, because neither of them heard it. Without checking its denomination, Charles tossed a bill onto the tray the waiter presented, then ignored the waiter's profuse gratitude when the man saw the amount. Getting to his feet, Charles extended a hand to help Sarah up, which she took and clung to as a deep, peaceful calm spread its way throughout her body, a calm that was disrupted only slightly by an underlying anticipation.

Outside the restaurant Charles hailed a taxi, and once they were settled in the back of it, he gave the cabbie the address of Sarah's apartment before settling back in the seat beside her and taking her hand in his own.

As they sat in the back of the taxi, their only contact that of their clasped hands, the only sound that of the traffic around them, the thread of excitement in Sarah began to build steadily until she felt detached from everything except Charles's hand and Charles's body, a body she longed to claim again and to have claim her.

At her apartment Sarah had her key out and Charles swept it from her hand quickly, opened the door, slammed the door behind them when they were inside, then leaned back against it and pulled her into his arms.

"Now!" he said, low-voiced, tensely hoarse. "Show me how much you love me, Sophie." His head came slowly down to hers as he spoke. "Take me apart and put me back together again," he whispered, "the way you used to."

Oh, God! Sarah thought on an inward shudder as Charles's mouth swept over hers and forced it open for the first of the deep, probing kisses he would take from her that night. *I want you so much, Charles. I need you, and God help me, I love you more than ever!*

Her capacity to think got lost somewhere after that, melting away into pure sensation as Charles drank and drank from her lips, his tongue an exquisite probe of exciting demand, his hands instruments of hynoptic, sensual warmth as they stroked the skin of her neck before pushing the white drawstringed blouse over her shoulders. He took her breasts into his hands to knead and stroke them, but he soon became impatient with their covering, and he stopped to pull the blouse up over her head and toss it aside before dispensing with her bra as well.

"Sophie," he muttered in a thick voice as he gazed at the full silkiness he had uncovered and now held, before he bent his head to taste the sweetness no other man had ever truly possessed.

And as his mouth closed over the throbbing tip he now owned, Sarah shuddered, moaning her pleasure at the dart of arousal his moist tongue and urgent lips transmitted from her nipple to her belly.

Sarah could stand very little of such attention before she had to thrust at his shoulders to make Charles straighten. When he had, she raised her hands to begin unfastening his tie with fingers made awkward by excitement. Charles didn't offer to help her. His own hands were busy at the waistband of her skirt, and even after it fell in a puddle at her feet and he had roughly disposed of her panty hose, he stood with quiet tenseness while Sarah pulled off the shirt she had finally managed to unbutton.

Her hands then moved to the waistband of his trousers, pausing as she slanted a liquid look of entreaty up at him.

"No, Sophie," he grated in a voice grown so hoarse, he could barely get the words out. "You do it. I want everything I've been denied all these years."

As though the intervening years since the last time they'd made love had never existed, Sarah understood exactly what he meant. It had always heightened his excitement to have her undress him, and she would never have thought to deny him that pleasure if she hadn't been so impatient herself, and so frustrated by the shaking of her hands that made such a simple task so difficult.

She took a deep breath in an attempt to still that shaking, then took her time undoing the simple fastening of his trousers, enjoying the flinch he gave when her knuckles brushed the bare skin of his waist. She tugged the trousers down, a soft intent smile curving her lips when Charles flinched again as her hair brushed his chest while she bent to her task. Then she heard a soft groan before his hands joined hers on the waistband of his briefs, and together they disposed of the last of his clothing.

Charles bent to rip his shoes and socks from his feet, and to pull some small packets from his pants pocket. Sarah smiled—it was so like him to want to protect her.

"You don't have to worry about that, sweetheart," she said softly. "I'm still taking the pill."

He looked at her sharply for a moment, his face tense with jealousy, then relaxed as he remembered that she'd told him years ago that she needed the pill for medical reasons. He lifted her into his arms, his breath coming in labored gasps as his eyes glittered blue fire down at her body before locking into her own softly liquid gaze.

"Bedroom?" he asked impatiently.

"That way," Sarah murmured as she gestured down the hallway behind them before returning her arm to Charles's neck, which she stroked and touched and clung to as he carried her along. Her lips were fastened to his throat, drawing sustenance for her seeking tongue and eliciting a deep groan from Charles's heaving chest.

He was entering her before her back had settled solidly onto the vividly patterned spread of her bed, and as he did, Sarah had the sudden, utterly shattering sensation of being transported from a cold, alien planet back to a beloved, warm, and secure, yet intensely exciting homeland. Her body remembered everything about Charles as though he had left her bed that morning instead of five years ago. Her soul expanded into the dimension Charles had carved to fit himself years earlier, while her heart gave a long, aching sigh of contented ecstasy.

Her tears melded with the slight film of perspiration on Charles's face as he guided her into their rhythm. Their voices mingled in incoherent, yet totally meaningful gasps and murmurs of love, while their bodies arched, demanded, molded, and melted, responding to their mutual need to satisfy desires too long suppressed, too long withheld from each other. And at last the final explosion rocked the two of them out of reality altogether before thrusting them back into it long before either of them was ready to return.

When it became possible for either of them to move, Charles rolled over onto his back, and as Sarah turned on her side to look at him, she saw that he had his eyes closed and that a muscle was working overtime in his jaw.

"God!" she heard him mutter in a tone of incredulity. And then again, "God!" in stronger tones of such painful intensity that she hurt for him. He then raised a hand to brush the moisture from his face, held out the hand to look with puzzled wonderment at the wetness, and shook his head as he closed his eyes again while he raked his hand through his hair.

"Charles?" Sarah said his name softly, reaching a hesitant hand to rest her fingers on the muscles of his upper arm. "Are you all right?" she asked anxiously.

He gave an unamused smile. "All right?" he echoed blankly. "Hell, I haven't been all right in five years, not until now." Sarah still regarded him anxiously as he turned to look at her, the harshness in his face fading to the natural gentleness she remembered so clearly and with so much love. "How about you?" he questioned her tenderly, cupping her tear-stained cheek in his large palm. "Are you all right?"

"I haven't been all right for five years either," she answered on a shuddering sob of emotion, then wished she'd kept quiet when she saw Charles wince before he stared at her with a bleakness it hurt her to see. So she echoed the assurance he had given her a few seconds ago. "Not until now," she whispered.

At that, he moved closer, pulling her into the curve of his body, while he tenderly kissed her temple, then her cheek, and finally her mouth, his lips moving over hers with a tasting reverence she returned in full measure.

When he pulled back his eyes held a promise. "We'll both be all right from now on," he murmured unsteadily, and at Sarah's nod he strained her to him for a full-length hug while he ran his hands over her back, her bottom, and her thighs, then tugged her closer into the curve of his body.

Sarah, reveling in the touch of his flesh against her, murmured, "Oh, that feels so good, Charles," as she ran her hands over the corded muscles of his shoulders and wriggled closer, raising one thigh to place it over his hip while she settled her own hips snugly against the hardness of his.

She heard a soft growl of laughter coming from his chest and tipped her head back to look inquiringly up at him. "You think I'm funny?" she asked with mock seriousness.

"No, I think you're asking for trouble if you keep that up," Charles answered, his chuckle low and sexy.

"Trouble?" Sarah inquired innocently. "Is that what it's called?"

"What you're doing is called extreme provocation," Charles mocked her softly, dipping his head to suck her lower lip into his mouth for an instant before he released it in favor of running his tongue over her lips.

"And what you're doing is not, I suppose," Sarah said shakily, her lids beginning to flutter sleepily over her eyes, not from exhaustion, but rather from the sensuous lethargy Charles was inducing in her.

"I admit freely to having an intense interest in provoking you," Charles answered, reaching a hand under her bottom to turn her so that he could slide over her.

"You're succeeding," Sarah gasped, arching her throat to allow his lips and tongue access when he dipped his head to her.

"Good," he whispered. "Let's go more slowly this time," he suggested as he slid an inch at a time down her body, seeming to savor the friction of contact between them as much as he enjoyed the taste of her skin against his mouth and tongue.

"That's easy for you to say," Sarah groaned on a shudder as his mouth covered the peak of one breast. "It takes you longer to—" She broke off on another gasp as Charles bit down on her nipple very gently, while his shoulders shook with suppressed laughter. "Sadist!" she hissed unconvincingly.

He lifted his head to give her a chiding look, though his eyes were dancing with mischief. "And I was just about to invite you not to wait for me," he mocked sternly. "I have the feeling I can catch you up and take you right along with me on a third trip down memory lane. And I remember clearly how greedy you can be, my lusty little Sophie."

With a contented sigh Sarah tugged his head back down to her breast, murmuring smugly, "Do you also remember that I'm impervious to insults as long as I get what I want?"

"I remember everything," Charles whispered, a sudden catch in his voice stirring the slumbering fire in Sarah's loins into a blazing flame that Charles devoted himself to quenching with his knowing palms and fingers and a mouth and tongue that had grown diabolically skillful.

Sarah had barely recovered from the unencumbered gift Charles had bestowed so generously when she became aware that he was in need of some generosity on her part.

"Come here," she crooned to him, exulting in the throbbing evidence of his manhood pressing against her with urgent demonstration of his need. An instant later her open mouth was smothered by Charles's hot, seeking lips, invaded by the demanding insistence of his tongue, and pleasantly bruised into submission by the urgency of his kiss.

She gave up trying to pleasure him actively when it became apparent his needs lay more in the direction of conquering her, making her pliant to his will, demonstrating graphically that he could have her anyway he wanted her. And even through the haze of sensuality his dominance induced, the fact registered in her subconscious that this was another way in which Charles was different now. But the difference was so headily exciting, she found no complaint to make at learning the man she loved had turned into a much more aggressive and absorbing lover than she could ever have anticipated when he had been such a fully satisfying one in the past.

And then she became wholly incapable of any coherent thought at all under the driving, exultant, roughly male possession Charles took of all she was and had to give, until he went over the edge of his own limits, taking her with him, and crying out his love in a hoarse expression of such complete joy that Sarah delighted in joining that cry with an expression of her own love and her own complete satisfaction.

CHAPTER SIX

"You know what I'd like?" Charles asked in the middle of a yawn as he stretched his powerfully muscled arms over his head.

"No, what?" Sarah responded with teasing wariness, giving him a look that suspected him of being about to ask for something kinkily outrageous.

He chuckled slyly as he brought one arm down to gather her close for a brief hug. "Well, I'd like whatever you've got on that dirty little mind of yours too," he said complacently, "but what I was going to say, is that I want one of your peanut butter and mustard sandwiches with lettuce. Suddenly I'm starving, and it's been a long time since I had one of your masterpieces."

Sarah laughed before giving a luxurious stretch of her own. "Sure, why not?" she agreed lazily as she sat up. "I'm hungry, too, and since you're the only other convert to that delicacy I've ever been able to make, it'll be nice to have one myself without having someone across the table glare at me with horrified disgust."

She swung her legs over the side of the bed and sat for a moment to stretch again before she turned to give Charles a saucy look over her shoulder, a look that faltered when she saw his expression. "What's the matter?" she asked, puzzled by the remoteness of his gaze.

"I was just wondering who it was you'd been making that sandwich for and wishing it could have been me," he said simply, and there was a touch of pained self-mockery in the statement.

"Jealous?" Sarah asked softly, knowing instinctively that he was trying not to be.

"Terribly," Charles answered, again with simple honesty.

Slanting an understanding glance at him, Sarah gave in to her innate softheartedness. "Would it make you feel better if I told you that I can count the people I've made that sandwich for on one hand, and all of them, except for you, were female?"

Charles's startled look of gratitude warmed Sarah, and when he then gave her a slow and easy grin, she grinned back. "Much better," he affirmed gently.

Lightening the mood, she tilted her mouth up to his. "Well, husband-to-be, if you want that sandwich, you'd better give me an incentive kiss to get me started. Looking at you is starting to make me hungry for something besides food."

Charles gave her a doubtful look. "And a kiss is supposed to divert me?" he asked dubiously.

Sarah nodded complacently. "Temporarily," she allowed. "How about it?" She wriggled her eyebrows suggestively at him, causing him to smile down at her warmly.

"You still have Sophia Loren eyes, Sophie," he commented, his tone matching his smile.

Diverted by his remark, Sarah's expression softened at his reference to how she'd gotten her "private" name. "And I'm still not a Sophia," she said quietly. "Sophie is the best I can do."

"And Sophie is quite enough for me," Charles responded huskily, "as long as you're *my* Sophie."

Sarah sighed with mock resignation. "I don't think there's much doubt of that after tonight, do you?"

"No," Charles agreed, a great deal of satisfaction in his tone, and to seal his possession, he leaned down to give her the kiss she'd requested, lingering over it until Sarah raised her arm to encircle his neck in a mute appeal to forget about the sandwich.

Charles drew back and gave her a mocking smile. "Food first, woman. Then we'll see if the laborer is worthy of her hire."

Sarah gave him a cross look of exasperation. "I've already labored enough tonight to earn my hire five times over," she groused, then yelped as Charles laughingly pinched her bottom before making her sit up and pushing her to the side of the bed again.

"Feed your man, lady," he ordered sternly. "This uppity female business won't do."

"Yes, sir," Sarah said meekly, placing her palms together

under her chin in a servile fashion, though her eyes danced mischievously over them. "Your wish is my command, master," she continued her mockery as she got to her feet and backed away, still bobbing in a parody of groveling servility.

"That's better." Charles yawned complacently, lying back to place his arms behind his head while he sprawled in kingly splendor over the sheets.

Sarah dropped her pose in order to don her white terry robe. "Does Master want his sandwich in bed?" she cooed dryly, "or is he willing to accompany his slave to the kitchen in order to be served his banquet?" As she spoke she couldn't keep her eyes off his superb body. His tanned, muscular physique made a startling contrast to the white sheets, and Sarah was extremely reluctant to let him out of her sight.

Charles gave another ostentatious yawn, patting it away with one hand. "I suppose I could get up," he admitted reluctantly.

"I suppose you could too," Sarah said sweetly. "That is, if you really do want that sandwich."

"Is that a threat?" Charles frowned sternly.

"You could say that," Sarah simpered, sashaying toward the bedroom door. "If you want to find out, why don't you just keep lying there, and if I haven't returned with your sandwich in a couple of hours, I think you can safely assume that—"

The rest of the sentence disappeared in a yelp as a pillow landed squarely across her backside. Sarah scowled at Charles over her shoulder and found him sitting up with a delighted grin plastered over his face that fairly reeked of satisfaction at having hit his target so accurately.

"Physical abuse is not the way to gain a peanut butter and mustard sandwich," she informed him with lofty dignity as she bent, daintily lifted the pillow from the floor, scowled at it, then dropped it distastefully onto a nearby chair.

"And defiance is not the way to end up back in my bed," Charles informed her smugly.

"It's not your bed," Sarah sniffed. "It's my bed."

"Not any longer," Charles answered with a quiet firmness that effectively ended the teasing between them, replacing it with undercurrents that feathered Sarah's senses.

Their gazes locked and held for a moment before Sarah smiled at Charles with languid arousal. "Come get your sandwich, Charles," she said gravely. "Our bed is waiting, and I'm not a very patient woman."

He was chuckling softly as Sarah turned away to go to the kitchen and begin preparation of their late supper. She was assembling the various ingredients when Charles appeared at the door in nothing but a towel wrapped around his lean hips, and as he leaned against the doorjamb in a casual stance while he inspected the room, Sarah found herself wishing the precarious knot in the towel would slip and leave the rest of him as bare as his magnificent chest and arms and legs.

"Nice room, honey," he commented as his eyes ran over the bright, cheerful oranges, yellows, and whites in the room. "You always did have a knack for decorating."

Sarah paused in the act of spreading peanut butter over a slice of bread and looked at him, her eyes widening. "Where will we live, Charles, here? I don't know what you plan to do now that this job of yours is almost over." She stopped and gave a helpless shrug. "I don't know any of your plans really."

Charles wandered into the room, his face bearing a thoughtful expression. He paused beside her and absently stuck a finger into the jar of peanut butter, lifting a swipe of the gooey substance to his mouth.

"I haven't got it all worked out yet, honey," he said thoughtfully around the bite. He lifted his eyes to hers, and the expression in them was casually wary. "I work as a finance officer now for an oil company—abroad. But they have an office in California, and I think they'd transfer me there if I requested it. Would you be willing to give up your business here and start again out there?"

Sarah watched him, suddenly feeling shut out and uneasily disturbed. When she answered, she did so absently. "I wouldn't mind," she said quietly. "I've already done some casting for various California studios, and I'm sure I could find work there." She wanted to ask him why he wanted to work in California instead of in New York, but she didn't get the chance.

Charles lifted his head, his gaze probing and curious, his smile expressing pride in her. "How did you get into casting, Sophie? You were going to be an actress."

76

Sarah shrugged, her mind not on her own career, but on Charles's. "When I came to New York after—" She broke off, shot him a cautious look, and started again. "When I came to New York," she repeated, "I lived in a domicile for single women, most of them aspiring actresses. In between auditions for jobs of my own, I found myself getting more and more involved in helping the others try out for roles that suited them rather than for ones they might prefer to go after. They had such success after listening to me, they told others, and the whole thing just seemed to snowball." She shook her head in remembrance. "I ended up having less and less time for my own auditions while I spent more and more time helping others get jobs. Finally it dawned on me that while I was no more than an adequate actress, I was a first-rate casting director. I worked hard at it, finally made enough money to start my own firm, and here I am," she finished, giving an open-handed gesture of fatalism.

"Are you happy with what you do?" Charles asked quietly.

"Very," Sarah answered with a quirking smile. "The work suits me better than the insecurities of acting. I suppose I was never a dedicated enough actress to enjoy having my ego stomped all over. I'm glad things worked out the way they did."

"Good," Charles said with sober honesty. "I don't know if I could take it if you were a successful actress. I'm afraid I might end up punching out your male fans regularly."

Sarah gave him a faint smile, thinking that five years ago she couldn't have pictured Charles in a fistfight, while now the image was all too real. She finished making the first sandwich, put it on a plate, and set it on her small, white enamel table, then gestured at Charles to seat himself, which he did with alacrity.

After she'd made her own sandwich, Sarah joined him, and for a while the two of them munched in a contented silence. But Sarah's thoughts were churning steadily, and at last, she raised solemn, serious eyes to Charles's face, and when she spoke, there was both entreaty and firmness in her tone.

"Charles, we need to talk more about what you do," she said levelly. "I'm not asking you to tell me any secrets," she added hastily as she saw his expression begin to close up. "But surely you can tell me the name of the firm that employs you, and the country where you work. That isn't asking too much, is it?" She hesitated, then added, "And I'm also curious about why you want to go to California. Doesn't the oil firm have offices here?"

The planes of Charles's face grew harder momentarily, but then he sighed and pushed his plate away. "I work for World Oil, Sophie," he said in a noncommittal tone. "And yes, they have offices here, but when I get free of my present commitment, I want to make a completely new start. I want to put the past behind me entirely." He gave her an intimate smile, then added, "Except for your part in it."

Sarah smiled back, but then encouraged him with a look to go on, and he did. "I'm one of World Oil's financial officers," he continued. "I have been for the past five years." He took a deep breath, then faced her unflinchingly. "And that's all I can say," he finished with soft firmness.

Feeling frustrated, but unwilling to press him further for the moment, Sarah gave a slight shrug. "All right, Charles," she said with equal softness. Then she eyed him hesitantly. "Will you ever be able to tell me about it?" she asked with subdued entreaty.

"Perhaps," was all the concession he would give, however. He rubbed his chin thoughtfully for a few moments with one long finger, then lifted his eyes to her again. "Sophie, all this secrecy is for your protection as much as for mine," he told her with quiet seriousness. "In fact, I'm going to ask you to keep our relationship quiet for the time being." And at her startled, protesting look, he grimaced, but his tone remained firm. "I'm sorry, Sophie, but in my situation, the less people know about my private life, the better. Until I'm out of this, you're my only area of vulnerability, and believe me, there are people who wouldn't hesitate to use you to get to me."

He sighed at Sarah's look of alarm, but continued steadily. "I realize your secretary and that other woman who was in your office today have seen me, but I'd appreciate it if you didn't go into any detail about why I was there. It would just be safer all around . . . for a while anyway."

"That other woman," Sarah repeated in a dazed tone. "Charles, are you seriously telling me you didn't know who that other woman was?"

He frowned in puzzlement, then shrugged. "No. Should I?"

Sarah shook her head in wonder. "That was Lila Benton, the hottest sex symbol in the entertainment business right now," she told him with wry incredulity.

Charles raised one eyebrow in an unconcerned expression. "I don't get to the movies much," he informed her in a matter-of-fact way.

Sarah stared at him in puzzlement for a moment, then her expression cleared. "Oh, that's right," she mused. "You said you worked out of the country." She eyed him with mocking interest. "It must be a pretty backward country if you haven't seen at least an advertisement for one of Lila's movies," she said speculatively.

Charles leaned back in his chair, folded his arms over the wide expanse of his chest, and just looked at her long and hard until Sarah had to drop her eyes.

"Oh, all right!" she muttered disgruntledly. "I'll stop playing detective, at least verbally," she added in an almost inaudible tone.

She gave Charles a defiant look when he continued to stare at her, disapproval written all over his masculine features. "Well, for heaven's sake, Charles," she protested grumpily as she got to her feet and snatched his now empty plate from in front of him. "You can't expect me to turn off my brain, can you? I do have a modicum of interest in how you've spent the last five years of your life, after all!"

She stomped to the sink, her shoulders rigid, but that rigidity relaxed when she heard Charles say, his tone lovingly amused, "*Spent my life* is the operative phrase, Sophie. That part of it is almost over, remember?"

She swung around, glaring at him in a half exasperated, half loving fashion, and opened her mouth to say something, when instead she jumped a foot in reaction to the shrill ring of the telephone.

"Now, who . . . ?" she grumbled with a frown as she marched over to the phone. She snatched up the receiver and said impatiently, "Hello!"

Then her expression turned puzzled as she lifted her eyes to Charles, who was staring at her with a brooding expression that alerted her to the fact that he wasn't as surprised as she was that their reunion had been interrupted by a third party. But who would he have given her number to, she wondered with uneasy puzzlement.

"Yes, he's here," Sarah said slowly, frowning at Charles. "Just a minute, please." She took the receiver away from her ear and nodded at Charles. "It's for you," she said quietly.

She watched as Charles slowly got to his feet, his face expressing absolutely nothing as he adopted a concealing mask, and suddenly Sarah had a sudden premonition of danger that made her heart beat faster. Concealing her reaction behind a smile, she whispered, "It sounds like someone who might very well spend his spare time making obscene calls. I hope he's not a close friend of yours," before she handed the receiver to Charles.

Charles returned her smile absently as he took the phone from her, but before he raised it to his ear, he hesitated, then said quietly, "Sophie, would you mind leaving the room for a few minutes? I have the feeling this isn't something you ought to hear."

Sarah stiffened momentarily, her eyes widening in shocked anxiety. Charles watched her, his expression calm, as he put out a hand to draw a lazy finger over her jaw, waiting for her to accede to his request. Lifting one shoulder in what she hoped was an unconcerned shrug, Sarah nodded, smiled halfheartedly and left the room.

As she moved into her Oriental-style living room, Sarah felt the strongest urge she'd ever experienced to eavesdrop on Charles's conversation, but she forced herself to continue across the room to the large windows on one side of it. Pulling back one of the thin, lime green panels at the window, she gazed blindly down at the dark street below her.

Until that moment Charles's revelations hadn't really registered. It had all seemed so unreal, so dramatic, that she had unconsciously discounted most of what he had been trying to tell her. Except for the moment in the restaurant when he had mentioned the possibility of his own death, she had continued to live in a dreamworld, anxious to grasp at anything that would explain satisfactorily Charles's desertion five years ago while she refused to accept the truth of what that explanation implied.

80

A shiver traced her backbone as she recalled the rasping, almost sinister voice of the man on the phone who had impatiently asked to speak to Charles. That voice was uncannily like one she would have sought in an actor to represent the villain of a play or a movie, and she reflected that even though Charles was undoubtedly on the side wearing the white hats in his cloak-and-dagger work, whoever had called him had sounded absolutely depraved. It made her wonder if his co-conspirators were as honest and filled with integrity as Charles was.

But the real problem was that Charles was in danger, whichever side he or his companions were on. Being on any side at all placed him in jeopardy. Sarah had to take deep breaths to calm herself after that thought, and she struggled for optimism as she reminded herself that it was all almost over. Charles had said his assignment would be finished in two months.

Hang on to that thought, Sarah, she advised herself grimly. *It's all you've got until he's safely yours again.*

"Sophie?" Charles's voice made her start before she whirled around to see him standing in the entranceway to the living room, hands on his hips, his expression determinedly cheerful. That expression alone would have made her aware that he'd had bad news even if she hadn't sensed it from the troubled look in his eyes he couldn't quite conceal.

"Yes, darling," she greeted him calmly, having determined in an instant that she wouldn't add to his unknown worries by making him concerned about her as well. "Do you want another sandwich?" she asked in a bright tone as she crossed the room to him and slid her arms around his waist.

His slow smile was deliciously sensuous. "No, I don't want another sandwich," he murmured in a suggestive voice. "I want to go back to bed."

Sarah employed all her acting skills to flutter her eyelashes at him coyly while she let her mouth slip into a smirk. "Why, certainly, master," she cooed at him. "I promised you anything your little heart desires."

A few moments later, when they were once again tucked closely together in Sarah's bed, Charles used one finger to tilt her head up. "You know, Sophie," he informed her huskily as the finger moved in bewitching twirls over her cheek and then to her

81

earlobe. "I've been having dreams of you for years, and I'm more than ready to trade them in for reality." And as Sarah answered his seductive tactics by slipping the back of her hand across the smooth skin of his abdomen below his navel, he groaned, "Ahhh, God, Sophie!" as he involuntarily closed his eyes against his abrupt arousal.

Then his arms drew her roughly to him, and his eyes came open, blazing with a desire that made Sarah catch her breath. "Come here to me, little Sophie," he growled, the sound starting from deep within his chest. "Let me show you what I dreamed."

And this time there was no rush, though there was just as much eager passion. There were words where before there had been mumbled incoherencies. And there was a wealth of love where before there had been a blind, instinctive searching for satisfaction of desperate needs as old as time.

CHAPTER SEVEN

The next morning as Charles walked Sarah to her subway stop, kissed her good-bye, then hailed a taxi for his own journey to a nondescript building ostensibly housing the offices of Ace Exports, he failed to notice a tall, slender, brown-haired, brown-eyed man strolling along behind them with a pleasant smile on his handsome face. The man had a general air of aimlessness about him as he walked along with his hands in the pockets of his well-cut, light tan suit, but that manner was sometimes belied by the sharp interest in his eyes when he occasionally let them rest on the couple walking in front of him.

Charles's own interest definitely would have been aroused had he seen the man and recognized him as a fellow passenger on the flight from Africa two days previously, and if Charles had not already planned, as a result of long habit, to use concealing tactics in getting to his destination that morning, he would certainly have chosen to do so after spotting someone whose presence in this neighborhood was too much of a coincidence to be dismissed lightly.

When Charles and Sarah split up, the man hesitated briefly, his gaze darting first to Charles as he caught the only visible taxi on the street, and then to Sarah as she disappeared down the steps of the subway entrance. With a fatalistic shrug the man then turned his steps after Sarah, his indolent stroll disappearing in a burst of speed as he narrowed the gap between them. Now that it was only Sarah he followed, he was far less careful about keeping groups of people between them, and his pace slackened only when he was a mere few paces behind her.

An easy smile of satisfaction curved the jaunty line of his aristocratic mouth as the man followed Sarah onto the subway

83

train, and he seated himself far enough away from her to be able to observe her clearly without her realizing that he was studying her lovely face and body with a great deal of interest. His smile turned slightly cynical as he noted the dreamy look in her eyes that would have told anyone that this woman had had a very enjoyable night indeed. And since the man watching Sarah made his living with his brain, it was not difficult to put two and two together and come up with Charles Trainer's part in putting that look on Sarah's beautiful face.

The man followed Sarah all the way into her office building, rode up in the same elevator with her along with several other people, and exited on her floor with Sarah and two other people. He hung back and watched carefully to see which door she would enter, and when she had disappeared inside, he paced softly down the hall to pause for a moment and inspect the lettering on the glass-paned door, which read BAILEY CASTING.

Fifteen minutes later the man was in the lobby of a hotel two buildings down from Sarah's, speaking earnestly into a pay telephone while his dark eyes darted restlessly around the lobby. Upon finishing his conversation, he bought a morning paper, seated himself in one of the plush, brown leather chairs situated near the same pay telephone, and proceeded to turn to the sports page, which he read with total concentration until the shrill summons of the telephone brought him up from his chair exactly one hour later.

Meanwhile Charles was pacing the shabbily carpeted floor of an equally shabbily furnished office as he waited for Foster and went over in his mind the conversation they'd had on the telephone the night before.

Once Sarah had disappeared out of the room, he had brought the receiver to his ear and clipped out an impatient "Yes" that spelled out how unhappy he was at being disturbed at Sarah's apartment.

"It's hit the fan," Foster's equally clipped tone had answered. "We've just learned there's been an announcement in Zwahola concerning the upcoming marriage of Lugubu's son and Njomo's granddaughter."

"What!" Charles's incredulous tone was followed a few moments later by a soft curse after Foster had given him more details. "Lugubu didn't waste any time, did he?" he commented in a grim, worried tone.

"I imagine he wanted to take advantage of the fact that most of the people who matter, especially Njomo, are in the States right now to attend the U.N. talks," Foster answered just as grimly.

"Yes," Charles acceded thoughtfully. "I should have suspected something when Lugubu delayed his departure instead of traveling with the rest of the party. Lugubu must have been working on the girl's father for some time, though, to get him to do something like this without Njomo's approval." He paused before speculating thoughtfully. "But perhaps that will work to Lugubu's disadvantage. Njomo isn't going to like the fact that the two of them acted behind his back."

"Well, you and I are going to have to talk about this," Foster said before adding hastily, "but I'm not suggesting we do it tonight. I wouldn't hesitate to break up your reunion if I thought it would help anything, but first thing in the morning should be soon enough."

"Thanks," Charles drawled with dry appreciation. "You're all heart."

"You know better than that," Foster chuckled raspingly. "Although I wouldn't even have bothered you tonight if I hadn't thought you could be thinking about this, if you can find the time," he added with a rather resentful suggestiveness in his voice.

"Foster," Charles warned in a low, threatening tone.

"Okay, okay," Foster grunted. "Maybe I'm just jealous." And then he got back to business. "Can you be here at nine tomorrow morning?"

"Same place?" Charles asked.

"Yeah. You know the way."

"All right," Charles agreed. The two men rang off, and Charles stood where he was for a moment, his face tautly grim as he thought about what Foster had told him, before he cleared his expression and went to find Sarah.

Now Charles paced impatiently as he waited for Foster, but his impatience sprang not so much because the other man had been delayed, but from his own inner conflict about what had happened.

For five years events in Zwahola had occupied him to the exclusion of all else. And though he looked forward to living a more normal life, with Sarah at the heart of it, he was still interested and concerned over matters that had figured so strongly in his past. Indeed, he thought wryly, it wasn't even appropriate as yet to term it his past. He was still on the job, and as long as he was, he knew he would do everything in his power to keep Zwahola at least nominally friendly to the West. His parents had given everything, including their lives, to that country, and while the present government there could not in any sense of the word be termed a democracy in the same sense an American would define it, it was at least a more desirable form of government than it could become if Lugubu and his friends came to power.

Charles's thoughts were interrupted as Foster came through the door and locked it carefully behind him. "Trainer," he nodded a greeting to Charles before taking off his hat and tossing it onto a nearby chair. He then seated himself wearily behind the scratched, battered desk in one corner of the room and rubbed his unshaven chin.

Charles noted that Foster's bloodshot eyes and the lack of a shave gave indication that if Foster had had any time to sleep at all the preceding night, he had not taken much advantage of it.

"I've been with the chief," Foster informed him. "He and your other employer, the chairman of the board, in fact, have been putting their heads together." Foster paused and tossed Charles a disgruntled look. "By the way," he added gruffly, "they're both furious because you couldn't be found last night. You owe me one, Trainer. I didn't tell them where you were."

Charles quirked one eyebrow, but his tone was sincere when he replied. "Thanks, Foster. I appreciate it. Did the chief say what, if anything, they've decided to do?"

"Hell, he didn't have to," Foster snorted. "World Oil knows what can happen if Lugubu gets more power than he already has. They don't want to get kicked out of Zwahola and have all their assets there confiscated. It would cost them millions. You know that. And the Agency doesn't want that to happen any more than World Oil does for their own reasons."

"They're being a little premature in worrying about it, aren't they?" Charles mused, though his own worried frown gave indication that he was just as concerned that the seemingly innocuous announcement of the engagement of two young people could have such far-reaching implications.

"Are they?" Foster responded rhetorically. "Anyway, everybody's prepared to do anything necessary to stop that marriage. But if we're lucky, we won't have to be the ones to interfere. Njomo's apparently as upset as we are. At least we assume that's why he called World Oil last night looking for you."

At Charles's alert glance, Foster's doleful face turned even more discouraged as he added, "And, of course, you couldn't be found, so the chief is mad as hell because he couldn't produce you on the spot. My tail is still sore from the chewing it got."

"Sorry, Foster," Charles remarked sympathetically as he momentarily stopped his restless pacing. "So should I call Njomo back now?" he then asked in a level, thoughtful tone.

"No, you should get your tail over to Njomo's hotel," Foster replied firmly. "The chairman made an appointment for you at ten, and the chief made it clear that if I didn't find you and get you there on time, my neck was on the chopping block."

Charles glanced at his watch before immediately starting for the door. But when he got there, he paused and looked at Foster again. "You and I will need to talk after I've seen Njomo, right?" he questioned, his brows raised in inquiry.

"Hell, yes!" Foster said in a tired voice as he raised a hand to pass it wearily over his untidy graying hair. "My instincts are twitching all over the place. I have the feeling things are going to go all to hell pretty quick, and I don't like surprises!"

"Then you should never have gotten in the business," Charles mocked with a slight quirk. "Surprises are the name of the game in our work."

"Not if I can help it," Foster snorted grimly.

"But that's the point," Charles said with soft irony as he opened the door and prepared to leave the room. "You can't."

His chuckle accompanied him out of the room, and Foster scowled at the door that had closed behind Charles for several moments before he moved his tired body to a lumpy, discolored sofa and threw himself down for a quick catnap before he had to start confronting any of those unwanted surprises.

Meanwhile, if Chelley hadn't been on the phone when Sarah sailed into her office that morning, Sarah would have given herself away within seconds of entering the room. Fortunately, however, Chelley's conversation was so distracting that she barely noticed the soft glow in Sarah's eyes and the complacent smile on her lips, and by the time Chelley had hung up and entered Sarah's inner office, Sarah had become sufficiently immersed in the business of the day that she gave the appearance of being her normal self.

"Light schedule today," Chelley announced prosaically as she brought the appointment book to Sarah's desk, "unless Bal Henderson decides to pay us a visit. If he does, we can shuffle people around to give you plenty of time with him."

"Thanks, Chel," Sarah said absently, her attention on a letter from a West Coast studio which was planning a New York City location for a forthcoming movie and wanted her to start contacting sufficient extras for some of the crowd scenes. "Get our file on standby weirdos, will you?" she requested.

"Sure," Chelley agreed, her eyes lighting with mild interest. "What's up?"

Sarah explained that the West Coast studio wanted a crowd scene with some distinct eccentrics scattered among the "normal" people, and Chelley shrugged. "Wonder why they're shooting it here then," she drawled. "I'd be willing to bet that the West Coast has more certifiable weirdos than we do."

Sarah shook her head, smiling at Chelley's droll sense of humor, and when she had the file she'd requested in hand, she began to make phone calls. She had just hung up from one of them when Chelley stuck her head around the door and hissed, "Bal's on his way, and he doesn't sound as though he's in a very good mood. Get ready," she advised, rolling her eyes to the ceiling to express her opinion of the temperament of one of the hottest playwrights going.

Sarah smiled, grateful for the warning as it gave her time to get her thoughts together before she tackled Bal on the subject of changing the focus of the character she wanted Lila Benton to play. By the time the tall, skinny, bespectacled, haphazardly dressed Bal Henderson appeared at her door with a prominent scowl plastered across his doleful face, Sarah was ready for him, and she greeted him with a gentle smile of affectionate respect.

"Hi, Bal," she said warmly. "How've you been?"

"Terrible," he informed her gloomily. "I hate this business!"

"Hmmm," Sarah said soothingly, gesturing Bal to a chair after kissing his cheek. "Sit down and have a cup of tea and tell me all about it."

Right on schedule, Chelley appeared with a cup of herbal tea for Bal and a cup of strong black coffee for Sarah before discreetly disappearing again. In between sips of his tea, Bal proceeded to bemoan the fate of any poor playwright who got entangled in the coils of insensitive producers and dictatorial directors in the insane business of producing plays.

"I'd have been better off digging ditches," he pronounced angrily, though it was apparent that the opportunity to get things off his chest and into Sarah's sympathetic ear had improved his mood considerably over what it had been when he'd first entered the room.

"Now, Bal," Sarah scolded him affectionately. "I for one am very glad you decided to write plays instead of digging ditches, as is the rest of the theatergoing public. You know you're fantastic, and you're certainly a big enough man to put up with the little irritants that go along with your work, aren't you?"

Relaxing further under the soothing balm of Sarah's praise, Bal's lined face smoothed into a complacent smile. "I suppose so," he admitted, taking her description of his talents as his due. "But it's distracting, Sarah," he added with grumpy irritability. "It puts me off my stroke."

"Not for long, I'm sure," Sarah returned confidently. "Now, Bal, let's talk about the Marilyn Mason play." And she proceeded to spend ten full minutes praising the work to the skies before she got down to the delicate, artful business of convincing Bal to change it slightly.

It was a testament to her skill that before another hour had passed Sarah had Bal not only agreeing to change the focus of the character, but enthusiastically accepting her compliments for having the vision to see where the play could be improved. His last comment before he took his leave was indicative of his belief that the changes were strictly his own idea.

"I'm surprised you didn't see all this yourself, Sarah," he pronounced with indulgent forgiveness of her lack of perspicacity. "You're usually pretty sharp about these things."

"Oh, well, Bal, I've been pretty busy lately," Sarah responded vaguely. "And you're the author, after all," she added admiringly. "It's only natural that you would have more insight than I do."

"Yes, I suppose so," Bal mused complacently. "And you really think Lila Benton is right for the part?" he then added with a touch of anxiety, though Sarah could see he'd already accepted the idea.

"She'll be perfect," Sarah assured him gravely. "But I'll set up a reading for you so you can make your own judgment, if you like."

"No, no, that's all right, Sarah." Bal hastily rejected the idea as Sarah had known he would. "I trust you."

"All right then, it's all settled," Sarah agreed, hiding a smile at Bal's reluctance to get involved in the nuts and bolts of producing one of his plays. He was really happy only when he was writing one, and though he liked to complain about everyone else's contribution to the actual production, he was secretly relieved to be spared such involvement.

After Bal had taken his leave, Chelley appeared in the door again, shaking her head in amazement when Sarah calmly informed her Bal was going to change his play in accordance with her very tactful suggestions.

"You're something else," Chelley declared with a sigh of exasperation and awe. "I don't know how you do it."

"It isn't easy," Sarah replied wryly before giving a huge yawn and reaching her arms over her head in a relaxing stretch.

"Rough night?" Chelley asked with suspicious innocence.

Sarah's acting talents came into play as she answered, very casually, "I had things on my mind." Whereupon Chelley, with a little pout of disappointment, disappeared back into her own office.

A few minutes later she was back, and after carefully closing

90

the door behind her, she approached Sarah's desk with a bemused half frown, half smile on her face.

"What is it?" Sarah asked curiously.

"There's a guy out there who's never been in before," Chelley informed Sarah almost eagerly. "He just dropped in, he says, to discuss the possibility of obtaining a 'spot on the telly' or some other sort of acting job," Chelley mocked the applicant's obviously English accent with a giggle. And at Sarah's skeptical look about seeing someone without an appointment who sounded naively unsophisticated about the acting profession, Chelley hastened to plead the man's case.

"I know, Sarah," she coaxed, "but he's really impressive looking, and he has sort of a lordly English air about him that got to me. Can't you just see him for a couple of minutes? That'll give me time to freshen my makeup and pretend I'm just leaving for a coffee break when he comes back out again. If I'm lucky, maybe he'll want to go with me."

Sarah eyed her secretary with humor. "Careful, Chel," she cautioned. "I'm aware you're a sucker for an English accent, but I would have thought you'd be a little wary after your last disastrous relationship with one of that breed."

Chelley sniffed unconcernedly. "I bounce back fast," she tossed off lightly. "What about it, Sarah?" she then continued her coaxing. "Just for a few minutes?"

Shaking her head with resigned exasperation, Sarah nevertheless hunched her shoulders in a why-not? gesture, while Chelley beamed her delight and spun on her heel to go fetch the unexpected visitor.

A few seconds later Chelley escorted a tall, slender, brown-haired, brown-eyed man into the room who was clad in a light tan suit and who sported a pleasant smile on his handsome face and an intelligent expression in his dark eyes that was somehow at odds with the air of general aristocratic boredom he exuded.

Sarah watched his approach with professional curiosity, automatically trying to fit him into a standard acting category, and feeling oddly disconcerted when he failed to fit any niche she tried to carve for him.

He came right up to her desk and leaned his hands on the wooden surface while he studied Sarah every bit as thoroughly as she had studied him. Finally he spoke, his tone thick with an accent that was nominally British, but which was tinged with some other patina Sarah couldn't identify.

"Has anyone ever told you you could pass for Sophia Loren's twin?" he inquired casually while he continued to peer at her with undisguised appreciation.

"No, I'm afraid not," Sarah returned with a smile, replying truthfully in the sense that Charles had only told her she had eyes like Sophia Loren's. She was nevertheless startled that this stranger had made the comparison when she herself considered the resemblance to be so remote as to be negligible.

"Blind clods." The man shrugged, the gesture and his tone both suave and utterly self-confident. With casual aplomb he then seated himself in the chair opposite the desk without waiting for an invitation. "And how are you today, Sophia?" he inquired then, smiling at her with a charm Sarah found herself succumbing to in spite of herself.

"The name is Sarah, and I'm just fine today, thank you very much, Mr.?" Sarah replied with humor, unable to explain to herself why she was so inexplicably drawn to this utter stranger who handled himself like a man born to the manner.

"Connors," the stranger introduced himself suavely. "Ian Connors." He paused, raising his eyebrows with humorous self-mockery. "Ever heard of me?"

"I'm afraid not," Sarah answered, imparting just a tinge of mocking regret to her tone. Something about the man made her want to puncture his self-confidence, albeit gently, while at the same time she could only admire his poise.

"Ah, well," he responded with insouciant good grace. "No reason why you should have, actually. I've only ever done a spot of . . . ah . . . character acting on the Continent."

"And what character was that?" Sarah asked curiously, certain that for some reason he was putting her on, though why he should, she couldn't fathom. Still, there was something so attractive about this man, she was in no hurry to conclude the interview, especially since she had time to fill anyway.

"Ahhh," he hesitated, eyeing her with delicious, complicitous humor. "Can't say as I remember myself, come to think of it. Something medieval, as I recall, where I had to wear a godawfully hot costume. An unpleasant experience altogether," he informed her with cheerful unconcern.

"But you'd like to try acting again?" Sarah suggested tongue-in-cheek, certain now that her visitor was not and never had been an actor. Actors never forgot their roles. But she was more curious than ever about why this man had come to her office at all, and she was willing to play along in the interest of finding out.

"Of course," Ian Connors agreed, widening his dark, intelligent eyes at her innocently. "As long as it's not a costume piece," he hastily qualified his statement. "I don't think I could stomach that again."

Unable to help herself, Sarah gurgled with laughter. "I don't think you're going to have to worry about it," she informed him through her giggles. "I get the feeling you'd do better as a suave James Bond than as a Shakespearean actor anytime."

The look of alert startlement she got as a result of her comment was gone so quickly in favor of a slow smile that Sarah wasn't certain she'd seen it. "Perhaps you're right," Ian agreed soberly. "I'm not much given to serious things."

"That doesn't surprise me," Sarah quipped, smiling, "but the fact that you came in here to see me does. Why did you come?"

Ian's face then dissolved into something as close to a sheepish grin as he seemed capable of. "Would you believe I was bored?" he asked innocently.

"I'm beginning to think I'd believe anything where you're concerned," Sarah offered dryly. This interview was certainly not what she'd expected when she'd agreed to see Ian Connors, and while she was strangely taken with the man, she was also beginning to feel a little disoriented by the strangeness of the encounter.

"Ah, a woman after my own heart." Ian gave an expansive sigh of satisfaction, his dark eyes twinkling charmingly. "A woman with a delightful sense of trust, a true beauty, a woman whose sympathetic charm is only equaled by her—"

"Lack of time," Sarah cut in sardonically since it looked like Ian's effusive compliments might continue indefinitely, and the warm look in his eyes that accompanied them was beginning to make her feel uncomfortable. "Now, Mr. Connors, if you could just . . ."

"Get to the point?" he suggested cheerfully, and at Sarah's nod, he lapsed into an appealing, beseeching smile. "Well, as it happens, Miss Bailey, you see before you a man afflicted with the curse of modern times."

As he paused, Sarah, thoroughly fascinated by Ian's conversation, despite the fact that it had no purpose whatsoever so far as she could ascertain, prompted him. "And your particular curse is?"

"Too much money," he informed her with grave sobriety, his brown eyes suggesting that he was a man much put upon by fate.

"Ohhh," Sarah sympathized with exaggerated pity. "What a shame!" she mocked, shaking her head with implied empathy.

"Yes, isn't it?" Ian sighed, though his eyes fairly sparkled with devilish mischief. "I've been everywhere, seen everything, done everything, had everything . . . well, almost." He made a deprecating gesture of modest denial. "What else is there?" he inquired dolefully. "Not bloody much."

For a long moment two sets of brown eyes contemplated each other with shared sympathetic understanding underscored with an equally shared dose of humor. Then Sarah brightened and suggested in a tone indicating she'd just had a staggeringly brilliant idea, "But as an actor you could experience other lives than your own, Mr. Connors! That is, of course, the answer to your problem, and no doubt the reason why you found your way to me," she finished, settling back in her chair with an air of satisfied accomplishment while she waited for Ian Connors to play out his side of their impromptu drama.

"By God, you're right!" he answered in a tone of amazement. "I'll bet Sir Laurence Olivier never gets bored!" he pronounced in a theatrical tone that fairly rolled across the room in waves of impressive import.

"Ah, let's not walk before we can run," Sarah cautioned him with gentle humor. "As a matter of fact, Mr. Connors," she then informed him with sweet modesty, "I think I have just the right job for you."

"Amazing!" he mocked in awestruck tones. "I haven't been in

her offices for more than ten minutes, and already the lady
. . ."

"Is offering you a job as an extra on the streets of New York
in two months' time," Sarah completed the sentence for him, as
certain as she'd ever been in her life that Ian Connors had no
intention of accepting such a job, which left her wondering in an
amused, intrigued way, how he was going to get out of accepting
it and why he had really come into her offices in the first place.

"Oh," he responded flatly, his expression suddenly crestfallen.

"Now, now, Mr. Connors," Sarah chided him briskly. "Think
of the experiences you can have starting at the bottom for a
change."

Ian Connors raised an aristocratic eyebrow as he eyed her
doubtfully. "Experiences, hmmm?" he mused thoughtfully.

"Tons of them," Sarah answered promptly. "What do you
say? No costumes, no lines to learn, nothing remotely medieval
about it. It sounds just your cup of tea," she added with a
straight face, causing him to groan aloud his disgust at her
atrocious reference to his English background.

"Well." He considered the matter thoughtfully before his expression brightened. "I don't suppose you'd care to have dinner
with me tonight to discuss the matter further?" he inquired with
smooth hopefulness.

"Sorry," Sarah declined, satisfied that she had at last discovered the real reason for Ian Connors's visit. He must have seen
her somewhere, sometime, and been attracted, and he was just
the sort of man who would go to these unusual, amusing lengths
to make her acquaintance.

"However," she added mischievously as Ian's face reflected
disappointment and then the rueful resignation of a gentleman
who had tried and lost, "if you'd care to extend that invitation
to my secretary, I'm sure she'd take you up on it. She was quite
taken with you, you know."

"Was she?" Ian inquired, interested speculation perking him
up noticeably. "She is a lovely little thing, isn't she?"

"Quite lovely," Sarah agreed soberly. "She's just bought a new
dress too," Sarah added as she got up from her chair, indicating
that the interview was about to end. "Which means she probably
doesn't have a thing to eat in her apartment because she can't

afford it. Do take her somewhere nice, Mr. Connors, and see that she orders anything she wants. You can afford it, can't you?" she ended the discussion with suspicious innocence dripping from her tones.

But Ian chose not to react to her teasing. "Capital idea!" he announced suavely as he got to his own feet. "I shall go straight-forth and put it into operation."

Smothering a laugh at his way of putting things, Sarah came around the desk to walk him to the door, not even aware that it was an unnecessary gesture, though the satisfied look in Ian Connors's dark eyes evidenced the fact that he was aware he had managed to charm Sarah to a limited degree. He took her by surprise by placing a firm, warm hand on her shoulder, but when she looked up at him in surprise at the familiarity, he slanted such an intelligent, appreciative glance down at her that her misgivings disappeared.

"It's been a pleasure, Sarah Bailey," he murmured in deep, drawling tones that were disconcertingly sexy after the mocking-ly humorous ones he had used earlier. "And I'm looking forward to seeing you again. I'm afraid the crowd scene doesn't appeal to me, but I feel certain if I keep turning up here from time to time, you'll find another role for me that will suit me better."

Sarah heard the suggestive note in his voice and ignored it. When they reached the door, she did, however, look up at him curiously. "Exactly what role do you see yourself playing, Mr. Connors?" she inquired dryly, wondering why she had sudden conflicting feelings about the man beside her. He seemed a man of many parts. He had wit and humor, an intelligence that was cloaked by a good deal of charm, and a certain masculine appeal that made her understand Chelley's reaction to him.

"Why, I thought we'd agreed I'm the James Bond type," he teased, his dark eyes twinkling down at her as he casually rested his hands on her shoulders, an act that Sarah only vaguely noted. And before she could answer, he changed the subject.

"You're a delightful woman, Sarah Bailey," he said more soberly, searching her face with something unfathomable in the depths of his brown eyes. "I can see why . . ." But he seemed to change direction abruptly after an infinitesimal pause. ". . . you have such a good reputation in the business."

"Where did you hear that?" Sarah asked curiously. "I wasn't aware the man on the street knew about my reputation."

"Ah, but I'm not just any man on the street," Ian replied, his eyes dancing wickedly. "We men of wealth have our ways," he added with exaggerated pompousness.

"Oh, yes," Sarah responded wryly. "I'd forgotten about your . . . ah . . . problem."

"Be careful how you speak to me," Ian teased, his grip on Sarah's shoulders imperceptibly tightening. "We British still know how to maintain the upper hand with you upstart colonists."

"Oh?" Sarah mocked him, endeavoring to look impressed. "And how do you British go about that?"

"Like this," Ian replied calmly, suddenly pulling her into the curve of his body. Before Sarah could react, he had dipped his head and kissed her with a brief thoroughness that left her in no doubt that when he spoke of having had everything, women undoubtedly held a prominent place on his list of accomplishments. But when he lifted his head, he was so boyishly pleased with himself and so unthreateningly amused at his cleverness that Sarah couldn't find it in her to give him the setdown he deserved.

"See what I mean?" he quipped as he let her go. "I learned that at my nanny's knee."

"Somehow I doubt that," Sarah drawled, her frown failing to quell his good humor.

"Ah, well, it makes a good line," Ian responded insouciantly, chuckling complacently before he turned in a graceful motion to open the door behind him. "I'll be seeing you, Sarah," he then promised in a tone that while it was cheerfully bland nevertheless contained a hint of steel that made Sarah convinced he was a man who meant what he said.

As Ian disappeared into the outer office, Sarah wandered back into her own, and for a few moments she contemplated a disturbingly vivid impression that Ian Connors was not at all what he seemed—that contrary to being a novice actor, he might just possibly be the most accomplished one she'd ever met. But as she resumed work, she forgot about him, since she had no intention of ever seeing him again, or at least not in the way he seemed to anticipate. It was all she could do to keep her mind on her job when enticing thoughts of the night before kept intruding and a wholehearted eagerness for the night to come kept demanding her attention as the hours passed before she would see Charles again.

CHAPTER EIGHT

Despite his hurry, upon spotting a public telephone in the lobby of the luxurious hotel where Njomo had his suite of rooms, Charles gave in to the impulse to telephone Sarah for a brief, reassuring "I love you," since he knew she was having trouble adjusting to his reappearance in her life. It would take time before she regained the complete trust she had had in him once before, and he meant to do all he could to speed up the process. It hurt him immeasurably to see, for however brief and unguarded an instant, the flicker of uncertainty she had displayed toward him upon occasion the night before, though he knew she was perfectly justified in having those doubts about his sincerity.

Upon hearing Sarah's crisp, businesslike, "Bailey Casting," when she answered his call, a warm smile curved his lips, and his eyes turned a darker shade of blue, a color resembling what pilots saw in the upper reaches of the atmosphere.

"Is it?" he said softly. "Good. I need a job."

"What sort of job did you have in mind, sir?" Sarah answered after a momentary pause and in a tone that told him she had recognized his voice.

"Well," he drawled with humor, "I see myself as a combination lover/husband type, and there's a certain lady I think will vouch for my qualifications."

"Hmmm," Sarah replied doubtfully. "You realize, of course, sir, that . . . ah . . . intimate acquaintances can't always be objective about one's attributes. I would certainly have to see you for myself and test you before I could be certain you fit the requirements."

"Certainly," Charles answered smoothly. "It's impossible for me to come into the office now for the . . . ah . . . testing, but

99

if you would be willing to have dinner with me tonight and then, perhaps, spend the evening with me?"

"Well," Sarah hesitated, feigning dubiousness. "That's not usually the way I handle interviews, but I must admit you sound sexy enough to make me bend the rules a little."

"Lady," Charles growled in his most sensual voice, "before I'm through with you, I can promise you're going to bend more than just the rules."

"Oh, yes?" Sarah projected a slight shiver of anticipation into her now husky tones that, had she known it, made Charles close his eyes briefly against a wave of desire. "Well, it's obvious you're a determined man, so I suppose I might as well give in to the inevitable, hadn't I? What time do you want to begin the—test?"

"Right now," Charles replied with wry huskiness. "But since that's impossible, I'll pick you up outside your offices at five thirty." He paused for a second, then asked with quiet insistence, "Love me, Sophie?"

"Love you, darling," Sarah replied, almost in a whisper.

"I love you, too, honey," he breathed into the telephone. "In a few hours I'll show you how much again. Until then, I can see I'm going to have my hands full keeping my mind on business."

He realized from the momentary silence that greeted his words that it had been the wrong thing to say, but other than giving a resigned grimace, his tone betrayed nothing.

"See you then, babe." He rang off quietly, and as he replaced the receiver, he shook his head slightly, regretting his inadvertent slip, before he straightened his shoulders and swung on his heel to stride toward the elevators.

Outside Njomo's suite of rooms he was greeted by a huge, hulking black man who looked as though he had been crammed forcibly into the gray Western-style suit he wore, and whose eyes had the calm, placid stare of a man who was prepared to do anything in his power to protect the man on the other side of the closed door behind him, up to and including murder.

"Mornin', Mr. Trainer," he growled, his eyes searching Charles's frame as though looking for something. "Step over here, please."

With a sigh of resigned patience, Charles moved in front of the man and lifted his arms while the huge hands patted over him, looking for any concealed weapons. When the guard was satisfied, he nodded at Charles and opened the door behind him.

Inside the suite of rooms Charles was confronted by another, more refined, yet equally intimidating personage whose coal black eyes surveyed him with a detachment that quickly changed to a limited warmth.

"Charles," the man nodded his head in a regal gesture that matched his Oxonian accent. "Glad to see you. Njomo is waiting."

"Hello, Yinka." Charles returned the greeting. "I'm not late, am I?"

"No, you're right on time." Then the black eyes pierced Charles with restrained curiosity. "Though he would have preferred to see you last night," Yinka added politely, a slight questioning tone at the end of his comment. When Charles remained silent in the face of that tone, however, Yinka shrugged. "In here." He directed Charles with an elegant sweep of one finely tailored arm toward the inner room.

As Charles stepped through the door and spotted Njomo ensconced amid a welter of brightly colored pillows that almost smothered his tiny frame, Charles's eyes went opaque momentarily while he remembered his youth. He had lived with his parents in Njomo's village and had been adopted, along with scores of black youths, into the circle of children that always followed Njomo around, waiting for him to teach them from his vast store of knowledge about the surrounding countryside, the animals that resided there, the history of the tribe, and Njomo's philosophy of life.

It had been a good time while it lasted, and as the gaily clothed women who now surrounded Njomo melted from the room after giving Charles shy smiles of recognition, Charles shook off his momentary journey into the past and stepped forward. He came to a stop in front of the withered old man and bowed from the waist.

"Grandfather," he greeted Njomo respectfully. "I am pleased to see you well and happy."

Two dark eyes deeply set into the lined, seamed face that seemed to radiate kindness and intelligence and even a spark of ironic humor, inspected Charles with fondness.

"Sit down, my son," he answered in his native language, which was the one Charles had used to address him. "I am well, yes, but no longer happy."

Charles sat down immediately in front of Njomo on the floor, crossing his legs under him as he continued to hold Njomo's gaze. "It distresses me to hear that," he said with quiet, respectful formality. "How may I serve you, Grandfather?" he asked simply.

The old man closed his eyes wearily for a moment before he opened them again to gaze into the distance. "I have not spent my seed to see the second generation fall into the thorn bush," he mused almost absently. "My son is already a lost cause. He has been since infancy, perhaps because I had so little time to spend with him. I do not know." He sighed gustily while Charles remained silent, accustomed as he was to Njomo's seemingly random discourses, which Charles knew from long experience were never random.

"But I have plans for my granddaughter I will not see disturbed," Njomo continued, his chin lifting proudly. "I will not see her cast to a swine like Ajayi."

Charles regarded his old friend and mentor steadily, waiting to learn how Njomo planned to prevent the marriage of his granddaughter to Lugubu's son.

"She thinks she loves him," Njomo said with a philosophical shrug. "But there is no substance to maintain love inside his soul. He is a handsome shell who brags and swaggers and causes the maiden's heart to pound with the excitement one feels at seeing a proud lion strut his path." He shook his head sadly. "Like the male lion, however, he does not mate without expecting the female to provide him with other than her sex. He will use her to provide something he wants. Then he will break her heart."

Charles waited quietly; he totally agreed with the old man's opinion. When Njomo's thoughtful silence had gone on long enough for Charles to show no disrespect at breaking it, however, he inquired softly, "And what is it you think Lugubu's son wants from Yetunde, Grandfather?"

Njomo returned his wise gaze to Charles and a quavering smile stretched his thin lips. "Why does my son ask a question when he knows the answer already?" he asked softly. And when

Charles hesitated, Njomo provided the answer. "Unless it is to probe what is in the answerer's mind?"

Charles smiled ruefully then, and it was a smile of combined affection and chastened recognition of the old man's wisdom. "Thou knowest the answer," he replied softly.

"Yes," Njomo nodded his gray head complacently. "You know as well as I do this marriage is a ploy of Lugubu's. He has wanted total power for a very long time. I am the only one who stands in his way. Since he cannot go over me, he expects to go around me. It is a good plan," he said, shrugging one thin, bony shoulder philosophically. "But it will not work," he added in a tone that was almost casual, but with a quality Charles recognized as springing from Njomo's powerful, inflexible will.

"What will you do?" he asked in a soft tone of admiration.

The thin lips stretched in another smile. "I will marry her to Kinte," he said simply.

It was all Charles could do to stop himself from sucking in a deep breath of astonishment. Kinte was the heir apparent to a neighboring nation, one which had never been friendly to Zwahola in the past. Despite himself, he found it shocked him to think that Njomo, while unwilling to sacrifice his granddaughter to Lugubu's plans, would willingly contemplate throwing her to an enemy equally as dangerous and quite as likely to cause her unhappiness.

"You are shocked," Njomo smiled complacently. "You think I am cruel?" he inquired with mild interest.

"I . . ." Charles hesitated, then opted for the truth, a commodity he and Njomo usually shared in their relations with each other. "Yes, Njomo," he said firmly. "I must admit it sounds cruel to me."

"Ah." The old man gave a sigh of satisfaction. "It sounds cruel, yes. But I know what I am doing. This is in confidence," he tossed off almost as an afterthought, an unconscious gesture that spelled out his trust in Charles, before he went on. "I have been meeting with Kinte in secret for some time now," he informed Charles, noting with sparkling satisfaction in his dark eyes that he had managed to surprise his young friend. "The man is honorable. The man is strong. He will make many changes when he comes to power."

Charles frowned, his gaze thoughtfully doubtful. "Are you sure, Grandfather?" he asked skeptically.

The old man nodded his head with firm assurance. "I am sure," he pronounced in a tone that left no room for argument. Then he smiled slyly. "He will also make a good husband for Yetunde once she is over her disappointment that she cannot have the strutting lion. Kinte is much man. He will treat her well, but he will tolerate no resistance from her. She needs a man like that, a man she can respect but not dominate." Njomo suddenly chortled, his old eyes taking on the leer of a much younger man briefly. "I would like to be a watching eye on the first night he demands his rights as a husband though. He will be in for a surprise."

Charles smiled with him, though his gaze was troubled. "But how will you accomplish this?" he inquired.

And suddenly Njomo was no longer an elderly, frail old man with wisdom in his deep-set eyes, but had the look of a young warrior who could be ruthless in accomplishing his objectives. "You leave that to me." He dismissed Charles's curiosity almost curtly. But then, as if he regretted his sharpness, he let his gaze fall on Charles with quiet inflexibility. "If I have to somehow remove Ajayi from Zwahola, I will do so. Let us hope it does not come to that, but if it does . . ." He shrugged, dismissing Ajayi's life as though it were of no consequence, and reminding Charles with chilling force that in the past, Njomo had found it necessary to remove other obstacles to what he wanted to accomplish, and he had not always done so in a gentle fashion.

"Now, my son." Njomo focused his attention on Charles with complete concentration. "I have something to ask of you. I will not press you for an answer now, but this is important to me, and I will be happy if you will consider long and hard before you give me your answer. I have need of you."

Charles, wondering why his back was suddenly traced by a slight, chilling whisper of danger, looked back at Njomo's steady gaze and dipped his head respectfully. "Ask, Grandfather," he said calmly, giving no sign that suddenly he dreaded to hear how Njomo needed him.

"You know my views on what is best for my country," Njomo said with quiet reflectiveness. "I do not wish for Zwahola to become involved in the tug-of-war between the superpowers. She will only be torn apart if she leaves the safety of neutrality. But it is becoming apparent that Lugubu and his friends on the one hand, and Hwala on the other, are determined to force her to one side or the other. Since it is inevitable that there will be a battle over the matter, I must plot strategy to foil them both."

Charles felt mildly uncomfortable then. Of course, his own government supported Hwala, and if it became a choice between Hwala and Lugubu, Charles knew which one he himself would support. But there was a niggling part of his mind that agreed with Njomo that Zwahola would be better off maintaining a strict neutrality in which to work out her own destiny. Still, he was an agent of his government, and his loyalty, while strained, held fast.

It would have been impolite to ask Njomo what that strategy was, but he was relieved when Njomo volunteered part of what Charles wanted to know.

"While I will work to maintain neutrality," the old man said musingly, "I will reserve judgment, outwardly at least, on which philosophy of government I will support should my efforts fail. It is never wise to burn one's hut behind him. A man may have need of its shelter again one day."

Charles almost winced at Njomo's phrase, having only recently realized how devastated he would have been after having burned his bridges between him and Sarah, if she had elected to maintain the gap between them. He was not sure he could face a life without her now that he'd had the opportunity to be with her again.

"Therefore," Njomo continued, "I will say to no man, not even to you, which course of action I will ultimately support should neutrality become impossible."

Charles looked at him in surprise, having thought Njomo's determination to keep Lugubu from power was a confession of where he stood.

Njomo shook his wise old head at seeing Charles's surprise. "I learned long ago to keep my inner self private," he said sadly. "One's intimates can often hurt one more than an enemy can. But I do have a plan I will share with you," he added, smiling a charmingly cunning smile at Charles.

"Yes, Grandfather," Charles encouraged him patiently.

"If," Njomo mused speculatively out loud, "if our exports could somehow catch up with our imports temporarily, thereby upgrading the standard of living for the populace, I think that populace would be very much inclined to support the government that made such enjoyable living possible, do you not agree, my son?"

Charles nodded cautiously, sensing where Njomo was heading, and again feeling that sense of warning.

"Lugubu tells everyone his Eastern friends can make such a thing possible," Njomo still mused out loud. "I think it is doubtful, but"—he spread his hands, which were heavily veined and shook slightly with a palsy that afflicted him in his old age—"who am I to say?" He disclaimed his own wisdom with modesty. "Hwala says the same of his Western friends. I assume you agree with Hwala?" he asked innocently.

"Yes, Grandfather," Charles admitted, a faint mocking smile hesitating on his lips. He knew that despite Njomo's seeming innocence, the old man was at his most dangerous when adopting such a façade.

"Suppose there were a way to test the matter," Njomo inquired casually. "Would it not be in Zwahola's best interest to do so?"

Again Charles had to agree, though, despite his puzzlement at where Njomo was heading, his senses were screaming a warning at him by now.

"Suppose," Njomo proposed thoughtfully, "suppose a Western man were put in charge of solving our economic problems and was at least partially successful. Would that not be somewhat of a test?"

Charles sat where he was, his body rigid with stillness while he fought to keep his gaze impassively nonrevealing. He knew exactly where Njomo was heading now, and the knowledge filled him with a sense of foreboding it was all he could do to conceal. He remained silent while Njomo's sharpened gaze ran over him like a laser beam propelled by an intelligence Charles had always respected in the past, but which now filled him with a totally selfish fear that his future was about to be recharted, and not to his liking.

"If such a position were offered, my son, you would be a very prominent candidate," Njomo said softly, watching like an aged hawk as his words fell into the silence between the two men. "In fact, I think I can safely say that you are the only man our government would consider for such a position," Njomo went on placidly, though his gaze was fiercely avid now. "And I believe you have been giving thought to leaving your . . . ah . . . position in Zwahola recently?" he asked very quietly.

Charles's head came up as he heard that note in Njomo's voice. It was common knowledge that he supposedly had left Zwahola for good when he had come back to New York this time. So why was Njomo putting his question in such a way, unless he knew about Charles's "other" position.

But, no, Charles reassured himself warily. Although Njomo might suspect, there was absolutely no way he could be sure. Still, Njomo was asking something of him other than his innocent words implied. Charles was certain of it.

"Yes, Grandfather," he said levelly. "In fact, my job in Zwahola is already over." He started to ask why Njomo had not been made aware of that fact, then hesitated. It would be bad form to ask such a question, though he was certain Njomo had known already, though he had been unavailable when Charles had attempted to see him to say good-bye in person.

"Then," Njomo said with satisfaction, "if such a position were offered to you, there would be nothing to stand in the way of your accepting."

It was not a question. Had it been, Charles was not certain how he could have answered when all his instincts were screaming at him to keep his involvement with Sarah a secret. Still, those same instincts were also screaming at him that this development could mean the end of his plans with Sarah. And after last night, the thought was intolerable. There was nothing he could do at the moment, however, except stall.

"I am certain you must be mistaken in thinking there are no other qualified candidates for the position, Grandfather," Charles said as smoothly as possible against the tight feeling in his throat, as though he were being choked by responsibilities he wanted no part of.

"And I am certain there are not, none that I would accept,"

Njomo replied with quiet arrogance. Though he was not the head of the government of Zwahola—that position was filled by Hwala at the moment—his influence and reputation were such that he could make such a statement with complete faith that he held the power to back it up.

"However"—Njomo then adopted a lighter tone—"this is all speculation at this point. Such a position has not as yet been created, and my government is not yet, therefore, in a position to offer it to anyone. I merely wanted you to give the matter some thought, and to come to a conclusion about what your answer would be should such an eventuality occur."

There was a tone of dismissal in his voice that was impossible to ignore, and Charles did not, though he felt a strong urge to argue with Njomo about other possible candidates for the hypothetical position. He could think of three men right off the top of his head who would give their souls to obtain it, but since one of them would have Lugubu's wholehearted approval, Charles was in no position to suggest that the man be considered. The other two, while competent, would, Charles knew without false modesty, be less effective than he himself would be in the job, but perhaps their enthusiasm would make up for his superior expertise. He was certain that his own complete lack of enthusiasm would be a major handicap he wasn't certain he could overcome.

He took his leave of Njomo after indulging in the ritual of departure that was expected, but his eyes were abstracted and hard, his lips forming a taut line in his handsome face as he left Njomo's presence and made his way toward Ace Exports to report to Foster.

And as he changed taxis in a precautionary maneuver in case he was being followed, the planes of his face were harshly outlined as he realized exactly what sort of pressure was going to be put upon him to accept Njomo's hypothetical position. For he knew without a doubt in his mind that the position would not remain hypothetical for long, and that both of his employers would stop at nothing to force him to accept it.

As he automatically made his way to the offices where Foster awaited him, he agonized over the conflict Njomo's proposal would bring about, knowing he would be in exactly the same position he had been in five years before when he had had to choose between Sarah and his duty. But he was not the naive young man he had been then, and he knew from personal experience what a decision for duty would entail. He didn't know if he could face another series of long, empty years without love—without Sarah. It was asking too much. God damn it, he had paid his dues, he thought viciously as he swung the door of a taxi closed behind him and strode across a street to a subway entrance.

And what about the effect on Sarah of all this? How would she face being told that he was again choosing duty over her, especially since she now knew some of what that duty entailed? She couldn't be expected to understand a second time. It was unfair. God, it was worse than unfair, Charles thought grimly. It would be criminal to hurt Sarah so badly again.

But he knew with an inner rage that consumed him that his superiors would not see matters his way. Which meant he would simply have to develop a cast iron shelter around that part of him they would attack with dedicated fervor in an attempt to make him subject to their will instead of his own—the part of him that still, despite all he'd done to satisfy its demands, whispered that duty had to be served, regardless of who got hurt in the process.

CHAPTER NINE

That evening, as Sarah waited outside her offices for Charles to pick her up, she thought she glimpsed a familiar figure in a light tan suit just disappearing around the corner, and though she couldn't be certain it was Ian Connors, the possibility that it might be brought a frown to her face.

Though Ian Connors was enormously attractive—so much so in fact that if Charles hadn't come back into her life, Sarah might have considered going out with him—she hoped he wasn't the sort of man who, once he was in the grip of infatuation, found it impossible to take no for an answer. And after what Chelley had told her when she had returned from having coffee with Ian, it looked as though Ian had somehow developed such an infatuation for Sarah, though how he'd even become aware of her existence was a mystery to her.

When Chelley had reappeared after taking her break in Ian's company that morning, she had not seemed nearly as cheerful as she had when she'd left with him, and Sarah had inquired tactfully about what had happened.

"It seems I made a fateful mistake," Chelley had replied with a rueful shrug.

"Oh? What was that?" Sarah had asked sympathetically.

"I insisted you talk to him first," Chelley had explained with wry fatalism. "That was obviously the wrong thing to do because you're all he talked about the whole time we were having coffee." And then with a disgusted frown, Chelley had amended, "Or, rather, asked about. He wanted your life history from the time you were born."

"Of all the luck," Chelley had gone on to complain disgustedly, while Sarah hid a sympathetic smile for her secretary's obvious disappointment. "First you have that gorgeous Viking appear out of your past, and now the second most exciting man ever to walk into our offices wants into your future. It's just not fair!" Chelley finished on a gloomy note. "Especially since you aren't even interested!"

Sarah had maintained her silence about her interest in the Viking, but she felt no qualms about discussing Ian Connors. "What did Ian ask you specifically, Chelley?" she had inquired with idle curiosity.

Chelley had reacted by giving Sarah a look of exaggerated astonishment. "You mean you *are* interested?" she had cried. "Greta Garbo's heir is actually curious about a man at last instead of 'vanting to be alone'?" And then Chelley had dropped her pose and said with good-natured crossness, "And about a man I'd give my eyeteeth to go out with!"

"I didn't say I was interested in Ian Connors," Sarah had replied mildly. "I'd just like to know what he asked and what you answered. There's nothing strange about that."

Looking resigned, Chelley had capitulated then and tossed off, "Oh, the usual things, like whether or not you're married or engaged or interested in anyone in particular. What type of man you like, what sort of interests you have, that sort of thing."

"And you told him?" Sarah had prompted dryly, hoping Chelley hadn't lost her sense of discretion under the impetus of her disappointment that Ian Connors's interest lay elsewhere.

"Aside from the fact that you're single and totally involved in your work, I didn't tell him anything." Chelley shrugged. "He's a stranger, after all, and I figured if you wanted him to know anything about your personal life, you'd tell him yourself."

The telephone had started ringing then, effectively ending the conversation, but as Sarah stood outside her building waiting for Charles, she idly speculated about why Ian Connors should have taken such an interest in her, and half decided to discuss the matter with Charles when he arrived.

But when a taxi drew up in front of her a few moments later and Charles thrust open the back door to gesture at her to join him, everything but the pleasure of seeing his beloved face again flew right out of Sarah's mind, and the kiss he gave her once she

111

was beside him in the taxi finished the job of wiping all extraneous matters from her consciousness.

When Charles at last raised his head and allowed her to breathe again, Sarah looked at him with all of her love shining from her soft brown eyes. "Now, that's the way to end a hard day's work," she said shakily, stroking his cheek with a loving hand.

Charles chuckled, a little breathless himself Sarah was pleased to note, and disputed her. "No, honey," he drawled. "There's another, much better way to end the day than with a kiss. Are you interested in learning what it is?"

His silky, husky tone made a shiver of anticipation run up Sarah's spine, and the expression in her eyes softened further as she gave him her lopsided smile. Unable to resist the temptation to tease him, however, she played innocent.

"Well, I am awfully hungry," she replied with artful gravity. "In fact, I thought we could stop by the market on the way home and pick up a couple of steaks and something for a salad. That is, if you don't mind eating in tonight?" she inquired innocently.

Charles's reply was half groan, half laugh. "Eating in suits me fine," he growled with mock ferocity. "But I'll be damned if I planned on having to shop for the menu."

Blushing slightly at the double meaning, Sarah nevertheless cuddled close to him. "It won't take a minute," she assured him shakily. "There's a market on the corner of my street. Just tell the driver to let us off there."

Charles did so before proceeding to kiss Sarah senseless again, and they were both slightly dazed when the taxi drew to a stop at their destination. The shopping was accomplished with a speed that left Sarah breathless, but it was nothing to what she felt a few moments later when, after depositing the bag of groceries purposefully on the kitchen table, Charles turned to her and swept her up into his arms.

"That meal can wait," he informed her in a low, rasping voice. "This one can't."

"No," Sarah agreed on a submissive sigh. "It can't."

His kiss as he carried her to the bedroom had all the hunger and urgency Sarah could wish for, drawing from her all the tensions and cares of the day and replacing them with an eager

112

passion that made her groan a protest when Charles set her on her feet beside the bed and started to draw away.

At her protest he wrapped his arms tightly about her. "I'm not going far, sweetheart, don't worry," he whispered, his voice strained with urgency. "But I've missed you like hell today, and I'm in a hurry. I was just going to get out of these clothes as fast as possible."

Sarah could feel the proof of that urgency pressing against her lower body and in the heat of Charles's mouth as he rained hungry, searching kisses on her face and neck. "I've missed you too," she groaned as she slid her hands around to his tie to loosen it. "I don't know why we have to wear all these clothes anyway. They just get in the way."

Charles's answer, given with a smothered chuckle as he drew back to speed the undressing process, was filled with a pleasing possessiveness it thrilled Sarah to hear.

"Thank God they do! If someone who looks as good as you do in the nude were to parade around the city naked, I'd spend all my time fighting off other men, in between ravishing you myself!" Then, with his eyes caressing her, he added, "However, if you really are in as big a hurry as I am, we can shorten the process a little."

He caught her waist in his strong hands then, lifting her to toss her gently back onto the bed where she fell with a faint gasp of surprise. An instant later his hands were on the waistband of her skirt, which he disposed of, along with her slip and panty hose, with a speed she viewed as little short of astonishing. He then drew off his jacket and tie, slipped out of his trousers and briefs, and spread himself atop her and entered her in one swift motion that erased her gasp of surprise in an instant and replaced it with a groan of pleasure that was echoed by Charles when he found that Sarah was more than ready for him.

"Now," he began in unsteady tones of arousal as he watched Sarah's eyes darken and begin to glaze with passion. "You take off my shirt, and I'll take off your blouse. There's no rule that says we have to undress—or make love—in any set order, is there?"

"Uh-uh," Sarah gasped before biting the reply off on a moan as Charles shifted position slightly to raise himself to give her

113

access to the buttons of his shirt, thereby increasing the pressure of the fullness within her.

"Uh-uh?" Charles inquired, his voice dropping into a lower register that crooned his pleasure at her reaction. "Does that mean you agree or disagree with me?"

"I don't know. I can't think . . ." Sarah whispered, barely able to focus her attention on the buttons that swam before her passion-clouded eyes. She somehow managed to find them with her fingers, but her progress in removing his shirt was slowed by her fumbling eagerness to touch Charles's flesh with erotically sensitized palms and fingertips. And when she was only halfway done, she became distracted by Charles's attempts to undo the buttons of her blouse. He seemed inordinately clumsy at the task. His hand kept slipping to the other taut buttons that were straining against the silk, and once there, it lingered and stroked and drove Sarah insane with sensations that enhanced the ones erupting from her lower body.

"God, Charles, don't!" she finally got out with strangled pleading. "Please, stop! I remember now why we take off all our clothes first!"

"Why?" He laughed from low in his throat, but even as he asked the question he was disposing of the last button, and when he had her blouse pushed aside, he helped her with his shirt, so that at last Sarah could feel the burning heat of his skin beneath her hands, an experience so pleasurable, she forgot about his question. She forgot absolutely everything when he deftly unfastened the front clip of her bra and lowered his head to nuzzle and kiss and liquidly stroke with his tongue the sweet, swollen firmness of her breasts.

But a few moments later, when the two of them were locked together from head to toe in a rhythmic, pulsating union as old as time, Sarah murmured unthinkingly, "This is why," on a sigh of such aching gratification, that Charles increased the strength of his hold on her to the point where she lost the distinction between his body and hers, while at the same time she reveled in the weight and heat of him pressed into her own flesh.

And then the crest was reached, the sweetness was shared. Their bodies were completely as one for one brief shattering moment while their hearts and souls exulted in the unity, and

Sarah was lifted into a world of exploding richness that made the lonely years behind her slide into oblivion in favor of experiencing the blinding excitement of the present.

Slowly, regretfully, reality resumed its place in Sarah's mind, and her pleasure in the physical oneness she and Charles had shared was replaced by another sort of pleasure as she stroked his heaving shoulders into a semblance of calmness. She felt absolutely contented as she whispered nonsensical murmurings of love into his ears and felt him gradually relax the muscles in his large frame until he pinned her with comforting solidity to the mattress beneath her, his body a bulwark against everything outside of the two of them.

They lay thus for long, uncounted moments, each savoring the affirmation that love existed beyond the spiraling excitement of physical need, until Charles lifted his head at last, his blue gaze bathing Sarah in an almost tormentedly loving look.

"I want nothing more from life than you, Sophie," he murmured in ragged tones. "You make me whole."

"As you do me," she whispered back, framing his strong, rugged face between her two fragile hands and feeling a wondering awe that their love was more complete than ever.

Their gentle, seeking, warmly affirming kiss then was a blending of physical sensation with emotional commitment, and after it was over they clung together with a mutual reluctance to let the moment go, with Sarah feeling she would never, ever, experience such total satisfaction again.

She resorted to humor to combat the tears that threatened to well up from her heart and overflow her eyes. "Now I suppose you're going to tell me you'd feel even more whole if you had a steak in your stomach?" she queried with mocking sternness.

Charles's seriousness fell away into a gently devilish smile. "Now, Sophie," he chided as though he took offense at her tone. "Am I the sort of man who would spoil a tender moment like this by thinking about something so mundane as a steak broiled to a luscious shade of pink, a salad crisp and green and mouthwateringly bathed in the tartness of Italian dressing, a potato baked just the way—"

"Heavens, no!" Sarah interrupted him. "It's plain that food is the last thing on your mind at the moment." She gave him a push to roll him off her, which he allowed with a suspicious lack of protest.

"No doubt you'd be content to go without dinner and live on love?" Sarah queried archly as she sat up and scooted to the edge of the bed, preparing to get up and fix the food he had denied an interest in.

"Oh, well," Charles said hesitantly as he rubbed his stomach as though to quell its demands. "I sort of thought we could have both love and food, if that's all right with you?"

"Hmpf!" Sarah said, adopting a cross tone. "You haven't changed a bit. First you ravish me, then the kitchen. I always did wonder if I came first simply because after you'd had me at your mercy, you could talk me into cooking what you really want but are too lazy to get for yourself."

"That's not logical," Charles teased her, watching with warm interest Sarah's graceful movements as she donned her robe. "It takes a lot more energy to satisfy you than it does to cook a simple meal."

"Oh, is that so!" Sarah turned on him, hands on her hips and a threatening scowl on her face. "Are you going to ruin all hope of getting that simple meal by telling me it's also just as much fun to cook as it is to . . . ah . . . er . . ." Her face reddened as she bit off an unthinkable description of their lovemaking that was highly indelicate and, in view of the quality of emotion underlying it, not at all appropriate either.

Charles supplied the word with bland helpfulness, his face contorting with the effort to control his laughter, which burst out anyway when Sarah's face displayed guilty discomfort at his bluntness.

"What's the matter, Sophie?" he asked through his chuckles as she scowled reproachfully at him. "Is that too descriptive a term for what we just did?"

Sarah flushed again at his question, and his expression softened. "Or is it that that was an inaccurate term for what we just did?" he said, watching her with loving gentleness. "We make love, Sophie," he assured her, his tone masculinely tender. "We always have, and we always will. You know that's true."

Sarah's expression slid into one matching Charles's as she whispered, "Yes, darling, you're absolutely right."

After they had exchanged a long look of mutual agreement and understanding, however, she reverted back to her teasing. "But the question was, do you like making love to me as well as you like cooking? You didn't answer."

He laughed then before saying soberly, "Sophie, I don't even know that much about cooking, if you remember, and I certainly never thought of it as being fun. Loving you, on the other hand, is not what I'd call fun either," he drawled, grinning as he saw her look of outrage. Hastily, he clarified his meaning. "I'd call it earthshakingly exciting, emotionally shattering, physically debilitating . . ."

He got no further as she pounced on him to cover his face with kisses, murmuring her satisfaction with his descriptions as she did so with a gratifying purr in her tones that soon had Charles returning her kisses with a fervor that threatened to deprive the two of them of dinner once again. At last Sarah drew back to inspect his seductively sleepy gaze with pleasure for a moment before she pulled herself out of his arms and got to her feet again.

"You keep talking like that, Mr. Trainer, and I'll follow you anywhere," she quipped as she strutted to the door to go to the kitchen. Since she had her back to him, she failed to see the instantaneous transformation from arousal to thoughtful sadness that crossed his features. When she paused at the door and turned back to him, he had his face under control again, though his eyes were more blankly unrevealing than she was used to seeing.

"You may lie there and rest your poor abused body for exactly thirty minutes," she informed him sternly. "Then you are to report to the kitchen for that dinner that doesn't interest you, because I have tickets to a movie tonight, and we're going to have to hurry to get there on time, you hear?"

"Yes, ma'am," he replied solemnly, looking suddenly like a small, adorable boy instead of the formidable man he was in truth, and causing Sarah to blow him a kiss before she departed from the room.

When she had gone, Charles did lie where he was, though the tenseness of his body belied the fact that he was resting. Instead, he was thinking of the four separate conversations he had had that day with four very different men who were for once united

117

in their desire to have him forgo his own plans for his future and substitute one that each, in his own way and for his own reasons, was determined would take precedence over what he had planned for himself.

Njomo had started the process with his suggestion that his government might create a position where Charles's financial skills would be requested. Foster had reacted to that news by beaming like a Cheshire cat and immediately launching into a hard sell about the benefits of such an arrangement, ending with a plea designed to play upon Charles's conscience should Charles contemplate refusing to accept the position.

When Charles had refused to give any assurance that he would accept the position should it be offered, Foster had gotten their immediate superior into the act by calling him and having Charles relate what had happened during the interview with Njomo. And naturally, the chief had begun to work on Charles, appealing to everything from his patriotism to Mom's apple pie to convince him he should take the job.

Next, the chairman of the board of World Oil had put in his plea when Charles, of necessity, had called in to report on his meeting with Njomo. By that time Charles was nearly at the end of his patience, but he had somehow managed to remain polite while refusing to capitulate.

Now, however, as Charles lay on his back staring up at the ceiling of Sarah's bedroom, one strongly muscled arm behind his head while the other lay beside him, his fingers absently folding and refolding the crisp, clean sheet that rested over his powerful thighs, it was not Njomo or Foster or either of his employers he was thinking of. Instead, he was remembering his own father, a tall, strong, powerfully motivated man who had always reminded Charles of one of the saints depicted in the Bible the elder Charles Trainer had always carried with him wherever he went.

Charles Trainer, Sr., had loved his wife and his son devoutly, but never so much that he had placed their welfare over what he saw as his mission and his duty. He had repeatedly placed all three of them—his beloved wife, Rachel, his son, Charles, and himself—in danger by defying local conventions and the status quo in Zwahola in favor of espousing his faith in his own God over the local religions. In the process he had made many power-

118

ful enemies, and those enemies, one of whom was Lugubu's father and consequently Lugubu himself, had finally triumphed, at least insofar as they had robbed Charles Trainer, Sr., and his wife, Rachel, of their very lives—all in the name of patriotism.

And now Charles, who had taken up the cudgel against Lugubu once he had his education, and at no little emotional cost to himself, was once again faced with the prospect of leaving Sarah in order to continue the battle.

As he lay thinking, Charles knew it would cost him far more this time should he give in and return to Zwahola, and furthermore, now that he was older and wiser, he was not even sure his contribution would make any real difference to the fate of that tiny African country that was his second homeland, or to his mother country, for that matter. The shaping of a nation's destiny often seemed to be as haphazard an undertaking as a volcanic eruption, due more to luck and chance than to the dedicated efforts of men who would enforce their own philosophies and desires upon a particular populace and geographical area. Charles was not so egotistical as to be certain he could make a substantial difference to the eventual fate of Zwahola.

On the other hand, he could not seem to get free of his father's early teaching. His father had not been ultimately concerned with any nation's destiny. He had been concerned with how well a man lived his life in accordance with certain ideals and principles. And he had instilled his own ideals and principles in Charles to such an extent that while Charles might question other things, he never questioned the fact that a man had to live with his own conscience. He knew Lugubu would lead his country into chaos and servitude to a tyrannical master while depriving the West of a crucial oil supply. Hwala, on the other hand, while in some ways a tyrant in his own right, would at least maintain a semblance of democracy in Zwahola.

But the single most crucial factor in whether he would be forced to return to Zwahola, Charles knew, would be how hard Njomo pressed the issue. Njomo was the man Charles had the most reason to fear right now. While though, in some ways, Charles felt more in tune with that old man than he had with any other, except his father, he also knew Njomo's strengths and weaknesses and his occasional capacity for sheer ruthlessness.

And Charles knew that if Njomo chose now to call in an old, outstanding debt Charles owed his old friend, Charles would have little option but to pay that debt in full.

As Charles vaguely listened to Sarah's lighthearted singing in the kitchen as she went about her work, perspiration broke out on his brow as he contemplated what he faced. He had spent five long, lonely years denying his own needs and desires, and he had forced that same loneliness onto Sarah. Could he go through that again? And could he live with himself if he had to make Sarah go through it again?

He found himself thinking futilely about taking Sarah with him this time, thereby satisfying both his conscience and his heart. But he had lived too long in the hotbed of intrigue and danger that infested Zwahola to allow himself to contemplate that alternative for long. He remembered his anguish at the death of his parents, and he knew that anguish would be tripled should such a fate befall Sarah. Should she come to harm, he was actually frightened at what violence he might do.

No, he thought with grim frustration as he rubbed strong fingers over his forehead in an expression of his inner conflict. If he went back to Zwahola, he couldn't take Sarah. Neither could he ask her to wait for him. And it was a certainty that when and if he ever came back again to find her, she would not be waiting placidly for him to come back into her life and upset it again.

"Charles?" Sarah's tentative query interrupted Charles's tormented thinking and brought his clear blue eyes open to see her standing in the doorway to the bedroom watching him with an anxious gravity that tore at his heart. "Are . . . are you all right, Charles?" Sarah asked hesitantly. "You look so—"

She couldn't say that he had looked so ferocious that she was actually frightened of this powerful stranger in her bed who resembled the man she loved, but who contained a terrifying difference that shook her into wondering if this was really the Charles Trainer she had grown to value as she valued her own life.

"Sure, babe," he said in deep reassuring tones as he sat up and made the effort to smile at her. "I'm . . . fine. Just fine."

But his tone left her unconvinced, and even when he shifted

his large frame to the side of the bed and got to his feet to come to her where she stood by the door and take her into his strong arms, the slight shudder she gave as she felt his touch was as much from her sudden fear of him and for him as it was from the instinctive pleasure she felt as her hands came in contact with his heated flesh.

CHAPTER TEN

That night at the movie Sarah endeavored to forget the mood she'd glimpsed in Charles earlier that evening by maintaining her own determined high spirits. She knew the actors who starred in the film they saw, and she kept whispering outrageous things about their personal lives into Charles's receptive ear until his smothered laughter had the people around them frowning and shushing him ill-temperedly, while Sarah stared blandly at the screen pretending she wasn't the one who'd instigated the disruption.

Charles was the object of censure by the time he grabbed Sarah's hand and pulled her out of the theater, and when they emerged outside, he threatened her with such dire retaliation that she cowered back and begged him—in a loud voice, of course—not to beat her again, whereupon a nearby policeman began to eye Charles with glowering suspicion. At that, Sarah meekly subsided to the point where Charles could bundle her into a taxi and begin to dispense some of the retaliation he'd promised her.

But though their lovemaking that night began with laughter, and though Sarah couldn't fault the ardency of that lovemaking once the laughter ceased, she was aware that something was wrong. She longed to ask what was bothering Charles, but after they were snuggled down together for sleep, and she had ventured one tentative query which he answered with a vaguely offputting reply, she realized whatever was on his mind must fall under the constraints of secrecy that bound him, and she lapsed into a silence that grew more and more uneasy as the weekend approached.

Finally, on the Friday morning following the Monday that

Charles had reappeared in her life, as they were dressing to go their separate ways, she decided she had to do something to break the tension she had felt growing in him daily, and with that objective in mind, she suggested they spend the weekend at a small inn in Connecticut she had heard about but never visited.

"I could use the break," she ventured, hoping that by making it appear that she was the one who needed a relaxing weekend, he would be more likely to agree to it.

Charles frowned in thought for a moment, but at seeing the pleading in Sarah's soft brown eyes, the frown disappeared and a look of determination replaced it.

"All right, honey," he agreed, smiling as he saw her eyes begin to dance with anticipation. "If you'll make the arrangements, I'll see about getting free for a while."

Sarah abruptly turned away in an attempt to hide the resentment she couldn't help feeling at the demands his "job" made upon him, and Charles, recognizing her reaction for what it was, firmed his mouth and approached her where she stood ostensibly searching for something in a drawer. He slid his arms around her waist and drew her back against his body, bending to place a kiss on the side of her neck.

"We'll have our weekend, Sophie," he promised in a low tone of grim determination. "You can count on it, even if I have to—" But instead of finishing the statement, he turned her into his arms, tilted her head up to search her wide, smiling eyes for a moment, then leaned down to cover her mouth with his own in a brief, almost desperately hungry kiss that sparked a renewal of Sarah's uneasiness. His lovemaking had been tinged with that hint of desperation for the last two days, as though he were trying to store up a lifetime of loving her and couldn't get enough to fill the empty spaces inside of him.

When he raised his head, however, he was smiling. "You make those reservations, darling," he instructed her with a promise in his tone that he would not disappoint her. "You'd better rent us a car too."

Sarah returned his smile, struggling to keep all the uncertainty she was feeling out of her expression. "Yes, sir," she said with teasing solemnity. "I'll get right on it, sir."

Charles laughed then and gave her an enveloping hug. "Did

I sound bossy?" he inquired with musing laziness, his hands roving her body with pleasure. Sarah loved the way he always seemed so aware of her. He touched her at every opportunity, and not in an absent way, but with alert enjoyment.

"If you did, I can't seem to mind," she replied with dreamy contentment. "In case you haven't noticed, I'm putty in your hands. I can't imagine resisting anything about you."

"Hmmm." Charles's laugh was low and seductive. "They say absolute power corrupts, You're tempting me to find out if that's true."

Sarah laughed with him before sobering somewhat. "I wish it worked the other way around," she said ruefully. "But I can't imagine anyone having absolute power over you."

Charles's gaze grew abstracted momentarily before his thoughtfulness gave way to a warm smile. "You come awfully close, Sophie," he whispered, bending to kiss her again, while Sarah had to accept what he was able to give, realizing she wouldn't change him if she could.

The rest of the day was a mad rush for Sarah, while Charles spent it in a battle to claim two short days as his own after having given over the last five years of his life without a substantial break of any kind. When Foster protested that things were too hot for Charles to disappear even for a brief weekend, Charles reminded him of his past sacrifices with a snarl in his voice that succeeded in making Foster not only back down himself, but to go so far as to intercede with the chief on Charles's behalf.

Choosing a time when Charles was out of the office to make the call, Foster used the argument that if they wanted Charles to renew his contract, they'd better give him some slack now. And at the chief's inevitable question as to why Charles wanted the time off, Foster, against his better judgment, remained silent about Sarah and instead merely remarked that Charles needed some "feminine diversion" for a change. To his relief, the chief accepted the argument, with the condition that Foster keep a tail on Charles all weekend—without Charles's knowledge, of course —and when Foster informed Charles later that he had his weekend, his hunch that Charles had intended to take it with or without permission was confirmed when Charles merely looked at him without expressing either gratitude or complaint.

124

A few hours later, as Charles and Sarah were driving to Connecticut oblivious to the fact that a relay team of escorts accompanied them, Sarah set herself to the enjoyable task of distracting Charles from his worries. That her jokes and chatter and even a couple of ribald songs were proving successful was evidenced as the lines of tension in Charles's face began to smooth out and his laughter began to ring through the automobile repeatedly.

It was dark by the time they arrived at the small, secluded inn on the shores of a lake, but Sarah could see enough to be delighted with her choice. She had specified privacy when making the reservation, and as she and Charles were directed through a charming, old-fashioned, comfortably furnished lobby to a newer wing at the back of the inn, which faced the lake, she felt as though they were being escorted to their own private domain, since their room was off to itself in a jutting extension of the building.

She was even more pleased when, upon entering a large room furnished with a king-size bed covered in an old-fashioned quilt that had, of necessity, to have been made in modern times, she saw they had sliding glass doors leading to a private balcony with steps leading down to a path to the lake.

"This is delightful, Sophie," Charles echoed her pleasure in their accommodations. "I'm glad you suggested we come here."

She swung around with an ear-to-ear smile, crossed the short distance that separated them, slid her arms around his waist, and rested her head on his broad chest. "Me too." She sighed contentedly. "But I'm already sorry it's only for two days. I could spend a year here with you."

"Greedy," Charles said on a laugh as he hugged her to him, but he sounded indulgently pleased by her greed.

"Of course," Sarah admitted complacently. "What woman wouldn't be at the prospect of having you all to herself?"

"And what man wouldn't want to be alone with you like this," he returned the compliment. "Aren't we lucky we have each other when there's all that competition?" he teased.

"Extremely lucky," Sarah agreed. Then she drew back and tilted her head up to eye him mischievously. "But I'm greedy in other ways besides my appetite for you. In fact, I'm starving to

125

death for some plain old food. Shall we go down to the dining room or order room service?"

Charles looked over her shoulder at a charming fireplace on one wall of the room, then returned his gaze to Sarah, his smile rakishly suggestive. "Room service," he said succinctly, pleasing her immeasurably with his reluctance to share her.

After they had selected a fresh seafood dinner from the menu in the room and called their order down, Sarah grabbed up the small bag she'd brought with her and headed toward the bathroom which, despite the old-fashioned decor of the inn, was satisfyingly modern, even to the extent of having a huge sunken tub.

"I'm going to bathe and change," she said, high spirits in her lilting voice.

"Into something more comfortable, I hope," Charles suggested, slanting a mocking blue leer in her direction.

"Yes," Sarah teased solemnly. "I brought along a pair of overalls and an old flannel shirt. I thought they would make a nice change from dresses and sexy nightgowns."

At Charles's growl of disapproval, she laughed and scooted into the bathroom, throwing off her clothing with careless abandon after turning on the taps in the large tub. She congratulated herself on having thought of everything as she sprinkled perfumed oil into the water and watched the bubbles start to foam up while steam rose enticingly to her nostrils.

Humming, she tied the long length of her silky hair atop her head, placed a huge burnt-orange bath towel where she could reach it, then stepped into the tub and let herself down into the deliciously hot water, sighing with utter contentment as the soothing liquid closed around her body.

The door to the bathroom was only partially closed and Sarah called drowsily to Charles as she let her eyelids close and leaned her head back. "This is wonderful, darling. You should take one, too, after I'm through. You'll love it."

For a couple of minutes she got no reply from him, and she was just about to open her eyes and call to him again when his voice came from directly above her, startling her into opening her eyes.

"Now, why would I want to wait until you're finished?" he

126

asked mockingly as he stepped into the tub himself, giving Sarah the opportunity to view him in all his magnificent nudity before he let himself down into the water beside her.

Delighted at his action, Sarah turned on her side to accommodate him, and cuddled close to his body, reveling in the slick feel of his hard muscles beneath the scented water. "Because you're going to smell like me if you bathe in this water?" she teased mischievously, chuckling from deep in her throat at the idea of Charles smelling feminine.

Charles cupped her bottom and gave her a playful pinch, but he seemed unperturbed at the prospect of absorbing the sweet smell of the bath water into his skin. "I think I would anyway," he murmured on a growing note of arousal when his pinch propelled Sarah more closely against him, "since I plan to stick pretty close to you tonight."

"How close?" Sarah asked throatily, exulting in the feel of their bodies pressed closely together beneath the warm, slippery water.

In answer to her question, Charles slid a leg between her thighs while he raised a hand to trace lazy circles around one slowly tautening nipple. "Is this close enough?" he asked with interest before pressing a soft kiss on her damp temple.

Sarah forced eyelids that had suddenly grown heavy slightly apart and considered the gleam of gentle mockery in Charles's blue eyes. "Not for me," she informed him, smiling when the words came out slurred and invitingly low-toned. "But if you're satisfied . . ." She shrugged a soapy shoulder in a languid gesture of feigned disinterest.

Charles slanted a look down at her that struggled for mild disappointment, but which was growing more aroused by the moment. "Hmmm," he mused. "Well, then, how about this?" And he increased the pressure of his thigh against the wet triangle between Sarah's legs while his thumb slid back and forth across her nipple.

Both attempts to satisfy her desire for more closeness made Sarah arch against him, and as her hip came in contact with Charles's swollen maleness, she instinctively began a rubbing motion of her own. "Better," she managed to get out shakily, "but . . ." The "but" contained reservations.

"My, you're hard to please, aren't you?" Charles scolded her gently as he slid the hand that had been tormenting her breast down the silky length of her before bringing it back up to cup her bottom and tug her closer into him. At the same time, he used his other hand to lift her shoulder blade slightly, exposing the breast that had been underwater to his fascinated gaze. For an instant he watched the spectacle of runnels of water sliding over the firm, taut fullness before he slowly lowered his head until his lips could close over the warm wetness of the flowering nipple, and then he began to tug gently with his mouth in between teasing swipes of his hot, moist tongue.

"I'm . . . not . . . hard . . . to please," Sarah said in a drugged voice, ending on a gasp as Charles bit gently down with his teeth on what he held in his mouth. "You're beginning to get . . . the idea," she faltered on a groan of pleasure as he returned to his earlier ministrations.

"I was always a fast learner," Charles informed her with satisfaction without removing his mouth from her breast. "How about you?" he then inquired suggestively.

"Oh, yes," Sarah responded with dazed comprehension, only then realizing she had been so caught up in receiving her own pleasure, she hadn't been reciprocating.

There were no more words then, at least not intelligible ones, as Sarah alternately skimmed and kneaded the slick wet muscles of Charles's body and reacted to his touch with writhing invitations for more and more. Their mutual explorations didn't last long before Charles pulled her astride him, adjusting her hips to take the thrust he launched the instant he had her in position for it. Then it was all an enchanting, mindlessly exciting blur of sliding, rhythmic absorption in their lovemaking until they simultaneously burst the boundaries of time and place and entered the realm of an exploding universe of ecstasy.

Afterward, Charles cuddled Sarah against him while each awaited the relaxation of their breathing and their trembling limbs and savored the complete contentment that always followed such journeys together.

Finally, Charles eased himself up, chuckling when Sarah, apart from shifting slightly to accommodate his movement, remained with her arms draped over his shoulders and her head propped on his chest with her eyes closed, the picture of exhausted contentment.

"Come on, lazybones," he murmured indulgently against the corner of her smiling mouth. "They'll be bringing our food and someone has to get up to take it."

"Not hungry anymore," Sarah informed him with lazy brevity.

"You will be," Charles promised, clearly meaning not for food. Then he gently slid her away from him, smiling at her pout at being disturbed. "I'll get out and be ready to take the food," he offered with mocking resignation. "You finish your bath."

He stood up, and Sarah tilted her head to gaze at every inch of him with a bemused, lopsided smile while he grinned down at her before climbing from the tub. She continued to watch as he dried off, his movements unhurried, but powerfully masculine. "You're so beautiful," she murmured unthinkingly.

Charles cocked one skeptical, yet gently appreciative eyebrow at her as he threw the towel down, then faced her with hands on his hips while she gazed her fill. "Maybe I should take offense at the way you put that," he said with teasing tenderness, "but I can't seem to work up a good anger about it."

"That's because you know it's true," Sarah rejoined complacently before lifting her arms in a stretch of contentment.

"I could return the compliment," Charles said, watching her movement with appreciation, "and I do, and I will . . . repeatedly."

Sarah gave him a sweet smile then, causing his eyes to darken with appreciation of the qualities about her he loved that had nothing to do with her physical attributes. "Thank you, darling," she said simply, loving him with her eyes as he stood loving her with his.

Finally he took a deep breath and pivoted to start toward the bathroom door. "I'd better put something on," he said roughly. "Whoever brings the food might not find me as beautiful as you do if I open the door to them like this."

Sarah smiled a pleased, secret smile that echoed her thought that she found it impossible to believe anyone wouldn't find Charles as beautiful as she did, before she devoted her energies to washing the body Charles had just worshipped with his own.

When she came out of the bathroom a few moments later, clad in a flowing ivory-colored nightgown and matching robe that made her damp skin glow with enticing color and set off the darkness of her hair and eyes to perfection, she found Charles standing in front of the fireplace with a glass of wine in his hand. A small table had been set up nearby, and on it was one glowing, perfect yellow rose in a crystal vase.

But Sarah had eyes only for Charles. He was wearing something that resembled an Arab robe. It was white, loosely folded around his tall, broad body, and it looked comfortable while it set off his tanned blondness in a way that set her pulses racing again.

"What are you wearing?" she asked, her voice warmly curious as her eyes scanned him from head to foot. "Whatever it is, you look great in it."

Charles's own gaze was more than appreciative as he took in Sarah's appearance, and his tone was distracted as he answered vaguely, "Just something I picked up in my . . . travels." He seemed to come to himself at the end of his explanation, and Sarah noted the slight hesitation before the last word.

She kept her expression from revealing the sudden knot she felt in her stomach, and her smile was normal, she hoped, as she crossed the room to him. "Oh, this looks good!" she exclaimed as she came to the table. "I think I am hungry after all."

"I thought you might change your mind," Charles teased as he came to the table to seat her, then sat down across from her. "You have a healthy appetite in every respect, don't you?"

"Yes," she teased back, "but believe it or not, I am capable of going on long fasts from all my appetites, though I certainly prefer not to. I much prefer to indulge them."

She was lifting the cover from one of the dishes as she spoke, and she missed the sudden sadness in Charles's gaze as he watched her with a look that wished, both for her and for himself, that Sarah would never have to fast again.

He was back to normal by the time she raised her eyes again, and they proceeded to eat the meal with enjoyment, chatting as they did so without urgency or purpose, while their eyes, as they met across the table occasionally, provided all the important communication needed.

When Charles at last leaned back, sated with food and lazily content, his eyes fell onto the empty fireplace. "Hell, I forgot to light the fire!" he remarked with astonishment.

"Never mind, darling." Sarah smiled, unconcerned. "It's too hot for one anyway, and it's likely to get hotter before the night is over," she suggested hopefully.

Charles turned his eyes back to her, and the expression in them confirmed her hope. "You have a point," he replied, a lazy, anticipatory smile curving his lips. "In fact, that bath and this wine have made me a little warm already. What do you say we go out on the balcony for a few minutes before we go to bed?"

"Go to bed?" Sarah asked with blank innocence. "But it's only nine o'clock, Charles. Are you tired?" she asked with solicitous sympathy.

"No, but I'm expecting to be," Charles drawled as he got to his feet and held out his hand for Sarah to take. "And so are you, so you might as well drop the innocent act. It isn't convincing."

Sarah pouted at him halfheartedly, but she took his hand too eagerly to give the pout any veracity, and with arms encircling each other, they walked to the sliding glass doors, which Charles opened, allowing them to step out onto the wooden deck outside their room.

A full moon shone gloriously over the waters of the lake, and the air was balmy and intoxicating as they lifted their heads to breathe it in while they leaned on the wooden rail encircling the balcony.

"Heavenly," Sarah murmured, leaning her head on Charles's shoulder. "I could spend my life here and be perfectly happy, as long as you were with me."

Charles dropped a kiss on the top of her head and hugged her to him. "I wouldn't care where we were," he said, deep emotion in his voice. "Having you beside me is all that matters."

Sarah turned into his arms then, lifting her own to encircle his neck while she stared into the blue glitter that encompassed her possessively and with such gentle power. "You're right, darling," she whispered, the love she felt imparting an ache to her voice. "Being together is all that really matters."

And as their lips met in an affirming kiss, neither could see or hear the man who stood several yards away in the shadow of a tall tree, giving a sigh of resigned frustration at having to watch while Charles Trainer had the privilege of holding such a delectable bundle of willing femininity in his arms. Another sigh escaped Foster as Charles broke the kiss and propelled Sarah back into their room with an urgency that bespoke his need for more than a kiss.

But as envious of Charles as Foster felt at that moment, his sense of fairness nudged him into a grudging acceptance that Charles Trainer deserved what he would be receiving this night, as well as a lot of other nights, if only the world were as fair a place as it should be. But it wasn't, and as Foster turned to speak to the man who would be taking his place for the long hours of the night to come, he muttered almost inaudibly, "You should have it pretty easy. I don't think they'll be poking their heads out again until morning. I know I sure as hell wouldn't."

And as he trudged off to find a lonely bed of his own, Charles and Sarah were entwined in a loving embrace that for all its excitement was as much a demonstration of a mutual emotional need as it was of a physical one. Neither of them was interested in sleep that night, and what little they got was interspersed with alternate explosions and tender explorations that were taken and given with a fervor only love could provide.

CHAPTER ELEVEN

The next morning, however, as Sarah sat across from Charles at the breakfast table in the delightful dining room of the inn, she knew that however conscious some of her motives were in setting up this weekend, at least part of her had wanted a chance for the two of them to talk as well as make love. The problem, she thought musingly as she nibbled a piece of golden toast, was how to go about holding a conversation with a man who, of necessity, must keep large areas of his life secret.

She let her eyes rove over Charles as he sat eating his eggs Benedict. He looked as vital and alert as though he hadn't just spent hours making love to her with enough energy expended as a stevedore after a long day's work. He had on a dark blue knit shirt that set off his blond good looks strikingly, and a pair of light blue slacks that molded his masculine hips in a way that made her want to forgo talk altogether for another loving session in their room. His thick, sunbleached hair was clean and crisp after his shower, and his face looked strong and tan and healthy.

Sarah's eyes traced the masculine firmness of his lips, which were incredibly sensitive and knowing in giving pleasure, rose to the straight strength of his nose, then stopped when her gaze became locked in a pleasurable duel with the clear blue of Charles's. She shrugged helplessly in the face of his teasing grin. "What can I say?" she said simply. "I like to look at you."

"Look all you want, honey," he invited her, his mouth quirking into a masculine smile that tugged at Sarah's senses. "I like to look at you too."

They smiled at each other in perfect understanding, until Sarah finally had to look away before her newly burgeoning sensuality ran away with her.

133

"Shall we go for a walk by the lake?" Charles inquired lazily when Sarah had finished her last bite of toast. "It's a beautiful day for it."

"Yes," Sarah agreed, her eyes lighting at the thought of sharing such a simple pleasure with him. "I'd love to."

A few moments later, as they strolled in a leisurely walk hand in hand beside the gently lapping waves of the small lake, blithely unaware that the couple who strolled a few yards behind them were anything other than another happy twosome, Sarah bent her head, her thoughts occupied with how to approach Charles about her need to talk. Charles slanted a perceptive look down at the top of her shiny hair and inquired quietly, "What's on your mind, honey? You've got that look I remember so well that says you're thinking hard about how to tell me something you think I don't want to hear."

But when Sarah raised her head to gaze up at him with an uncertain look in her eyes, he paused, bent down to brush a reassuring kiss across her softly parted lips, then straightened. "I'm sorry, babe," he murmured. "I didn't intend to make you afraid to talk to me. You can tell me anything. You know that." He cupped a hand around the back of her neck and tilted her face so that she would look at him and know that he meant what he said.

"It's not so much that I want to tell you anything, Charles," Sarah started out hesitantly. "It's just that I think we need to talk—about a lot of things. The past, the future—" She stopped, looking up at him with clear-eyed urgency. "The present is beautiful, but . . ."

"But," Charles echoed on a resigned sigh. He guided her to a grassy knoll overlooking the lake and shaded by a tall tree. He sat down with his back against the tree and pulled Sarah down beside him.

"You're right, Sophie," he agreed with musing thoughtfulness. "There are a thousand questions I want to ask about how you've spent the last five years, and a thousand things I want to share with you about how I spent mine. But since I can't tell you much about my experiences, suppose you let me be selfish and you tell me about how you spent those years when I wanted to be with you and couldn't be."

134

It was a start, Sarah reflected, and so she did as he'd asked and began to talk about the years without him, choosing to dwell on the happier memories rather than distress him by recounting the emptiness that had been her constant companion for so much of the time.

After listening for a long time with a fascination that was gratifying, Charles himself chose to introduce the more painful memories.

"Were you angry with me all those years, Sophie?" he asked with quiet regret. "Or did you get over the hurt and forgive me?"

Sarah hesitated before answering with part of the truth. "The first two years were pretty bad," she understated badly. "But after that I buried you away somewhere so that I could stop merely existing and get on with living." She lifted one shoulder in a rueful gesture. "I thought I'd gotten over you entirely until the day you walked into my offices." She raised her eyes to his and looked at him helplessly. "But it's evident I hadn't, isn't it?" She sighed and shook her head. "Sometimes I think I'm a fool. And I suppose a lot of people would consider me a fool for forgetting what I went through so quickly and falling back into your arms the way I have. But I don't feel foolish, Charles," she finished softly, telling him with her tone and with her eyes that she loved him so much, pride came second to what they shared.

Charles cupped her cheek in a large palm, the lines of his face suddenly prominent under the strength of some strong emotion that made her ache to wipe away the strain she saw in his features.

"What we have together is too special to throw away for the sake of old hurts, Charles," Sarah told him in an effort to make that look go away. "You were worth the wait."

"Was I?" he said, sounding faintly bitter, though the bitterness was wiped away an instant later by a smile so sweetly reminiscent of how he had been in the past that Sarah had to close her eyes against a wave of emotion that gripped her heart in a vise of steel.

"Don't close your eyes, Sophie," Charles whispered on an intake of breath. "I can never get enough of seeing your beautiful, loving eyes."

Sarah did as he asked, opening her eyes fully, and for a long moment they exchanged nonverbal vows.

"Maybe we'd better talk about the future," she suggested shakily then, after swallowing down the lump in her throat. "The past is done. Neither of us can change it now, but we can make the future better."

She had dropped her gaze and therefore didn't see the despairing, bitter look in Charles's eyes before he got himself under control.

"I don't know about you," Sarah went on in a low, quiet voice, "but I'd like to have a child right away. I work with children sometimes, and I love doing it. I'd like one of my own as soon as possible."

Sarah had kept her head down while telling Charles this, fearing he might not feel the same. But when he said nothing and the silence had stretched to an uncomfortable length, she raised her head to look at him anxiously. He leaned his head back against the trunk of the tree with his eyes closed, and his mouth was a tight line that made fear strike at her heart.

"Of course, if you'd rather wait awhile . . ." Sarah ventured hesitantly, the fear in her heart leaking into her tones uncontrollably.

Charles's eyes flew open, and the look he gave her was one of blazing, if tortured, love, before it cleared to a warm sincerity. "Sophie, there's nothing I'd rather do than plant my seed inside your lovely body and watch you grow with our child. There's nothing I want more than you as my wife and the mother of our children, to live with you and laugh with you, to love you again and again and share everything with you—"

He broke off, his mouth firming into that grim line again as he pulled her into his arms and held her with a fierce strength that almost hurt. But Sarah was beyond reacting to that kind of hurt when she was besieged with another kind that had the power to destroy her completely. Suddenly she was filled with a sense of frustration and anger at whatever was causing Charles's paradoxical behavior, and she drew back and took his face into her hands, scorching him with her look of determined ferocity.

"Charles, what's wrong?" she demanded fiercely. "I know you

love me! I know you want a life with me! What is it that's coming between us? Is it your job again?"

Her voice contained all the bitterness she felt about the occupation that had robbed her of him once and which she was convinced was at the heart of his ambiguous behavior now.

"Are you in trouble?" she demanded at seeing her frustration echoed in his steady blue gaze. "Tell me, Charles! We can't live with secrets always between us. Don't you trust me?"

Her frustration grew as she heard Charles sigh, though his eyes said he did trust her and that everything else she'd thought was true. "Sarah . . ." he began, but the moment he said her given name and she heard the tone in which he said it, she knew her outburst had been useless.

"Sarah . . ." he repeated at seeing her close her eyes and firm her lips into a visible expression of her frustration. "Darling, don't you think I'd tell you anything you want to know if I could?" he asked with quiet firmness. "Don't you know I want to share everything with you now the way I always did in the past?"

"But you didn't!" Sarah burst out, unable to help herself. "You never told me anything but the bare facts of your childhood. You shut me out then, just as you're doing now!" She bit her lip in an effort to gain control of her temper and the tears that were threatening, and when she continued, it was in a calmer tone. "I'm sorry, darling," she said, her apology slightly weary. "But I get so tired of knowing you completely on one level and not knowing you at all on another."

Charles murmured, "I know, baby, I know," as he pulled her into his arms and began to stroke her hair and her back with soothing, gentling hands. When she had quieted, he took a deep breath and said, "Well, we can talk about part of my past, if we can't talk about all of it."

And then he began in a steady, almost emotionless tone that told Sarah vividly that he was feeling anything but unemotional. He talked about his boyhood in a small African nation where he had grown up, the son of a strong missionary father and a loving, devoted mother. He told her small details she had longed to hear, interspersed with a broader picture of what his life had been like. And it was only as he began to speak of the growing political

137

turmoil during those years that his voice began to take on a shaky quality that made Sarah hold him tighter and long to help him over this part of his recitation.

"Even when he was threatened directly, my father refused to leave, Sarah," Charles explained as he drew near the torturous part of his disclosures. "He wouldn't stop speaking out against what he considered the barbarous, godless acts of some of the rebels. He wouldn't hide. And he refused even to send my mother to safety."

Sarah's voice was soft as she broke in to inquire about what mattered to her. "And you, Charles?" she ventured quietly. "Wouldn't he send you to safety either?"

Charles shrugged, dismissing the question as self-evident. "No," he said with no regret in his tone that such had been the case. "I was his son. He wanted me to see how a man should behave when everything he believed in was threatened. And I wanted to stay," Charles added soberly. "I wanted to help."

And as he said that, Sarah's vision of his character began to clear. She had always known he was a man of principle, and she had always loved his integrity. Now she was finally beginning to understand the people and events that had shaped him into the man she loved, though she wasn't sure she entirely approved of his father, who had forced Charles to mature in such a drastic fashion.

She became aware once again of Charles's inner strength as she watched and listened to him tell her about the death of his parents. She saw the anger and the hurt that still lingered in his heart after all this time, and though she couldn't blame him for his feelings, she could hurt for him, and she did as he forced himself to say the words he had kept bottled up inside himself for such a long time.

"One guerrilla group had its roots in the village where we lived," Charles said with stoic calm, "and the leader of it was my father's biggest enemy. He vowed that if my father didn't leave the country and stop trying to rally the people against his rebels, he would kill my father. And one Sunday he did," Charles stated flatly, his voice unemotional while his hands were clenched into tight fists so that the knuckles showed white, while the planes of his face had grown starkly outlined and pallid beneath his tan.

"My father was preaching his Sunday sermon when the rebels came," Charles went on. "When the leader strode down the aisle of the church while the people cowered away, my father challenged him, defying him to commit an act of violence in the house of God." Charles swallowed down the bile in his throat as he relived his memories. "The man laughed at him and said, 'Your God is not mine, white man,' and then he shot my father with an automatic pistol provided by his secret backers."

Charles's face had turned to stone while Sarah's had whitened, her eyes huge and liquid with the vicarious pain she was feeling for Charles. But he wasn't done yet, and Sarah gave a moan as he finished his tale.

"Then the man shot my mother in front of my eyes," Charles continued, breathing hard now, his blue eyes staring in front of him as though he were seeing that ghastly scene out of the past. "I went for him," Charles said in low, guttural tones of remembered rage. "But I was a boy, and he was a man, and he threw me to the side with one hand. He leveled the pistol at me then, and would have shot me, but a man the people held in too much respect to be ignored stopped him before he could pull the trigger."

Charles's voice died away, and Sarah, the tears streaming from her eyes, waited quietly, to give him time to come back to her from the memories that still held the power to infuse him with emotions she had never seen in him before and prayed she would never see again.

Finally Charles closed his eyes for a moment, then blinked them open again as he turned to look at her seemingly surprised to see her there waiting. He appeared even more surprised to see that she was crying, and he lifted a hand to stroke her tears away. His look was puzzled before understanding brought him back to the present.

"Sophie," he murmured, gathering her to him and increasing the strength of his hold when he felt her shoulders shake with a sob she couldn't suppress. "It was a long time ago, Sophie," he said in a quiet, bleak voice that hurt her to hear. "It's over," he added, but in a tone that told her it wasn't—that he was simply trying to calm and comfort her when it was he who needed the real comforting.

139

"Is it?" she choked. "Is the man who killed your parents still alive?" she asked, hoping he wasn't, hoping that if he were dead now, his death had somehow eased Charles's burden.

"No, he's dead, Sophie," Charles assured her. "But his son—" He broke off suddenly, as though he realized he was about to say too much.

Sarah drew back and studied the closed, hard look on his face. "You've been working in that country, haven't you, Charles?" she asked, her realization coloring her tones with mingled relief and dread.

He shifted a brief look at her that told her she was right, but that he would say nothing about his more recent past. And considering what he had just put himself through at her request, Sarah didn't probe him for any more information, though what he had revealed already answered a great many questions that had plagued her not only through the years when he had been absent from her life, but during the past week after he had reentered it. And it raised other questions she knew she couldn't ask just yet. Not now, not when all her instincts were screaming at her that Charles didn't need any further inquisitions, but rather the healing wholeness of love.

"Let's go back, darling," she said gently as she moved to her knees and encouraged him with love in her voice and eyes. "I want to love you. I want to make you forget all this for a while. Let me make you whole again, darling."

Charles looked at her without seeing her for a moment before her tone and her look got through to him. Slowly he relaxed the tension in his muscles and his mouth curved first into a semblance of a smile, and then into a real one after Sarah had kissed the tautness from his mouth.

"Yes," he agreed on a deep breath of relief. "Let's go back. You make me forget everything but you and how good it feels to be back with you."

They took their time as they strolled back to the room which would provide a refuge from the world for each of them for a little while and envelop them in a world all their own, safe from everything but the pleasure of loving and the contentment that came from being loved.

And throughout the rest of the weekend Sarah concentrated

140

on restoring the wholeness she had inadvertently disturbed, while she knew deep within herself that if only Charles could be healed of the remaining bitterness he still felt at those who had murdered his parents, he would be able to free himself from old loyalties, old hatreds, and an unrelenting compulsion to submit to the call of his perceived duty.

CHAPTER TWELVE

"Your time's running out, Trainer," Foster prodded as Charles prepared to depart for another interview with Njomo at the old man's request that Wednesday. "You know as well as I do what Njomo wants. You saw the interview we taped of him on that Sunday talk show. He all but spelled out Hwala wants help in dealing with Zwahola's economic problems, and you know what sort of help they have in mind. Njomo's going to ask you for a decision today, and I hope you come up with the right answer or you may find yourself without many friends in the near future."

Charles paused in the act of opening the door to leave and glanced back at Foster over his shoulder, his expression unmoved by the mild threat. "You think so?" he rejoined politely, but it was a politeness that frustrated Foster since he realized he'd taken the wrong tack. Any man who had Sarah Bailey in his life wasn't going to worry too much about losing friends.

"All right." Foster quickly changed tactics. "So you've got a woman who would walk through fire for you. But have you given any thought to how you're going to make a living once you've burned your bridges at World Oil? Do you really think you'll have a future there if you let them down on this?"

Foster's normally swarthy complexion paled when Charles laughed at that threat. "Foster," Charles said when his chuckles had died down. "I haven't spent a penny on myself other than for the bare necessities in five years. If I want to set up a business of my own, I've got the means to do it. The only reason I haven't given it much consideration before is that I happen to like working in the oil business, and I haven't got quite enough money stashed away to set myself up on the scale of World Oil."

This last was said with mocking understatement, but at seeing Foster's dejection at his answer, and because he had a fondness for the man, Charles relented enough to add, "Foster, I don't know myself what answer I'll give Njomo if he offers me that job. It will depend on—" But he didn't finish that thought. Instead, he gave another mocking smile. "But if I decide to turn Njomo down, you won't need to worry about my future. I'm positive it will be one to envy, not to pity."

With that, Charles let himself out of the room, realizing that his words had not succeeded in extinguishing the anxiety Foster was displaying. Once out of sight, however, Charles's own expression became disturbed as he contemplated the interview he faced.

He had spoken the truth when he had said he didn't know how he would answer Njomo if Njomo offered him the job in question. He knew what he wanted to answer. He wanted to be finished, once and for all, with his past and get started on a future with Sarah. The preceding weekend had brought them closer than ever, and the astonishing rapport they'd established in the year they'd lived together had been reestablished on an even deeper level in Connecticut and had grown in the few days he'd been back, as Sarah had made a determined effort to reintroduce him to American life and to the joys of having someone with whom to share that life.

And though he was plagued by the fear that Njomo would at last press for payment of the debt Charles owed him, and by guilt that he was creating in Sarah an ever-growing dependence on the love they shared, Charles had found himself grabbing greedily with both hands for everything that might be denied him if he could find no alternative to paying that debt. It was all happening again, just as it had in the past when he had known that someday he and Sarah would have to pay for today's happiness with tomorrow's grief. And he was no more capable of stopping the process now, no more able to resist Sarah's warmth and love and almost mystical ability to reach him on every level that counted than he had been six years ago.

It remained to be seen, of course, just how strongly Njomo would press for payment of that debt. He never had before. But Charles had the desperate feeling that this time Njomo thought

143

the game was worth any price that had to be paid, whether by himself or by Charles or by anyone else who could aid Zwahola.

After Charles had once again passed through the wall of bodyguards that surrounded Njomo and was at last seated cross-legged in front of the old man, he braced himself for whatever was coming, feeling as he had only once before in his life that he was at a crossroad, and that a wrong turn would strip him of every chance for real happiness he'd ever envisioned.

And after Njomo had greeted him warmly and offered him refreshment, which Charles refused politely, Charles felt his heart begin to freeze within him when Njomo started out the conversation by saying, "I have been reminiscing, my son, remembering earlier days in my life, and in yours." He spoke quietly, bringing his ancient dark eyes to bear on Charles in an unblinking stare that was as unyielding as a block of obsidian.

Over the next hour Charles sat while Njomo bludgeoned him emotionally, reminding him in subtle, skillful, cunning yet affectionate tones of the debt that existed between them. Njomo recalled his own respect and affection for Charles's father, and reminded Charles in the process of how much store the elder Trainer had placed in doing one's duty. He rambled on about the happy days of a bygone time when Charles had been a boy in Njomo's native village. He recounted with sadness the growing political unrest in those days and touched gently on the death of Charles's parents, leaving unsaid his own part in sparing Charles's life, while the memory nevertheless palpated between the two of them like a heavy weapon with blunt edges.

And finally, when Charles was showing signs of becoming increasingly torn by Njomo's reminiscences, Njomo administered the final thrust with such gentleness that Charles barely felt the blade until it had already severed his heart in two.

"Do you remember my first wife, Mary?" Njomo asked quietly. "She used to feed you when you would come by our hut after a hard day's play."

"Yes," Charles barely murmured, only now remembering that he had never heard what had become of Mary. She had been a frail woman when he had known her as a boy, and if he had thought anything, he had assumed she'd died of her ailments. "Is she still alive?" he asked abstractedly, his mind filled with the

144

obligations Njomo had been applying to his weary shoulders over the past hour.

"No," Njomo replied sadly. "Lugubu's father had her killed . . . secretly, with poison, so that nothing could ever be proven. But I knew, just as he meant that I should know."

Charles lifted his head at that, staring at Njomo and sensing that something was coming to add to his already unbearable burden. "Why?" he asked in a hoarse voice, unable to help himself.

"It was after your parents were killed and you had left for your own country," Njomo answered gently. "I knew revenge would be extracted for my part in saving you, but I was called away to meet with Hwala's men, and while I was gone . . ." He spread his hands in a weary gesture of fatalistic resignation, their trembling seeming to emphasize the sacrifices he had had to make in the name of ethics and patriotism.

For a long moment the two men stared at each other, Charles in a state of shocked anguish and Njomo steadily patient. Then Njomo, with the utmost kindness in his voice, said, "I hear you have a woman now, too, Charles."

Instantly, the anguish in Charles's blue eyes departed, though the shock grew more apparent, to be followed by a stone-hard wariness and a coldness that Njomo viewed with interest.

Almost apologetically, Njomo explained. "As with any government, Charles, when we contemplate employing a man, we make it our business to find out everything about him." He shrugged his shrunken shoulders in a slightly pitiful gesture. "I had no idea when I followed Hwala's instructions and set the surveillance in motion that any secrets about you would be revealed. You have always been . . . honorable."

The slight hesitation before the last word told Charles clearly that Njomo was aware Charles had two masters. But whether Njomo had shared that knowledge with anyone else was debatable. The old man was a master gamesman, and it was entirely conceivable that given the inevitability of someone from the American government keeping an eye on Zwaholan affairs, he preferred that it be a man like Charles, who was basically sympathetic, and, yes, honorable.

As long as it was only Njomo who knew, Charles felt he could rest reasonably easy about the rent in his cover. And he very much doubted that anyone who had been investigating him on Njomo's behalf had been able to link him in any way with an agency of the United States government. Charles had been far too careful—except in the matter of having Foster pick him up at the airport and take him to Sarah's offices. That had obviously been a mistake. But Charles knew Foster would have shaken off any tail before they had ended up at Ace Exports. It was only Charles's involvement with Sarah that had been exposed, though he would, at that moment, have preferred it had been the other way around.

Njomo's voice interrupted Charles's thoughts. "Hwala has decided to employ a Western financier in the position I outlined to you at our last meeting, Charles." The old man finally got to the point of the interview. "And he and I will accept only you." Njomo hesitated momentarily before saying with exquisite delicacy, "I realize accepting the position will mean you will have to make some sacrifices, my son. I am waiting to hear if you are man enough to make them."

The old man settled back against his pillows while Charles sat silent for a long time, his back held straight though it felt as though he had the weight of the universe across his broad shoulders, and contemplated the trap Njomo had set with such consummate, unflinching, and, Charles was sure, even sadly regretful skill. There was no doubt in Charles's mind that Njomo was fond of him, and that in other circumstances the old man wished Charles a happy and fulfilling life. But Charles also knew that under the present circumstances Njomo would stop at nothing to steer Zwahola in a course that would result in its ultimate rescue from the quagmire of a growing national debt, a frustrated populace, and, perhaps, the threat of Lugubu and his ilk coming to power.

Finally, Charles accepted the inevitability of his choice, but it was a while before he could put that acceptance into words. When at last he opened his mouth to do so, he felt older than the ancient man waiting patiently for his answer.

"I bow to your will, Grandfather," Charles uttered in a tone devoid of all animation.

For the barest instant Njomo's black eyes contained a gleam

of satisfaction, but it was followed by a regretful sadness, backed by an inflexible will.

"No, my son," the old man said with soft certainty. "You do not bow to my will, but to your own. It is true that I proposed the burden. But it is also true that you took it up of your own free will. You are a strong man, Charles Trainer, a man of conscience. You know, of course, that I counted on that."

"Yes," Charles grated as he felt the trap close around him. His thoughts were with Sarah and how brutal he was being in letting her down—again.

"Is she a good woman?" Njomo asked with soft sympathy, as though he fathomed completely what was on Charles's mind.

Charles looked at Njomo, his expression hard and cold and withdrawn. He was in no mood to discuss the woman he would be giving up, this time for good.

"She is better than a good woman!" he clipped out, however, his tone ragged despite his efforts to control it.

"Ah, then there is that between you," Njomo replied thoughtfully, his dark eyes becoming contemplative for a moment as though he were remembering someone from his own past who had been more than a "good woman." "I am sorry, Charles," he then said with eloquent simplicity. "I don't suppose—" he started to suggest tentatively, but Charles cut him off.

"No!" Charles rapped out, his inner pain coloring his voice and graying his blue eyes with bleakness. "I won't risk her," he added after a moment, and more quietly.

"It is perhaps better so," Njomo agreed with the fatalism of his age.

"Excuse me, Grandfather, but I'd like to go now," Charles said, his distress evidenced by his rudeness in requesting to leave rather than waiting for Njomo's dismissal.

"Yes, go, my son." Njomo ignored the lapse and waved a shaking hand at Charles. "You must accompany me to the United Nations tomorrow, however," he added sharply. "There are matters that need your immediate attention."

With a curt nod of his head Charles accepted the directive before getting to his feet and going numbly through the ritual of departure. And it was only after he was back out on the street that Charles gave vent to his feelings with a string of short, explicit, hopeless curses that failed to alleviate the sense of loss he was already feeling.

His mood was so explosive that Foster, and even the chief and the chairman of the board, wisely muted their exuberant feelings of relief and satisfaction that Charles was safely back in the fold. And Foster, with an unexpected wash of sympathy that obviously embarrassed and irritated him, encouraged Charles to take the rest of the day off. Foster knew Charles needed time to prepare to break the news to Sarah, though he was unaware of the depth of bitterness in Charles's heart as he faced the prospect of telling Sarah she had made the mistake of giving her heart twice now to a man who could only throw it back to her broken.

When Sarah returned home from work that evening, feeling puzzled because Charles hadn't picked her up as usual, she found him sprawled in one of her wicker armchairs looking haggard and disheveled, and in a mood so strangely turbulent, she had the immediate reaction of wanting to walk on tiptoe around him and speak to him in whispers. Instead, she approached him with confidence that she could somehow retrieve him from the black despair she read in his features and felt emanating from his powerful body.

"Need a backrub?" she asked with gentle, sympathetic teasing as she came to a stop beside him and ran a caressing hand over his tousled hair. "You look as though you had a hard day."

For a moment Charles simply stared at her, his expression so filled with pain, Sarah felt a lump of anxiety begin to form in her stomach.

"God, Sophie, I need you!" he finally answered in a low tone of such force, Sarah felt it reverberate in her chest. An instant later he was on his feet and had his arms around her, straining her to him with a strength that made her cringe physically while she stared wide-eyed over his shoulder and realized he did need her, just as he'd said, but on some powerful level she wasn't sure she could handle.

At last Charles muttered hoarsely, "Come to bed, Sophie," and drew her with him toward the bedroom, his grip on her wrist so painfully tight, she knew she would have bruises in the morning. But she didn't care about a few bruises. She cared only about

148

Charles and what it was that was driving him as he stripped the clothes from his own and her body with an urgency that left buttonholes stretched and their clothing torn.

His lovemaking was driven as well, alternating between an almost brutal ferocity and a tender, worshipful gentleness that made Sarah want to cry. She did cry at the last, when Charles drove himself into her as though he wanted to bury himself within her body for all time.

He was hurting her, and yet at the same time he reduced her to a shaken state of awe that she could inspire such powerful emotions in him, she knew she would never forget this night of love . . . never *want* to lose the memory of what he was giving and taking with every concentrated cell of his body and mind. And though he allowed her little room for response, what she did manage to give was received with such shatteringly eloquent evidence of the effect she had on him, Sarah actually feared to give as much as she wanted to.

She was stunned when, after the loving, she thought she detected tears in Charles's blue eyes before he closed them and turned his head away. Not knowing what to do or what to say, she lay silent beneath him for a long time, bestowing the stroking, soothing touches Charles seemed to require above all else.

He stirred at last, raising himself to look down at her. He frowned when he saw the faint discolorations on her skin that would turn to bruises by morning. "I'm sorry, Sophie," he whispered with bleak regret. "I never meant to be so rough."

"It doesn't matter," Sarah reassured him softly. "You needed me. I'm glad I was here."

Charles's face contorted with bitter cynicism at that, surprising Sarah, the reaction was so unexpected. His words startled her even more, and then frightened her. "And you deserve a man who will be there for you when you need him," he said, his voice expressing harsh self-disgust.

Sarah lay where she was as he thrust himself off her and got up from the bed. As he threw on a robe and paced to the bathroom, a feeling of dread began to consume her until she felt like a numbed mass of quivering nerve endings anesthetized by shock. She had felt this way once before, she remembered with a growing sense of panic, the morning Charles had told her he

149

was leaving her. And if what she feared proved to be true, she prayed the numbness would never wear off and expose her to the agony that had almost destroyed her then.

An instant later, however, she was chastizing herself for her morbid thoughts. Charles wouldn't do that to her again, she assured herself, struggling for calmness. She got up from the bed and donned a pair of dark brown slacks and a tailored yellow blouse while she tried to force her thoughts to what she would fix for dinner. But as she passed the closed bathroom door, she gave it no more than a flickering look, superstitious that if she let herself dwell on the fears she was trying to fight down, they might overwhelm her, and they might become real.

With deceptively calm movements, Sarah searched the refrigerator and the cabinets for something to put together for a meal, finally deciding on a simple salad made with cold chicken left over from the night before. She was preparing vegetables for the salad when she sensed Charles behind her, though he had said nothing, and she swung around to find him in the doorway to the kitchen, watching her with such sadness that it made her heart begin to pound.

"What are we having?" he asked, and it was obvious he was struggling to sound normal, even cheerful, though he failed miserably. Sarah elected to follow his lead, however, not willing to precipitate what she instinctively knew was coming.

"Salad and leftover chicken," she replied in a determinedly light tone. "I haven't gotten to the store yet, so we're having to make do."

Charles shrugged and shook his head slightly, as though it didn't matter, and it was clear to Sarah that food was the last thing on his mind. But she had known that already, and the knowledge increased the desperation with which she maintained her false calm.

While she worked she forced herself to chat about her own day, merely to fill the silence Charles maintained. He apparently heard little or nothing of what she said, but that didn't matter either. Sarah wasn't talking to be heard.

When they sat down to eat, meager though the meal was, neither did more than pick at it, though Charles kept refilling his glass with wine, which made Sarah eye him anxiously each time

150

he did so, until she realized that she herself was drinking far more than was normal for her in reaction to the stress building within her with inexorable force.

At last she pushed her glass away and sat with her eyes fastened on Charles's taut, grim features until he looked up at her and went still. "What's wrong?" he asked, trying for gentle concern but succeeding only in sounding abrupt.

"You tell me," Sarah answered quietly, a slight tremor in her voice.

Charles went very still then, and Sarah thought he looked as though he were gathering himself together to face something that would take all his strength. She had seen him look like that once before, she remembered, her eyes widening, her face whitening.

Charles closed his eyes briefly, then opened them, displaying an expression as bleak as a barren ice cap. "Let's go into the living room, Sophie," he suggested, this time succeeding in sounding gentle. "We have to talk."

He got up from his chair, his movements slow and deliberate and somehow unutterably weary. He paused beside Sarah—she was still frozen in her chair—and extended his hand to help her up. When she didn't immediately take it, he put both of his hands on her shoulders and drew her up in front of him, wrapping his arms around her to enfold her against his body for a moment before he gently steered her toward the living room.

Charles seated himself on an exotically patterned, dark green love seat and drew Sarah down onto his lap. He held her for a long time in a gentle, cuddling embrace with his cheek against her hair, his eyes closed, and his hands gently roving her body as though he sought to imprint the memory of her skin and form on them.

"You have a scent all your own, Sophie," he murmured once, rubbing his mouth and nose against her hair. "It fills me up every time I'm near you, and when we're apart, I remember it and want you near."

"So do you," she whispered, hugging him close to her as though she could absorb him into her body. But as close as they were, she felt a sense of being torn from him, which only made her hold him all the tighter.

151

"I love everything about you," he went on, his throbbing tones exposing the deep emotion that rode him. "I wanted you the first moment we bumped into each other in that hallway at the university, and I've never stopped. I don't think I ever will."

"I feel the same," Sarah replied with haunting simplicity. "I suppose we were meant for each other. We never had to play the games most couples do, did we?"

"No," Charles said on a deep note. "We never did."

After a long silence Charles shifted slightly so that he could look into Sarah's face, and his expression was pleading. "Sophie," he begged, "you know I wouldn't hurt you for the world, don't you? You know I love you. You know I want you to be my wife, to bear my children, to be with me all the days of my life?"

"I know, Charles," Sarah said in dull, flat tones, knowing what was coming on some deep, inevitable level she was familiar with now and which would tear her to pieces if she let it. She was grateful that suddenly she felt as though she were wrapped in layers of absorbent cotton. The numbness made everything seem remote, as though it were happening at a distance. It still hurt, but it was a muffled, anesthetized pain that probed and tried to find an opening where it could grow and dispense its agony without hindrance. Sarah didn't know what was keeping it away, but she was unutterably thankful that something was—temporarily.

"I shouldn't have come back into your life," Charles continued, guilt and self-disgust coloring his voice while his arms gripped Sarah tighter. "But I couldn't help myself. And God help me, I would probably do the same again after what you've given me these past few days. Except for the year we lived together, this has been the happiest time of my life."

Sarah sagged a little in his arms then, and Charles, feeling it, bent his head to her neck and burrowed there, straining her to him as though she were trying to pull away, which she wasn't. She couldn't have. She wasn't strong enough.

"Sophie . . . Sophie . . ." Charles murmured over and over, his voice aching with despair and love and hopelessness, and propelling Sarah into making the effort to offer him the comfort he seemed to need so badly. She encircled his shoulders with her arms and held on to him as he rocked her and murmured her name with anticipation of his loss in his tones.

At last he fell silent and sat back, drawing her head to his chest with one hand cupping her cheek. The important communication had been done, but Sarah felt the questions being drawn from her without volition.

"When do you have to go?" she asked dully.

Charles hesitated, then said, very softly, "Tonight," and the finality devastated her.

After another few moments of silence, during which she regathered her strength, she ventured, "Will there be times when you can call me? Or write me? Or see me?" The dull hopelessness with which she spoke spelled out that she knew the answers to her questions already.

"No, darling," Charles answered with gentle, utterly brutal truthfulness. "I'll be out of the country for a long time. Too long to ask you to wait."

The numbness slipped a little then, and Sarah's voice contained a slight bitterness when she spoke again. "Like before."

She felt Charles's muscles tense beneath her body, but when he answered, his voice was quietly serious and utterly sincere. "No, Sophie. It's not like before. When I left you five years ago, I did so as a young man filled with idealism. It was a reluctantly voluntary move, but it *was* voluntary. This time, nothing could tear me away from you except the strongest coercion possible." His tone was now grim. "Believe me, it took a lot to make me agree to go again."

His admission helped Sarah in a way, and yet it didn't. The brutal fact remained that Charles was leaving her again, regardless of his reasons, and she felt her bitterness rising, beginning to choke her. It made it difficult to speak.

"Why don't you want me to wait?" she said in a strangled, harshly forced voice.

Charles's tones were equally harsh when he answered. "Because you're twenty-nine years old, Sophie. Because you've already wasted five years you could have spent with a man you could count on, having his children, sharing his life . . ."

Charles could barely get the words out, his pain was so intense at spelling out what it was he wanted to give her and couldn't.

His jealousy and envy of whoever would give Sarah those things was eating him alive.

"Because I don't know when, if ever, I'll be back," he continued grimly. "Because it isn't fair to keep doing this to you. Because if you or I let ourselves believe we can ever get together again, and then it doesn't happen—"

He stopped, taking a long, shuddering breath before he was able to continue. "Sophie, if I let myself think about you, I can't function. And in the sort of work I'll be doing, if I don't function well, I may cease to function at all. Do you understand me?" he asked harshly.

Sarah went rigid in his arms for an instant before she thrust backward and held Charles's gaze fiercely. "Are you being cruel again, Charles?" she asked with shaken disbelief. "So that I'll get over you faster?"

The lines in Charles's face deepened before he slowly shook his head. "No, darling," he replied quietly. "I'm trying to be honest with you this time. If it sounds like cruelty, I'm sorry, but the facts of life are often cruel." He paused briefly, and when he went on, it was with bleak self-mockery. "And if I wanted to carry this honesty to the extreme, I'd tell you that I don't want you to get over me." His blue gaze roamed her sad face. "But that would be my selfishness speaking, Sophie. I tend to be selfish where you're concerned.

"But I also love you very much," he added on a deep breath of resignation. "And because I love you, I can't and won't deny you the chance for a normal, happy life without me, though God help me, the baser part of my nature would like to!" He looked at her with such blazing possessiveness as he spoke that Sarah felt herself begin to dissolve into splintered pieces of emotion, with Charles owning every single piece of her that was sparking off her inner core.

"Then ask me to wait, Charles," she found herself begging him in a low-voiced whisper. "I will. You know I will. Even if it takes—"

"No!" The word exploded from him as though if he didn't pronounce it forcefully, he couldn't say it at all. At seeing Sarah flinch, he softened his tone. "Don't you think I want to?" he asked harshly. "Don't you know what it does to me to think of you with another man? Do you realize how hard it is for me, even though I love you so much, to put aside what I want so that you'll have a chance for a decent life?"

Sarah stared at him, the animation that was normally so much a part of her slowly draining away until her eyes were blank and dull. "I don't think I'll ever understand, Charles," she said lifelessly. "I suppose I'm more selfish than you claim to be, but I can't imagine anything being important enough for me to put it first over what you and I have together."

She started to disentangle herself from his arms, suddenly feeling rejected, as though, despite Charles's assurances to the contrary, he didn't really love her. At least not in the way she understood love.

But Charles tightened his grip, refusing to let her up. He took her chin in his large hand and forced her to look at him, and when she did, he looked frighteningly strong and rigidly purposeful.

"I don't believe that, Sophie," he grated. "You know the meaning of duty as well as I do. And if you owed your very life to someone, as I do, you wouldn't put me first. You'd do just as I'm doing and pay your debt! You know you would!"

But Sarah didn't know any such thing. Not at this particular moment. All she knew was that the man she loved was leaving her—again—because his sense of duty was stronger than his love for her.

"I'm sorry, Charles, but you're wrong." She shook her head. "I'm not as principled as you are. I'm not as strong as you are. If it came to a choice between you and duty, I'd take you every time."

She was too tired to resist when, after closing his eyes against what he saw in hers, Charles wrapped her in his arms and held her to him fiercely, rocking her slightly as he might have a hurt child. She lay against him without returning the embrace, but without resistance either.

After a while, Charles slipped his arm beneath her legs, and with the other behind her back, he got to his feet, holding her close to his chest like a sleepy child he was carrying to bed. He started toward the bedroom, and when he got there, he laid her gently down on the bed and stood over her, his hands braced on either side of her body. His strong face was a study in tortured love as he gazed down at her, and his voice echoed that love in deep, shaken tones.

"I'm going to love you one last time, my darling Sophie," he whispered, a catch in his voice making her heart lurch in her breast. "Please, love me back. Don't shut me out now. I need everything you have to give me. I need to give you everything I have. I have the feeling this is the last time I'll ever make love with everything that's in me."

After a long moment that hung between them like a pulsing knife-edge of destiny, Sarah gave a sob from deep in her throat, then raised her arms to gather him close to her. He came willingly, with restrained, gentle tenderness in his touch and in the kiss Sarah met with open-mouthed helplessness. Her lips were trembling, and she groaned with mingled despair and loving awe when she realized Charles's were as well, and that his hands, as they skimmed her body worshipfully, were shaking from the emotions that held him captive.

It was that evidence that Charles's strength had limits that calmed Sarah somewhat and made her determined to give him what he had requested and more. Vaguely, through a mist of passion that increased as Charles gently undressed her, she at last realized how very hard it was for him to leave her again. And though she could not have done what he was doing, and put duty before love, she finally understood a portion of the strength of will he embodied. She resolved to stretch her own will to its limits to make his departure as memorable as he needed it to be.

It was not a time for light, loving teasing, but it was a time for innovation. Sarah searched her drugged mind for ways to show Charles how much she cared. He seemed content to run his hands over every inch of her, followed by his mouth, as if he wanted to commit each inch of her body to memory. His earlier urgent forcefulness was gone in favor of a quiet, thorough exploration and a murmured, husky approbation of what he touched.

When he had finished his worshipful inventory and was giving every indication he meant to start another one, Sarah gave one brief, spasmodic shudder before pushing him with gentle force onto his back.

156

"It's my turn," she whispered hoarsely when he made a slight movement of protest.

He relaxed then, letting his muscles slowly settle into passive tension as Sarah got to her knees and bent over him. She cupped his face in her hands while she covered it with soft kisses. She closed his eyes, which had been wide open, with those kisses. They opened again when she was done, and stayed open as she moved slowly down him, her mouth feathering his skin, her tongue tasting and savoring his flesh.

Sarah felt Charles's heartbeat increase as she moved from his chest to his stomach, felt his muscles clench as she moved to his navel and dipped her tongue delicately into its hollow, then heard him groan from deep within himself as she moved lower.

"Sophie?" he half questioned, half begged, as her hand closed around him and then he gasped and trembled as she began to kiss and stroke that part of him which she considered was as much hers as his on this last loving, poignant journey into intimacy they would ever take together.

She had not intended to push him over the edge with her offering, but she was afraid she might have when, after one strong, suckling caress with her tongue, she released him and moved lower and began to kiss his thigh. After a moment, his fingers threaded lightly through her hair, he guided her back to what she had been doing before.

She slanted her head to give him a questioning look, asking him if this was what he really wanted, and he smiled tautly. "Oh, Sophie," he breathed.

With a tiny understanding smile, Sarah bent to him again, and as she did so, her hair slid across her face, concealing it from Charles. He gathered the silken tresses and drew them to the back of her neck and, with her hair as a cushion, cupped her nape and rubbed it through her hair with gentle encouragement.

Sarah became immersed in her loving, her mind drifting in and out of reality in accompaniment to the rhythm of her breathing as she lay relaxed against Charles, one hand stretched to his chest to feel his heartbeat while the other caressed his abdomen.

From time to time she opened her heavy-lidded eyes to inspect Charles's face, and it was always to find him watching her with intent concentration, his strong features held taut in mingled ecstasy and torment.

At last, after a deeply probing, liquid stroke with her tongue, Sarah felt Charles's stomach convulse slightly before he tugged her hair gently, lifting her away from him.

"Enough." He uttered a strangled command as he drew her up beside him. When he had her in his arms he gazed down at her as he passed his hand from her neck, down over her breasts, across her stomach, and finally to the throbbing center of her passion, which he cupped possessively.

"You're *mine!*" he said in a strangled voice while the blue of his eyes darkened to a midnight shade and Sarah arched into his hand with a low groan of submission. Her eyes were opaque with passion. "You'll never be like this for anyone else," Charles said in a tone that was part command, part wish.

"Never . . ." Sarah moaned with conviction, and Charles's possessive, tortured smile said that he believed her.

He continued his tantalizing exploration, holding Sarah close as she twisted against his delicious, intimate invasion as her body took on a life separate from her mind. It was ravenously greedy for satisfaction, intent on having it at all cost.

Charles reduced the sweet torment slightly, whispering, "Not yet, my darling. Wait for me." He gentled her, keeping her at a pitch of excitement that approached being unbearable without pushing her into that final all-encompassing excitement he wanted to put off until the last possible moment.

But the time came when Sarah couldn't wait any longer, despite his skill, and she begged for release in a whimpering plea. "Charles, my darling, please! I'm not as strong as you are. I need you now!"

"Yes, Sophie," Charles whispered rawly as he moved over her. "I need you too."

But still he moved with patient slowness as he settled himself between her thighs, then paused to take a deep, drugging kiss before he began very gently, very slowly, to push himself into the secret, mysterious treasure he claimed as his alone.

Sarah tried to accommodate his need to stretch out their loving. She tried her best. But she couldn't contain her impatience, and in a beautifully graceful surge, her body leapt to his,

158

taking him deeply inside her, making both of them gasp with the impact.

Her action broke Charles's resolve, and from there on he took over, his patience falling away in a burst of rhythmic energy that became a driving, overpowering, elemental force. They exploded together in a shattering moment of oneness that left them both shaken, and Sarah, at least, sobbing. And it took a very long time before either of them could break what was going to be their last contact.

Afterward, in the grip of the little death that follows such an experience, Sarah could take no comfort from the murmured, achingly sweet declarations of love Charles whispered to her, nor from the stroking, calming influence of his hands on her. She could only lie limp in his hold, her body racked occasionally by the remnants of the sobs that had followed his loving.

When the sobs finally ceased, Charles tilted her face up and kissed away her tears, ending in one last searching, tender kiss on her mouth, which Sarah accepted, trying to make the effort to return what he was offering. He drew back at last, his eyes dark with sadness.

"I have to go now, Sophie," he said with a finality that filled the aching void inside her with numbness. She was beyond speech and could only nod her acceptance.

She watched him all the time he dressed. And it was only when he had finished packing and straightened to look at her where she lay sprawled limply in the bed that she was able to make the effort to sit up, then stand and draw a robe over herself while Charles took his last look at her body with a grim intentness that spelled out his concentrated effort to memorize in detail what he was seeing.

Silently they walked to the front door of the apartment, where they paused, each of them searching the other's face for something that would ease the pain of parting. There was nothing that could do that, however, and finally Charles raised a hand to cup the back of Sarah's head and drew her to him. He bent to her, and with his mouth a breath away from hers, he whispered, "Be happy, my darling. But don't ever forget me. I couldn't stand to think you would ever forget me."

He kissed her as though she were the most fragile, delicate

object in the universe, and when he drew back, she started crying again at the look of anguish in his eyes.

He hesitated, then turned away and opened the door, but as he was about to step through, Sarah stopped him.

"Charles!" she demanded in a harsh, hurtful rasp. When he turned back, she faced him stonily, her mouth trembling under the force of her emotions. Her moist, gold-flecked eyes were steady beneath the shimmer of her tears.

"Will there ever come a time when your debts are paid in full?" she asked shakily. "Or will you spend all of your life trying to ease your conscience?"

Charles regarded her just as steadily, the taut lines of his face stretched to grimness. But his blue eyes were softened against the pain he saw in hers.

"I don't know about my other debts, Sophie," he answered quietly. "Maybe someday they'll be paid, even if it's after it's too late to do us any good. But the debt I owe you will never be paid," he continued, his voice dropping to a whisper. "You'll be in my heart and in my mind until the day I die."

After holding her gaze for a long, soul-shattering moment, he turned away and strode down the hall to the elevator which, to Sarah's mingled relief and resentment, came immediately. Its doors closed against Charles's broad back with a finality that made Sarah want to scream her anguish at her loss. She didn't want to be in his mind! She wanted to be a part of his life, every day, in every way, until the end of time.

But her throat was closed to contain her sobs, and she was barely capable of closing the door of her apartment behind her before she collapsed against the wooden panel and slid down to the floor where she buried her head against her updrawn knees and began to weep the first of many long, wracking bouts of tears that were to punctuate her days for weeks to come.

CHAPTER THIRTEEN

Most of the next day was a sojourn in hell for Sarah. She called Chelley to say she was ill and wouldn't be in the office that day, and then spent her time alternately crying or huddled in agony, unable to eat, unable to sleep, and unable to think of anything but her loss.

The fact that this time she knew at least part of the reason why Charles had left proved to be of only marginal comfort. The aching void was still there. The brutal loneliness still consumed her, and the sheer emptiness of her future, after the plans she'd been making since Charles had reappeared in her life, almost overwhelmed her.

Around dinnertime the reverberating silence in the apartment made her switch on the television, not to watch, but to hear other human voices, though she paid no attention to what was being said.

She sat huddled on the love seat where Charles had held her on his lap the night before, staring unseeing at the small square of light across the room, which, at the moment, was filled with the face of a well-known news commentator. Vaguely she took in the fact that the news commentator was disappearing from the screen, to be replaced with an on-the-spot interview at the United Nations of a tiny, wizened old man who looked too ancient to be able to stand unaided, but whose black eyes still sparkled with life and intelligence. He was saying something about a new economic policy his nation intended to implement, but Sarah's attention wasn't focused enough to understand much of what he said.

It was not until the camera panned the crowd milling behind

the elderly man that Sarah sat up abruptly as she found herself looking straight into the vivid blue eyes of the man she loved.

Perhaps if Charles had not been almost the sole Caucasian in a sea of black faces, she might have missed his presence in the crowd. Or perhaps she wouldn't have. But the fact was, that for one brief second, he stood out from those surrounding him like the Viking Chelley described him, and then he was gone, and Sarah flew across the room to the television set to turn up the volume so that she could hear what the tiny old man was now being asked.

The reporter was just saying, "Mr. Njomo, it is well known that there is a faction in your country that will oppose any policy of your government that may result in closer ties to the West. You, as an established neutral in the controversy, seem now to be endorsing such ties. Is that a correct statement?"

The reporter thrust the microphone at the elderly man, who faced the camera with the calm demeanor of a veteran speaker.

"You are correct in referring to me as a neutral," he replied, his quavering voice nevertheless projecting dignity and power for all its tremors. "A better term, however, might be a patriot. I am seeking the path which will result in a better life for the Zwaholan people and stability for the country as a whole." His black eyes twinkled with humor as he finished his statement. "And you will recall that, at the moment, I am simply the spokesman for the present Zwaholan government."

Before the reporter could ask another question, the little man made an unobtrusive gesture with a shaking hand, and immediately a huge black man inserted himself between the reporter and Njomo, effectively ending the interview.

Sarah's hope that the camera would again scan the crowd was dashed as the scene abruptly switched back to the commentator in the newsroom, who said, "And so Zwahola, despite its oil wealth, is faced with the problem afflicting so many emerging nations these days—that of balancing its imports and exports and maintaining a stable currency. Let us hope they can solve their internal problems, both political and economical, and become a stable bulwark against the chaos that has too often swept third-world nations in the past few decades."

He then went on to another subject while Sarah, crouched in

front of the set, ceased to hear or see what that subject was. Her mind was focused on the bits and pieces Charles had told her about his background and his work and integrating those pieces with what she'd just seen and heard.

Of course she had known where Charles had spent his early years. She knew he spoke the Zwaholan language and was thoroughly familiar with its varying cultures. And after what he'd revealed to her during their weekend in Connecticut, she had realized that was where he'd spent the last five years and where he would be returning now. What she didn't know was what his role would be this time. But given his presence in the midst of a Zwaholan delegation, coupled with his financial background, she suspected that where before he had ostensibly been an employee of an American oil firm, now he would be more intimately involved with the Zwaholan government itself, yet she was not so politically naive as to believe that that involvement meant he had severed his ties with the American government.

Sarah moved her cramped body, switched off the television set, and got to her feet to pace the room while she thought. She remembered other things now, such as Charles revealing his education had been paid for with the expectation that he would reimburse that payment with his services. Bitterly she reflected that he had probably been recruited for the work he did before he had ever met her, and at an age—and after experiences that would make him easy prey—when he was too young to evaluate the costs.

A chill traced her back as the full force of the risks he had faced, and still did, slammed into her mind like a sledgehammer. For surely the risks would be even greater now if he was going to work directly for the Zwaholan government.

She slumped into a chair, her face white with fear for him, as she contemplated what his dual role could mean. Hadn't the newscaster mentioned something about there being political turmoil in Zwahola? And wasn't assassination the rule rather than the exception nowadays? Whatever that "other faction" was, they might not think twice about disposing of a Westerner who threatened whatever political ideology they espoused.

Since Sarah didn't know exactly what role Charles was to play in Zwaholan affairs, she wasn't sure just how big a target he was going to be, but a soft moan escaped her lips as she remembered that he had told her he couldn't have her with him because if he had to worry about her, he couldn't function well, and that if he didn't function well, he might cease to function at all.

The fear swamping her became so unbearable, Sarah had to find some relief from it, even if that relief took the form of mere physical activity. Hardly realizing what she was doing or why, she fled to her bedroom to throw on a pair of jeans and a casual top. Forcing her feet into a pair of sandals, she grabbed up her handbag and keys and let herself out of the apartment. Once out on the street, she calmed down enough to determine a destination, and made her way to the market on the corner.

At the market she headed straight for the rack of newspapers, fighting down the desire to read then and there the one she snatched up. The market clerk hailed her in a friendly fashion, asking if she needed anything else, and Sarah forced herself to answer calmly, requesting a few articles she did actually need, as if that little bit of normality could force down the terror threatening to swamp her mind.

Back in her apartment, she settled herself at the kitchen table and leafed methodically through the pages until she found the article she sought. And what she read confirmed her dread that Charles would, indeed, have a responsible position in the Zwaholan bureaucracy. He was not referred to by name, but the mention of a former World Oil financial expert was all the identification she needed.

A sob caught in her throat as she threw the newspaper aside and leaned her head on her clenched fists. "Damn you, Charles!" she raged to the empty room around her. "*Why!* Why must you do this to me . . . and to yourself!"

He had said it had taken a lot to make him undertake this new job, but the small, traitorous thought began to grow in Sarah's mind that despite what he'd said, Charles wanted the life he had chosen over one with her. She knew his strength of will, and it seemed almost impossible to her that anyone could force him to do something he didn't want to do.

She remembered he had said something also about owing a debt to someone who had saved his life once. But couldn't that be the excuse he used to justify what he wanted to do anyway?

Sarah wondered, her inner bitterness growing. Surely his five years of service had already wiped out any such debt.

A small flame of rage began to build inside her, which she failed to recognize as a self-protective measure to wipe out her fear for Charles and, at the same time, prevent another long episode of grieving for her loss. The anger she felt began to take the place of the empty void inside her that Charles had left, filling it instead with the healing energy of purposefulnes.

As the anger grew, Sarah fed it, reliving her pain over Charles's desertion five years ago while she determined she would not let him ruin any part of her future. He had asked her not to forget him, she remembered with wrathful cynicism. As if she could! As if she wanted to! No, far better that she did remember what could happen when she gave herself over completely, heart, mind, and soul, to a man who never returned the commitment.

Sarah jumped to her feet to give physical expression to the resolution churning within her. Crossing her arms over her chest, she paced back and forth as she charted the course of her future without Charles, and without the naive, starry-eyed vision of love that had stayed with her even through the long years without him after he'd betrayed her before.

Her wanderings took her into the living room, and as she braced her hands on the windowsill and stared out at the city below her, she whispered, "Never again!" Her mouth set and firm, her eyes wide and staring and, for the first time in her life, displaying a hard cynicism, she determined that from now on she would protect herself from her own forgiving, foolish, loving nature.

"You've taught me my lesson, Charles," she whispered to nothing and nobody but herself. "I hope you enjoy your life of duty!" And then the bitter thought intruded that he probably would. Probably, he was so caught up in the little-boy excitement of living life dangerously on the edge that he could never have left such a life even if there hadn't been a convenient reason to return to it.

Sarah straightened and lounged by the window as a brief, unamused smile twisted her lips into almost a grimace. "You wanted me to have the chance to get on with a decent life, Charles?" she asked her absent lover in a cynical tone. "Well, I intend to. I intend to play the game the way everyone else does. And when I get ready to marry, I will marry someone else and have his children. But I will never, ever, make the same mistake I did with you and turn my whole life over to him. Not again!"

And with that resolution ringing in the otherwise silent air around her, Sarah swung on her heel and made her way back to the kitchen to prepare, deliberately, a peanut butter and mustard sandwich, which she determinedly choked down against the lump of mingled anger and disgust that seemed to have settled in her throat permanently.

When she had finished and was rinsing the dishes in the sink, the sound of the telephone made her jump in reaction to the instantaneous, stinging, futile thought that it might be Charles. She slammed the plate she was washing into the sink, dried her hands, and reached for the telephone with an abrupt, impatient gesture that was echoed in her tone as she snarled, "Hello!"

"Hey, it's only me," Chelley's plaintive voice came over the line. "If you're still sick, I can hang up. I don't have anything that important to tell you anyway."

Taking a deep breath to calm herself, Sarah made her voice quieter. "No, it's all right, Chelley. I'm feeling better now. How did things go at the office today?"

"It was dull," Chelley said flatly. "Nothing exciting ever happens when you're not there, except—" She paused, and since her voice had taken on a lightly teasing note, Sarah took the cue and prompted her.

"Except?" she asked dryly.

"Except that Ian Connors came in looking for you," Chelley replied in arch tones. "He was devastated when you weren't here."

Since Chelley didn't sound in the least bit jealous now, Sarah asked, "Well, did you make it up to him?"

"Ha! Fat chance!" Chelley responded, blithely unconcerned. "I don't fight losing battles. Besides, I met the cutest guy last night, and I—"

"Spare me," Sarah ruefully interrupted. "What did Ian Connors want, Chelley?"

"What do you think he wanted?" Chelley answered flippantly. "He wanted to make time with you. And I have the feeling you aren't going to be as successful at brushing him off as you usually are with men. Underneath all that suave British charm beats the heart of a relentless pursuer. I can tell."

Sarah went silent for a moment as she thought over Chelley's remarks. Then she literally stunned her secretary by replying, "Maybe I don't want to brush him off, Chelley. Maybe he's just what I need right now."

"What!" Chelley gasped over the phone. "I can't believe it! What happened? Did your Viking let you down?"

Sarah winced at that, and the pain she felt was momentarily reflected in the sadness of her brown eyes before she pulled herself together enough to reply in a manner that would lead Chelley away from the truth. "What Viking?" she asked with idle puzzlement.

"What Viking!" Chelley snorted. But an instant later she said impatiently, "Oh, never mind! I'll never understand you, Sarah Bailey. Nature gave you twice what she gave me in the looks and brains department, but you haven't got the slightest idea what to do with them! It isn't fair!"

Sarah managed a saucy chuckle before replying, "I might surprise you yet, Chelley. Maybe I'm just a late bloomer."

"Well, if anyone could make you bloom, I would have thought it was the Viking, but obviously I was wrong. Oh, well, maybe Ian Connors will have better luck."

"Maybe he will, Chelley," Sarah murmured thoughtfully, "maybe he will." And then she projected more authority into her voice as she asked, "Was there anything else, Chelley? I'm still a little weak in the pins and I thought I'd have an early night, but I'll be in the office early tomorrow."

"No, nothing else," Chelley said, sounding sympathetic. "Sorry you're sick. And there's nothing really important on the schedule tomorrow if you want to stay home again."

"Thanks, Chelley, but I'll be in," Sarah replied, warming her tones. "Good night. Thanks for calling."

"Good night, Sarah. See you tomorrow." Chelley rang off.

Sarah finished her chores in the kitchen, took a long, hot shower, then went to bed early, though not to sleep. Instead, she lay awake hour after hour, trying not to sense the empty space beside her, trying instead to plot out a new role for herself as a

167

modern woman, self-sufficient within herself. She had been that way before Charles reentered her life, and she would be again, she determined grimly. But now there would be a new twist. Now she would become liberated in every sense.

And as sleep came at last to twist her reminiscences into random, disjointed patterns, her last clear thought was that Ian Connors would be just the man to help her evolve into a woman who could never get hurt again. He was sophisticated and wouldn't expect more than she could give for a while. For she knew it would take some time before she could take some of the steps she was contemplating.

But in the morning, when the alarm brought her awake to the sound of her own sobs, her determination wavered, and as she crawled from bed to begin a new day and a new life, she could only hope that her subconscious would, in time, come to have less power over her when she lay defenseless in sleep, unable to combat the dreams of Charles that had brought on the tears that racked her still.

CHAPTER FOURTEEN

Over the next few weeks Sarah thanked God for her work. And gradually, as Ian Connors slowly insinuated himself into her life, she began to thank God for him.

The day after she made her resolution to put her love for Charles behind her and adopt a new life-style, she entered her offices with a frown of concentration on her lovely face rather than the warm smile she usually bore, causing Chelley to look at her with wary concern, especially after Sarah ordered her to begin bringing in every single file they had in bunches of a dozen or so at a time.

"What's up?" Chelley asked cautiously, something in Sarah's manner alerting Chelley that now was not the time for her usual flippancy.

"We've been stagnating," Sarah informed her secretary, much to that young woman's surprise, since Chelley was of the opinion that Sarah worked hard enough for two people. Sarah ignored Chelley's widened eyes and skeptical look. "I want to tackle the California studios more aggressively," Sarah continued. "That's why I want to look through all our files. And another thing," she added as she turned on her heel and started toward her office, "get on the phone to our contacts on the West Coast and see if you can't scare up some more scripts. They've been trickling in lately. I want an avalanche from now on."

With that, Sarah entered her office and closed the door behind her with a decided thud, leaving Chelley staring after her in open-mouthed astonishment.

As Sarah crossed the burnt-orange carpet to her Danish modern desk, the first thing that caught her eye was a huge bouquet of assorted, brightly colored flowers in a beautiful white porcelain vase resting in the very center of her desk. For an instant her breath caught in her throat as she wondered if they were from Charles, but when she read the small white card, a look of mingled disappointment and wry amusement replaced her earlier stricken look.

The card read, "Sorry you were under the weather. Hope these brighten your day." Ian Connors. And beneath Ian's name was a brief P.S. "Have lunch with me?"

Sarah tossed the card aside, removed her beige linen jacket, draped it over the back of her chair, then settled down to read yesterday's mail. When Chelley staggered in a few moments later bearing the first batch of files, Sarah glanced up, then hastily removed the vase of flowers to the credenza behind her.

When Chelley spotted the flowers, her eyes lightened into mischievous teasing. "Where did those come from?" she asked lightly. "Do you have a secret admirer?"

Sarah raised her dark, winged eyebrows in surprise as she looked behind her at the flowers. "They're from Ian," she informed Chelley in a puzzled tone. "You mean you didn't know they were here? Didn't he send them yesterday?"

"Nope," Chelley said, then gave a sigh of relief as she dumped the files onto the vacant space on Sarah's desk. "They weren't here last night when I left, and I haven't been in here yet this morning." Chelley moved to the credenza and buried her nose in the flowers, giving a sigh of pleasure. "Mmm, they smell heavenly, don't they?" She turned back to Sarah then, her eyes dancing. "What did the card say?"

Sarah shrugged, though a slight smile tugged at her generous mouth. "Sorry you're sick. Have lunch with me," she told Chelley casually. Then the smile disappeared into a faint frown. "How do you suppose he got them in here?" she murmured thoughtfully.

"He probably bribed Willy, the night watchman, to bring them," Chelley suggested unconcernedly as she retraced her steps to the door. "Are you going to?" she tossed off over her shoulder casually.

"Am I going to what?" Sarah inquired in an abstracted manner as she began to leaf through the first file.

"Are you going to have lunch with Ian Connors?" Chelley answered with exaggerated patience.

"Oh," Sarah replied, a thoughtful look entering her eyes. "I'm not sure. Maybe." And then she bent back to her work, and in the process missed seeing Chelley's delighted grin.

Ian appeared in the outer office around 11:30, looking dapper and handsome in a new version of the tan suit he favored. Chelley glanced up at him and smiled as he came to a stop beside her desk and withdrew his hand from behind him. In it was a single red rose, which he presented to Chelley with a flourishing bow as he gave her a wicked smile.

"What's this for?" Chelley asked, taking the rose and bringing it to her nose while her eyes twinkled at him over the lovely blossom.

"It's a bribe," Ian confided unashamedly in a whisper, slanting his dark eyes toward Sarah's closed office door. "I'm starting a campaign to win your lovely boss's heart, and I have the feeling I'm going to need all the help I can get."

"Wellll." Chelley considered the matter with teasing soberness. "Usually my bribes run to quite a bit more than one rose, but since I think it's time *somebody* won Sarah's heart, I'm going to subdue my mercenary nature and cooperate with you." She leaned toward him in a conspiratorial manner and whispered, "What's your plan?"

Ian beamed down at her approvingly before adopting a considering manner. "I think a slow process would be the best bet, don't you?" he asked. "She isn't the type to be swept off her feet, is she?"

Chelley nodded emphatically. "You're right," she approved. "Rushing her never works with Sarah." And then she looked whimsical for a moment, unaware of how little truth there had been in her last statement or in her next one. "But, then, I don't know of anything that *does* work with her," she muttered frustratedly.

Ian apparently didn't hear the last part, and he nodded thoughtfully. "That's what I thought," he commented. "Slow but sure is the ticket, I think." And then his manner turned brisk. "Now what about my chances of getting her to join me for lunch? Do you think I should leave things alone for a while after sending the flowers, or should I get on with it?" And at Chelley's skeptical look, Ian turned earnest. "It's just a bloody lunch, for God's sake!" he protested. "I don't plan to ravish her at the table!"

Chelley giggled, then eyed Sarah's door consideringly. "I'll tell you what," she said thoughtfully. "She's buried in work today, and I have the feeling she's going to ask me to order out for her. Why don't I just accidentally order enough for two, and then you just accidentally show up at her door while I'm out having my own lunch." She looked at Ian sternly then, and added, "But if you ever tell her about my part in all this . . ." And as Ian looked back at her with earnest innocence, she shrugged. "To tell you the truth, I don't know why I *am* helping you. Maybe it's just my matchmaking instincts, or maybe you just have a way about you." She shrugged again. "Well, whatever it is, I guess you can count me in as a conspirator."

"Done!" Ian agreed, holding out his hand for Chelley to take, which she did, shaking it enthusiastically. "Now suppose I just disappear for a while," Ian suggested. "I'll be in the coffee shop. Come by and give me the high sign when it's time for me to 'accidentally' appear, all right?"

Chelley formed her thumb and finger into an okay sign as a broad grin split her pixieish face. And a few minutes later, when Sarah buzzed her to ask her to send out for a sandwich, Chelley's grin grew even broader as she called downstairs to order two Reuben sandwiches, two potato salads, and two colas.

When the food came and Chelley delivered it to Sarah's office, Sarah looked at the array of food and raised her eyes to Chelley inquiringly.

"I didn't mean you had to stay in, too, Chelley," she said with surprise. "But since you've ordered enough for yourself . . ."

Chelley looked suitably distressed. "Well, the fact is, Sarah, I *meant* to eat in, but after I'd ordered the food, that cute guy I was telling you about on the phone last night called and asked me to lunch. It was too late to cancel my part of the order, and I hoped you were hungrier than usual today."

Sarah shook her head in rueful denial as she contemplated the large sandwiches. "I can't possibly eat all that, Chelley." And then at seeing Chelley's disappointed look, she added, "But leave

172

it here. If I can't eat it, we'll either pitch it or save it for a snack later this afternoon. Go on and meet your date, Chelley. It's all right."

Chelley's woebegone face brightened immediately as she thanked Sarah and departed the room hastily, taking care to leave the door to Sarah's office open as she left.

Ten minutes later, after Sarah had closed the file she was studying and was reaching for her sandwich, Ian Connors appeared in the doorway, looking at first delighted to see her, and then chagrined and disappointed when he saw the sandwich in her hand.

"Bloody hell!" he exclaimed, doing an admirable job of appearing to be both cross and charming at the same time. "You're already eating!" he accused her, woeful hurt in his brown eyes.

Sarah leaned back in her chair and viewed him with tolerant speculation. "So I am," she agreed calmly. "After all, you didn't specify *when* you were asking me out to lunch."

"But it was evident I meant today," Ian complained as he moved into the room and made his way to her desk where he stood looking down at the food hungrily.

Sarah found herself laughing at his expression, and since she also found herself surprisingly glad to see Ian Connors, she gestured at the food and asked him to sit down. "I'm sorry," she said soothingly. "Why don't you join me? Chelley ordered enough for two, and I certainly can't eat all of it."

Ian accepted the invitation with alacrity, his hand reaching for the other sandwich before the words were barely out of Sarah's mouth. "Don't mind if I do," he mumbled around his first bite. "I'm perfectly starved, as a matter of fact."

"Obviously," Sarah grinned, softening her observation with a warm look at Ian that made him pause in his chewing.

When he had swallowed the bite in his mouth, he murmured teasingly, "You should do that more often."

"What?" Sarah asked, puzzlement in her voice.

"Look at me like that," Ian said as he seated himself in the chair across from her desk. "It could get to be a habit, and if it did, I won't deny I'd be delighted."

Momentarily, Sarah experienced the same wary reaction she always had when a man flirted with her. But Ian's teasing look and open smile erased the feeling immediately, and she found herself smiling at him again without adopting the offputting manner that had been her shield in years past.

On that first day their conversation over their meal was so casual and relaxed, and Sarah felt so easy with Ian, that she was actually surprised when Chelley appeared in the doorway and Sarah realized a whole hour had passed. When Chelley appeared, Ian immediately got to his feet, eyeing the stack of files in front of Sarah with respect.

"Well, I can see you have lots to do," he remarked, "so I'll be on my way. Delightful lunch, my dear. We must do it again soon."

And Sarah, much to her surprise, found herself replying, "Yes, I'd like that, Ian." Whereupon Ian gave her such a warm, approving smile, coupled with a look that contained just the faintest hint of sexual interest, that Sarah gave him one of her warm looks again, which made him pause momentarily in the act of turning away. His gaze sharpened for an instant into something that changed his whole personality, and as Sarah watched, startled by the transformation, she saw him become, however briefly, the exact opposite of an easy, charming, unhurried, and relaxed man of humor. Instead, he assumed the mantle of a very virile, very male, very intelligent predator. But then he returned to his usual manner so quickly, Sarah doubted she'd seen any such thing at all.

He had reached the door before he turned back and snapped his fingers, as though he'd just remembered something. "Oh, yes," he said with utterly convincing casualness. "I knew there was something I meant to mention." He reached into his jacket pocket, withdrew two tickets, and waved them at Sarah. "Are you a fan of the ballet by any chance?"

"I don't know," Sarah said simply. "In my job I always attend the theater or the movies. I've been to the ballet only once, and that was years ago."

"Well, then, it's time you did again!" Ian snorted, sounding outraged that Sarah had been so deprived. He retraced his steps to her desk and tossed the tickets down in front of her. "Those are for Saturday night," he informed her sternly. "See that you use them!"

"But, Ian," Sarah protested, startled by his action.

"No buts!" he denied her protest, assuming an exaggerated masterfulness. And then his eyes started to twinkle and he rocked back on his heels and looked up at the ceiling as though he found it of supreme interest. "Of course, you'll need an escort," he suggested mildly.

And Sarah, her lips twitching with amusement, replied gravely, "Of course."

"Have anyone in mind?" Ian asked, returning an innocent gaze to her face.

"Not a soul," Sarah replied, maintaining her gravity. "Any suggestions?"

Ian beamed at her, then tried without too much success to look modestly tentative. "Well, as it happens," he remarked casually, "I'm free Saturday evening myself." He shrugged an impressive shoulder offhandedly. "And as it happens," he went on, "I've always been a devoted fan of the ballet." He paused, lifting his eyebrows suggestively. "But, of course, I'm not suggesting that the two of us . . ."

"Of course, you're not," Sarah agreed with suspicious innocence. Then she dropped her pose and grinned at Ian. "Why don't you pick me up about seven?" And she gave him her address, delighting in the boyishly eager light that sprang up in his dark eyes.

"Dinner before or after?" Ian inquired, his answering grin imparting a mischievous charm to his handsome face that Sarah found very pleasing. "After," he decided emphatically, answering his own question. "It will give me that much more time to impress you with my sterling qualities."

"Oh, Ian," Sarah laughed. "You're incorrigible."

"And a lot of other things as well." He came right back with a wicked leer before turning on his heel to return to the door. "See you Saturday, Sarah." He took his leave with a rakish little wave and a self-satisfied smile that made Sarah begin to think she was going to have her work cut out for her keeping one step ahead of him in the romantic game they were about to play. She decided she had better spell out to him Saturday evening that, despite his undoubted charm, he was going to find it harder to put the next stage of his no doubt complicated game plan into operation. For she was convinced that Ian Connors would be a master at playing his hand.

Between working herself to the point of exhaustion and Ian's coming into her life, Sarah had very little time or energy to spend thinking about Charles, though at night, alone in her bed, it was inevitable that there were still bouts of tears—crying jags that left her drained and empty and lonely for the one man she was determined to put behind her.

However, under the self-delusion that she was merely feeding her anger at Charles, she watched the evening news programs faithfully, waiting for any mention of Zwahola and its problems. But there was very little mention of that country, and without conscious purpose, Sarah began to find herself at the library in her few off hours, where she scanned the reference books for material on Zwahola and looked up old newspaper articles where the country was featured.

In that way she learned more about Zwahola's financial difficulties, which were caused by a period of enormous oil revenues flowing in, followed by a temporary glut of oil on the market that reduced those revenues drastically just at a time when they were most needed. For during the good times, so many projects had been started and so many people had come to the major cities to find employment in the oil business, that now there was a real problem in finishing those projects and providing employment for the workers.

Zwahola was now experiencing riots by the newly unemployed, crime by the poverty-stricken, and a corruption in its government that was appalling, but which was generally covered up by convenient fires that burned records of investigations. It was clear that some solution had to be found, and soon and it was equally clear to Sarah that Charles's new job in the Zwaholan government was one attempt to find such a solution.

Despite the temporary glut, Sarah learned that the United States government was concerned with keeping Zwahola's oil available due to the volatile situation in the Middle East, which could possibly deteriorate rapidly at some time in the future, leaving the United States with an insufficient oil supply. And then she realized that in addition to being important to the

Zwaholan government's plans, Charles was equally crucial to the plans of the American government.

She came away from her studies feeling a combination of renewed anger at Charles and a reluctant acknowledgment that she and her desires were very low on the scale when placed against such world events as he was involved in. And she also felt that there was no way to change the situation. She had lost Charles for good, and it was time she accepted the fact and made a life for herself without him.

Therefore she was doubly grateful to Ian Connors for having the knack of turning up just when she needed him the most. Invariably, when she was feeling down and depressed, Ian would appear with an invitation to dinner or to the theater or the ballet or a movie. He was always unfailingly cheerful, and before the evening was done he had somehow managed to lighten Sarah's own mood to the point where she was able to forget for a few hours the empty, yawning gap in her life that Charles had filled, however briefly.

On the first night she had gone out with Ian, when he had brought her home and somehow managed to get himself invited in for coffee, Sarah had accepted his first kiss with wary reluctance. And Ian, noting ruefully that his kiss had not been as well-received as he had planned and expected, had drawn back and eyed her searchingly.

"You're not ready for this, are you?" he had asked quietly. And at Sarah's agreement to his observation, he had smiled warmly at her. "You will be," he had promised self-confidently. "But until you are I'll keep my advances to the bare minimum." He had then added teasingly, "But I do insist on at least *one* reciprocal kiss on our dates." And despite the teasing note in his voice, Sarah had sensed an underlying seriousness that told her Ian might be patient, but he certainly wasn't a saint.

"All right," she had answered hesitantly, thinking one kiss wasn't too much to ask for the pleasure he gave her.

"Well?" Ian had then raised his brows inquiringly. And at Sarah's puzzled look, he added, "I haven't had it yet." And as she had still looked puzzled, he had sighed, and said patiently, "My kiss. I haven't had my one kiss tonight."

And so Sarah, with reluctance and a certain remote curiosity, had raised her mouth to his and had found his subdued, but obviously expert exploration of her lips to be both pleasant and, oddly, dangerous. He did nothing to alarm her, but there was a certain quality in his very restraint that set off warning bells somewhere in her mind. She decided Ian was not a man to be underestimated. She had the feeling if the restraint ever fell away, he would be very hard to handle indeed—perhaps even unstoppable.

But after that first night, her warning bells ceased to function as Ian behaved with unfailing politeness, though gradually she found that he was taking two kisses instead of one, and then it was three, until finally one night when she had had more to drink than usual and was feeling lonelier than usual as a result of a particularly vivid dream about Charles the night before, the warning bells went off again as Ian took his kisses on her living room love seat instead of at the door, where he usually received them.

She didn't remember clearly how they had gotten there. Her head was fuzzy from the wine she'd drunk, and Ian was being unusually masterful despite maintaining his normally cheerful demeanor. But by the time Ian was on his third kiss, which had graduated from gentle exploration to a muted urgency, Sarah pulled back and gazed up at him, noting the slightly glittering arousal in his dark eyes.

"Ian—" She started to protest, but Ian placed a finger over her lips to silence her.

"Shhh . . ." he murmured in a lazy, complacent tone. "You have my word of honor I won't push you too far. But I need more than tame kisses tonight. And it's time you found out what can happen when I let out some of the stops I've been imposing on myself for far too long."

Still anxious, still wary, Sarah nevertheless allowed him to push her back into the sofa cushions and take her mouth in another kiss. And this time, after gently biting her lower lip until she opened her mouth to protest the slight sting, Ian seized the opportunity to thrust his tongue inside the sweet cavern and begin a tantalizingly expert seduction that, despite Sarah's inner warnings, began to have a physical effect on her that she almost welcomed after her long weeks of abstinence, and yet despaired because it was only a physical response, and nothing like the conflagration Charles could excite in her.

For a while Ian tolerated Sarah's passive acceptance of his kisses and his tentative, grazing explorations with his hands. Finally, however, he drew back slightly and gave her a humorous, glittering look that increased her pulse rate, it was so demandingly male.

"Trust me, Sarah," he said in a low voice. "Help me a little. I've told you I'll stop, but I need more from you than you're giving. Don't you think I deserve more than this?"

His words elicited a sense of shame in Sarah. For weeks now he had been escorting her out, teasing her out of her occasional black moods, and just being there when she needed someone. And he had demanded nothing in return except her company. And he had said she could trust him—that he wouldn't push her too far. Surely she could give him some encouragement.

She had grown so fond of him, too, that she was afraid if she didn't make an effort to show him some of that fondness, he would disappear from sheer lack of attention. And hadn't she determined she was going to change the way she behaved with men? And wasn't Ian the perfect man to help her put her new resolution into effect?

"All right, Ian," she murmured softly, trying not to look as anxious as she felt. "But not too fast, please?" She backed up slightly when she saw the gleam of anticipation spring into his eyes. "I'm really not . . . not used to . . ."

"I know, my sweet," he answered on a low chuckle. "That's what's so special about you. You're such a combination of provocative outward sexuality and inward chastity that you're driving me wild with yearning to reverse the process." He cupped the back of her head and drew her toward him, his mouth curved into a seductive smile. "Come here, darling Sarah. Come here and help me start the transformation."

And Sarah moved that last little inch on her own, meeting Ian's open-mouthed kiss with a yielding softness of her lips and a first tentative stroking with her tongue until Ian groaned a little and pulled her lower body closer to his in a convulsive movement that restrained her just enough to keep her from jerking back in an instinctive defensive movement.

179

That kiss enhanced the muted physical arousal Ian had managed to provoke earlier, and Sarah began to relax under his carefully coordinated exploration of her body, feeling her nipples tauten when his fingers grazed them outside her dress, feeling a shiver trace her back when his mouth moved to her ear and his tongue took a delicate path over the outward curve of it.

"That's it, darling," Ian whispered huskily against her ear. "Relax. Let me learn that delectable body of yours. Let me show you mine."

He took one of Sarah's hands from his shoulder and moved it to his chest, encouraging her to open the buttons of his shirt. After a moment's hesitation, she undid two of them, then slipped a finger inside to run it lightly over the mat of hair that covered the heated chest beneath.

"God, that feels good," Ian approved her action, his tone dropping further into an erotically soft growl. He gripped her waist tighter with his hands, then suddenly lifted her onto his lap. "Go on," he urged her softly when she paused in what she was doing as a result of his action. "I love your touch," he muttered. "Give me more of it."

Under his somehow soothing encouragement, Sarah resumed her stroking, pausing to open two more of the buttons of his shirt so that she could slip her whole hand inside and run it over his chest. She paused again when Ian's hand came up to one of her breasts and covered it, closing convulsively into a gentle squeeze that sent darting shafts of pleasure through her body. He moved his thumb to her nipple and began a back and forth motion that increased the pleasure until Sarah's head dropped to his shoulder and she resumed her own exploration, rubbing her palm and fingers against his chest, feeling his heart rate increase as a result of her action.

Her pale-lime silk dress had a row of tiny, fabric-covered buttons down the front, and Sarah vaguely realized that Ian had moved his hand to them and was unfastening them one by one. She felt a remote sense of pleasurable anticipation about what would happen when he was done, and she wasn't disappointed when at last he slid his hand inside to skim it softly over her lacy bra before inserting one tantalizing finger inside the upper rim

180

of the cup to run it back and forth just above the already taut-ened nipple.

Beneath her thighs, Sarah could feel the pulsing hardness of Ian's arousal, and while one part of her was pleased at this evidence of how she affected him, another part was dimly trying to issue a warning that this game couldn't go on much longer before Ian might forget his promise not to push her too far.

But then he was deftly unfastening the front closure of her bra, and as her breasts sprang free, he gathered one of them up into his warm hand and commenced his previous erotic game of passing a thumb back and forth across the nipple, only this time the pleasure was enhanced many times over because of the flesh against flesh friction.

Sarah drew in her breath on a gasp, and as though reminded that her mouth could provide pleasures he had neglected, Ian dipped his head to capture her lips, forcing them wider and wider apart until it seemed to Sarah that the whole world consisted of his demanding, marauding mouth and his erotically tormenting thumb. Her hand clenched against his chest, gathering a handful of the hair covering it which she pulled at until she felt Ian's muscles harden under the inviting, erotic effect.

Still, the whole episode seemed to have a slow-motion quality that Sarah dimly sensed Ian was deliberately encouraging in order to lead her further and further along the path he intended for her to travel. But he was so damned good at what he was doing, she couldn't find the will to stop him, though she knew somewhere, somehow, there would come a time where she either had to stop this or plunge into the total experience with no road back.

Ian released her mouth at last, but it was only so that he could move it to take the place of his thumb, and when Sarah felt his warm, moist tongue stroking her nipple and the gently suckling action of his lips, and then the warm pressure of his freed hand traveling inexorably up along one thigh until it came dangerous-ly close to where she was beginning to want it with every part of her sensual nature, she struggled for sanity, yet abruptly lost it when Ian closed in on her secret desire.

With her eyes closed and her body totally dedicated to finding its own pleasure, Sarah slid into instinctive response rather than thought. And since Charles Trainer was the only man whose touch she truly desired, she slid quickly into the delusion that it was Charles who was giving her pleasure now, Charles who was making her want to tear off the impeding clothing she wore and which prevented her ultimate satisfaction.

In muted complaint her lover's name left her lips, and it was only when the man who held her stiffened into stillness that she realized it was Charles's name she had called, not Ian's.

Her eyes came open in a stunned blink, and she drew in her breath on a shocked gasp as she realized what she'd done, hated what she'd done, regretted what she'd done so unthinkingly. "Ian . . ." She started to apologize, her tone miserable and still shaken by the tremors of arousal he had instigated.

Ian's head came up, and when Sarah looked into his eyes, everything in her froze in shock when she saw the sheer cold rage they displayed for an instant before the look was concealed beneath mere anger. But Sarah had seen enough to feel afraid of Ian for the first time since she'd come to know him, and all her physical arousal departed in a flash of cold, shaking fear that must have shown in her eyes because suddenly Ian's expression reverted to rueful sadness.

"That's the first time that's ever happened to me," he said in an oddly formal tone that struggled for humor and failed. "I find I didn't like it much," he added with more sharpness than he'd obviously intended because his mouth then twisted into a shape displaying self-mockery. He relaxed back against the sofa, and it seemed to Sarah that he had to take absolute control of every one of his muscles in order to accomplish such a simple action.

"I'm sorry, Ian," Sarah said softly, misery in every syllable.

"I'm sure you didn't plan it," he answered, again in that oddly clipped, oddly formal tone. "Hop up, my dear," he then suggested flatly. "This little episode is obviously over. I don't think we're going to be able to recapture the mood tonight."

Sarah scooted from his lap and hunched miserably in the other corner of the love seat, resting her elbow on its arm and her head in her hand. She felt as though she'd just been on an emotional roller coaster, and try as she would, she couldn't erase the memory of that look in Ian's eyes that had frightened her so much.

"Don't take it so badly, Sarah," Ian said in a flat tone as he stretched his arm over the back of the sofa and clasped her shoulder. "I don't know who this Charles is, but I assure you, I have every intention of wiping him so thoroughly from your mind that this sort of thing will never happen again."

Sarah raised her head and turned it to stare at him, her expression disclosing the fearful puzzlement she was feeling. Ian held her eyes, his own displaying dangerous purposefulness, so much so in fact that Sarah again felt afraid of him, though he was doing nothing remotely threatening at the moment except looking at her.

"Oh, yes, my dear," Ian continued with soft inflexibility. "You didn't think this would make me give up on you, did you?" He chuckled softly, dangerously. "Quite the contrary. It only makes me more determined to unwrap you step by step until you give me everything you thought you were giving this Charles."

He practically sneered Charles's name, though he did so with an upper-crust, snobbish dismissal that was actually worse than a sneer. But Sarah had the eerie sensation that if Charles were in the room with them right then, Ian's British reserve would fall away without a trace, to be replaced with as much savagery as a barbarian who believed in fighting to control what was his own. A shiver racked her, and she felt helpless, thoroughly confused and intensely frightened by Ian's complex, contradictory nature.

"I think I'd better leave now," Ian said, giving her a much more natural smile, though it was strained and his eyes had gone blank, concealing his thoughts from her.

He got up, casually buttoned his shirt with steady hands, straightened his tie, shrugged his shoulders into his suit jacket, then turned and looked down at where Sarah still sat watching him, her eyes as huge as saucers.

"Don't look at me like that, darling," he chided her, reaching a hand for her to take so that he could pull her up beside him. When she was on her feet, he grasped her waist lightly and planted a light kiss on her cheek.

"I'm not a boy, my dear," he said with a slight grimace of his lips. "I won't pretend that what just happened didn't affect me, and badly at that. But I'm not going to storm off into the night nursing my bruised feelings, never to return. I'll be back," he promised with a return of that hard inflexibility that somehow frightened Sarah unreasonably. "And one of these days," Ian continued, "you'll be mine. I won't be satisfied until I own you as completely as this Charles obviously did at one time." He gave her an unflinching look straight into her eyes. "You'll notice I used the past tense," he said with a mockery that came nowhere close to humor. "And that's exactly how it's going to be. Charles is past. I'm the here and now."

He kissed her fully then, and it was a kiss that echoed his words. There was nothing gentle or tentative or even erotic about the kiss. It was simply a physical statement that he did intend to own her. It was a form of possession, not a kiss between lovers.

Sarah accepted it passively, though it made her uneasy and in some ways repelled her even while it was vaguely, though very vaguely, exciting. She felt sick that she had put Ian through such an experience, and she wanted to make things up to him. But she was also confused by her new view of him as a man who had an uncivilized savagery beneath his suave charm and sophistication.

When he released her, Ian gave her one last flashing look of hard determination, then he moved to the front door of the apartment. "I'll call you tomorrow," he said casually, as though nothing in the least unusual had just happened between them. "I think I can get tickets to that concert you've been wanting to attend. I'll let you know, all right?"

"All right," Sarah whispered hoarsely, watching him with a helpless lack of understanding of who the real Ian Connors was.

"Cheerio, my love." He took his departure with a return of his normal good humor, which departed instantly once he was outside the door and invisible to those huge, searching eyes of Sarah's, those eyes that got to him far too deeply for him to pretend any longer that his assignment was merely a pleasant interlude between other, more dangerous ones.

While Sarah prepared for bed and tried to sort out in her mind why she was having such conflicting feelings about Ian, he was in his rented rooms placing a call to a nameless, guttural voice to ask for further instructions. And if Sarah could have heard the content of that call, she would have been more than simply a little afraid of Ian Connors. She would have been terrified of him.

"Anything new?" Ian asked in a clipped voice when his call was answered.

184

"Yes," the guttural voice answered. "Our friend is having much more success than our employers can tolerate."

"So?" Ian responded impatiently. "Then why don't our employers remove our . . . ah . . . friend from the scene?"

"Too many repercussions," the voice answered. "Besides, it is not necessary. All we have to do is put him on a leash."

Ian's dark eyebrows rose and a sardonic smile played on his firm mouth. "And that involves my particular charge, I presume?" he inquired with mocking humor. "If you want me to take her away from all this for a while, I assure you I'll be delighted to do so. This job is turning out to have some interesting side issues that intrigue me enormously." The smile slid away from his mouth then, while his eyes took on a chilling, thoughtful purposefulness that would have made Sarah doubt she had ever seen an easy, relaxed, cheerful Ian Connors.

"No, not yet," the voice answered. "If it comes to that, we'll let you know. Right now all we want is to issue a warning to our friend."

Ian frowned slightly. "What sort of warning?" he asked.

"Our friend is coming to New York in two weeks for some meetings with certain bankers who hold notes we would prefer not to see repaid. Do you understand?"

"Of course," Ian shrugged. "But what's the plan?"

"There will be a certain reception our friend will attend. You will attend also, and you will bring your charge with you."

Ian's frown deepened then, and his voice was clipped and cold as he objected. "I say, old chap, do you think that's wise? You know what sort of connections we suspect our friend has. Surely they know who I am. Hell," he snorted disgustedly, "our *friend* must know who I am. I'm certain that in the position he holds now, he'll have been briefed about all the people who do my sort of work in that part of the world. I'm not in business for fun, you know, and I'll be damned if I'll take any unnecessary risks. I have plans for my retirement that have nothing to do with the bars of a prison cell."

A harsh chuckle greeted his outburst. "Don't worry," the voice sneered. "Nobody knows you've been seeing her, so they won't be prepared. And our friend, once he gets the message we're conveying to him, will be afraid to do anything about you.

185

He'll be too concerned about what might happen to your charge to take any risks." The voice changed to an order then. "I'll send you the details in the usual manner. You just get her there. That's what you're being paid for."

The buzz of the dial tone signaled that the conversation was over, and Ian replaced the receiver, a dark scowl distorting his face into a caricature of its usual bland pleasantness.

He paced to the window, whistling between his teeth as he stared out into the night. He had his hands on his hips and a blank look in his eyes that showed he was thinking hard and fast. Finally a smile curved his mouth again. It seemed the time schedule for Sarah's eventual seduction had just been stepped up. But after tonight he didn't think it mattered. She was ready for him. More than ready, in fact. And he didn't intend to let her near Charles Trainer again until he'd succeeded in dividing her loyalties into a pattern more to his liking. Before he was through with her, she was going to be willing to follow him anywhere for as long as he wanted. And he knew he would want her for much longer than he'd wanted any woman.

With a satisfied chuckle Ian stepped away from the window and entered the adjoining bedroom to take a long, cold shower before he got into bed and lay with his hands behind his head replaying the evening with Sarah in his mind. He took it step by step until he figured out where he'd gone wrong, and when he had, he nodded his head with satisfaction.

A small, self-satisfied smile played on his mouth as he plotted out how to avoid such a conclusion to an otherwise delightful evening in the future, and then he fell asleep with that smile still curving his lips, to dream about Sarah Bailey and what would happen the next time they were together and he had the opportunity to erase Charles Trainer's hold on her senses and replace it with his own—until such time as he'd had all he wanted from her and was ready to toss her back to Trainer like so much damaged goods.

CHAPTER FIFTEEN

It was oppressively hot and muggy as Charles climbed from his small car in the parking lot of the office building where he worked, and the tight feeling behind his forehead presaged another headache, an affliction he was becoming resigned to lately. He knew it was not only the coming of the rainy season that was causing them, but the frenetic pace he maintained. His fatigue told him he was going to have to reduce that pace before too much longer, or he would have a lot more to contend with than headaches. He was making himself a sitting duck for one of the serious illnesses that infested Zwahola, and all it would take would be exposure to some germ or other to lay him low.

As he passed his secretary's desk, however, he forgot about resting and concentrated his thoughts on the business at hand. "Bring me the rest of the loan files, Ironsi," he instructed the man more curtly than was his usual wont. "We've got a lot of work to do to get ready for the New York meetings."

His secretary gave him a wounded look that said more clearly than words that he had taken offense to Charles's tone, and Charles gave an inaudible sigh as he continued into his office and dropped his briefcase onto his desk. The Zwaholans were an excessively polite people, and he knew he should have taken more care in greeting Ironsi, but he had other things on his mind at the moment.

With a mental reminder to soothe Ironsi later, Charles poured himself a cup of coffee from the pot Ironsi kept filled in his office, then seated himself behind his desk to open his briefcase and take out the files he had worked on the preceding night until the early hours. But at seeing the name of a prominent New York bank on the first file, his lips tightened, and he braced himself to try

187

to repress the thoughts of Sarah that his forthcoming trip to New York provoked far too often lately.

During the early weeks of his return to Zwahola, he had thrown himself into his work so fervently, and had had so few hours of the night to sleep, that he had managed to keep her out of his thoughts most of the time, if not out of his dreams. But she had been safely in New York then, and he had been thousands of miles away. Now he found himself asking how in God's name he was going to keep from calling or seeing her on his brief return to the States.

He knew he couldn't give in. It would be unspeakably cruel to Sarah to contact her and bring everything between them back into focus for a few brief, unsatisfactory meetings. For that matter, it would be unspeakably cruel to himself, he admitted as he leaned back in his chair and stared unseeingly at the portrait of Hwala that hung on the far wall of his office. If he could help it, he had no intention of giving in even to the almost overwhelming desire to view Sarah from a distance. He wanted to spare her the pain of possibly seeing him again, and himself the exquisite torment of looking when he couldn't touch.

He had even told Foster to discontinue his sporadic surveillance of Sarah once Njomo had assured him that there was no reason for the Zwaholan government to be interested in her any longer. He had done so in order that he wouldn't know when she fell in love with someone else, married someone else, bore another man's children.

"God, Trainer, stop it!" Charles instructed himself wearily in a harsh whisper at realizing he was falling into the self-destructive pattern of hashing over what he had lost. He then reminded himself to be quiet, since he was certain his office was bugged, if not by Hwala, then certainly by Lugubu, and possibly by both. But there was little point in trying to hide most of what he was accomplishing anyway. What he was doing was the subject of endless gossip among the bureaucrats—gossip and speculation and, depending upon the political bent of the gossiper, either excited hope or dour resentment or even hatred.

Charles knew that Lugubu's hatred of him was virulent by now and would continue to grow as Charles slowly made inroads on the financial difficulties facing Zwahola. But since both Hwala and Njomo went to exceptional lengths to protect Charles and had made it abundantly clear that should Charles meet with an untimely accident, certain people would be arrested without benefit of a trial and thrown into prison with the possible threat of execution, Charles spent very little time worrying about Lugubu's hatred. But he knew also that the closer he got to obtaining his goals, the more risks Lugubu would take to get rid of him, and Charles had already made arrangements to protect his back in New York even more strenuously than he did in Zwahola. For if Lugubu was going to try anything, Charles knew the man would try it there, where someone else might be blamed for a possible "accident."

"Sir!" Ironsi appeared in front of him with a stack of files in his arms, while his face portrayed the same offended dignity it had earlier.

With an inward sigh of resignation, Charles made the effort to smile warmly at Ironsi as he took the files and thanked the man for bringing them.

"And how is your new son, Ironsi?" Charles then started the ritual which would take at least fifteen minutes he could ill afford to lose, but which he knew from experience would succeed in erasing Ironsi's resentment and turn him into a productive employee for the rest of the day.

A broad white smile greeted his question, and Charles again gave an inward sigh as he recognized from the change in the man's stance that Ironsi was settling in for a lengthy chat about his brand-new baby son, a subject that brought painful envy in its wake for Charles.

Exactly fifteen minutes later a fortuitous telephone call brought Ironsi's recitation to a halt, but Charles had the satisfaction of seeing that Ironsi's brisk departure to his own office to answer the call gave every indication the man was now ready to settle down to work.

A moment later Charles's eyebrows rose as Ironsi came back, his face slyly inquisitive as he informed Charles that Yetunde, Njomo's granddaughter, was on the phone and wished to speak to him. Charles hesitated—he really didn't have time to cater to Yetunde right now, but he knew he would suffer pangs of guilt for the rest of the day if he didn't—then he nodded to Ironsi and picked up the receiver on his desk.

"Hello, Yetunde," he said with gentle respect. "How are you today?"

When it came, Yetunde's tearful response made Charles close his eyes in weary sympathy. "I've got to get away from here for a while, Charles," Yetunde half demanded, half cried. "You've got to talk Grandfather into letting me come to New York with you. I can't stand it here any longer without Ajayi!"

"Yetunde, dear, please." Charles tried to persuade her to drop the matter, but Yetunde was determined.

"No, Charles, don't try to talk me out of it!" Yetunde cried almost hysterically. "Everywhere I look, everywhere I go, I'm reminded of Ajayi! If I don't get away from here soon, I'll . . . I'll . . . kill myself!" she finished dramatically. And then her voice dropped to a low, threatening tone. "And I swear to you, if Grandfather won't let me go to New York willingly, I'll run away on my own! This is not the old days any longer. I have some rights now!"

"Yes, of course you do, Yetunde," Charles soothed her. "And believe me, I know how you feel." He hesitated briefly, then relented. "I'll try once more, Yetunde. But you know your grandfather as well as I do. If he doesn't intend for you to go, your rights won't mean much. You won't be going."

Yetunde was mollified somewhat by Charles's promise to speak to her grandfather on her behalf, and after a few more pitiful, irrational threats, she hung up. Charles then placed a call to make an appointment to see Njomo that evening, then got down to the business at hand, which was to consolidate his plea to several New York banks to renegotiate the loans they'd extended to Zwahola.

At the end of a long, hard day, Charles made his way to Njomo's home, an unpretentious building in the middle of a compound containing the rest of his family, and after being ushered inside, he accepted the offer of a cool glass of palm wine. When he was seated in front of Njomo, the old man looked at him critically.

"You look weary, my son," Njomo sympathized. "You work

too hard. But then," he added with sly satisfaction, "I understand your work is beginning to pay off."

Charles lowered his glass after taking a long swallow and nodded. "Yes, Grandfather, I think it is. If we can get those loans renegotiated, get the back-to-the-farm program off the ground, and negotiate a better contract with World Oil, we should be looking forward to a breathing space for a while." At seeing Njomo's pleased look, however, Charles hastily cautioned him not to get overconfident. "But we're not out of the woods yet, Grandfather. There are a lot of other measures that need to be taken, and most of them won't be popular. These things take time. The worldwide economy is not all that good right now, as you well know, and there's going to be a long haul before any country with Zwahola's problems is permanently stabilized."

Njomo waved a dismissing hand at Charles. "I know, I know," he said, impatient over Charles's caution. "But we are on our way, and that is what is important!" He paused and eyed Charles with shrewd concern. "You realize, of course, that Lugubu is certain to make a move soon to defeat all this progress?"

Charles's expression turned grim. "Yes, I know. He can't wait much longer. He can't afford even to let me pull the bank deals off. If I do, Hwala will have enough confidence in me to put some muscle into the other projects. He's been dragging his feet, you know," Charles said with wry cynicism.

Njomo chuckled. "Of course, he has. Hwala is a politician, after all. What did you expect? He stuck his neck out more than he likes when he hired you. He is certainly not going to stick it out any further until you bring him something to make it worth his while to do so again." The old man relaxed back among his cushions, a confident smile creasing his lined skin into a thousand pieces. "You will do it, Charles. I know you will."

"If Lugubu doesn't kill me first," Charles qualified wryly. "Nothing would please him more for a number of reasons." He hesitated briefly, eyed Njomo cautiously, and added, "I've heard he even blames me for his son's accident."

All at once Njomo's smile disappeared, to be replaced by a look of stony impassivity that revealed nothing. "Lugubu is paranoid where you are concerned," he said in level tones, his old black eyes unwavering in their regard of Charles. "Ajayi's death *was* an accident. Lugubu should accept that."

Charles regarded Njomo steadily, knowing he would never learn the real truth of the matter. "Yetunde is having an equally hard time accepting Ajayi's death," he offered quietly into the ensuing silence. Njomo frowned then, his gaze becoming sadly troubled.

"Yes, she is taking it harder than I would have thought," he said in a musing tone of regret.

"She called me today," Charles said with a careful lack of expression in his tone. "She's threatening to do something desperate if she isn't allowed to come to New York with my delegation. I think she means it," he concluded quietly.

Njomo frowned, looking arrogantly determined for a moment, before he let his seamed face dissolve into an expression of uncertain sympathy. "Are you recommending that I let her go, Charles?" he asked with uncharacteristic deference. "Do you think it will help her?"

Charles paused for an instant, then nodded his head. "I would recommend it, Grandfather. She needs a change of scene to help her get over her loss."

For a moment Njomo thought the matter over, and at last he nodded. "You are right, Charles," he agreed. "I will send a bodyguard for her, of course, but you must look out for her also. She is spoiled, but at times she will listen to you."

"Grandfather," Charles protested, "I'm already going to have my hands full with business. I won't have time to look after Yetunde as well."

"I do not mean that you have to be at her beck and call," Njomo said gently. "Merely that, if she needs you, you will be available to help. I know she cries in the night sometimes," Njomo said sadly. And then he drew himself up and added more briskly, "But that will pass. I am going to introduce her to Kinte soon, and he knows what he must do. He is a charming man with much appeal to women, and he will do his part well. I have hopes that there might even come to be love between the two of them."

Charles passed a tired hand over his aching forehead, thinking that, for all his years in Zwahola, he would never become accustomed to parts of their culture.

"Very well," he said. "I'll keep an eye on her when I can. She'll be very happy to learn she's going to be allowed to come. Perhaps just getting away for a while will help."

"Let us hope so." Njomo echoed the thought, but it was clear his mind was already turning to something else. Charles looked at him inquiringly, and when Njomo spoke again, it was in his warrior voice.

"You must be very careful in New York, my son. You know that is where Lugubu will strike if he can."

"I know," Charles answered with tight grimness. "I'll be careful."

"*You* will, I know," Njomo said, "but he may not attack you directly. There is another area where you are vulnerable, my son."

Charles looked at him in puzzlement, obviously not following what Njomo meant, whereupon Njomo sighed tiredly. "Your woman, Charles. She lives in New York, does she not?"

At that, Charles stiffened abruptly, every muscle in his body tightening with tensile strength while his eyes became a glacial blue.

"But no one knows about Sarah but you and whoever tracked her down, Njomo," he said with dangerous quietness in his voice. After a pause he said even more quietly, "Who *did* track her down, Njomo?" and there was deadly intent in his voice and in his cold blue eyes.

Njomo looked distressed, both at Charles's lapse into addressing him by name and not the affectionate appellation he normally employed, and at what his own answer had to be.

"A man named Ian Connors, Charles," he nevertheless answered without dropping his steady gaze. "Time was short, and we had to use what resources were available. This man Connors is well known in Africa for selling such services. He is not necessarily a dangerous man." He made an attempt to reassure Charles. "He normally does not use violence, though he can if he is pushed. But he is an amoral man. He sells himself to the highest bidder." Njomo paused, then added with soft regret, "And lately I have begun to wonder if I am the only one he might have sold the information about your woman to. Lugubu would certainly pay a high price for such knowledge."

Charles stared back at Njomo, the pounding in his temple becoming almost unbearable under the stress Njomo's revelation had imparted. At that moment he came as close as he would ever come to hating the old man who had been his friend, his mentor, and, in a way, a second father to him all these years. But now Njomo had inadvertently placed Sarah in jeopardy, and no man who had done that could claim Charles's loyalty.

"I do not know this to be true, Charles," Njomo added hastily, the quaver in his voice becoming more pronounced under Charles's glacial stare. "But it is something to be considered. If you have any resources," he suggested delicately, "with which to provide your woman protection, I suggest you use them. We cannot afford to lose you now."

Charles's jaw tensed with the inner disgust he felt at those words. He supposed it was predictable that Njomo's real concern should lie with Charles's value to Zwahola, but the fact did little to alleviate the inner rage he felt beginning to burn a hole in his chest.

"Grandfather," he then said with slow, deliberate, enunciation, "if any harm comes to Sarah Bailey, you will have to afford to lose me." He stressed the last five words with rage in his tone. "Because my involvement with you and with Zwahola will come to an end then and there. I could not, I *will* not, live with the knowledge that in my efforts to help you and your government, I was responsible for harming Sarah."

Charles got to his feet and stood towering over the frail old man at his feet who was staring up at him in surprise. "And God help any man who does harm her," Charles added with implacable purpose in his tone, which was very quiet, very sure, and very deadly. "He'd better kill me first, because when I get my hands on him, he won't live long enough to regret his bad judgment."

With that, Charles turned on his heel and left the room and a very badly shaken old man to go straight to his contact at the American embassy in order to send a message to Foster to resume his surveillance of Sarah immediately. He marked the message urgent and added a code that spelled out danger in the strongest possible terms. And then he returned to his barren, lonely room to sit on his bed and hold his aching head in his hands while he cursed himself, Zwahola, and the American agency that employed him with every bit of strength left in him, before getting quietly and thoroughly drunk on a bottle of nearly undrinkable local liquor given to him by an ecstatic Ironsi on the occasion of the birth of his first son.

CHAPTER SIXTEEN

Two days after Sarah had almost succumbed to Ian Connors's seduction, she was on a plane winging toward California and feeling relieved yet guilty at the opportunity to put her normal life behind her, even if only for a short time.

She had woken up the morning after the disastrous evening with Ian, feeling besieged and harassed by any number of conflicting emotions, one of which was a vague sense of anxiety about Ian. There had been something about Ian's reaction that had unnerved her that night and still did when she thought about it, which was strange, since he'd certainly been more of a gentleman about the whole thing than many men would have been.

And besides her confusion where Ian was concerned, she was having to contend with an unreasonable sense of guilt about what she herself had done the night before. To her anger and astonishment, she found herself in the frame of mind that might afflict a wife who had betrayed her husband with another man. Which was patently ridiculous, she had fumed silently to herself as she had dressed that morning. In the first place, Charles was not her husband. In fact, he was out of her life entirely. And in the second place, she had made a conscious decision to start changing her life-style because of what had happened with Charles. So why was she behaving like such an idiot now when she hadn't even gone to bed with Ian?

She had therefore not been in the best of moods when she'd arrived at her office, and as usually happened when a day started out wrong, it went rapidly from bad to worse.

Her very first call had been from the director of Bal Henderson's new play. Dick Bradley was an old friend, and Sarah had picked up the phone, her pleasure in hearing from him evident in her cheerful "Hello, Dick! How are the rehearsals going?"

That her question had been the wrong one to ask became evident when Dick, instead of bantering and teasing with her as he normally did, came back with "They'd be going fine if that bitch you stuck us with would ever show up for them, or if, when she does show up for them, she was in some sort of shape to actually rehearse!"

Dick's snarling, sarcastic tone had made Sarah wince, and her voice was resigned as she had inquired what was going on.

"Lila Benton's infatuation with Jocko Norwood is what is going on," Dick had responded with another snarl. "She leaves early on Fridays to be with him, and half the time she doesn't show up again until the following Tuesday. And when she does finally get here, she looks like she's been through the wringer while she falls asleep over her lines!"

Sarah's groan had been audible over the phone, and Dick Bradley had evidently gotten a sort of satisfaction in it. "You might well groan, Sarah baby, because if you don't straighten Lila out and be quick about it, hers is not the only career that's going to take a nose dive."

Alarmed by that statement, but nevertheless angered on her own behalf now by Dick's attitude, Sarah had sounded decidedly clipped when she'd answered.

"Well, you're the director, Dick. If there's any straightening out to be done, it's your job to do it. Just because I—"

Dick had cut her off. "Just because you practically crammed Lila down our throats, you don't think you have any responsibility toward her anymore?" he had asked sarcastically. "Is that what you're saying, Sarah? Because if it is," he had added before she could speak, "I can tell you right now that most of the producers and directors in this town aren't going to see it that way, and you'd damned well better take note of that fact before the day is over, because I'm not going to waste another twenty-four hours on that blond prima donna! She either straightens up or she's out of the play!"

After making his threat, Dick had slammed down the phone, causing Sarah to jerk the receiver away from her ear, and her anger had been prodigious as she'd barked at Chelley to get Lila Benton into the office within an hour, if not sooner.

When Lila had shown up looking washed out and cowed because she'd been in the business long enough to know what was coming, Sarah had sat her down in a chair and proceeded to spell out in detail and without bothering to lower her voice in the process, just exactly what Lila was risking, not only for herself but for Sarah as well.

"And another thing," Sarah had raged at a thoroughly downbeaten Lila toward the end of the interview. "I warned you about Jocko Norwood when you first mentioned him! You wouldn't listen, and now look at you! Are you so besotted with him that you can't see what he's doing to you?"

At that point Lila had dissolved into tears, and it had taken a good half hour to calm her down, but when she had been calmed, she admitted that Jocko was no good for her, and that she valued her career more than she cared for him anyway. Then she apologized to Sarah for her behavior and departed with the promise that from there on she would begin to behave like a professional actress again.

The only good thing that had happened that whole day was a late afternoon call from a major California studio asking Sarah to fly out there and assist in casting a blockbuster movie they were planning. It seemed the new energy she had thrown into her business lately was paying off, since one of Chelley's requests for scripts had occurred just at a time when the producers were looking for new talent. One of them had worked with Sarah before with fantastic results, and had been instrumental in suggesting her as an temporary addition to their regular casting crew.

By that time, Sarah had seized the opportunity with the desperation of a drowning swimmer. And her very alacrity in accepting the offer, despite the fact that it made sense from a business standpoint, had told her she was badly in need of a change for emotional, if not for professional, reasons.

Ian's reaction to her California trip made her even more grateful to be getting away for a while.

He had started out as suavely cheerful as usual. "I got those tickets for tonight, darling," he had purred into her ear. "I'll pick you up at seven, all right?"

Sarah had stumbled for a reply, realizing with a sense of shock that she really didn't want to see Ian that night, or for some time, for that matter, not until she'd had a chance to sort things out in her own mind.

"Ah . . . er . . . no, Ian," she had replied hesitantly. "I'm leaving for California in the morning, and I have to spend this evening packing."

"You're *what*?" Ian had practically snarled back at her, his tone stopping her in mid-pace as she'd taken the call standing up, and in her nervousnes, had been walking back and forth.

"I'm going to California tomorrow—on business," Sarah had answered patiently, still feeling slightly guilty over what she'd done to him the night before, though his attitude was beginning to irritate her.

Ian had greeted that information with a long silence—a silence that had somehow taken on an air of menace.

"How long will you be gone?" Ian had then asked, his tone quieter, but sounding more curt than she'd ever heard it.

"I'm not sure. Not longer than a couple of weeks," Sarah had replied, her relief that Ian was back to normal, at least *almost* back to normal she felt, evident in her voice.

Another silence had ensued, but when Ian had finally spoken again, he had sounded more like his cheerful self. "Why don't I come with you?" he had asked, managing to insert a suggestive note into the question. "I'm free, and it would be fun to travel with you—in fact, I'm certain it would be more than fun. Exciting might be a better word."

But Sarah had refused, feeling strangely relieved that she had a perfectly good excuse for doing so. "I'm afraid not, Ian. I'll be working very hard with little or no time off for pleasure. It just wouldn't be worth your time."

Ian hadn't been willing to drop the matter, however. "Come now, Sarah," he had coaxed. "You're not feeling . . . ah . . . uncomfortable about what happened last night, are you? I assure you it will make no difference at all to our relationship. There's no reason to worry. Please, let me come. I promise I won't get in the way, and I'll wait patiently for whatever time you can spare me."

Had there been a grating insincerity in that last statement, or had she been imagining things again, Sarah wondered. In any event, she remained adamant. "I'm sorry, Ian. It has nothing to do with last night. It's just that I really will be too busy to spend any time with you."

Inwardly, Sarah was feeling guilty because her refusal to let Ian accompany her did have a great deal to do with what had happened the night before. Furthermore, she had every intention of sight-seeing a little or just spending some time by her hotel pool getting some sun. Nevertheless, she was glad she had stretched the truth when Ian turned belligerent again.

"Come now, Sarah," he had grated. "You don't expect me to believe that, do you?"

"Yes, I do, Ian," Sarah had replied quietly, but with a quality in her tone that must have alerted Ian that he was pushing too hard, for after a long pause, he had sounded more reasonable.

"Very well, Sarah. But I'll be waiting for you when you get back. If you think running away is going to solve anything, you're wrong. I fully intend to take up where we left off the next time I see you."

"Oh, Ian, I'm not running away," Sarah had started to protest somewhat untruthfully, but Ian had simply said good-bye and had hung up.

While she was packing that night, however, he had called again, and this time he had seemed to be trying to make up for his earlier behavior.

"Darling, let me bring over some Chinese food," he had suggested soothingly. "I won't stay long, but you have to eat, and I'm sure you're too busy to cook."

"Oh, Ian, I'm sorry," Sarah had replied wearily. "But I've already had a sandwich, and I'm tired. I have to get up at five to catch my flight, and I'm going to bed in another few moments. Thank you, but . . ." She had let the rest trail off and then braced herself for his reaction. But after another long silence, it had been surprisingly mild.

"Very well, Sarah," he had said with quiet smoothness. "They say that absence makes the heart grow fonder, and I know that will be true for me. I only hope it will turn out to be true for you too. We have spent rather a lot of time together these past few weeks, you know, and I'm going to flatter myself that you'll miss me."

After they had hung up, Sarah reflected upon his statement, thinking sadly that she hoped the old cliché didn't hold true where Charles was concerned, while she hoped it did where Ian was. After all, Charles was gone for good. Ian could represent the future if she let him.

And over the next two weeks, in what little time Sarah had to think about anything other than work, she was grateful to find that she did miss Ian. She forgot her doubts as though the distance between them wiped them from her mind. Instead, she remembered the good times they'd had together, and she found herself looking forward to seeing him again.

But if Sarah could have known about the black rage Ian had fallen into when she had removed herself from his reach just at the time when he had planned to consolidate their relationship and build upon it in preparation for their scheduled encounter with Charles Trainer again, she would have changed her view of Ian considerably.

Meanwhile, however, blissfully unaware that one of the bellboys at her hotel, the driver of the car the studio had provided her, and one of the gofers who ran errands at the studio were anything other than what they seemed, Sarah worked harder than she ever had in her life, loving every minute of it, and in the process, impressed a great many important people with her uncanny ability to pluck just the right actor or actress out of the crowd of eager applicants.

At the end of the two weeks, she boarded a flight back to New York, tired and drained, but with a final accolade ringing happily in her ears. Both the producer and the director of the forthcoming film had sought her out before her departure, and the director, acting as spokesman, had assured her that if she ever wanted to come to California to work permanently, she would receive a hearty welcome.

"You've got something a person has to be born with, Sarah," the director had said admiringly. "I've heard you wanted to be an actress yourself, but believe me, you fell into the right niche when you went into casting instead. I've never worked on a film before where I felt so confident that every single role was cast as if the actor or actress were born to play the character. You're fantastic!"

The producer had echoed that assessment, and Sarah had come away from the interview feeling as though she were walking on air.

Now, however, as she leaned wearily back in her seat on board the flight to New York and closed her eyes, she realized it was time to concentrate on her personal, rather than her professional life, and that meant she had to decide what to do about Ian.

But she'd already decided, she realized with a faintly contented smile curving her mouth. Ian might not be Charles. He might not elicit the total sense of rightness she felt with Charles. But he was as close as she was ever likely to come. And if he still wanted her when she got back, then she intended to explore a more intimate relationship with him. She was not going to spend the rest of her life lonely and unfulfilled because Charles Trainer preferred duty to her.

It was late when she got back to New York, however, and she was too tired to confront Ian just yet. So instead, she went to bed, woke late, and then had to hurry to the office, as she knew already from having kept in touch with Chelley that there was a backlog of work only she could handle.

On her way to work she was much too preoccupied to notice that Foster, with a relieved look on his face, stayed right behind her. And since Ian Connors was sleeping soundly in his rooms at the time, there was no one to see that Foster, like a hovering guardian angel, was taking no chances that Charles Trainer would have any reason to be distracted from his work or to explode with the violence Foster suspected he was capable of if any harm came to Sarah Bailey.

CHAPTER SEVENTEEN

The first thing Sarah did at work was to call Dick Bradley to see how Lila was doing.

"Hello, Sarah," Dick's voice answered, sounding cheerfully delighted to hear from her. "I hear you've been making quite a reputation for yourself on the West Coast. Congratulations!"

The rate at which industry gossip traveled was no news to Sarah, but she was a little surprised, and a lot relieved, to learn that Dick was apparently no longer angry with her.

"Thanks, Dick," she answered without going into any details about her California venture. "But I called to see how *you're* doing. How's Lila? Any complaints?"

"Complaints?" Dick sounded astonished that she'd asked. "Are you kidding? We've got the hit of the century on our hands thanks to you. Lila's a peach!"

Sarah cast her eyes to the ceiling, both in relief and exasperation at how Dick had changed his tune. "She's not causing you any more trouble then?" she asked cautiously, hesitating about introducing a sour note into Dick's apparent euphoria.

"Hell, no!" Dick responded cheerfully. "After you talked to her she settled down like a dream. She doesn't even argue with my direction anymore, and that's a relief, I can tell you. For a while there I thought her brain was solid cement under the glamorous exterior. But now that she's behaving like a professional, we get along fine. And she's exactly right for the part, Sarah," he added gratefully. "You did good."

"Well, uh, thank you, Dick," Sarah said with rather weak gratitude. She reminded herself not to remind Dick that his tune had changed considerably since the last time they'd talked. Instead, she asked, "When's the opening?"

"On the twenty-third," Dick answered with satisfaction. "And you can have all the tickets you want. Bring your friends, your family, and any strangers off the street that appeal to you if you like. The way I feel right now, I'd kick my own mother out of her seat to give it to you."

"I don't think you need to go that far," Sarah responded wryly, "but thanks for the offer." With a sigh of relief she concluded the conversation. "Well, now that I know everything's all right, I can sleep a lot better at night. Good luck with the opening, Dick."

"Thanks, kid. See you," Dick rang off, and Sarah gave a satisfied chuckle before tackling the mountain of work that lay on her desk awaiting her attention.

Try as she might, it was two days before she felt able to notify Ian that she was back in town. She had come home so tired the first two nights that she knew she couldn't give Ian the attention he deserved if she tried to start their relationship off in the way she wanted it to go, but on the third day, at finding she'd made enough progress so that she could be reasonably certain she wouldn't go home feeling like a wrung-out rag, she dialed the number he'd given her where he could be reached, intending to invite him over for dinner that night—dinner and whatever else happened to come about.

But when she got him on the line, his snarling greeting made her draw back and eye the telephone receiver as though it were likely to bite her at any moment.

"Where the hell have you been?" he demanded heatedly.

"Why, California, of course," Sarah answered after a slight hesitation. "You know where I've been."

"All this time?" he asked nastily. "Someone I know said they thought they saw you on the street yesterday evening."

Wincing a little at having been found out, Sarah explained. "Well, actually I got back a couple of days ago, Ian, but I was so tired and I had so much work to do here at the office that I—"

"Nice of you to finally let me know you were back," Ian cut in sarcastically. "I'm surprised you bothered to call at all."

Puzzled and angered by his attitude at first, then realizing the ego she'd damaged severely before she had left was probably at the root of Ian's belligerence, Sarah set out to soothe him in the fastest way possible.

"Ian, I called to ask you over for dinner tonight," she said with a note in her voice that was deliberately provocative. "Just the two of us."

A short silence followed her invitation, and just when Sarah was beginning to think he was going to refuse her invitation, Ian spoke, his voice suavely charming at last.

"Darling, nothing would please me more," he said smoothly, regret in his tone. "You know that. But as it happens, I have an engagement planned for this evening which I simply have to attend. But I'd like you to come with me," he added, cutting through Sarah's disappointment and lifting her spirits again. "Afterward, perhaps, you'll invite me home for coffee?" The sensual note in his question indicated that coffee was the least of what he hoped she would be inviting him home to enjoy.

"Of course," Sarah agreed softly. "What sort of affair is it, Ian? What should I wear?"

"Best bib and tucker, darling," Ian responded cheerfully, his mood completely different from what it had been when he'd first answered the call. "I'm wearing black tie."

"Really?" Sarah asked, intrigued by the idea. "Why?"

Ian laughed mysteriously. "That's a secret. You'll find out when we get there. Just look your best, darling. I want to make every other man there envious of my good fortune."

Sarah thought she detected a slight hint of maliciousness in his tone, but she dismissed the idea impatiently, wondering why it was that she always seemed to read things into Ian's tones that were ridiculously inappropriate.

"I'll do my best," she assured him with a laugh. "What time will you pick me up?"

"Eight o'clock," Ian responded smoothly, then added in a lower tone, "And plan to make a late night of it, darling. I've been looking forward to this evening for a long time."

"That's nice, Ian," Sarah said, lowering her own tone to one of guarded intimacy. "I'm looking forward to it as well. See you then."

"Yes, darling," Ian said with a note of promise in his voice that shivered Sarah's spine. "You certainly will see me then." He rang off on a low chuckle, and Sarah sat back in her chair, suddenly feeling as nervous as if she were about to embark on her first date.

That evening, as Sarah lay in her bathtub trying to let the luxuriously scented hot water soothe her growing tenseness, she grew increasingly impatient with herself. No matter how many deep breaths she took or how many times she consciously relaxed her muscles, the knot of tension in her stomach refused to go away.

She felt ridiculous. How many women, she wondered wryly, after having reached the ripe age of twenty-nine, became a bundle of nerves at the prospect of embarking on an affair? Perhaps an eighteen-year-old virgin could be forgiven such immaturity, but at her age? It was not only ridiculous, it was just plain dumb. She knew what she was doing and why. She should be anticipating the night to come, not lying here feeling as awkward as a refugee from a children's story.

Well, she decided, as she gave up trying for that elusive relaxation and stood up to dry herself off, perhaps this first night with Ian would not turn out to be the stuff that dreams were made of. But if he was as skillful a lover as he had shown himself to be on that other occasion, it should be very pleasurable. And she was a good enough actress to cover up if she became seized by these ridiculous qualms at the critical moment. In fact, it might be better if she didn't lose her head completely, since the last time she'd done so, she had ruined everything by calling Charles's name instead of Ian's.

As she gazed rather sadly at her own image in the bathroom mirror, however, she realized her features were far too woebegone to reflect those of a woman who should be anticipating a new love affair, and a sparkle of anger lightened her eyes. She stuck out her tongue at that image before turning on her heel to go to the bedroom.

"Grow up!" she hissed at herself disgustedly. "There's no percentage in comparing every man and every relationship to Charles and what you had with him. Take what's available and like it, you idiot!"

She dressed carefully in a gold lamé gown that hugged her curves as though it were part of her. It was strapless, but there

206

was a short-sleeve jacket of the same material to impart a modesty sufficient to carry her through any type of function Ian had in mind. Once the jacket came off, however, as it certainly would later in the evening, her image was all sultry, sexy woman, just waiting to be unwrapped by any man she allowed the privilege.

She had dabbed perfume in all the secret places Ian would undoubtedly be exploring before the morning came, and the scent wafted around her, creating an elusive, tantalizing sexual aura. In a way, she wanted him to take her and get it over with this first time, leaving no opportunity for doubts and anxieties to creep in and ruin things.

"Oh, Sarah," she addressed her image resignedly as she tilted her head to affix a long, dangling golden earring. "Are you sure you know what you're doing?"

But her mind didn't supply an answer, and as she brushed her long sable hair into a cloud of satin around her smooth, elegant face, she deliberately made her mind go blank rather than continue to feed her doubts.

She put on gold high-heeled sandals, and when she'd finished fastening the straps, she straightened to survey her image in her full-length mirror and nodded her head in satisfaction. Immodestly, she knew she would make Ian proud of her tonight, and that was all to the good, considering that she might disappoint him in other ways.

She was ready when the knock finally came at her door, and as she pulled it open to see Ian looking formidably handsome in his tuxedo, she smiled at the instantaneous dilation of his dark pupils as he took in her own appearance.

"My God, woman!" he breathed a little unsteadily. "I wanted you to look beautiful, but I didn't mean for you to place me in the position of having to knock men off you with a stick all night!"

Sarah laughed and held out her hand to him to draw him into the room. "Don't worry, Ian," she teased, primly demure. "I perfected the art of enforcing the look-but-don't-touch dictum on men a long time ago. But I am pleased that you like the way I look."

"I think you've mastered the art of understatement as well," Ian mocked as he shut the door behind him. "*Like* is a mild way of putting my reaction." His dark eyes roved over her possessively as he came closer. "Come here," he murmured. "I want a personal demonstration that all this is mine before I have to share your outward image with others."

Sarah went into his arms, relieved when she found herself able to do so without hesitation. Ian looked splendid, and since his good humor seemed to be firmly in place—indeed, he seemed to emanate an aura of excited anticipation that was gratifying to her ego—Sarah felt relaxed and comfortable with him again. She pooh-poohed her earlier nervousness as she lifted her mouth for his kiss, thinking that things were going to turn out just fine. And as Ian's mouth came down on hers with exquisite consideration for her makeup coupled with an erotic playfulness that warmed her pleasurably, she relaxed even further. Ian's kiss was so skillfully executed that she felt another layer of inhibition fall away, and she was certain that tonight was going to be very enjoyable indeed.

When he drew back, Sarah's eyes were shining liquidly with the sensuality that was so much a part of her nature, and Ian's darkened as he smiled his satisfaction at having brought that look into her eyes.

"I have the feeling this is going to be one of the best nights of my life," he chuckled complacently, while Sarah, angry at herself for once again thinking she had detected a certain maliciousness in Ian's anticipation, smiled hesitantly back at him.

"I hope so, Ian," she said more seriously than she'd meant to. "I hope I don't disappoint you."

Ian's smile grew broader while an eager, predatory light sprang up in his eyes that somehow made Sarah uneasy. He seemed almost hyperactive, as though he were infused with an energy and excitement that seemed more pronounced than it should have been.

"I have no intention of letting you disappoint me," he said with such mocking self-confidence that Sarah reacted with a tremor of annoyance. Immediately she castigated herself, wondering incredulously why she seemed always to be looking for things to be upset with Ian about. Was she that afraid of their coming intimacy? she wondered crossly.

"Let's go, darling," Ian distracted her from her thoughts.

"We're on the verge of being late, and this is one night when I definitely want to be on time."

"Why?" Sarah asked curiously as she went to pick up her evening bag. "Is this function special to you in some way?"

Since Sarah had turned her head away as she reached for her bag, she missed the hard, cold glint in Ian's dark eyes which disappeared immediately as she faced him again.

"Special?" he mused in an enigmatic tone. "Why, no, Sarah. Actually it's rather a duty night. Do you think I'd be spending it anywhere but here alone with you if it wasn't?"

His suggestive teasing made her flush slightly, and she scolded herself for being so uptight about this. Her own behavior made no sense to her at all in light of how uninhibited she'd always been with Charles, and even with Clive, she hadn't been this nervous. She didn't like it one bit that somehow she found it so hard to behave naturally with Ian.

Ian during the taxi ride to their destination reminded her of boys she'd known who played sports and were getting all keyed up for the big game. She was half amused, half puzzled by the excitement in his eyes and the tension in his body she could feel even from across the width of the automobile seat. She had a great deal of difficulty accepting herself as the cause of all his inner alertness, but she gave a mental shrug, accepting that there were always new facets of any personality to be discovered.

She didn't recognize the building where the taxi let them off, and she was a little startled when two huge black men dressed in tuxedos inspected the printed invitation Ian held out to them with unusual intensity before waving them on.

Sarah looked at Ian with wide-eyed puzzlement. "Ian, where are we?" she murmured to him quietly as they came into a large room and stopped to look out over a crowd of people in evening dress. Most of the occupants were black and were speaking a language Sarah didn't recognize.

"This is a diplomatic function, my dear," Ian replied as though her question amused him, then he flicked her a sardonic look she found disconcerting. He returned his attention to the room in front of him, his eyes scanning the crowd as though he were looking for someone in particular, and before Sarah could ask him what country the function was in honor of, he said, "One of my . . . ah . . . family is some mucky-muck or other with this crowd, darling. He prevailed upon me to come here and combine a family visit with business. He doesn't have time to get together in the normal way."

Ian took her arm and started pushing her forward toward a waiter with a tray of drinks. "Have some champagne, dear. It will help the medicine go down. These things are usually rather dreary."

Finding Ian's explanation credible, if a little vague, Sarah allowed him to fetch her a drink. When it was in her hand, he escorted her to a row of chairs along one wall and seated her, though he remained standing.

"Will you allow me to be incredibly rude for a short while, my darling?" he asked smoothly without looking at her. He was still scanning the crowd with his eyes. "I can see I'm going to have to fight my way through this mob in order to find my man, and I don't want you to get crushed in the process. When I've located him, I'll be back for introductions."

He shot her a brief, abstracted, rather tense smile, and without waiting for her to agree or disagree, left her to start making his way through the crush of people in front of them. Sarah shrugged, thinking Ian hadn't exaggerated when he'd described this affair as dreary, and she lifted her glass of champagne to her lips while she began to watch the people immediately in front of her.

Idly she speculated about what the occasion was in honor of. It had to be one of the African nations, but as Ian hadn't bothered to give out any details, she had no idea which one. The very fact that this soirée was obviously African-oriented, however, made her start to think of Charles, and she wished sadly that Ian had chosen somewhere else to take her on this of all nights. Charles was the last person she wanted to think about.

She sat for some time in lonely splendor, and just as she was beginning to feel self-conscious about the number of interested stares she was getting, a small group of people directly in front of her moved away, and through the space they'd vacated, she had an unrestricted view of Charles Trainer bending toward a beautiful, statuesque young black woman who was looking up at him as though he were the sun and the moon and the stars all blended into one entity and presented to her for her delectation.

As Sarah watched in stunned dismay, Charles, with an indulgent smile on his lips, cupped the young woman's beautifully sculpted face in his hand and kissed her temple gently.

For one frozen instant Sarah doubted her own sanity. Every cell in her body seemed to contract and withdraw into abnegation of what she was seeing. Her hand, holding her now empty champagne glass, was suspended in mid-air in front of her as though she were a store mannequin devoid of living blood and tissue, and her huge eyes were blank with shock.

She had no idea how long she sat there in suspended animation like that, but at last Charles turned his head to survey the room around him idly, and when his blue eyes found Sarah, she saw a replay of what she herself must have looked like enacted with uncanny similarity.

Charles's large body froze, his mouth slightly parted as though he'd been about to say something to his companion, and his hand, which he had been about to raise to rub the back of his neck, stayed outstretched halfway there as though he were conducting an orchestra.

The scene dissolved when Ian abruptly appeared in front of Sarah. He smiled down at her in a way that left no doubt of the intimacy, or at least of the about-to-be-consummated intimacy, of their relationship.

"Sorry to be so long, darling," he crooned to her in a clear, projected voice that Charles heard.

At that, Charles's body moved in an almost imperceptible jerk, and Sarah, her eyes still fixed in a locked stare on his face, could actually see a vein begin to throb in his temple. His mouth closed in a grim line that seemed to represent not only suffering, but danger—a danger Sarah dazedly recognized but could barely accept, since she'd never seen Charles look like that before.

"Darling, pay attention," Ian chided her, reaching down to cup Sarah's chin in his hand and turn her face up to his. "What has you so distracted?" he asked, idly curious.

Ian then turned his head to follow Sarah's gaze, for though her head had necessarily turned toward Ian, her eyes hadn't. They shifted to stay fastened on Charles in hurting, horrified fascina-

211

tion. Therefore, she couldn't see Ian's face, and so she missed the maliciously dangerous challenge he was directing at Charles.

But though Sarah couldn't see Ian's expression, she could see Charles's, and what she saw made her moan under her breath in mingled hurt and fear. Charles looked fully at Ian, and his eyes widened, focused sharply, then went rapidly through a series of emotions that ranged from shock to understanding to agony and then to an icy rage that made the blue of his eyes glitter like sunlight bouncing off an iceberg. That last look struck a chill of fear in Sarah, reaching to the depths of her soul.

Vaguely she noted that the woman with Charles was tugging on his arm in an effort to get his attention. Her lovely face bore a pout that spelled out the fact that she felt she had a right to claim Charles's complete attention, and it was that fact that finally brought Sarah out of her shocked immobility and pushed her into a blazing rage of her own that leapt across the room at Charles and would have scorched him had it had tangible force.

Through her mind ran a series of thoughts at lightning speed. So Charles was unable to call or write or see her because he would be out of the country? Yet here he was, and she doubted if he'd ever been anywhere else over the past few weeks.

So Charles had no intention of becoming seriously involved with another woman because he had to concentrate so hard on his own survival? Yet the woman with him was obviously no stranger. Indeed, her behavior toward him, and his toward her, was much too familiar to have sprung up overnight. They had obviously been intimately involved with each other for quite some time, and the sick jealousy Sarah was feeling gave birth to some very ugly questions indeed. One of those questions was whether anything Charles had told her had been the truth.

All the time those thoughts were ravaging her, Sarah was acting instinctively. She felt a need to hurt Charles that was much more than a need; it was a compulsion. And from the expression in his eyes, she knew that although he might have lied to her about everything else, he still had some feelings toward her, and was apparently experiencing a gnawing jealousy of his own at seeing her with another man. Since Ian was the only weapon she had to use against Charles, she used him with all her might.

Reaching a hand up to Ian's neck, Sarah drew his face down to hers and pressed a lingering, sensual kiss on his mouth. Since they were in a public place, the kiss was necessarily a short one, but Sarah used every acting trick she'd ever learned to make it a work of art. No one who saw it could be left in any doubt that she and the man she was kissing were on very intimate terms indeed.

When it was over, and she turned her gaze back to Charles, she had the dubious satisfaction of seeing that Charles had gone white under his tan, and that his mouth and eyes were displaying the living torment she had wanted to see. Then she very deliberately let her gaze slide to the woman still clinging to Charles's arm while she smiled indifferently, as though that woman's very image wasn't piercing her soul like a well-honed knife.

That last gesture proved to be a mistake, however. Charles's gaze turned puzzled at first, and then as enlightenment dawned, his eyes opened wider, and he looked at Sarah with stunned understanding blazing at her from the depths of his blue eyes while he involuntarily made a short, negative gesture with his head.

But Sarah, using Ian's demand for her attention as an excuse to turn away, could stand no more of what she considered Charles's extraordinary talent for deception. She was sick with a feeling of betrayal, and all she wanted was to crawl away somewhere and nurse her wounds. But first she knew she had to find a ladies' room in order to bathe her face and overcome the physical nausea that accompanied her mental and emotional sickness.

"Darling, are you all right?" Ian asked solicitously. Sarah barely registered the fact that he seemed insincerely effusive with his sympathy, and in any event, she didn't care about Ian Connors at the moment.

"The champagne . . ." she managed to stammer. "I'm afraid it's gone to my head. I need a ladies' room, Ian. Help me, please."

"Of course," Ian agreed smoothly as he helped her to her feet and started to steer her toward a nearby door. But his eyes continued to watch Charles, and they narrowed when Charles said something to his partner, then left her to start toward Ian and Sarah.

Sarah became aware that Ian's pace was frustratingly slow, and she looked at him with sick, weary impatience and pleading. She was about to ask him as forcefully as possible to hurry, when he came to a complete stop just as Charles came up to the two of them.

Without so much as a greeting, Charles addressed Sarah in an abrupt, harsh fashion. "I need to talk to you, Sarah. Right now!"

Sarah used every last bit of her willpower to draw herself up and give him the benefit of an icy stare. "I can't imagine why," she drawled with just the right amount of indifferent puzzlement in her voice as she gave the performance of her life. "You've already said it all—more than once, as I recall." She started to turn away, but Charles reached out in a lightning move and grasped her wrist.

"Sarah!" He started to say in a low, rasping, urgent tone, but Ian cut him off.

"Take your hand off her, please!" Ian rapped out in a tone that while outwardly polite, contained a sinister threat as well that made Sarah dart a glance of alarm at him. She might be in a confused, agonized state of mind, but her training made her extremely sensitive to the nuances of tone, and what she'd heard in Ian's made a shiver trace her spine.

Charles directed his attention briefly, dismissingly, to Ian in a manner that made another dart of alarm pierce Sarah's heart. "I'll deal with you later," he said in a tone every bit as dangerous as Ian's had been, if not more so, and Sarah had the unnerving impression that the two men were rapidly approaching a point where they might tear into each other in a fight to the death in full view of everyone in the room.

"Please . . ." she interjected hastily, darting a glance of pleading at Ian, then one of dismissal at Charles. Then her glance grew momentarily puzzled as she saw that Charles's face had tightened into a grim mask as he looked at Ian's right side, the one facing away from Sarah.

"I don't think you really want to argue about this, do you, old man?" Ian drawled, an underlying harshness in his tone that feathered Sarah's spine. "Sarah's not feeling well. She wants to

214

go to the ladies' room. I think you'd better let her, don't you?" Ian finished on a note that was nowhere near being a question.

Charles's gaze remained riveted for an instant longer at where Ian's hand rested in his jacket pocket, before he raised eyes that were as cold as death to Ian's face. "Whatever you say," he uttered in a voice Sarah had never heard him use before and which frightened her badly. "For the present," Charles added with harsh coldness.

Beneath her fear Sarah felt a sad, despairing sense of futility at hearing that Charles wasn't going to dispute Ian's claim on her—that he was going to let her go, as always.

Her eyes were bleakly cold in their own right as she gave Charles one last scathing look that contained all the betrayal she was feeling, and then she stared pointedly at where he still held her wrist. Charles let her go, his eyes passing over her in a blank, remote fashion that made her wonder if he had already forgotten she existed. And as she turned away, leaning heavily on Ian's arm, she wondered how long it was going to take her to forget that Charles had ever existed, for she knew now that that was exactly what she was going to have to do.

If she had seen the look of savagery on Charles's face once she and Ian had passed through the door leading to a hallway where the rest rooms were located, or had been able to watch as he spun on his heel and practically ran to the nearest exit leading outside the main room, she would have been at the very least puzzled, and at the most, frightened by his actions.

Ian's voice was casual as he led her along the hallway to the door they sought. "Who *was* that fellow, darling? Nasty sort of character, isn't he?"

"Very," Sarah answered bleakly. "Excuse me, Ian," she added with weary despair. "I'll be out in a few minutes." And without answering his question about Charles, she pushed through the door to the ladies' lounge, feeling unutterably grateful when the room proved to be empty for the moment. She made her way to a sink, where she ran cold water, and without regard for her makeup splashed it on her face repeatedly in an attempt to dispel the nausea that was boiling in her throat. When she felt a little better, she dried her face and collapsed into a chair to sit, dazed,

215

staring at nothing while she tried to close her mind to what had just happened.

It was perhaps just as well, for the sake of her own safety, that Sarah was unaware of the frantic efforts Charles was making at that moment to find Foster, who he learned from a hasty telephone call was waiting outside the building after having followed Ian and Sarah that night. Foster had been calling in reinforcements from the moment he realized what was likely to happen.

When Charles joined Foster outside, he made his evaluation of Foster's efforts to protect Sarah crystal-clear in explicit, harshly delivered language that might have scorched the ears of a less world-weary man.

"Calm down," Foster finally interrupted with a terse harshness of his own. "Tonight is the first we knew of Sarah's involvement with Connors. He must have learned about her during his investigation of you for Njomo and moved in on her at Lugubu's instructions. He knows Zwahola politics well enough to have seen the opportunity to make an extra buck once his initial assignment was over."

"I *know* all that, Foster!" Charles responded with harsh impatience. "What I don't know is what you plan to do about it! He's got a gun and Sarah trusts him." It was obvious that the admission hurt him to make, but his sense of urgency made him override his personal feelings. "She's furious with me and wouldn't listen when I tried to talk to her to warn her about Connors."

Foster grimaced at hearing that, but he didn't ask for details about why Sarah was furious at Charles. There wasn't time. "Do you think she'd listen to me?" he asked grimly.

"Hell, Foster, she doesn't even know you!" Charles replied angrily. "And I don't think she's in any state to listen to anyone —except maybe Connors!" he added bitterly. Then he turned purposeful. "No, Foster, we've got to act, and we've got to do it now!"

"I realize that, Trainer," Foster replied with calm professionalism. "I admit I hadn't counted on her not listening to you, which just makes things harder, but I've got a plan." He hesitated, eyeing Charles warily. But his dark eyes were steady as he told Charles what that plan was, then watched as Charles re-

216

coiled from the idea, then gradually accepted it as the only alternative available under the circumstances.

At seeing that reluctant acceptance in Charles's eyes, Foster turned brisk. "All right, then," he said firmly. "You get back in there and give Connors the impression that he's got you under his thumb." He sighed as Charles's thunderous expression said more clearly than words how he viewed such a course of action. "I know, I know," he said wearily. "But it's the only way. Your part of the job is in there. Leave the rest to me. You have my word I'll take care of her."

Charles directed a look at Foster that promised what would happen if Foster failed, but Foster's calm, professional demeanor reassured him somewhat. Nevertheless, even as he made a conscious effort to relax the tension in his muscles, his eyes still betrayed his tormented desire to take care of Sarah himself.

"Don't blow it, Foster," he said in a low, tight voice. "If the plan would work any other way, you can believe I wouldn't be leaving this to you or anybody else. Don't make me sorry I did it your way."

"You're making the right decision, Trainer. You're too emotionally involved to handle the next stage, and I'm better trained in this sort of operation than you are, anyway. If anyone were to blow it right now, it would more likely be you than me. Keep that in mind." He started to turn away, then paused and added, "Besides, you know the whole issue of whether Zwahola gets a breather on their loans or not rests on what happens back in that room tonight. You still have a job to do."

Charles's expression indicated how he felt about his "job" right then, and contempt echoed in his tone when he spoke. "Oh, I'll do my *job*, Foster, don't worry. But this is the last time. You tell the bosses they've got me for a maximum of six more weeks. That's about how long it will take me to wrap things up back in Zwahola and brief my successor. After that, I'm finished!"

Foster gave him a look filled with consternation, and Charles laughed harshly. "You don't think Lugubu will give up if he fails this time, do you? The alternative is to keep Sarah under lock and key for however long it would take me to straighten out Zwahola's economy, and in the world of economics, that's a lifetime project. No, Foster," he said with determined grimness.

"Even if that weren't the case, I'd be finished after tonight anyway. Ian Connors just taught me what it would be like to live the rest of my life without Sarah, and he woke me up to the fact that nothing is worth such a sacrifice. I intend to live my life the way I've wanted to all along!"

For a moment, the two men stared at each other, Charles with absolute certitude carving his rugged face as though in stone, while Foster looked first speculative, and then resigned. Foster then gave a short nod of his head and started to walk away, speaking urgently into a small communications device he held in his hand. He climbed into a dark sedan parked at the curb, and the moment the door closed behind him, the car started moving in the direction of Sarah's apartment.

Charles stood where he was until the automobile's red taillights were out of sight, his expression rigidly controlled. Then he turned away, and forced his body to take him back inside the building where his duty lay.

CHAPTER EIGHTEEN

As Sarah sat back in the taxi Ian had hailed, she wrapped her arms around her middle to try to control the shaking that had started after the second confrontation between Ian and Charles. After coming out of the ladies' room she had asked Ian to take her home, explaining that she was ill. It was no more than the truth, but it served a dual purpose. She couldn't face the thought of spending the night with Ian after what had happened. She needed time to recuperate from the latest blow Charles had dealt her.

Ian had seemed sympathetic, if disappointed, and as he escorted her through the main room, Sarah kept her eyes down, dreading the thought of seeing Charles with that woman again. As they passed through the door to the outside corridor, Charles loomed up in front of them.

Raising her eyes, she saw Charles look at her with a concern that seemed real, and at the same time, strangely false, and with a sick cynicism she decided it was all an act. He didn't really care how upset she was. He'd never cared. And she wondered why he bothered even going to the trouble of pretending he did.

"Are you all right, Sarah?" Charles had asked in a tone that was as mixed as his look was, and Sarah just looked back at him, incapable of responding to his farcical charade.

"No need to worry," Ian had put in with smooth coolness underscored with something else Sarah was too heartsick to identify. "I'll take care of her," Ian added, and if Sarah had bothered to look at him right then, she would have seen a triumphant sneer on his face that would have disgusted her.

Charles removed his gaze from Sarah to look directly at Ian.

"You'd better," he said with a soft coolness of his own. "Or I'll take care of you. Do you take my meaning?"

Sarah frowned as she felt Ian's grip on her arm tighten convulsively, but that was only a peripheral distraction. What really held her was the tone in Charles's voice and the look on his face that turned him into a complete stranger to her. At the moment he looked capable of murder, and that thought had started the shaking that gripped her still as she huddled in her corner of the taxi and prayed with all her heart for this night to be over.

Shortly before the taxi arrived at her building, she found the strength to say to Ian, in a cracked, shaken voice, "Ian, I'm really feeling very ill. I'm sorry, but I'm afraid we'll have to end the evening early. Perhaps another time . . ."

But even as she said the words, she knew there would be no other time. She was through with men for a while, perhaps forever, and was wondering how she'd ever thought she could allow Ian to become her lover. It wasn't Ian's fault, and she hated to disappoint him, but she couldn't stand the thought of him, or of any other man, including Charles, touching her for a long, long time.

"But darling," Ian came back with smooth soft concern. "I can't possibly leave you in this state. I insist I come up with you and get you settled comfortably for the night. I'd never forgive myself otherwise."

There was such unbreachable finality in his tone, and Sarah was feeling so inadequately prepared to argue with anyone about anything at the moment, that she lapsed into silence. She stiffened slightly when Ian moved closer, put an arm around her shoulder, and with a light caress on her cheek insisted she put her head on his shoulder. But he was so obviously trying to be tender and comforting that she allowed him the gesture, though she felt stifled by his hold on her and wished for nothing more than to be alone.

When they arrived at her apartment Ian supported her with an arm around her waist as they walked to her door. She made an attempt to have him leave her there rather than come in, but before she could gather the necessary strength to protest forcefully, he had already taken her key from her numb fingers, opened the door, and moved them both inside.

"Come along, darling," he said soothingly as he steered her toward her bedroom. "You get undressed and get into bed and I'll bring you something for your tummy. You'll be feeling better before you know it."

Ian would have accompanied her into her bedroom, but Sarah stopped him, not liking the dark glitter of excitement in his eyes nor the unnatural tautness of his smile. "I can manage, Ian," she said stiffly, thinking that it was fortunate that she had the excuse of her illness to fend him off tonight. Otherwise, the strange mood that had gripped him all evening might be transformed into a sexual tension she was in no mood to deal with.

"All right, darling," he said lightly as he moved toward the kitchen. "You get comfortable, and I'll be right back."

In her bedroom Sarah hastily undressed, donned an enveloping cotton nightgown, and remembering the look in Ian's eyes, a robe as well. She then slipped into bed, welcoming the crisp coolness of the pillowcase under her flushed cheek.

Closing her eyes, she huddled into a little ball while she fought off the thoughts that she knew could swallow her into a fathomless pit of despair every bit as painful and debilitating as the one she'd been in for an entire year after Charles had left her five years ago. She was determined not to let that happen. It was enough that he had destroyed her attempt to form another relationship. She was not going to lose herself in another long round of agonized days and nights as a result of Charles Trainer.

It seemed to take an inordinately long time for Ian to find the medication he sought, and at one time she thought she heard his voice raised in a heated argument with someone over the telephone extension in the kitchen. She couldn't imagine whom he could be calling at this hour and under these circumstances, and she was too miserable to care. She only wished he'd have done with it, give her the medication, and leave.

At last he came back with a glass of foaming liquid in his hand. He seated himself on the edge of her bed and put an arm behind her to raise her up. "Drink this, love," he coaxed her when she eyed the concoction with distaste. "It will help."

Sarah obeyed, nearly choking over the ghastly taste, but determined to get it down and be done with it so Ian would disappear at last. Once she had finished it and was allowed to lie back against her pillow again, however, it slowly began to dawn on her that Ian might have no intention of leaving. He was looking at her with an excitement in his eyes that brought back all of her earlier uneasiness.

"Ian, thank you . . ." she faltered unsteadily. "But you can go now. I'll be all right. I just want to go to sleep."

Her voice grew low as Ian greeted her words with an indulgent chuckle. She stared as he got to his feet and shrugged out of his jacket, then started to undo his tie.

"Ian, stop!" She started to protest, but she had to struggle against the scream rising in her throat. "Don't, please don't! I need to be alone right now."

"Now that's exactly what you don't need," Ian said complacently as he disposed of his tie and started on the buttons of his shirt. "What you need is some tender loving care, and I'm the man who's going to give it to you."

He smiled an inflexible, rather nasty sort of smile as Sarah, after staring at him incredulously, started to shake her head.

"Come now, Sarah," he said with smooth patience as he continued to unbutton his shirt. "Do you think I don't know what brought all of this on? Do you think I'm blind and deaf and half-witted?" He shook his head chidingly. "You and your friend back at the party are—or have been—intimately involved, right? That was Charles, wasn't it?" During the last sentence an edge had crept into his voice that disturbed Sarah immensely.

"Ian, please," she said, sounding more curt than pleading. "That's none of your business. I've said I want to be alone, and I mean it. Please respect my wishes. I'll be happy to see you tomorrow, but right now I want to be alone!"

"No, Sarah," Ian said with soft finality. He drew off the shirt and as Sarah started to get up, he moved quickly to seat himself on the bed beside her and stop her.

He had a magnificently appealing body, but Sarah was in no mood to appreciate it at the moment, and she drew back as Ian reached a hand to cup her cheek. He interrupted her movement, however, seizing her chin and turning her back to face him.

"I told you I was going to wipe Charles out of your mind, Sarah," he purred nastily. "And I intend to start the process right now. Tomorrow morning some friends of mine are going to drive us to a little hideaway where I'm going to finish the job, and before very much longer you're going to have trouble remembering Charles Trainer's name, much less what he once meant to you."

"No, Ian, stop!" Sarah protested, her tone growing stronger in direct proportion to the fear Ian was starting to inspire in her. But Ian ignored her resistance. His head was coming down toward her and Sarah began frantically to try to scoot away from him.

Ian stopped her by grasping one of her shoulders with such strength that Sarah involuntarily gasped.

"Don't force me to hurt you, darling," Ian said grimly as he contained her struggles and came down on the bed to lie half over her. "I'm a very good lover, and this will be a night to remember, if you'll just relax."

The next few moments were like a living nightmare as Sarah fought Ian with all her might, loathing the touch of his mouth and hands and his frighteningly muscular body. She began to cry as all her struggles proved useless. She was getting weaker and weaker while Ian seemed to get stronger, and she was sickeningly aware that in this battle of strength, he was going to be the winner.

She thought she might faint as Ian started to strip her robe from her, when over his shoulder, through the veil of tears, she saw a dark-haired, dark-eyed stranger enter the room and begin moving toward the bed.

She opened her mouth to scream, and the man quickly raised a finger to his mouth. The scream died while Sarah tried to decide which man posed the bigger threat to her.

The stranger held a cloth in his hand, and as he came closer, Sarah caught the cloying scent of some chemical on the air. Ian must have caught the smell as well, because he started to turn away from her. The stranger grabbed him in mid-turn and held the cloth over Ian's face. Ian reacted violently, but within a matter of seconds he fell into a heap atop Sarah, who frantically started trying to push him off her.

"Don't be afraid," the stranger said quickly, obviously trying to calm her, but Sarah was beyond calm by now. When the stranger pulled Ian off her, she scrambled out from under the inert body and continued off the bed. The stranger quickly moved to intercept her attempt to run out of the bedroom, and Sarah, her eyes wild with fear, gave a soft little moan of terror and started backing away from him.

"Miss Bailey, it's all right," the man said in soothing, calming tones. "I'm not going to hurt you." He started toward her, but seeing Sarah shrink back in terror, he stopped and ran a hand over his hair in frustration.

"Listen, Miss Bailey," he tried again, projecting confident gentleness into his voice. "I work with Charles Trainer. *Charles Trainer,* Miss Bailey," he repeated forcefully when it did not seem to register with Sarah. "Charles asked me to look out for you," he went on, then gestured at the bed where Ian still lay unconscious. "That man isn't what he seems to be. He's not your friend." And as Sarah still stared at him with wide, stricken, uncomprehending eyes, he added exasperatedly, "Well, for God's sake, Miss Bailey, think about what he was trying to do to you! I got here just in time. Surely you don't think I have the same thing in mind Connors did!"

But that was the wrong thing to say, because in Sarah's confused, terrified state of mind she couldn't comprehend Foster's assurances. All she got out of his words was that he was somehow connected with Charles, whom she considered had betrayed her, and that he was discussing rape, which she'd almost just experienced. So she backed away again when Foster started toward her once more.

"I'm sorry, Miss Bailey," he apologized with a resigned look on his face, "but you leave me no choice. I don't have any more time to argue with you." And then he grabbed her, subdued her struggles with an ease that was as frightening as everything else about him, and applied the cloth to her face until she collapsed into his arms.

Foster picked her up and carried her to the bed. He hesitated, his expression displaying distaste at the necessity of putting her down beside Ian Connors, but after giving a disgusted grimace, he did so, before turning away to find some clothes to put in a suitcase for her.

When he was done with the packing at last, he left the room

with the suitcase in his hand, opened the front door of the apartment, handed the suitcase to a young man who stood there waiting, and spoke for a few minutes in a low voice. As he went back inside the apartment to fetch Sarah, the young man began to speak quietly into a communication device he held, and when Foster reappeared with Sarah thrown over his shoulder in a fireman's carry, the young man grinned and said, "The car's ready and waiting downstairs. I'll go ahead and make sure there's no one around to see us leave. Hugo's coming up to get rid of Connors."

Foster nodded and followed the young man at a slower pace. Fortunately, they met no one on the outside, and within a very few minutes Foster had Sarah propped in the back seat of a neutral-colored sedan and was shutting the door behind the two of them. "Get moving!" he instructed the driver in curt tones, and the driver obeyed.

Once they were on their way, Foster settled Sarah more comfortably, then leaned forward to address the man in the passenger seat in the front.

"Did anyone turn up to watch the apartment after we last checked?" he asked tersely, his harried expression showing that he didn't like the hurried, haphazard fashion in which they had had to act.

The man shook his head. "No. I don't understand it, but it looks as though Ian Connors is the only one they had on her. That tap on the lady's phone finally paid off though," he added with a satisfied grin. "Connors made a call from her apartment asking for help in getting her away for a while. Apparently, Trainer scared the hell out of him during that last confrontation back at the party, and since Connors is more of a sneaking weasel than a trained operative, he didn't want to take the chance that Trainer might change his mind and come looking for him."

"Anything else?" Foster asked with an appreciative snort for what he'd heard so far.

"Yeah," the man replied with an edge to his voice. "We don't know precisely who Connors talked to, but they were on the line long enough for us to trace the call. It was to the Zwaholan embassy in Washington. Apparently, Lugubu has one of his men

225

in place there. But that's only to be expected," he added with a shrug.

"Connors had to argue like hell to get the help he wanted," the man then went on. "The man he talked to seemed to think Trainer would fall in line just on the basis of what happened tonight, which is what Trainer was supposed to make Connors think, wasn't it?" He slanted an inquiring look back at Foster, and when Foster nodded, the man shrugged. "Well, I don't know what Trainer did or said to put the fear of God into Connors, but he threatened to pull out of the whole thing completely if he didn't get some help by morning, so the guy he talked to finally agreed to have someone here by early tomorrow to take Connors and the woman away for a while."

The man hitched around and regarded Foster with a cynical smile. "They're going to be a little disappointed when they learn Miss Bailey's disappeared and Connors is snoring away in his rooms." When Foster nodded distractedly, the man went on to say, "You know, somehow I get the feeling Lugubu's pretty short on manpower to attempt something like this. If it was going to take until tomorrow morning to bring in some extra help, I'm not surprised they blew it. We'd have had someone here in ten minutes."

Foster snorted. "Sure, but it might have been a different story if we were working in Zwahola instead of in our own territory. Just be glad Lugubu's the one operating on unfriendly ground." He shook his head thoughtfully, and remarked almost inaudibly, "I don't know how Trainer's stood it all these years. I'm glad my field days are over. I'm too old for . . ." His voice trailed off as he suddenly remembered what Charles had said to him and realized he'd better report to his superiors that Charles Trainer wouldn't be a field man much longer either.

"Pull over at the next public phone booth, Dryson," he instructed the driver, who shrugged and did as he was told.

Foster started to climb out of the car when Dryson pulled in to the curb, then turned back momentarily. "Keep an eye on her," he instructed both men. "I hate to think what her reaction would be if she came to and found herself locked up in a car with a couple of thuggy-looking chumps like you two."

He ignored the looks of mock offense his statement evoked

226

from the two men, got out, and strode to the nearby phone booth where he placed a call to his chief.

Although his colleagues couldn't hear the ensuing conversation, Foster's mood when he got back into the car was foul enough to warn them that things were not going well.

His men gave him one cautious glance, exchanged another one between themselves, and then carefully kept quiet until spoken to.

For three hours the car sped through the night with Foster constantly casting anxious glances at Sarah's pale face. He was wondering if he'd dosed her with too much of the chemical, or if she was allergic to it. He was much relieved when, by the time the car pulled up at a lonely farmhouse in the countryside of New York State, Sarah's color had improved considerably.

She was still sufficiently drugged to be no problem when Foster pulled her out of the car and put her across his shoulder. He then spoke tersely through the window to the man who had been in the passenger seat as Dryson, the driver, climbed out of the car as well.

"When you get back, check to make sure that Hugo took care of Connors, then tell him to get his tail out here."

The man nodded before scooting under the wheel, and Foster turned away to carry Sarah into the farmhouse. Her eyes barely fluttered as he put her down on a bed in a sparsely furnished upstairs bedroom, then closed again in a more natural sleep.

"That's right, you sleep, honey," Foster muttered abstractedly as he removed her robe and then covered her with a quilt. "You're all right now. Nobody's going to hurt you."

He stood over her for a moment as she snuggled down beneath the quilt as though his soothing words had reached and calmed her, and when she had relaxed into a quiet sleep, Foster regarded her with gloomy resignation.

"I'll bet you're going to be a handful when you do wake up, aren't you, honey?" he muttered on a weary sigh. "And I don't envy Trainer one little bit when he tries to explain all of this to you." He turned away and started for the door, but when he reached it, he paused and cast one last envious, almost affectionate glance back at Sarah. "But I do envy that son of a gun for

227

what's he going to get after he's done all that explaining. You're everything I ever imagined you were and then some, sweetheart, and that Trainer is one lucky bastard."

Foster exited the room then and closed the door softly behind him. He shuffled down to the kitchen where Dryson was putting together a meal of bacon and eggs.

"Everything okay?" Dryson ventured to ask hesitantly, obviously not sure as yet whether it was safe to talk to his boss again.

"Ye-ah," Foster replied, a tired yawn interrupting the word. "She's still asleep." He raised his arms in a powerful stretch, then settled down at the table. "When she wakes up, let me handle it. She's going to be ready to take somebody apart, and it might as well be me. The chief's already had a piece of me, and I'm getting used to being chewed out."

Dryson grinned sympathetically as he brought a pot of hot coffee to the round oak table and placed it in front of Foster, who pulled it and a cup and saucer that were already there toward him.

"What about some food to go with that?" Dryson asked as he went back to an old-fashioned gas stove to turn the bacon.

"Might as well," Foster replied glumly before giving another yawn. "I'd better eat good while it's free. I'm liable to be standing in an unemployment line soon, since I hung up on the chief."

Dryson turned and shot him a look of startled surprise, then gave a low whistle of admiration. "How come?" he asked cautiously.

Foster scowled. "I just got sick and tired of being regarded as a machine without any human feelings!" he practically snarled. And at raising his head and seeing that Dryson was regarding him with open-mouthed astonishment, his scowl grew fiercer. "Well, I *am* a human being, you know!" he informed Dryson in a challenging tone that made the younger man turn hastily back to the stove.

"Sure," Dryson said after the silence had stretched just an iota too long. "Sure, Foster," he added more positively, though there was still an element of doubt in his tone that anyone in their line of work could have room for a plethora of human feelings. "We're all human beings," he asserted more strongly as he

228

seemed to think over the question and begin to have some definite opinions about the subject.

Foster bent to his coffee cup without answering, and both men subsided into a silence, each possibly contemplating the task they faced of baby-sitting a detainee, which was usually a long, boring job that wore on the nerves steadily, even if this particular detainee was a beautiful, charming woman.

CHAPTER NINETEEN

Just as the Eastern sky was beginning to pinken slightly, Sarah began to stir a little, aware even in her groggy state that she felt peculiar. Her limbs ached, her mind was foggier than usual, even for this early hour, and she felt a sense of danger prodding her, insisting she wake up and deal with it.

She tried to open her eyes, but it took some doing. Her lids felt as though there were stones lying on top of them, and when she did manage to keep them apart for a few seconds, the dark world surrounding her swam crazily in a disorienting fashion. Furthermore, though she was no more than half awake, she was aware that there was definitely something wrong about those surroundings. She could see almost nothing, but everything felt wrong.

After a long, slow process of gathering her senses together into a stuporous wakefulness, Sarah lay quietly, straining to figure out why the atmosphere in her apartment seemed so different. And as the first faint grayness of dawn crept into the room, she finally realized that she wasn't in her apartment at all. She was in a completely strange bed, in a completely strange room, in a completely strange house.

With that realization her memory of what had happened the night before returned, and Sarah was suddenly wide awake, staring at her surroundings with huge, dilated pupils as the beginnings of panic stirred in her mind. She took several deep breaths to quiet her galloping pulse, while she cautioned herself not to give in to fear.

"Easy, Sarah, easy," she murmured inaudibly. "Going off the deep end is the last thing you need right now." Then she jerked as the faint ringing of a telephone in another part of the house startled her. She lay rigid as the ringing abruptly stopped.

With slow, cautious movements Sarah sat up, then clutched her head as her vision blurred and dizziness overwhelmed her. Gradually the blurring ceased and the dizziness went away, and Sarah eased her legs over the side of the bed.

At last, clutching the headboard of the bed for support, she slowly got to her feet, feeling greatly relieved when her legs cooperated. Then with slow, faltering steps, she moved to where a faint line of light revealed a door. She turned the knob slowly and quietly, and frowned when the door refused to open. It was locked.

The panic started closing in on her again, but Sarah fought it down while she turned to look at the rest of the room. There was a window on the opposite wall, and she crossed to it on tiptoe. A groan almost escaped her throat when, at looking out, she discovered that she was on the second floor of the house, and directly beneath the window was a steep ravine that made the drop, should she be able to open the window, even more precipitous than it would normally have been.

"Okay," Sarah breathed quietly to herself in an attempt to steady her nerves. "It's the door or nothing."

She searched the dim room with her eyes, looking for anything that might help her open the lock. But as she was doing so, the door swung open suddenly, and standing there, looking rumpled and tired and immediately wary, was the dark-haired, dark-eyed man who had invaded her bedroom the night before.

"Oh, good, you're up," the man said calmly. "You're wanted on the phone," he added quickly at seeing Sarah open her mouth. Even Sarah wasn't sure whether she'd laugh hysterically or scream.

"It's Charles Trainer on the phone, Miss Bailey," the man said with wary politeness. "He wants to explain to you why you're here."

He paused to let that sink in, and while Sarah was grappling with the stunned disbelief his words inspired, he stood back and held the door open wider for her. "Will you talk to him, Miss Bailey?" the man asked in almost a pleading tone. "He won't believe you're all right until you tell him."

Sarah closed her mouth, gulped, then nodded, thinking that even if it wasn't Charles on the phone, at least she would get out of this room, which was the first step in getting out of the house altogether. She started toward the man waiting at the door, but he held up a hand and pointed to where her robe lay neatly folded on the foot of the bed.

"Better grab your robe and shoes," he suggested calmly. "It's chilly this morning."

Sarah stopped and shot him a wary glance, thinking her kidnapper's suggestion showed that he wasn't very smart. The shoes and robe would only make it easier for her to run away, which she planned to do at her first opportunity. It didn't matter that she had no idea where she was. Anywhere was better than staying here with this total stranger who had broken into her apartment, drugged her, kidnapped her, and who now seemed to be trying to make her believe nothing unusual had happened the night before.

Remembering the previous night made her think of Ian. "What have you done with Ian Connors?" she asked as she crossed the room and donned her robe. "Is he . . . is he . . ." She couldn't get the words out. Surely this man hadn't killed Ian. Despite what Ian had done the night before, or had almost done, she was almost paralyzed with fear that this man had murdered him.

"Oh, I imagine Mr. Connors is waking up in his own rooms right about now wondering how the hell he got there," the stranger answered with a chuckle that made Sarah relax somewhat—until she remembered that her abductor might be lying. He had seemed almost charming there for a moment, but charm was no indication of a person's innate character, as Ian had shown her. She tensed again as she crossed to the door, guided by the man holding it, and stepped out into a dimly lit hallway that looked as though it belonged in a bygone century.

"How old is this place?" she asked nervously as she spotted the curlicue carving on the stairwell they were descending.

"Maybe one hundred years," the man answered rather apologetically, as though he was ashamed at having to offer her less than superior accommodations.

Encouraged by that attitude, Sarah grew bolder. "Where are

232

we?" she asked, trying to sound casual so that the man might be taken off-guard and answer her before he thought better of it.

It didn't work. The man simply gave her another apologetic smile and shook his head, his dark eyes containing a hint of reproach at her attempt to get around him.

Sarah frowned, and her tone was crisper as she asked the next question. "And who are you?" she demanded, giving the man an up-and-down look that was far from complimentary.

"You can call me Foster," the man answered in a way that made Sarah wonder if that was his real name. But they were at the bottom of the stairs now, and the man, Foster, was gesturing at a small stand. A black telephone sat on the stand with the receiver off the hook. "Over here," Foster directed her. "Trainer's waiting."

Up until that moment Sarah hadn't believed that Charles was on the other end of the line, nor that he could possibly be involved in her kidnapping. But now she did, and the fact made sheer fury boil up inside her, which was reflected in her tone when she snatched up the receiver and snarled into it, "Hello!"

"Sarah!" The emotion in Charles's voice as he said her name caught at Sarah's heart for an instant until she remembered how he had betrayed her and that she couldn't believe anything he said. She opened her mouth to reply in a scathing manner, but Charles interrupted her.

"Thank God you're all right!" he said with such evident relief that Sarah almost fell into the trap of believing he loved her. But only for a moment. Then she concentrated on how he had lied to her, and on the sight of him with that woman, and how he had kissed that woman, and she let loose with a vengeance.

"No thanks to you!" she snarled. "I don't know what makes you think you have the right to talk to me, Charles Trainer, much less have me kidnapped, but let me tell you—"

"Sarah, hush!"

There was such authority in Charles's order, yet it was coupled with such loving undertones, that Sarah found herself obeying him. Her pause gave Charles the opportunity to say what he wanted.

"Sarah, darling, listen closely," Charles went on in that same authoritative manner. "I'm sorry about what's happened, but it was for your own safety. You were in danger, darling. There are people who are trying to get to me through you. They want me to fail at the work I'm doing. We had to get you out of the way for a while."

Sarah's anger was rekindled at the mention of Charles's work, which she felt he had used as an excuse for too many things for far too long.

"How kind of you." She found her voice and it was filled with false sweetness. "But did it ever occur to you that kidnapping is a crime? That I have a business to run and clients and friends who might be just the tiniest bit concerned if I suddenly drop off the face of the earth? That I don't appreciate having my life turned upside down *again* for the sake of you and your god-damned work? And another thing!" She began to gather steam, her voice taking on a grating harshness. "I don't want to hear anything more about how dangerous your work is! You didn't look like you were in any danger last night, unless it was from overstimulation from that woman you were—"

A sudden thought made Sarah break off, a ferocious scowl taking control of her flushed face. "Wait a minute!" she demanded heatedly. "What do you mean *I'm* in danger!" She asked the question with cross suspicion in her voice. She had been too upset to pay attention to much of what Charles had been trying to tell her earlier, and in any event, she wasn't prepared to believe much of anything he said. Still, here she was in a decrepit old farmhouse being guarded by a man who, despite his occasional charm, looked decidedly hard enough not to have spent his life growing roses, and there must be some reason for all this.

She was not prepared to take things on face value, however. "Is this another one of your ploys to justify what you want to do anyway, Charles?" she demanded harshly. "What's the matter, don't you like it when I play your sort of game? Did seeing me with another man make you decide that while you don't want me, you don't want anyone else to have me either?" A certain bleakness crept into her tone at the last, despite her best efforts to keep it scorchingly nasty.

"Sarah," Charles answered, his obvious impatience tempered with regret and, she hoped, with love. "I don't have much time to talk, but I want you to understand one thing. The woman you saw me with last night is a friend, nothing more. I've never loved any woman but you, and I never will. I'm going to spend the next six weeks working my butt off so that I can spend the rest of my life proving that to you. When I saw you last night with Ian Connors, it hurt. But it wasn't only jealousy I was feeling. It was sheer terror that because of me, you might be killed!"

Charles paused to take a breath, and it was obvious to Sarah, despite her distrust of him now, that unless he were a better actor than she thought he was, he was laboring under some very sincere, very strong emotions.

"Anyway," he continued more steadily. "What happened woke me up at last. I've decided I can't take it without you any longer. I'm getting out."

Despite her longing to believe what Charles was telling her, Sarah could only think of his past abandonment.

"Sure," she answered with flat insincerity. "Just like last time."

She heard Charles give a deep sigh before he replied, "Sarah, I'm running out of time. I don't blame you for thinking I'm lying, but when I see you again, I'll convince you I'm not. Meanwhile, just sit tight until I've wrapped things up and can get there."

"For six weeks?" Sarah shrieked disbelievingly. "You can't be serious, Charles! What about my business? What about—"

"I'm sorry, Sarah," Charles responded with what sounded like real regret, but which was nevertheless a firm refusal to yield. "Foster will let you keep in touch with Chelley. Tell her you had a family emergency. Tell her anything you want, except the truth. There's just no other way to handle this other than to keep you out of harm's way until I finish what I started out to do or, rather, get things under way to the point where someone else can carry on."

Charles paused and Sarah started to sputter another protest, but he cut her off. "Sarah, if Ian Connors had had his way, you would have been out of action anyway, and believe me, you'd have liked what he had in mind far less than you're going to dislike staying where you are for a while."

The grimness and the apparent jealousy in Charles's tone was convincing, but Sarah, out of sheer stubbornness, found herself defending Ian despite what he'd attempted the night before.

"What do you know about Ian Connors?" she challenged Charles with sulky defensiveness. "He was very . . . ah . . . kind to me, and . . ." She sputtered to a stop as her memory of Ian's attempted rape robbed her statement of the veracity she'd intended to give it. In any event, Charles was not prepared to listen to any defense of Ian Connors.

"That bastard is the scum of the earth," he grated so harshly that Sarah winced at hearing him sound so bitter. "If I could get my hands on him, I'd kill him for what he tried to do to you last night, Sarah, so don't talk like that about him to me!"

Sarah bit her lip at learning that Charles knew what Ian had tried to do. She would have much preferred to keep that knowledge to herself, but she supposed it was unrealistic to ask that Foster would feel the same. Charles went on, and Sarah shivered at the deadly coldness in his voice.

"The only thing stopping me from taking Connors apart piece by piece is that I'd rather spend my life with you than behind prison bars, Sarah. That's where he belongs, by the way, but since there are reasons why we have to keep his part in this quiet, I'm going to settle for getting him run out of the country with no chance of ever getting back in." He took a deep breath to calm himself, and when he continued, his voice was quieter, but no less grim. "Forget Ian Connors, Sarah. You're not going to see him again, and you're lucky you're not. In fact, he's luckier than he deserves to get off as easily as he's going to."

Sarah could think of nothing to say to Charles, in view of his present mood, that wouldn't make things worse, and when he paused, she remained silent, though the glance she gave Foster, who still stood within hearing distance and who was now shaking his head at her as though he couldn't believe that she had actually defended Ian Connors to Charles of all people, was wary and anxious.

"Sarah?" Charles was back to normal now, or at least reasonably so, and Sarah let out her breath in relief before answering.

"Yes?" she responded cautiously.

"Just remember that I love you, Sarah," Charles said, dropping his tone into one of such loving intimacy that Sarah's eyes moistened with tears. "Be patient, darling," he continued. "I'll come for you in six weeks." He paused, and then with a soft, teasing chuckle, he added, "Keep busy thinking up what you want to name our first child. I promise you it won't be long before we have one. I'm through paying dues to other people. I'm ready to have a life of my own, and I want you to share it with me."

Sarah swallowed down a lump that had risen in her throat. She knew she shouldn't fall into the same trap Charles had once spun so well, but she was unable to challenge him further after hearing that tone in his voice. She wasn't sure as yet that she could believe him, but since there was nothing she could do at the moment except do as he asked, she remained silent.

"Sarah, I need to hear you say you love me too," Charles urged her with gentle persistence. "Do you? Please tell me I haven't lost you to that—" He abruptly cut off what he'd been about to call Ian, but Sarah could imagine what he'd been about to say.

Helpless against the entreaty in his voice and the truth of her own feelings, Sarah said the only thing she could. "I . . . I still love you, Charles," she answered with something approaching despair in her tone. "I'm not sure I trust you, but I do love you," she finished quietly.

"I'm so glad," Charles said, soft relief in his voice. "And you will learn to trust me again, darling," he said with utter certainty. "We were made for each other, remember? There are no games between us. There never will be."

"If . . . if you say so," was all Sarah could give him as encouragement.

It seemed enough for Charles, and though he sounded extremely weary when he spoke again, he also sounded immensely relieved and expectant as he drew the conversation to a close.

"It won't be long now, Sophie," he promised, using his special name for her for the first time during the conversation. His tone lightened to humor as he added, "And don't give Foster too hard a time, will you? He's risked a lot for us, and we have a lot to thank him for. He deserves some sympathy and cooperation."

Sarah shot a belligerent look at Foster, who was lounging in a nearby doorway trying to look as though he wasn't hanging on

237

to every one of Sarah's words and wishing he could hear Charles's side of the conversation.

"I'm not making any promises," Sarah responded somewhat sourly. "It's a little hard to be nice to a man who drugs and kidnaps you!"

She was gratified to see Foster's head snap up, indicating without a doubt that he was listening. Furthermore, his somewhat shamed and defensive look disclosed that he was feeling guilty about the tactics he'd had to use to get her here. Sarah smiled at him with false sweetness, and he hung his head and began to fidget with a nail file he'd pulled out of his pocket.

Charles, however, was upset by her words. "Honey, I'm sorry about that," he said with weary regret. "Foster wouldn't have done it if he'd had any choice in the matter, but he said you were hysterical."

"I was not!" Sarah bristled immediately into indignant self-defense before backing off slightly. "I was just a little . . . ah . . . upset," she finished weakly.

"And with good reason," Charles retorted, grimness returning to his voice. "God, if Foster had been one minute later—" He stopped, obviously struggling for control of his rage, and Sarah hastened to short-circuit the emotion she had aroused without meaning to.

"It didn't happen, Charles!" she interjected sharply. And then she repeated more quietly, "It didn't happen. Remember that, darling." The endearment slipped out, and Sarah, at hearing herself say it, frowned at realizing how strongly Charles was still embedded in her heart.

"It's the only thing keeping me sane," Charles answered bleakly. "That and concentrating on our future." And after a momentary hesitation he added softly, "I've got to go now, darling. If you need to contact me, you can do so through Foster, but it will take some time, and—"

"I know," Sarah interrupted, weary resignation tinged with disgust in her tone. "And it had better be extremely important or Foster won't take the trouble to bother you at all." The slight sarcasm with which she spoke made Foster stare at her with an apology in his eyes. He shrugged in resignation, and Sarah turned her back on him.

"Sarah," Charles chided her gently.

"Never mind," Sarah said fatalistically. "I'm beginning to learn the rules of the game by heart." Then she relented somewhat as she sensed Charles's distress over the phone. "Well, I'll see you in six weeks then, I suppose," she said, striving for breezy unconcern, which was spoiled when her voice broke in the middle as she realized this would be the last contact she would have with Charles for some time.

"I love you, darling," he said, quietly sincere.

"I—I love you too, Charles," Sarah answered, equally sincere, but almost hating herself and him because of it.

They each murmured good-bye, and Sarah hung on to the phone until she heard the dial tone. She hung up then, but still she stood with head bowed, trying to fight the tears that were welling behind her lids. She felt a warm hand on her shoulder and stiffened slightly as she swung her head up to look into Foster's sympathetic eyes.

"How about a cup of coffee?" he asked gently. "There's some made in the kitchen."

Sarah nodded, turning to accompany him there. Then she stopped and looked up at him in consternation. "What time is it?" she demanded urgently.

"Don't worry," he assured her, understanding without being told what was on her mind. "You've got another hour before you need to call your secretary."

Sarah sagged with relief, and as they started toward the kitchen again, Foster asked curiously, "What are you going to tell her?"

"I don't know," Sarah responded with a shrug. "I guess I'll have to make up some desperately ill relative, though I think I told her once I didn't have any that close." She shrugged dispiritedly again. "Maybe she wasn't listening."

"You'll think of something," Foster said confidently as he escorted her through a door into a rather dreary kitchen that looked as though no one had taken any trouble with it for at least 50 of the 100 years it may have been in existence.

When Foster saw Sarah's unhappy glance at her surroundings, he apologized again. "We don't use this place much," he said glumly. "And when we do, the occupants aren't usually the type who—" He broke off and looked at the faded paint on the walls, at the decrepit hutch in one corner, and at the scarred oak table in the center of the room. "It's a mess, isn't it?" he commented unnecessarily. "Funny, I never noticed before how bad it is," he mused apologetically.

Sarah smiled at him, finding it impossible to remain at odds with him when it was obvious he was uncomfortable enough with his role in all this.

"Don't worry about it," she said, struggling for cheerfulness. "It's no worse than some of the dressing rooms I had to put up with in my acting days."

She almost couldn't contain a laugh when she saw a startled, appreciative look come into Foster's dark eyes at her change of attitude, and then when his look changed to puzzlement, she smiled wryly to herself, realizing he had no way of knowing she was an expert at making the best of a bad situation. But at the same time she knew she'd go crazy cooped up here for six weeks if she didn't find something to do with herself, and she was already searching desperately in her mind for something to do to alleviate the boredom that would soon set in.

"Where's that coffee?" she asked, giving Foster a bland smile that was belied by the flashing light of determination in her gold-flecked eyes. "And what about breakfast? I'm starved!"

Foster went to the hutch to extract a cup and saucer, but Sarah noticed he kept giving her those puzzled, uncertain looks over his shoulder. Well, if he was puzzled by her behavior now, she thought grimly, it was nothing to what he was going to feel before she got through with him. He was all she had to work out her frustration on over the next six weeks, and she intended to use at least part of her time finding out some things she felt she had every right to know.

A second later she found out Foster wasn't to be her only companion during those forthcoming weeks, however, and she jumped a foot when an unfamiliar voice greeted Foster from behind her. "Morning, Foster. Where's the coffee?"

Sarah swung around to find herself looking up at a huge young blond giant with the features of a boxer who hadn't learned to duck very successfully in the ring. She stared at him in alarm, then relaxed somewhat when he gave her a shyly crooked smile. "Morning, Miss Bailey. You feeling all right today?"

"Ah, yes, thank you, Mr. er . . ." She raised her eyebrows, indicating that she didn't know the man's name, and Foster took the hint and introduced the two of them.

"This is Hugo, Miss Bailey. He helped . . . er . . . kidnap you last night."

The blond giant looked offended at Foster's way of putting what had happened, and Sarah relaxed.

"Don't look so put out," she said with dry humor. "If anyone has a right to be offended, it's me."

As Hugo looked at her dubiously, Dryson walked into the room, and being a tad more sophisticated than Hugo, his greeting was accompanied by an unrepentant grin. "Ah, I see Sleeping Beauty is awake," he teased good-humoredly. Then he made a show of inspecting Foster for damages. "Doesn't look like she took off too many strips, Foster," he drawled cheerfully. "You ought to recover in no time."

Foster grinned a little sheepishly. "Trainer deflected most of the blows," he commented dryly. And then he turned to Sarah. "This is Dryson, Miss Bailey." He introduced the newcomer. "He's okay as long as you don't believe half of what he says."

Sarah smiled sweetly, unable to resist the opportunity Foster had handed her on a platter. "Oh, but isn't that a prerequisite for the sort of work you men do?" she said innocently, making all three men give her rueful, wincing looks, which she ignored. "How do you do, Dryson?" She then acknowledged the introduction blandly. And at his nod, given with a dancing look of respect in his eyes, she inspected him thoroughly.

He was shorter than Hugo, with the build of a Mack truck. There wasn't an ounce of spare flesh on him, and despite that dancing sparkle in his clear blue eyes, he looked every bit as formidable as his companions.

"My, my," Sarah commented thoughtfully. "I wouldn't have thought it would take three of you to keep an eye on me. Did you have the mistaken idea I was an amazon or something?"

Foster looked slightly uncomfortable at her question, and Sarah felt a chill as she realized these men were here for her protection, not to keep her from running away. So apparently

241

she *was* in danger, just as Charles had said, and the knowledge, aside from frightening her, made her more determined than ever to find out more about what was going on.

Dryson covered nicely. "We just like to make sure we have enough people on hand to play a game of bridge," he said with mocking blandness. "It gets boring around here, and we have to find things to distract us."

Sarah let that go, ignoring the slight flirtatiousness in Dryson's teasing reply. She shrugged and pretended to accept the answer he'd given. "Well, I'm in the mood to be distracted by breakfast," she said firmly. "Who's doing the cooking?"

There followed a session of cheerful persuasion on the men's part, and a lot of discussion of women's rights on Sarah's part before she finally convinced them the cooking chores were definitely going to be shared. Foster then pulled rank and instructed Dryson to do the honors, which the man did after a great deal of good-natured griping. After breakfast, Hugo and Dryson departed to make a tour of the grounds, and after the two men had left and Foster turned back to Sarah, who still sat at the kitchen table fiddling with a now empty coffee cup, Sarah raised eyes from which all humor had departed.

"I have to call Chelley in a minute, Foster," she said with level determination. "But when I get back, you and I are going to have a little talk."

Foster withdrew a little, but at seeing the absolute resolve to have her way in Sarah's steady brown eyes, he relaxed a little and shrugged, though his eyes were displaying a distinct caution. "I'll tell you what I can, Miss Bailey," he said matter-of-factly, "but I have to warn you, it won't be much."

"That's what you think," Sarah muttered in a flat tone as she got to her feet and slammed her coffee cup down on the table. She started to leave the room, but paused at the door to turn back and deliver a parting shot.

"And stop calling me Miss Bailey. My name is Sarah! Use it from now on!"

With that, she departed the room, every line in her lovely body displaying a fine temper and a dogged purposefulness that made Foster blink with alarm. After a moment he sighed heavily, then went to fix another pot of coffee in preparation for what looked like a rather lengthy interrogation he would have preferred not to face. He had the uneasy feeling it was going to take all his skill to avoid or circumvent the questions Sarah Bailey was going to pose, and he found himself thinking rather wistfully of the days when all a man in his line of work had to worry about was dodging a few bullets or remaining strong under physically rougher, but possibly less effective, methods of interrogation. He hadn't been trained to combat Sarah's brand, composed of gentle humor, charming sweetness, and a ruthlessness that would have done credit to an agent of the KGB.

CHAPTER TWENTY

"Your father would be disappointed in you, Charles," Njomo said stiffly. He was obviously having trouble keeping a tight rein on his autocratic temper, and his own disappointment over Charles's decision showed in every imperious line of his small body.

Charles regarded the old man steadily. He had expected Njomo to pull out all stops in trying to get him to change his mind about leaving Zwahola, and so far he hadn't been disappointed. Njomo had run the gamut of his considerable arsenal of manipulative techniques, and was now becoming angry in the face of Charles's intransigence.

"Would he?" Charles replied to Njomo's statement, quiet reflection in his voice. "I'm not so sure, Grandfather. It's true that my father dedicated his own life to what he saw as his duty, but the substance of that duty, as he saw it, was the principle of letting every person choose for himself or herself how to live their lives."

Charles moved slightly to ease his cramped muscles. It had been a long session so far, and it didn't look as though it were anywhere near being over yet. Then he continued speaking, keeping his tone level and quiet.

"I remember my father telling me once that some men were destined to give their whole lives in dedication to a cause, while some men would give a part of themselves and no more. And then there are always those who will give nothing at all."

Charles's blue gaze was calmly accepting of his own course as he spelled it out for Njomo. "I'm one of those who can give a part and no more, Grandfather," he said gently. "I'm not my father. And while I thought, at one time, that I could follow his

244

example, experience has shown me that sacrificing my own needs and desires is one thing. Sacrificing the safety of someone I love is quite another."

Njomo's disagreement was evident in the gesture of negation he gave of Charles's reasoning. "But she is only a woman," he complained. "And she is safe now, you tell me. Can she not remain safe while you do your work?"

Charles's lids drooped slightly in weary frustration. He had been working almost around the clock for six weeks now, and this last bit of clearing up—his interview with Njomo—before he could go to Sarah, was proving to be even harder than he'd expected. Wisely he decided to leave the question of Sarah out of things from here on, since Njomo would never understand how a man could let a woman mean so much to him. He seized instead on Njomo's reference to his work.

"The work will go on without me, Grandfather," he said patiently. "Everything is in motion, and it will go forward. The bank loans and the contract with World Oil have been renegotiated in Zwahola's favor, and as a result Lugubu has been neutralized for the time being."

Charles took a breath, then continued to enumerate the things he had set in motion over the last difficult six weeks. "I've left detailed instructions for my successor," he went on. "Some of the measures will be rough, such as the devaluation of the currency, the freeze on wages, a new round of price increases, and a decrease in imports. But if Hwala is serious about turning things around, they'll have to be done. And if he wants to stay in power, he'll do them. I had a long talk with him, and I think I was able to make him understand that short-term thinking isn't going to work any longer. The days when the money flowed in by the bucket are over."

"Bah!" Njomo dismissed Hwala's understanding with a wave of his hand. "At the first sign of dissent, Hwala will cave in like a riverbank at the height of the rains. The first riot will have him promising the moon to the people!" He gave Charles a coaxing, almost pleading look of entreaty that was enhanced by his frailty. "But if you were here to keep him strong, perhaps he could be persuaded to remain firm."

Charles shook his head, his gaze steady and unyielding. "I am not Zwahola's savior, Grandfather," he said with gentle force. "The measures to take are clear, but it's up to Zwaholans to take them. Your destiny is in your own hands. I've done all I can."

When Njomo looked as though he was far from accepting Charles's view, Charles decided to use some of Njomo's own manipulative techniques.

"It was you who taught me that, Grandfather," he said with quiet respect. "You have always said Zwahola should not rely on the superpowers for anything, but should develop its own inner strength and resources. I am a citizen of one of the superpowers. You have citizens of your own who are capable of taking up the fight now. My successor is one of them. He may be young, but he is well trained, and I've made every effort to include him on all the planning. He knows what has to be done, and I think he has the courage and intelligence to do it."

Njomo's black eyes flashed with anger for an instant. Then, as he accepted the fact that Charles had effectively turned the tables on him for once, they began to gleam with grudging respect. Finally his thin mouth curved into a reluctant smile.

"You have learned your lessons well, my son." He admitted his defeat with thin humor.

Charles bowed his head in a gesture of respect. "Yes, Grandfather," he agreed quietly. "And one of the most important things you've taught me is to go after what *I* want. I intend to do that now. I almost waited too long to put my own desires first."

"A woman!" Njomo shook his head with bewilderment.

Charles smiled at Njomo indulgently. "Not just a woman," he said softly. "My other half. A man is no good to anyone when part of him is missing."

That, Njomo could understand, though he didn't apply it in the same way Charles did. "True," he agreed, eyeing Charles thoughtfully, as though he were beginning to realize for the first time what Charles had been trying to tell him all along. Then Njomo smiled reminiscently. "Ah, well," he said from the vast experience of old age, "you are young. Perhaps someday when the fever leaves your blood, you will be back."

"Perhaps," Charles said doubtfully. "But I'm hoping you won't ever need me again," he added with a light touch of humor. "Surely you wish that for your country also, Grandfather?"

The old man smiled slyly, his eyes twinkling at Charles's subtle point. "Yes," he allowed with an emphatic shake of his head. "That is exactly what I wish, though any nation can always use good men of your caliber."

The old man gave a sigh of resignation then and fixed Charles with a look of affection mingled with petulance. "You realize this may be the last time we have such a talk as this, my son?" he asked in a quavering, pitiful tone.

"I realize that, Grandfather," Charles replied with soft regret, his own clear blue eyes returning the affection if not the petulance.

"I will miss you," Njomo said, the quaver becoming more pronounced.

"As I will you," Charles responded. But then he smiled, his look gently teasing. "But you will soon have blood grandsons to replace me, won't you?" he said suggestively, his smile turning to a grin as Njomo brightened.

"Ah, yes!" he responded eagerly. "Yetunde has told you then that Kinte has managed to place his bait carefully?"

Charles nodded, then laughed. "Yes, she is definitely intrigued by Kinte's reserve where she is concerned. Ajayi comes less and less into her conversation, while Kinte carves his own space relentlessly. I have the feeling it won't be long before you can suggest a marriage without Yetunde going into a fit of screaming hysterics."

Njomo tittered, looking like a small boy with a delicious secret. "Did I not tell you I know best?" he asked with complacent self-satisfaction. "I know people, Charles. It has always been my strength." But then he looked at Charles with grudging respect and muttered, "Though even I can miscalculate upon occasion." And that remark was as close as he would ever come to admitting he had done so where Charles was concerned.

He held out a trembling, aged hand for Charles to take. Charles did so, and the resultant clasp was warm and strong, affectionate and respectful, on the part of both men.

"Go then, my son," Njomo concluded. "Perhaps your father's God will be merciful, and we will meet again in the spirit world."

"I hope so," Charles agreed, his voice tightening with emotion. "Farewell, Grandfather. Take care of yourself. Your memory will always rest in my heart."

Njomo nodded, his old eyes filming slightly with tears before he dropped them to preserve his dignity.

Charles got to his feet, hesitated, then turned on his heel to leave the presence of the man who had been almost as much of a father to him as his real father had been.

Once he was back out in Zwahola's hot, burning sunlight, however, Charles's mouth twisted into an anticipatory smile, and his step was eager as he made his way back to his quarters to finish the last bit of packing he had to do before he could board a plane to the States—and to Sarah.

And on the other side of the world, Sarah herself sat in a patch of autumn sunlight on a grassy hillock behind the farmhouse where she had spent the last six weeks preserving her sanity by working on an experimental play she had long had in the back of her mind, and working on Foster to force him to dispense with his professional reserve and tell her things she wanted to know.

She had started out bluntly. "Did you recruit Charles, Foster?" Her no-nonsense tone was intended to inform Foster that she wasn't a complete innocent about Charles's work.

He had looked startled for an instant before warily shaking his head, a mask descending over his face and eyes that was second nature to him.

"No," was his brief answer.

"Who did?" Sarah then asked.

"I can't tell you that," Foster responded, a sigh escaping him despite his best efforts. It was the first of many such sighs he was to give before Sarah was done with him, and for a man not given to sighing, he soon developed a remarkable repertoire of them that Sarah learned to read like a book. They ranged all the way from mild annoyance to deep despair.

"All right." Sarah learned immediately to accept his flat "I can't tell you's" as a matter of course, since nothing would break through Foster's resistance when he answered in that way. It was his "perhaps" and "maybe" and "probably not" replies that she attacked with dedicated fervor.

"Then did you train him?" She launched another question.

248

"Perhaps," had been Foster's cautious reply, which Sarah interpreted the same as yes.

The interrogation had proceeded throughout the weeks they had been cooped up together, and whether through sheer persistence, or the eventual winning of Foster's trust, Sarah finally began to get some meaningful answers. She pondered one of those answers now as she shifted to lie on her back and squint up at the blue cloud-bedotted sky above her.

She had asked Foster once if Charles was good at his undercover work, and Foster had pondered long and hard over his answer while Sarah waited patiently for it. At last he had answered slowly and thoughtfully.

"He's one of the best I've ever seen. He could have been *the* best, if . . ."

"If?" Sarah had prompted.

Foster had shrugged. "It's hard to explain to a civilian," he had hedged.

"Try," Sarah had persisted.

Foster had given one of his loudest sighs then, but he had answered. "His heart's not in it," he started out cautiously, then began to warm to his subject. "It's all sort of like a game, Sarah." And as she had given him a patently skeptical look, he had insisted. "All right, so it's a dangerous game, but sometimes the only way to go about it is to treat it like a game. Otherwise, you might freeze up."

He had then given her another cautious look, as though wondering if he might frighten her, but as Sarah had looked back at him with steady interest, he had continued.

"Charles went at it like a job," he went on. "Like something he had no real taste for, but just something that had to be accomplished." Foster shook his head and fumbled for the words to explain what he meant. "He's too . . . ah . . . decent for the work, I suppose. He had a real problem with the deception involved in it. He did it all right, and he always got what he went after, but he didn't enjoy doing it. Do you see what I mean?"

Sarah had just looked at him, and Foster had sighed again. "Trainer liked the real part of his work—the financial part— more than he did the cloak-and-dagger part. The only reason he agreed to work for us in the first place was that his recruiter was a master at psychology—at putting on the pressure. We wanted Trainer badly. He had all the qualifications we needed. He spoke the language, he knew the culture, and he had a first-rate mind— the ability to think on his feet. And after he got his degree in economics, we were able to slip him into Zwahola with a perfect cover."

"Working for World Oil," Sarah had inserted dryly. And at Foster's wary nod, she had encouraged him to go on.

"The only problem with him," Foster continued, "was his distaste for lying and his feeling that he was betraying the trust of his friends in Zwahola." Foster had hesitated slightly before adding, "Well, there was also the fact that some of the people he had to work with were pretty low in the ethics department, and he didn't like that much either."

"So you people are happy with Charles's contribution?" she had asked thoughtfully.

"Happy?" Foster had snorted. "That's too tame a word for it. He's been a gold mine for us." His expression had turned woebegone then, however. "We're sure going to miss him. He's going to leave a very large gap when he drops out."

Sarah had stared at him with thoughtful interest. "Drops out," she repeated his way of putting it. "Is that how you look at it, Foster? That sounded judgmental."

Foster had looked slightly uncomfortable then, but he had answered honestly in accordance with his own thinking. "Yeah, sort of," he had answered with subdued belligerence.

"You don't think over five years of his life is enough to give?" Sarah had bristled slightly. "That's longer than most men serve in the armed forces, isn't it?" And when Foster hadn't answered, Sarah had challenged him in stronger terms. "And he's been under a constant strain all that time. It's easy for you to condemn him when you're able to sit out here in the country taking your ease, isn't it?" She had gestured wildly around the room they were in to prove her point. "Charles has been in a foreign country all this time putting his life on the line every second of the day and night!"

It had been Foster's turn to bristle then. "Hey, I served my time in—" He had had to catch himself up before he revealed exactly where he had served. "In the field," he had finished jerkily. "I haven't always had to spend my off-duty hours chasing after some female in an effort to pacify some poor guy so he'd have peace of mind enough to do his job, and I haven't always had to baby-sit that same woman for weeks at a time for the same reason!"

Sarah had stared at him, confused and alarmed. "What are you talking about, Foster?" she had asked in a puzzled way.

"Nothing!" Foster had tried to backtrack fast, but he had been unsuccessful. His very reaction had made Sarah increasingly suspicious.

"Out with it, Foster!" she had demanded and he had burst out with the truth.

"Why do you think he showed up on your doorstep after all this time?" Foster had practically yelled at her. "Because I kept track of you and sent him reports, that's why! He knew you weren't married. He even knew all about your love life—or your lack of one after that one fellow. That's why he thought he had a chance with you again," he had finished on a quieter note, obviously feeling guilty at having said as much as he had.

Sarah had drawn herself up in shock for a moment, feeling as though her private life had been suddenly displayed on the evening news for everyone's enjoyment. After a while, with Foster's help, she had been able to gather her dignity together again. He was obviously feeling ashamed of his outburst, both on professional and personal grounds.

"Ah, Sarah," he had pleaded disgustedly. "Trainer needed something. It tore him apart to give you up. We needed his mind on his business, so I volunteered to keep tabs on you from time to time. We didn't bug your apartment or anything like that during those years." Sarah didn't notice his hesitation over the last three words and she didn't see the guilty look on his face that would have told her that qualification wasn't always the case, at least not lately. "I just . . . ah . . . checked on you occasionally," Foster finished on a weak note.

Sarah had given him her frostiest glare and had been about to question him further before she decided that she really didn't want to know just how thoroughly Foster had invaded her private life. But it was definitely disconcerting to realize that this man, though she'd actually grown fond of him, had been privy to such a large part of her life for such a long time, though it was equally reassuring to know that Charles had been telling the truth when he'd said he'd never stopped loving her. Why else would he have kept up Foster's surveillance?

She had changed the subject then, focusing on more recent events and learning more about Ian Connors. The realization that Ian had lied to her from beginning to end was not a particularly pleasant one, but since Sarah had no real interest in him any longer, she accepted the knowledge philosophically.

But now, as she lay staring up at the sky and facing her future and some hard decisions, a deep sigh escaped her.

Despite her protests to Foster that Charles had given enough of himself to duty, and despite Foster's assessment that Charles was too "decent" for undercover work, the facts were that Charles was good at it, he was needed, and the only reason he was giving it up was to assure her safety.

Sarah sighed heavily and turned over onto her stomach to rest her head on her crossed arms. With her eyes closed she wrestled with a solution to the quandary. Short of hiring a full-time bodyguard and living in fear for the rest of her life, she could think of nothing she could do to release Charles from the burden of feeling responsible for her safety. She loved her work and was not prepared to give it up for the dubious security of working at something she hated, in some little out-of-the-way place she hated, in the hope that Charles's enemies couldn't find her again.

But didn't Charles love his work too? Sarah frowned in concentration, because now she was at the heart of the issue. Foster thought Charles didn't love his work—at least not the undercover part of it. And Charles had been going to give it up when he had reappeared in her life all those weeks ago, hadn't he?

Sarah's eyes popped open and her heart rate picked up as she remembered that fact. If it were true that Charles was coming to her out of love, without making a tremendous sacrifice on her behalf, she could be happy. Happy? She scoffed at such a tame way of putting what she would feel. Ecstatic would be a better way of putting it. It would be like finding the pot of gold at the end of the rainbow.

She sat up and rested her chin on her updrawn knees, trying to contain the excitement that coursed through her veins at just the thought of finally belonging completely to Charles and having him belong completely to her. She didn't trust expectations of that sort any longer. She had been disappointed too many times in the past.

Too, there was the matter of her own patriotism to be considered. She was the only thing standing in the way of Charles's valued service to their country. And while she had once told Charles that she would never put duty above him, now that she was faced with the prospect, she didn't feel so positive that she was worth putting her own needs and desires above what was best for the majority. At the same time, however, she wasn't at all sure she could do as Charles had done and give up everything, drop out of sight completely in fact, so that her country would have the benefit of Charles's services.

"God!" she said on a weary sigh as she felt overwhelmed by the choices facing her. "Why me?"

Well, she thought, as she got to her feet and brushed the grass and twigs from her jeans, so much for decision-making. It would be impossible to decide anything until she saw and talked to Charles and discovered for herself how he really felt about all this.

Since it was time to start dinner, she returned to the farmhouse to check on the spaghetti sauce she'd left simmering and to prepare the pasta to go with it. No one was around when she entered the kitchen, and she was glad as she donned an apron and began to stir the large pot of sauce. She wasn't in a mood for putting on a happy face and chatting as though her whole life wasn't about to be decided on what happened within the next day or so.

As she stirred the sauce she heard a car coming up the lane to the farmhouse, and she frowned, wondering who on earth it could be since she knew Foster, Hugo, and Dryson hadn't gone anywhere, and it wasn't time for Charles to be arriving.

She was disgusted when she felt a clutch of fear twist her stomach as she remembered some of the things Foster had told her about Ian Connors and people like him. But surely Ian was out of the country by now, and even if he wasn't, how could he know about this place?

"Foster?" she called out, uncertain whether he was in the

house or outside. She hated the small quiver of fear in her voice as she called, but she couldn't seem to shake the panic beginning to curl in her stomach.

There was no answer from Foster, and Sarah nervously wiped her hands on her apron as she went to peer out the window. The car was almost at the house, and Sarah didn't recognize it, nor did she recognize the two men in the front seat, even though she couldn't see them clearly.

"Foster!" she called louder this time, and when she still got no answer, she swung on her heel to go to the hallway outside the kitchen. "Hugo? Dryson?" she called, then waited for an answer which never came.

Biting her full lower lip against the panic that was growing steadily, Sarah went back to the kitchen to check on the car again. It had just come to a stop, and one of the back doors was opening. Sarah held her breath, and then as she saw Charles climbing out of the back seat, she froze where she was, her pupils dilated into huge dark circles as she looked at the one man in all the world who had the power to affect her like this.

Dimly, she took in the fact that Foster was approaching the car from around one corner of the house while Hugo did the same from the other corner. She should have been relieved that the two of them had been doing their job after all, but she was beyond such considerations. Her heart was pounding with such force, she felt as if her whole body were vibrating to its rhythm. She was finding it hard to breathe as well, and her mouth was beginning to tremble.

She watched, dazed, as Charles talked to Foster and Hugo for a few moments before reaching into the back of the car for his suitcase, and her state of chaos increased as she realized that even as Charles had been speaking to the two men, his eyes kept returning again and again to the farmhouse as though he were looking for something or someone.

With a start Sarah realized he was probably expecting her to run to greet him. Should she? she wondered. She wanted to with all her heart. Every inch of her body was crying out to him, wanting his large, warm, comforting body against her while his arms held her tight.

But she continued to stand where she was, somehow reluctant

254

to see what his eyes would tell her, hear what would be in his voice, perhaps feel a certain reluctance in that embrace she longed for so wholeheartedly.

The men were moving toward the house now, while the car that had brought Charles backed up and started moving away. Sarah gulped and lifted a hand to run it over her wind-tousled hair. She looked down at herself and gasped as she saw the sauce-stained apron around her waist. She reached down and tried to take the apron off, but her hands were trembling so much that she succeeded only in tangling the ties into such a knot, they would have defeated an experienced sailor.

Defeated by the apron, Sarah raised her hands to the comfortable, shabby old sweater Foster had packed for her in his rush to get her out of her apartment. She clutched folds of the beige material in her hands as she gave a small moan of distress at her appearance, thinking that if Charles had been reluctant to give up his work for her before now, he would be twice as reluctant once he saw her in this getup.

The back screen door creaked and Sarah tensed, her large eyes focused on the wooden inner door in horrified fascination. Her breathing stopped altogether when she heard Charles speaking to the two other men, the deep tones of his beloved voice mesmerizing her where she stood.

"Give us a few moments alone, will you, Foster?" he said with barely concealed impatience in his tone.

Sarah heard Foster mutter something in reply, and then her heart jumped as Charles crossed the last barrier between them. He stepped across the threshold, dropped his suitcase on the floor, and slammed the door behind him so quickly, Sarah could barely take in the fact that he was finally here . . . right now! . . . standing across the room looking at her out of red-rimmed, hazy blue eyes set in a face so drawn and haggard-looking that Sarah gasped.

"Sarah . . ." Her name on his lips was like a sigh of homecoming that leapt from the depths of his broad chest and sprang across the room to envelop her in a wave of intimacy.

"Charles . . ." she choked out in an echo of his tone. And then they were moving toward each other as though they were each being reeled in on an invisible tether that was as strong as steel, yet as delicate as silk.

Charles's strong arms enfolded Sarah, and she gasped at the strength in them as he lifted her off her feet for a moment and buried his head in the warm hollow of her neck while he muttered her name over and over again against her smooth skin. She clung to him, feeling momentarily disoriented from the dizziness of the emotions that raged through her like a forest fire.

The feel of him was so overpoweringly invasive, she wondered how she had lived all these weeks without his touch to spark life into her soul and body. The smell of him was like incense. It went to her head and increased her dizziness. And the sound of her name on his lips affirmed her being, as though she existed only when he was there to acknowledge the fact that she did.

And then she was sliding down him as he let her find her feet again, but he didn't let her go, and she couldn't have stood unaided if he had.

"My beautiful Sophie," he muttered, and his mouth found hers and possessed it totally, as though he himself couldn't exist without the sustenance to be found within the warm, dark interior. Sarah's head lolled back under the pressure of that kiss, and Charles's large hand came up to support it so that he could increase the pressure. He hadn't shaved in some time, and the bristles on his face penetrated her delicate skin, but Sarah was unaware of any pain. She was unaware of anything but the solid, exciting warmth of his body straining against hers, the moist hotness of his seeking tongue, and the reassuring firmness of his muscles under her hands.

When neither of them could stand another second without oxygen, Charles broke the kiss and drew back slightly, but only for an instant. Then his lips were roaming hers again, sliding, sipping, draining, the breath from her lips as he took his fill of what Sarah offered, then returned in full measure.

His hands slid down to her firm, rounded bottom, and he lifted her into the hollow of his hips to tuck her against the raging heat flaming there, straining to break the barrier of his clothing and make her wholly his.

"God, Sophie!" Charles murmured in strangled tones between kisses. "I thought I remembered what it felt like to hold you like this." Then his mouth found hers for another draining kiss, and Sarah understood what he had meant, for it was the same with her. Memory was no substitute at all for the reality of this, and perhaps it was a blessing that that was true. She didn't think she could have stood their separation otherwise.

The sound of Foster's and Hugo's voices outside the door finally intruded on the intimate spell Charles and Sarah were weaving and slowly, reluctantly, Charles put a tiny amount of space between them, though their mouths still clung in hungry, stinging greed for the taste of each other.

At last they stood a bare few inches apart, brown eyes and blue taking inventory with the same greed their mouths had displayed. "This is the first time I've felt all of a piece since we parted," Charles said on a shaking breath. "The first time I've been certain that you were really safe."

Sarah ignored the tiny darting chill his remark aroused in her, and her eyes were soft with loving care as she took in his haggard appearance. "You look so tired, darling," she murmured haltingly. "What have you done to yourself?"

"You're just seeing the results of a lack of sleep and a lot of hard work." He dismissed her concern with a fleeting smile while his eyes roamed her face and neck and body hungrily. When they came back to her mouth, he frowned slightly. "I should have shaved," he said regretfully. "I've burned your skin with my beard."

"Have you?" Sarah asked dreamily, a shudder passing over her at the intimacy in Charles's blue gaze. "I didn't feel it." Her look invited him to burn her again, but the voices outside grew slightly louder for an instant, and Charles dragged his gaze from her face to glance at the door.

"I suppose they want in," he said with a frown of annoyance.

"I suppose they do," Sarah answered, showing no concern for what Foster and Hugo might want. And then both she and Charles started as a voice came from behind them.

"Oh, excuse m-me!" Dryson stammered the words as he came to a stop in the doorway leading from the hall.

Charles and Sarah swung to look at him, Charles with a scowl on his face and Sarah with an expression of rueful resignation that made Dryson look guilty for having intruded.

"I . . . well, I'll just go and, uh . . ." Dryson's stammering showed his embarrassment, and Sarah took pity on him.

"It's all right, Dryson," she sighed. "Foster and Hugo are outside the back door waiting to get in anyway. Go ahead and let them in, and I'll get everyone fed before—" She stopped what she'd been about to say abruptly, pinkening a little as she realized she'd been about to say something decidedly indiscreet.

She darted a look at Charles, whose slow smile and burning gaze informed her that he was in total agreement with the plans she was making for what would happen after dinner. She flashed him an intimate, slightly chastizing look, then started backing away from him in the direction of the stove.

"I'll . . . ah . . . finish the cooking," she volunteered a little shakily before turning away to the stove where the spaghetti sauce bubbled gently, its red color finding an echo in Sarah's flushed cheeks.

Foster and Hugo came in with muted excitement in their faces and voices, and before long the curious glances they directed between Sarah and Charles ceased as they drew Charles into a discussion about his latest experiences.

Sarah went quickly about her work, but her eyes rested on Charles's tired face time and again as she did so, and she had trouble concentrating on his weary recitation of how he'd left things in Zwahola for worrying about him.

Finally Sarah had dinner on the table, and while Foster, Hugo, and Dryson fell to eating with eager appetites, she merely pushed the food around on her plate while she watched Charles struggle to get a few bites down. It was evident he was on the verge of exhaustion, and at last he pushed his half-empty plate away and leaned wearily back in his chair.

"Is there a shower in this place?" he asked heavily, though his eyes smiled at Sarah as he talked. "I need a bath—and a shave." His slight hesitation before the last three words was for her benefit, and Sarah colored slightly even as she met his gaze with a sweet smile of anticipation.

"Upstairs." Foster volunteered the information around a bite of spaghetti. "You can have the green bedroom . . ." he started to add before he remembered what was between Sarah and Charles and raised his eyes in a startled, apologetic glance that

Sarah ignored while Charles merely gave his coworker a sardonic smile.

"I know exactly where I'll be sleeping tonight," Charles drawled with an intimate note in his voice as he looked at Sarah. The three other men exchanged bland, noncommittal glances while Sarah remained locked in the promise of love Charles offered with his eyes until he pushed his chair back and got to his feet.

Sarah's bemused look changed to one of alarm as Charles staggered slightly and caught the table with one hand to steady himself. "Jet lag." He offered that brief explanation as he drew himself up and came around the table to where Sarah was seated.

He placed a hand on her shoulder and squeezed it before moving on toward the hallway, and Sarah followed his progress with her eyes until he was at the door. He turned, slanted her a lazy look of promise, said, "I'll see you in a few minutes, Sarah," and with a smile left the room.

There was a silence at the table for a few minutes until Foster finished his meal, then stood up and picked up his plate. "It's my turn to do the dishes tonight, Sarah," he said in an unusually gruff voice. "You'd better go see to your man. He looked tired enough to drown in the shower."

Sarah flashed him a look of gratitude before springing to her feet. Without a word she was off to follow Charles, leaving three very envious men gazing after her.

Sarah heard the water running in the bathroom, but when she tapped at the door, there was no answer. Alarmed, she pushed the door open, and when she saw that Charles was sprawled in the tub with the faucets open full blast while he rested his head on the back of the tub with his eyes closed, the brown in her eyes softened to a combination of maternal and very adult warmth.

She crossed to the tub and shut off the water, since the tub was full almost to overflowing, then picked up the soap and a cloth and very gently began to wash her lover. Charles's eyes fluttered open briefly and he smiled, but then they fell closed again and Sarah could tell from his breathing that he slept while she continued soaping him.

When she was done, she cupped his bristly face in her hand

259

and said with soft gentleness, "Wake up, darling. You need your bed."

It took some time before she could rouse him enough to get him to stand up so that she could dry him off, which she did with loving pride in his beautiful, tanned, muscular body, and more than a little breathlessness at her reaction to its magnificence.

"Come on, dearest," she coaxed him into stepping from the tub. When he was out, she wrapped him in a towel and guided him from the bathroom, down the hall, and into her room. The way he collapsed onto the bed convinced her that there was no way they were going to get the loving they had counted on this night, but just having him with her was feast enough for her for the time being, and after she'd covered him tenderly with the bedclothes, she sat beside him for a few moments to stroke his hair away from his temple while she murmured her love to him.

When she withdrew her hand, he struggled to wake up, but it was a losing battle, and Sarah crooned to him, "Sleep, darling. Go to sleep. I'll be back in a little while." He settled again into a deep sleep that bespoke his exhaustion, and Sarah got to her feet.

She searched out the nicest of the nightgowns Foster had packed for her, and though it certainly wasn't the one she would have chosen had she been doing the packing with a reunion with Charles in mind, it would have to do. She took it with her to the bathroom where she showered, washed her hair, and then lamented the fact that Foster hadn't packed any perfume.

At last she was back in the bedroom, and though it was still early, she slid into bed next to Charles, cuddled up against his broad back, and wrapped her arm around his solid middle. When she was assured that her touch wouldn't wake him, she started a slow exploration of the planes and curves of his body, reveling in the warmth and strength of him, in the clean smell he exuded, and in the sense of rightness she felt at sleeping with him again.

All her doubts and worries went into abeyance as she cuddled him, stroked him, and murmured to him all the love she felt. And at last she fell asleep, feeling contented, safe, warm, and complete with her arm around the man she loved and her face pressed against the solid strength of his shoulder while a smile curved her mouth into angelic satisfaction.

CHAPTER TWENTY-ONE

Sometime in the wee hours Charles woke abruptly, as was his habit. He never came awake in stages. But this time he was momentarily confused at finding it still dark in his bedroom, while the bedroom itself had a strange feel to it.

Then he became aware that there was a soft warmth pressed up against his back, and he was so accustomed to sleeping alone that it took him a moment to identify what the object was, as well as where he was. When understanding dawned, a broad smile curved his mouth, and he began to turn, very slowly and carefully, onto his back.

As Sarah's position was disturbed by his movement, she gave a soft, sleepy mumble of protest, but when Charles had settled himself and wrapped her close to him in his arms, the mumble died away, and her deep breathing told Charles she was asleep again.

Content for the time being just to hold her against him, Charles felt a sense of wonder that so little a thing as waking up in the middle of the night to find that he was not alone could impart such a feeling of contented happiness. But upon further reflection, he realized it had always been this way with Sarah. He smiled and enjoyed the sensation, and it was all the more enjoyable because he knew he would never be alone again, that Sarah would always be there beside him in the night to chase away the cold emptiness that had been his companion for so long.

He relaxed into his contentment, savoring every detail of it, aware that this was one of those rare moments when, with nothing to distract him, he could contemplate his blessings with complete awareness of their sweetness. And Sarah, of course, was the fount of those blessings.

God, she feels good! he thought, his drowsy smile expressing his pleasure. He wished he could see her face, but it was too dark in the room, so he had to content himself with taking a gentle inventory with his hands, though he was careful not to disturb her sleep. She had on something that felt silkily delicious, but it was the skin of her shoulders and arms that he found intoxicating. Silkier than the fabric of her nightgown, warm with the life that pulsed in her lovely body, her skin was an aphrodisiac of the most powerful sort. But while his arousal was growing, it was as yet not urgent. He was too steeped in the slow savoring of her to go on to more exotic pleasures.

He wrapped a satiny length of her hair around his finger and rubbed it with his thumb while he inhaled the distinctive scent that was Sarah, and savored her femininity. She was all woman and all his, and he meant to enjoy her with a fervor that had been denied him for far too long. But there was a certain piquancy in the waiting as well.

He lost track of everything but the small pleasures Sarah gave even in her sleep. But finally the small pleasures weren't enough any longer, yet still she slept on. With a self-mocking smile Charles rubbed a hand over his face in frustration, and what he felt there made him frown. He'd better shave before Sarah did wake up, because when she did, there would be no time or inclination to delay their pleasure.

Carefully he eased out of bed, smiling when Sarah again made that small mumbled protest at being jostled and at losing his body warmth. He covered her bare shoulder, then padded to the door and let himself out into the dimly lit hallway. The rest of the house was silent, and Charles took care to be quiet as he let himself into the bathroom.

His shaving kit was where he'd left it the night before, and as he lathered his face, he whistled softly. When his skin was at last smooth again and he'd slapped on aftershave, he winked at himself in the mirror. Then he let himself out of the bathroom and returned to the bedroom.

There was a small bedside lamp on a table beside the headboard, and Charles switched it on, determined not to be deprived of the pleasure of seeing Sarah as well as touching her. He eased himself back under the covers and as he gently moved Sarah over a little to give himself room, her lashes fluttered open, revealing sleepy brown eyes.

Grateful that she was waking up, Charles stretched out beside her and took her into his arms, his smile rueful, but nevertheless pleased. Sarah's drowsy blinking ceased at his movement. "Oh . . ." she mumbled softly as she awoke enough to realize Charles was there. "Oh!" she repeated, as it came to her that he was really there.

"Good morning, darling," Charles whispered teasingly as he planted a soft kiss on her parted lips.

She returned the kiss rather ineptly in her sleepy state, then drew back to look at him, her eyes widening farther and farther as she became used to the light. "What time is it?" she whispered back.

"I don't know," Charles murmured huskily. "And I don't care. Do you?" He bent his head to nuzzle her neck, savoring the warmth of her skin and the seductive smell that was all her own. His tongue came out to taste what his lips told him would be delicious. It was, and Charles felt himself responding rapidly. Sarah felt it, too, and she leaned back in his arms, her eyes sleepily bemused, but encouraging.

"Still tired?" she asked, languidly teasing.

Charles tightened his arms around her. "I never felt less tired in my life," he informed her in a seductive growl. "How about you? Want to go back to sleep?" He challenged her with a blue glitter, daring her to say yes.

"Would you let me?" she posed, the gold flecks in her lovely eyes dancing with mischief as they softened with arousal.

"You'd have to be very determined about it if you managed to sleep through what I have in mind," he returned, a self-confident smile tugging at his sensuous mouth. "And I would much prefer your full cooperation right now," he added, lifting a finger to trace the clean line of her jaw while his eyes dropped to her inviting mouth.

"Then I guess I'll stay awake," Sarah decided, and lifted her lips invitingly toward his mouth. Then her eyes widened as she noticed his clean-shaven jaw. "When did you shave?" she asked in surprise.

"A few minutes ago," Charles smiled. "I've been awake for a

long time enjoying you, Miss Bailey, before it occurred to me that you might enjoy me more if I didn't scrape your face raw while you welcomed me home."

Sarah lifted her arms to place them around his neck. She arched her body to get closer to him and looked gratified when his heavy-lidded eyes half closed in pleasure at her movement.

"That was thoughtful of you," she murmured, "but I doubt I would have noticed. I didn't last night."

"But you're going to get a lot more of me now than you did last night," Charles pointed out as he slid a large warm hand over her silk-encased bottom. At feeling the fabric of her nightgown, he frowned. "There seems to be something between us," he mused thoughtfully, fingering the material with muted distaste.

Sarah pouted charmingly. "That's a nightgown," she informed him as she flashed a look of exaggerated patience up at him. "Women often wear them to bed at night, especially when their men are the type to fall asleep the moment their heads touch the pillow."

Charles looked down at her, a skeptical disbelief tinging his eyes. "Now why would they want to do that," he pondered, "when that type of man is usually the sort who wakes up anxious for some loving?" He eyed her sternly. "It seems to me," he said with an exaggerated patience that matched the look she had given him, "that a woman ought to realize that and not waste time by wearing something that's likely to get ripped to shreds."

Sarah studied him briefly, then gave an exaggerated sigh of resignation. "All right," she said as she pulled out of his arms and sat up to pull the nightgown over her head and toss it aside. "I certainly don't want to encourage wanton destruction of personal property. There's a recession going on, in case you didn't know it; Mr. International Financier."

She started to lie down again, but Charles, leaning on one arm, lifted his other hand to place it on her smooth shoulder and keep her where she was while he let his eyes roam over her with lazy, aroused appreciation. Sarah sat still under his inspection, though her breasts soon began to rise and fall with ever-increasing agitation.

"Are you assessing the merchandise before you decide to

buy?" she asked unsteadily. "I assure you it's prime quality. The previous owner, a tall, blond man with a mysterious past, used it well, but sparingly, and it's almost like new."

Charles raised his eyebrows doubtfully as he scanned the offering, before returning his blue eyes to Sarah's face. "Does it come with a guarantee of satisfaction?" he inquired with low-toned interest, a rasping purr beginning to feather his tones.

"That depends," Sarah replied, again unsteadily. "The previous owner seemed satisfied, but, of course, everyone's different. Some people are just hard to please." She paused to lick lips that had gone dry under the burning intensity of Charles's inspection of her breasts.

"I suppose you're wondering why he traded it in?" she inquired, her voice faltering as Charles removed his hand from her shoulder and traced a finger over her collarbone before moving it lower to trace lazy circles that enflamed Sarah.

"He was a damned fool?" Charles murmured inquiringly, his voice abstracted as he studied the effect his touch was having on Sarah's nipple.

"Ah . . . no . . ." Sarah whispered shakily as Charles's finger stroked on, "He-he had to move away, and . . . ah . . . he couldn't take it with him. I think he hated to give it up, but—"

Charles interrupted her by placing a large hand on her neck and pulling her down beside him while he moved quickly to pin her half beneath his body.

"I don't think he ever intended to give it up," he muttered thickly. "I think he always knew he would come back for it. And I don't think he's ever going to let it get away from him again!"

Sarah's moan was smothered by Charles's mouth as he seized her lips, forced them open, and thrust with a tongue made urgent by need too long denied. As he felt her body yield beneath his, Charles became abruptly aware that he wasn't going to be able to exercise the control he'd intended. He was suddenly on fire. And Sarah's instinctive molding of herself to fit his body fed the flames into a blazing inferno.

He felt his body move completely over hers without his realizing it was going to happen, and it was a struggle to warn her that he was not going to be able to be as slow and gentle and tender as she might wish.

265

"God, Sarah, I hope I don't hurt you!" he heard himself saying in a strange, ragged voice he didn't recognize. "But I'm out of control! I've got to . . ."

His words died on a graphic demonstration of what he had to do, and as he felt the sweet, hot, moistness of her closing around the center of his need, a shudder worked its way up from his toes to his shoulders.

With some dim, abstracted part of his mind he realized he was perhaps gripping Sarah's hips too roughly when he tilted her upward to receive more of him, but that far-off part of his consciousness couldn't make him stop. His body wanted more and more.

He heard his own breath as he started the mindless rhythm his body demanded, then his own voice urging Sarah. "Give me everything, Sophie—everything—help me!" he cried, and as her legs came up and her hips lifted into his rhythm, he moaned, "Yes, oh, God, yes, Sophie! That's it! That's what I want!"

The feel of her nipples grazing his chest was a sweet counterpoint to the aching, raging need between his thighs. The sight of her parted mouth and the glaze of passion filming her dazed brown eyes fed his appetite until it was rapacious. The moist heat of the feminine cavern he plundered incited his nature into a need to dominate, to ravish, to possess with total exclusion. He felt gloriously primitive and released of inhibitions, and the only thing that mattered in the world was taking what he wanted from this woman who gloried in that taking and who was urging him to take even more with her soft, whimpering cries of passion. He felt as strong and as powerful as a god.

"Sophie," he growled in a savage mutter as he felt that last welling of mindless ecstasy starting and began to give himself to it without reservation. "Join me now!" he urged Sarah. "I can't wait!"

And as he felt Sarah begin to obey him, her body convulsing into a rippling expression of passion gone wild, he let go of everything but a total concentration on his own ecstatic convulsion. It went on and on in waves of pleasure so intense, he cried out in hoarse exultation, cries that died away as the pleasure diminished, and vanished completely as the last shudder wracked his body until he collapsed onto the yielding warmth of Sarah's body under him.

He lay completely drained for a long time without moving or thinking. But then he felt Sarah's arms come up around his neck and heard her murmurs of love, and he was then consumed by such a wealth of tenderness and love for her that he felt tears spring up behind his closed eyes. It was as though the mindless passion they'd shared had made his emotional commitment even stronger, the ache of love even sharper, the sweetness of knowing that Sarah belonged to him, and he to her, almost intolerably precious.

He wanted to show her what he was feeling, and so he raised himself to look down at her. His smile was ragged when he saw that there were tears overlying the love in her eyes.

"You beautiful sorceress," he murmured hoarsely. "You really took me apart that time. I may never be the same."

"You'd better be," Sarah gulped on a trembling smile. "That was too good not to be repeated."

"I didn't hurt you?" he asked softly, a slight anxiety in his warm gaze.

Sarah shook her head, and then a tired chuckle bubbled in her throat. "If that's pain, then I don't know what pleasure is," she teased him, though there was nothing frivolous about the love in her gaze.

"I love you." Charles found himself saying the words without knowing he was going to, yet feeling their truth to the depths of his soul.

"And I love you." The sweet affirmation nestled in his ears like honey. "Always, forever, totally, without reservation," Sarah went on extravagantly.

Charles let his pleasure show in his smile and in his voice. "You must be practicing for the wedding vows," he said tenderly. "And that's good, because I'm not waiting any longer than absolutely necessary to marry you. I want you safely mine, and soon."

He saw an anxiousness spring up in her brown eyes as a result of his words, and it made him frown. "What's wrong?" he demanded, trying not to sound grim, but determined that nothing was going to interfere with making Sarah completely his at last.

"We should talk, Charles," she offered tentatively, then winced as Charles involuntarily squeezed her shoulders tighter than he'd meant to.

"So talk," he said in a deliberately level voice as he loosened his grip.

Sarah squirmed beneath him. "You're heavy," she complained, and Charles knew she was deliberately stalling. Nevertheless, he moved off her, but without letting her out from under the arm he stretched across her body. When she would have turned her face away, he caught her chin in his hand and gently forced her head back.

"Talk," he instructed flatly.

Sarah sighed, eyed him a little resentfully, then let the expression dissolve into a serious solemnity that made Charles's chest tighten up. Whatever she had to say was obviously serious, and possibly ominous for the future he had planned for the two of them.

"Charles, don't look at me like that," she said in a soft plea. "It's hard to think when you do."

"Do what?" he asked, aware that his face must look grim, but somehow unable to force his features into a lighter expression.

"When you look—dangerous," Sarah answered uncomfortably, her eyes darting from his eyes to his set mouth and back again.

Abruptly impatient, Charles didn't try to keep his tones level any longer. "I'm sorry," he grated, "but you're scaring the hell out of me. Maybe it's my guilty conscience for abandoning you in the past, but if you're about to tell me you don't want to marry me, I think you're going to end up kidnapped again. And this time *I'll* be doing the kidnapping!"

Sarah's uncertain look made him wild with frustration. "What's on your mind, Sophie?" He forced his tone to gentleness. "Put me out of my misery, will you?"

"Well, it's about getting married, Charles," she replied, sounding defensive. And then at something she saw in his eyes, she hastened to add, "It's not that I don't want to marry you. I do. It's that I have to know exactly why you suddenly want to get married."

"Suddenly?" he asked incredulously, though the relief he felt

268

at hearing Sarah say she did want to marry him was enormous. "Are you serious?" he exclaimed. "I've wanted to marry you since the day I met you! I thought you knew that!"

"Well, sort of," Sarah answered rather crossly, and Charles couldn't contain a smile. She looked like a sulky little girl with her tousled hair and her flushed cheeks, and he wanted to pull her onto his lap and cuddle her into a better mood. But that would have to come later. She obviously had something going on in that mercurial mind of hers he had to straighten out.

"Sort of," he mocked her sardonically, indicating with a lift of his brows that she should go on.

"Well, you certainly never got around to it!" Sarah answered heatedly, and Charles, wondering if she had a need to get some of her anger at him out of her system before she could settle down to loving him without reserve again, decided to let her do just that. God knew, she deserved the chance to express herself.

But apparently that wasn't really what she had on her mind, Charles realized as he saw her fight to contain her irritation before returning to seriousness. She took a deep breath, then held his gaze for several long moments. And just when he was about to drown in those huge, soft, gold and brown depths that had always enchanted him, she spoke, and her question tore at his heart.

"Charles, are you sure you're marrying me for the right reasons?" she asked him quietly. "Are you marrying me because you really want to or just to keep me safe from harm? And are you going to hate me someday because I came between you and your—duty?"

Charles felt his throat close up at the break in her voice when she said the last word. And he felt as much a heel as he ever had in his life at causing the anguish he saw in her eyes and heard in her voice. It took him a moment to get control of his emotions and be able to reply to her in a way that would still the doubts that were tearing her apart.

"Sarah, darling . . ." he started slowly, then had to clear his throat against the constriction that had appeared there. "When I left you that first time, I was young, naive, and idealistic. I thought I had to pay dues. That was the way I was raised. I thought I could make a difference in the world."

He wanted to close his eyes against the wide, vulnerable look in Sarah's, but she deserved to see what was in his own, so he held her gaze with complete openness as he continued.

"I don't know if I really made a difference or not," he went on, "but I hope so. But regardless of whether I did or not, at that time I couldn't have done anything differently. I couldn't have lived with myself if I hadn't tried, and I did what I had to."

He paused to take a breath before going on. "But the second time I was no longer so naive or so young, and I felt satisfied that I'd given enough to salve my conscience. I wanted nothing more than to stay with you and make a life together, just the two of us." He smiled then, and his eyes became softly abstracted for an instant as he added, "And our children, of course."

Sarah's fragile smile in reaction to his words pleased him, tore at him, unmanned him. He had to force himself to go on rather than take her into his arms again.

"But that second time I really did owe a debt I had to pay," he added quietly. "Do you remember the story I told you about the man who saved my life after my parents were killed?" Sarah nodded. "Well, he finally asked for payment," Charles continued in a low voice. "And I couldn't refuse him. That's why I had to leave you again."

He paused for an instant, and Sarah interjected a question. "And do you feel you've paid him back, Charles?" she asked trembling.

Charles reached a hand to stroke her smooth cheek. "Yes, darling," he said with utter certainty. "I did what I could. It was only when you were threatened because of me that I realized I didn't have to give my whole life over to my old friend in order to pay my debt, that I could set what he wanted in motion and be done with it, leaving others to handle the day-to-day operation. I'm convinced that my contribution will give him what he wants, and that my staying in Zwahola wouldn't affect the course of events appreciably either way."

He thought for a moment, and when he went on his tone was forceful. "Once duty was my master, Sarah. But now I'm master of my duty. My conscience is clear. My debt is paid in full. And the only duty that interests me right now is the duty of a husband and a father."

270

Sarah searched his face with her eyes, and he hid nothing from her, confident that she would see that he meant what he'd said. He watched as the glimmer of uncertainty in her huge eyes diminished, and he greeted the thrust of her body as she flung herself into his arms with a convulsive hug and a laugh.

When Sarah finally eased her stranglehold on him and leaned back slightly, he couldn't resist asking, "Satisfied?" though he knew he sounded smugly complacent.

"Yes," she answered, breathless. And then they both jumped as they heard a thump from the lower floor, followed by a muffled curse.

Sarah returned her gaze to Charles, and now it was woeful. "But I don't think Foster will be," she said sadly. "I have the feeling he's going to continue to work on you to change your mind."

Charles, his mind distracted by the feel of Sarah's nude body pressed against his, managed to shake his head. "No," he responded huskily. "I told Foster yesterday that I would be available for consultation, but not for active duty. You and I are moving to California, Sarah. I'll be working for World Oil there, and my contributions to my ex-employer will be strictly minimal. They can pick my brain from time to time, but from now on the rest of me belongs to you."

He took her hand and slid it between his thighs, showing her the truth of his statement. "I'm all yours," he said on an intake of breath as Sarah's fingers began to stroke him. "Use me any way you want to."

Sarah's smile was deliciously mischievous and sultry as she closed her hand around him and squeezed. "Good," she murmured seductively. "I know just what I'm going to do with you."

Charles felt his lids begin to droop over his eyes as his body filled up with tantalizing heat. "Show me," he invited in a lazy growl.

"Now?" Sarah asked, flashing a glance over his shoulder at the door to the bedroom. "Are you sure the other members of the household will respect our privacy?" She returned her gaze to Charles and pouted. "Foster never has in the past."

Charles ignored her reference to Foster's history of spying on her, preferring to leave that subject to another time. "Foster knows what will happen to him if he comes within ten feet of that door," he assured Sarah with enough toughness in his tone to convince her. "I've told him if he wants my help in the future, he'd damned well better make himself scarce in the meantime."

Sarah widened her eyes admiringly at his masterfulness, but then they slid around the room consideringly. "You don't think he has this room bugged?" she inquired doubtfully.

"He wouldn't dare," Charles replied, and having had enough of conversation when there were other, better ways of communicating, he turned Sarah over onto her back.

"Now," he asked huskily, "don't you think you ought to take advantage of what I gave you? I do. I think you ought to make me pay for what I've put you through in the past. I'm a sucker for paying debts."

He saw the gleam come into Sarah's eyes and chuckled contentedly.

She stretched with catlike sinuousness while he watched the movement with fascination. "How long do I own all this magnificence you're offering?" she asked in dreamy tones.

"Long term or short term?" he answered interestedly. "If it's long term, the answer is for life. If it's short term, it's all day if you want it or maybe two days or three or . . ."

Sarah shook her head firmly. "An hour or so should do for the time being. Then we have to get up and go get a marriage license. I don't trust Foster. He's entirely too good at the kidnapping business."

"Whatever you say," Charles answered blandly, though he knew an hour or so would definitely not do as far as he was concerned. She would find that out later.

"Okay," Sarah breathed with satisfaction as she slanted a greedy, speculative look up at him. "I'm going to take you at your word and tell you exactly what I want."

"Go ahead," Charles answered complacently, giving her an open invitation with his eyes to do just that.

"Well," Sarah drawled with a tiny smile curving her mouth, "I've always fancied a tongue bath. All over. Slowly. With feeling." The smile deepened as she cast her eyes up at Charles to see his reaction.

Charles took his time about reacting in any way at all, merely running his eyes over her from the top of her head to the soles of her feet. "What happens if I refuse?" he inquired lazily, meaning only to tease.

Sarah broke into a giggle. "Then I'll give you one," she answered with happy anticipation. "I planned to anyway. It's a secret form of torture I learned from one of my dirty books."

"Are you still reading those?" Charles asked with a stern frown, though his eyes indicated a smile was trying to break out.

"Don't *you*?" Sarah exclaimed, shock and disapproval redolent in her tone. "Then how did you learn some of those things you showed me at my apartment the last time we—"

"I have a creative imagination." Charles cut her off, moving over her and taking a liquid swipe at her throat with his tongue as a warm-up for the rest of what she'd requested. "Now, be quiet," he whispered. "I don't want to hear anything out of you for the next hour except moans and groans of appreciation for what you're about to receive."

"Oh, good!" Sarah purred. "I took Moans and Groans 103 in college. I got an A," she added with pride, which turned to a gasp as Charles bent to treat one of her breasts to another preparatory swipe.

"Don't tell me, show me!" he muttered abstractedly between warm laps with his moist tongue.

And Sarah did, over and over again, as Charles worked his way from her shoulders to her little toe, then started all over again until Sarah gave a frustrated cry midway through his return journey and pulled him up to lie atop her while she wordlessly showed him what she wanted now.

"Hmmm?" he mused obtusely as Sarah wriggled beneath him. "Was there something else you wanted?"

But his ragged tone spoiled the effect, and Sarah nodded vigorously. "You promised me this"—she touched him intimately, making him shudder—"belongs to me too. And I want it now!"

"How?" he asked, almost strangling on the word.

"Like this!" Sarah demanded, thrusting her hips at him, and he plunged deeply into her in a convulsive movement that made her cry out in pleasure.

"Oh, like this?" Charles muttered, pushing deeper before beginning the rhythm Sarah answered with all the eager passion in her, answering his question with her actions, not words.

He broke the rhythm just once in order to turn Sarah's head toward him so that he could take her mouth as he was taking her body, and then the rhythm spiraled out of control, and their breaths mingled in a mutual cry of ecstasy that seemed to fill the room long after they had collapsed into each other's arms to savor the aftermath of the loving that had taken them to the heights before dropping them back down into an almost equally pleasurable reality.

CHAPTER TWENTY-TWO

Sarah stood on the red-tiled patio of her home in southern California looking down at the twinkling lights of other residences scattered over the hills beneath her while the soft breeze soothed the slight headache she had as a result of a long, hard day.

Her arms rested protectively over the slight swell of her stomach, and she smiled as she felt her baby kick. She would have time to enjoy her pregnancy after today, and she was looking forward to it enormously, though the project she had just finished had given her the pleasure of another sort of birth. The play she had written while staying at the New York farmhouse was being produced at a small theater noted for its experimental work, and she had finished casting it today. It might not turn out to be a success—time would tell—but it had been sheer joy to get it started.

Her mind turned from her own career to Charles's as she waited for him and Foster to join her. Foster was here to consult with Charles over something to do with Zwahola, and as she squinted at her watch in the dim light she realized they'd been in the study over two hours.

Perhaps she should go on to bed, she mused tiredly. She and Foster had had a nice visit over dinner, so she didn't think it would hurt his feelings if she neglected to stay up to see him out.

"Tired, baby?" Charles's low voice brought a smile to her face, and she started to turn around, but he was already so close, his arms came around her from behind and held her where she was.

"Yes," she answered contentedly as she rested against his warm, solid body. "Where's Foster?"

"He left," Charles told her, nuzzling his cheek against her hair. "He said you were probably ready to throw him out, so he

275

thought he'd save you the trouble." His soft chuckle echoed pleasantly in her ear, and Sarah smiled as well.

"That man," she jokingly protested, affection in her tone. "Is he coming back tomorrow?"

"No, he's catching a late flight back to New York tonight," Charles said, his hands moving over her stomach protectively. "But he'll be back. If he doesn't have a real problem to consult with me about, he'll make one up. He's looking forward to being godfather to junior here."

Sarah grinned at the mental picture she had of the rugged Foster bouncing an infant on his knee. "It's too bad he never had a family of his own," she commented idly.

She felt Charles shrug behind her. "He made his choices," he answered matter-of-factly. "And I made mine," he added with quiet satisfaction.

He paused and stared abstractedly out over the valley beneath them. "Maybe I should be grateful to Ian Connors and Lugubu for their part in helping me make my choice," he mused thoughtfully, "since if it hadn't been for them, I might still be sweating it out in Zwahola instead of being the happiest man on earth."

"Lugubu?" Sarah questioned interestedly as she turned into Charles's arms and wrapped her arms around his waist.

"Never mind," Charles said with a smile in his voice. And then he deftly changed the subject. "Say, you're getting kind of hard to snuggle up to. Been putting on weight lately, have you?"

Sarah sniffed her disgust at his diversion, but she played along with it nevertheless. "Yes," she pronounced without apology. "Didn't you know that once a woman has caught her man, she doesn't need to bother staying slim and trim any longer?" She rubbed her tummy against Charles's and gave him a bland smile. "I did decide that I'd stop at three hundred pounds though," she said with an attempt at earnest solemnity while Charles slanted a laughing glance down at her. "I trust you, but not entirely. You might bolt at three hundred five."

"You think so?" Charles raised his eyebrows in a doubtful expression. Then he bent to slip an arm under her knees and lifted her into his arms. He hefted her once or twice, as though trying to guess her weight. "Hmmm," he mused with a frown of concentration creasing his brow. "Feels like about three hundred two. You'd better watch it," he warned as he pivoted to carry her toward the interior of the house. "You've only got three pounds to go before I've got carte blanche to stray."

"Try it," Sarah suggested with a dangerously sweet smile. "Just *try* it," she added more forcefully as she had a sudden vision of how Charles had looked when she'd seen him with Yetunde and remembered the jealousy that had ripped her apart.

"Is that an invitation?" Charles asked seriously as he pushed the door to their bedroom open with one shoulder and carried her inside.

"An invitation to suicide," Sarah snorted, pulling him down with her as he lowered her to their king-size bed. "Come here," she invited ominously, "and I'll give you a taste of what happens to a straying husband once his wife finds out about it and gets her hands on him."

Charles eyed her warily as she began to undo the buttons of his blue denim shirt. "What does she do?" he asked with mock anxiety. "Does she use whips and chains? Leather straps? Needles?" He yelped the final word as Sarah raked a long fingernail down his bare chest.

"Pooh," she scoffed as she lowered her hand to his belt. "How tame! You've led a sheltered life if you think I'd use such flimsy excuses for torture."

Charles sucked in his breath as she dallied about unfastening his belt and then even more so about unzipping his trousers. Finally, when her teasing fingers had pulled the zipper slowly down to the last stop, he seized her hand and used it to lever her onto her back.

"Woman, you're playing with fire," he warned in a low growl as he reached one hand behind her to capture her wrist while he used his free hand to begin unbuttoning her white silk blouse. "I think it's time to teach you your place again," he informed her sternly as she pretended to struggle.

Sarah stopped her struggles and looked at him mournfully. "Again?" she complained in sorrowful tones. "This must be the millionth time you've taught me my place."

"True," he grunted as he moved to get more comfortable before returning his attention to the buttons of her blouse. "And I can't remember you ever complaining about it once the lesson

277

got under way. I'm beginning to think you like this sort of lesson," he said suspiciously.

"Who, me?" Sarah batted her eyes at him innocently. "Why, I'm a liberated woman!" she asserted stoutly. "I find male chauvinism disgusting!"

"Yes, isn't it?" Charles drawled as he slanted an evil smile down at the swollen, delectably silken breasts he'd uncovered. And then he sighed and shook his head. "It's a good thing my parents can't know how you've perverted my character," he said sadly. "I used to be a nice guy until I fell into your clutches."

"Oh, piffle!" Sarah dismissed such an idea. "They'd love—"

"Piffle?" Charles interrupted, incredulity in his tone at her vocabulary. "Did you say *piffle*?" he crowed.

Sarah nodded complacently. "One of the actors who read for me today used that word, and I kind of took a fancy to it. Don't you like it?" And then without waiting for his answer she went on with what she'd been about to say before he interrupted her.

"Your parents would love me," she informed Charles with utter certainty. "After all, aren't I about to be fruitful and multiply? And isn't that in accordance with—"

"Sarah." Charles interrupted her with a stifled laugh. "I concede the point. My parents would love you just the way I do. And just the way our son or daughter is going to love you," he added tenderly as he ran a hand over her abdomen. "Has he or she been giving you a hard time today?" he asked on a smile as a slight undulation feathered beneath his hand.

"Not until a little while ago," Sarah said. "I think junior acts up when you're around. He probably wants some attention from his daddy."

She watched, a tender look softening her features, as Charles moved his blond-streaked head down to her stomach and rubbed his cheek against it. Sarah stroked his hair, content to remain quiet as Charles savored his coming fatherhood. When he moved back up to wrap her in his arms, she rested her head on his shoulder, and they lay in contentment together for a short while.

"Did Foster get what he came for?" She finally broke the silence.

Charles didn't answer, but Sarah could feel his chuckle at her persistent curiosity about the "secret" side of his life. "Yes," he finally answered. "I was able to help this time."

Sarah digested that information for a moment, and then asked the question that had arisen with Foster's visit and which she had to put to rest.

"Do—do you ever miss not being more actively involved?" she inquired hesitantly.

Charles answered her question by asking one. "Do you ever miss your business in New York?" he asked matter-of-factly.

"Why, no," Sarah answered, surprised that he'd had to ask. "I'm as busy or busier out here, and I'm more successful than I've ever been. And now that Chelley has finally taken the plunge and decided to move here and work for me again, there's no one I miss from back there that much . . . except . . ."

Charles frowned at her pause. "Except?" he prodded.

"Except the kids I worked with on Sundays," Sarah replied reminiscently. "But I'm going to have a child of my own now, and if I want to get involved in that sort of thing out here once I have the time, there are organizations available." She leaned her head back and looked up at Charles, her eyes rounded with sincerity. "And I have you, Charles," she added. "There's nothing I'll ever miss as long as you're beside me."

Charles's smiling look answered her earlier question to him. "Exactly," he mocked tenderly. "No, Sarah, I don't miss anything. I'm still interested in what happens in Zwahola, but I wouldn't leave you to go back there for anything in the world. I've got all I want right here."

Sarah twisted in his arms and wrapped her own around his neck, beaming her love at him.

"And now that we've got that settled once again," Charles teased as he trailed his hand over her thigh and stomach and then cupped her breast, "there's something *I'm* curious about."

"Ummm, what's that?" Sarah answered lazily as she nuzzled his cheek.

"I've always wondered," Charles said innocently, trying to smother his laughter, "what it's like to make love to a woman who weighs three hundred pounds."

Sarah tilted her head back and gave him a mock glare. "Well, don't count on finding out," she informed him haughtily, "because I was joking about weighing that much."

"Well, but just in case you ever do," Charles suggested helpfully, "don't you think we ought to practice?"

Sarah eyed him speculatively for an instant before she gave an elaborate faked yawn, patting her hand over her mouth while she let her eyelids droop. "Not tonight," she sighed at the end of the yawn. "I have a headache."

"You promised you wouldn't have headaches after we were married," Charles scolded with mock grimness.

"Oh, well, promises, promises," Sarah said with a vague wave of her hand, then yelped as Charles pinched her bottom. "All right," she said on a giggle. "Then suppose you make it go away with some of your cloak-and-dagger magic. There must be a few tricks you learned during all those years that can be useful in everyday life."

"Sarah," Charles said on a warning growl. "I learned some tricks I really don't think you want to know about as well. They're only supposed to be used against people who are . . . ah . . . uncooperative in giving me what I want."

"Oh," Sarah cooed in fascinated wonder. "Like what?"

Charles gave her an evil smile as he unfastened her wraparound skirt and flipped it away from her body with a flourish. "Did you ever hear of the side-to-side hustle?" he asked with cool dangerousness.

"No," Sarah breathed fearfully, mock terror in her eyes.

"Well, you're about to experience it firsthand," Charles informed her in a menacing tone as he sat up and divested Sarah of the rest of her clothing with efficiency before ridding himself of his own. He then slid down beside her, turned her on her side, tugged one of her legs under his waist and the other one over it so that they were nose to nose and informed her in a superior tone, "I'm an expert at it."

"You certainly are!" Sarah gave an admiring gasp as she felt Charles move against her.

"Note the freedom of access this particular hold affords the perpetrator," Charles instructed as he moved backward slightly to allow himself room to take Sarah's breasts in his hands. As he began to stroke and knead the fullness he held, he pressed his hips forward until Sarah felt a very slight penetration between her thighs. And as she moaned in anticipation, he smiled sensuously. "It works every time," he murmured huskily.

At that, Sarah's eyes came open slightly, and in their drugged depths was a struggle against losing all capacity for thought. "How do you know?" she queried raggedly, and then her eyes closed again as Charles pushed deeper into her, temporarily distracting her from her question. She dug her fingernails into his shoulders, and as Charles growled in response, she forced out, "How did you learn this anyway?"

"That's classified," he moaned, moving one hand to her hip to pull her closer as he thrust harder, "and you know you're not supposed to ask questions about my murky past."

"Well, if you don't answer this one, you're going to have an even murkier future," Sarah responded with shaky determination as Charles completed his journey at last and reached the depths of her inner being.

"Is that a threat?" Charles purred silkily as he slid a thumb over the aroused peak of one of Sarah's breasts.

"Definitely," Sarah groaned weakly, unable to quell the shudder his touch evoked.

Charles pulled her closer and whispered into her ear. "All right, then," he capitulated on a shiver as Sarah kissed his neck. "I got this out of one of your dirty books."

Momentarily diverted from all the delicious sensations Charles was instigating in her, Sarah pulled her head back and blinked drowsily at him, her eyes softened with passion and love. "Oh, darling," she whispered, "then I have succeeded in corrupting you, haven't I? Which one was it? The one with the amazon wearing a tiger-skin bikini on the cover?"

"No," Charles denied with a lazy, sensuous smile. "The one with the pregnant woman on the cover. You brought it home after your last checkup."

"Oh," Sarah responded disappointedly. "Then you're still as pure as the driven snow."

With a smothered laugh Charles shook his head. "Not exactly, honey," he denied, punctuating that denial with another thrust of his hips. "I haven't had a pure thought since the day I ran into you years ago."

His tone had deteriorated into an aroused growl by the time he finished his explanation, and it was Sarah's turn to smile.

"Wonderful," she crooned from deep in her throat. "I'm so glad I was able to wake you up to one of the finer things in life."

"Not *one* of the finer things . . ." Charles muttered hoarsely as he began the age-old rhythm of love. "The *only* thing I can't live without now. You, this, loving you."

And his mutter died away as he took Sarah's lips in a searing kiss that echoed the heat in their bodies and displayed the depth of his love.

LOOK FOR NEXT MONTH'S CANDLELIGHT ECSTASY SUPREMES

17 RED MIDNIGHT, *Heather Graham*
18 A HEART DIVIDED, *Ginger Chambers*
19 SHADOW GAMES, *Elise Randolph*
20 JUST HIS TOUCH, *Emily Elliott*

The primitive new world
of these lovers was
like their passion—
savage and untamed.

This first book in the
New Zealander series
sweeps through exotic
New Zealand with a tale of
adventure and passion. It is the story
of William Pollard, a deserter from a
British warship, and Tairata, a
beautiful Maori princess. Together
they embark on a perilous journey
through a primitive land. 11125-0-99
$3.95

THE CASTAWAY

Aaron Fletcher

Rebels and outcasts, they fled halfway across the earth to settle the harsh Australian wastelands. Decades later—ennobled by love and strengthened by tragedy—they had transformed a wilderness into fertile land. And themselves into

The Australians

WILLIAM STUART LONG

THE EXILES, #1	12374-7-12	$3.95
THE SETTLERS, #2	17929-7-45	$3.95
THE TRAITORS, #3	18131-3-21	$3.95
THE EXPLORERS, #4	12391-7-11	$3.50
THE ADVENTURERS, #5	10330-4-40	$3.95